WITH YOU
FOREVER

Risen Halo Publishing

Copyright © 2019 by M.L. Bull

Scripture quotations are used from the Holy Bible, King James Version ® KJV ®. Copyright © 1611.

Author's Note: This is a work of fiction. Names, characters, businesses, places, events, and incidents are either the products of the author's imagination or used in a fictitious manner. Any resemblance to actual persons, living or dead, or actual events is purely coincidental.

ISBN: 978-1-7333248-7-8 (paperback), 978-1-7333248-0-9 (e-book)

Cover designed by M.L. Bull using Derek Murphy's free DYI cover creator

Keychain of cover design handcrafted by Regina Boger, owner of small business Regina Lynn Boger in Fort Wayne, IN.

Edited by M.L. Bull and HugeOrange from Ephrata, PA.

Visit M.L. Bull's website at www.mlbull.com for more information about her and her other works.

Printed in the United States of America

For Family & Friends

WITH YOU FOREVER

M.L. BULL

Risen Halo Publishing

EPIGRAPH

"Charity suffered long, and is kind; charity envieth not; charity vaunteth not itself, is not puffed up, doth not behave itself unseemly, seeketh not her own, is not easily provoked, thinketh no evil; rejoiceth not in iniquity, but rejoiceth in truth; beareth all things, believeth all things, hopeth all things, endureth all things."

-1 Corinthians 13:4-7

PROLOGUE

TWENTY-SIX-YEAR-OLD EVA ROSE CONWAY braced herself for the new beginning of her life. It was an unusually cool afternoon, feeling more like early October instead of late August. Bright green oak leaves rattled in the gentle breeze, relevant to the present ceremony. She drew a deep breath and exchanged glances with her fiancé's grandfather, holding a colorful flower bouquet tied with a shiny blue ribbon.

Her bouquet stuck out of the white rose scenery like a sore thumb, but it was the only one she could get before the outdoor wedding. Grandpa Ricardo Felipe Morales was the only father Eva had, never knowing her biological father in Rome. He gave her a lopsided grin, wearing his favorite gray cowboy hat, which matched his thick, western mustache, double-breast suit, and leather boots.

"You look beautiful," he whispered as the hired male pianist played "Canon in D" by Pachelbel.

Eva smiled shyly. "Thank you, Papa." Growing up, she had been self-conscious of her appearance, worried she'd be noticed for something misplaced, or worse, not noticed at all. But today differed from her high school days. As all eyes set upon her, Eva realized this time *she* was the guest of honor—and for good reason. Her wedding dress was made of a white silk bodice and flowing skirt, sewn with lace embroidery, sheer-and-lace sleeves, and pearl buttons. Her raven-black hair with wavy end curls rested on her shoulders, draped with a hair net veil.

Grandpa Ricardo held her arm and sauntered with her down the mossy lawn aisle scattered with white rose petals. Two-year-old Emily Witherspoon—her daycare student—was her flower girl. Before Eva's big reveal, she overheard the oohs and ahhs of the guests seated on the black folding chairs. She presumed the little girl had captivated them with her angelic smile and big, blue eyes as she walked the aisle with her mother. Eva gave a timid wave at a few attendees. She locked eyes with her husband-to-be at the decorated altar.

He looked so handsome, so strong and confident, towering over the shorter, bald Pastor Joe Tyson. He smiled and watched her every step as she approached him.

Her fiancé—Andre Lucas—was dressed in a navy-blue tuxedo with black lapels, a white dress shirt, a navy-blue bow tie, black pants, and navy-blue Stacy Adams. Though he was a skinny kid of a measly five-foot-four, he had changed much after puberty. Now he was a six-foot, one hundred and eighty-five pounds, muscular giant. His small haircut of lustrous black curls glistened in the sun, his reddish-brown eyes glinting with tears.

For eight years they waited to marry.

They got engaged right after high school, but Pastor Tyson advised they hold off until they finish college. Eva and Andre agreed, but it wasn't easy. They struggled to keep their focus on their studies instead of each other, making small talk on campus whenever they traced each other's path. Eva finished her education first. As advised by her mother, she earned her Associates' degree in Early Childhood Ed, deserting the ambition of her true passion.

Though she enjoyed working with kids, sometimes within she kicked herself. But in a single-parent, low-income home, it always seemed her mom knew best. It took longer for Andre to earn his degree, majoring to become a veterinarian. But when he crossed the graduating stage and received his Doctorate in Veterinary Medicine, the gaze he and Eva shared said it all.

Their long wait was finally over.

Eva stood beside Andre and handed her bridal bouquet to her mother, who acted as her maid of honor. She lifted her face to her fiancé, her married name echoing in her mind. *Mrs. Lucas . . . Mrs. Eva Lucas . . .* Her new last name would take getting used to, she'd been a Conway since the day she was born. Goosebumps rose on her smooth, olive skin, her heart thumping anxiously in her chest.

She released a slow exhale and felt her pulse relax as they held each other's hands, but it appeared her fiancé was more of a bundle of nerves.

Andre's forehead beaded with sweat, and his hands were moist and cold as ice. He dropped his shoulders as the soft piano music ended.

Pastor Tyson cleared his throat. "Dearly beloved, we're gathered here today in the sight of God to join this man and woman in holy matrimony. Who gives this woman to join to this man?" He glanced around the outside assembly.

"I do," her mom said, sniffling with a hankie.

Eva glanced at her mother with teary eyes and whispered, "Thanks, Mom."

Her mother having a tight rein on her, she knew witnessing her only child leave the nest formed a pit of loneliness. Ever since her mom was a teenager, she had been under her mother's wings and kept her company after her parents' long-distance breakup.

She faced the pastor as he inquired for her fiancé's consent to their wedding vows.

"I do," Andre said, gazing in her eyes.

The pastor turned toward Eva. "And do you, Eva Rose Conway, take Andre to be your lawfully wedded husband and live together forever in the estate of holy matrimony? Do you promise to love, comfort, honor, and keep him, in sickness and in health, for richer or poorer, for better or worse . . . as long as you both shall live?"

"I do." Eva wore a dreamy smile.

Pastor Tyson grinned, slipped on his eyeglasses, and opened his Holy Bible to a page he bookmarked with his forefinger. "As stated in Mark chapter ten verse nine, 'What God hath joined together, let not man put asunder.' By the power vested in me, I now pronounce you husband and wife. You may kiss the bride."

Andre and Eva faced each other with nervous expressions, hoping they don't embarrass themselves in front of everybody. Neither of them had dated or kissed before—not even while they were engaged. Now that they could was both scary and alluring. Being six inches taller than her, Andre bent his back to reach her. He gulped and closed his eyes.

"I love you, Eva Rose," Andre whispered, leaning his forehead against hers.

"I love you too, Andre," Eva whispered back.

She closed her eyes and felt Andre's lips touch hers for the first time.

Regardless of the whistles of celebration and applause, to them, time had stopped. They were in their own palace, taken away to a faraway land. They had to make their exit, but they hated for their first kiss to end.

Pastor Tyson cleared his throat, giving them a cue.

Eva and Andre broke their smooch and blushed.

"Oh, sorry," Andre said with a chuckle, "I guess we got carried away." He shrugged and wore a wry grin.

Eva giggled. She brushed a wisp of her dark hair from her face and embraced Andre's bicep.

They faced the gathering and waved at them, strolling down the aisle as the people congratulated them. Their wedding was the start of a lifetime of adventures.

While the pages in their book of marriage filled with memories, there would also be hardships along the way. Life was unpredictable, a journey down a bumpy road of many twists and turns. But no matter what tests their future held, Eva would keep her word and believed Andre would do the same. As the crowd followed them to the limo, she looked above at the partly cloudy sky.

She prayed their marriage would survive.

1
Andre

THIRTY-FOUR-YEAR-OLD DR. ANDRE LUCAS glanced at the wall clock in his clinic every two minutes. He hoped he'd finish treating his animal patients in time to meet his wife at The Redfish Grill, their favorite restaurant. Eva hated him being late for special occasions, and this year he wanted their wedding anniversary to be a moment neither of them would forget. As he was in previous years, today he aimed to keep his promise and arranged with his boss to leave work earlier. Besides, after not being present during Eva's agony of childbirth, he owed it to her—big-time.

He had rushed in the hospital from the showering rain, worried sick about her and their child's health and well-being. Heavy bleeding and shortness of breath were major issues. She was diagnosed with amniotic fluid embolism, a rare pregnancy complication. During Eva's contractions, amniotic fluid entered her bloodstream, causing a life-threatening reaction. With only minutes to spare, doctors and nurses had worked promptly to save his wife's life and the baby. Thankfully, the delivery worked out, and a year and four months ago, she bore him one incredible, little boy. Andrew was an angel, always smiling and ready to give a hug.

Their son was one of the best things he'd ever received, and he made it his mission to be the father he'd never had. His dad—Derek Lucas, was African American, and his mom—Marie Morales, was Latina. But sometimes he wondered if he were adopted.

He acted so much different from them. His parents were drug addicts and shared a love-hate relationship, which resulted in heated arguments and petty apologies.

When he was five his grandfather took custody of him, moving him from the city of Philadelphia to his farm in Garden Ridge, North Carolina. Grandpa Ricardo told him he and Andre's mother were from a northwestern Mexican city called Chihuahua, like the small dog.

Andre and Eva visited the place for their honeymoon, but he wasn't thrilled about flying on a plane. His wife held his sweaty hand the whole six-hour flight there, comforting him when they flew against turbulence. Easy for Eva though, who had flown with her mother to Garden Ridge over two thousand miles from Seattle the start of their freshmen year of high school.

This was when they met and became friends.

However, their love for each other hadn't happened instantly, at least not for Eva. For a long time, she had been drawn to a stellar point guard of the basketball team. His name was Caleb Williams, an attractive jock who was one of the most popular boys of Garden Ridge High School. It wasn't until their senior year their friendship changed, and Andre had finally told her how he felt about her. Neither of them with a date to the prom, they watched *The Grapes of*

Wrath, played rounds of UNO, and ate dinner with his grandfather.

Outside on the porch that night, Andre had talked to Eva about building a relationship with Jesus Christ. He'd also told her she shouldn't feel like she had to be popular to be important because she already meant an awful lot to God and to him. His kind words had made her cry, overwhelmed since ninth grade, the *one* guy who accepted her was under her nose the entire time.

Andre shuffled a stack of patient records, placed them in his folder, and put the folder into his leather briefcase. He glanced at the ticking wall clock above the wooden cabinets again. *Tick-tock . . . tick-tock . . . tick-tock . . .*

It was six-thirty in the evening, and this morning at breakfast he said he'd meet Eva no later than seven tonight.

He fastened the latches of his briefcase and toted it along his side, hustling toward the exit door.

A small knock on the front door froze him.

Andre sighed and glanced over his shoulder at the entrance. *Oh, no. Not again.* He flared his nostrils and opened the door. "Yes?" His tone was flat and weary.

"I'm sorry. Dr. Lucas," Mrs. Witherspoon said with an embarrassed look, holding her two-year-old son Tyler on her hip. "Emily wouldn't stop crying until I brought her here again."

Andre gritted his teeth and scratched his temple. With Eva on his case about managing his time and working late, he wasn't in the mood for a last-minute checkup. He looked at the nine-year-old girl in a lavender T-shirt and jean jumper dress, standing in front of her mother.

Except for her two braided ponytails and bulky, round glasses, Emily was the spitting image of her mom. He imagined her in her puffy, flower girl dress and white rose crown when she was two and couldn't help but smile. In her arms, she cradled Halo—an orange, seven-weeks-old tabby kitten.

Emily raised her head, her rosy cheeks stained with fresh tears. After three times in a row, Andre understood her obsessed checkups.

Her former cat Mittens died in a roadkill accident.

Since she was six, Mittens was Emily's best friend, and her sudden death to a taxi cab broke the little girl's heart for weeks. Recently, her mom bought her a new kitten for acing a spelling test in school. Emily named it Halo because the fur on top of the kitten's head glows in the sunlight.

Andre thought the name suited the endearing little tiger, and being as sensitive about animals as she was, he couldn't turn the child away. At the same time, he wanted to relieve Emily of her anxiety and save her the trouble of making unnecessary doctor visits.

Emily sniffled. "Dr. Lucas, Halo is sick."

Andre angled his head and sighed. "Okay. Bring him to my exam table."

Emily and her mother entered the air-conditioned office.

"Thanks for letting us in, doctor." Mrs. Witherspoon sat in a chair and adjusted her sleepy toddler son from her hip to her lap. Her daughter Emily placed her kitten on the exam table in the center of the small room.

Andre released the heavy door and let it close itself. "So, what's the problem?" He walked over to the feline and stood across the table from Emily.

"Umm . . ." Emily nibbled her lip, trying to think of another excuse.

"How about I give Halo a complete exam?" Andre glanced at Mrs. Witherspoon, and they shared an amused smile, each knowing there was more than likely nothing wrong with Halo again. But if it would ease a little girl's nerves and help her feel better, Andre figured another checkup before his next annual couldn't hurt.

Emily's face brightened. "Okay."

Andre stroked Halo's head and the back of his fur coat, inspecting for fleas. "Hey, Halo. It's nice to see you again. Your coat looks clean and beautiful. Do you mind if I check your eyes and ears, buddy?" He opened a drawer of the counter behind him and pulled out his exam instruments.

Emily watched as Andre checked Halo's eyes and ears.

Halo meowed when Andre removed an otoscope from its right ear.

"Looks like his eyes and ears are perfectly healthy," Andre said. "No retinal damage, and no ear mites or signs of infection."

"What about his heartbeat, Dr. Lucas?" Emily asked.

Andre smiled. "Alright, let me have a listen here." He unclipped his stethoscope from his hip holder and plugged the earpieces in his ears. Andre held the metal diaphragm over Halo's chest, listening to the kitten's heart and lungs. "Halo's heart sounds like a steady beating drum. And I heard no sign of congestion." He linked the earpieces around his neck.

"That's good," Mrs. Witherspoon said. "Emily complained about Halo's breathing before at home. I caught her sleeping by his kennel in the kitchen yesterday morning."

"Hmm . . ." Andre arched his brow and snapped on a pair of latex gloves. "Well, let's check Halo's mouth, shall we?"

"Okay," Emily said with a half-shrug.

Andre opened Halo's mouth and examined the kitten's tiny white teeth, tongue, and tonsils. "Nope. No signs of cleft palates or inflammation. Everything looks good." Halo meowed again as Andre picked up the squirmy critter in his hands and felt around the abdomen of the kitten. "No signs of umbilical hernia. I guess there's one thing left to check." Andre put Halo down on the exam table, raised his tail and coated the kitten's rectum with Vaseline from a jar. Finally, he inserted a baby rectal thermometer to check Halo's temperature.

The thermometer chirped.

Andre removed it from Halo and read the digital degrees. "His temperature is . . . a hundred and one point five, which is normal for kittens—unlike humans. Halo's healthy as a horse and caught up with his vaccinations. No worries here."

"I keep telling her, doctor." Mrs. Witherspoon wrapped a lock of her straight, blonde hair behind an ear and rocked Tyler in her arms.

"Here you go." Andre smiled and handed Halo back to the little girl, who held him in her arms.

"Thank you, Dr. Lucas." Emily grinned hard, revealing her missing front tooth. She scratched her fingers behind Halo's pointed ears, making him purr.

"You're welcome, sweetheart," Andre replied, "but try not to worry yourself. Sometimes we can think something is wrong to the point we expect to find something. I know after losing Mittens, you're scared something bad will happen to Halo too. But if you take good care of your kitten—which you clearly have been doing—Halo should be fine, okay?"

Emily nodded and wiggled her glasses up her nose. "Yes, Dr. Lucas."

Her mother stood with Tyler in her arms, who was still fast asleep, sucking his thumb. She smiled and held out a hand. "Thank you, Dr. Lucas, for your patience."

Andre shook her hand. "No problem, Mrs. Witherspoon."

Mrs. Witherspoon watched Emily walk a distance away toward the entrance door and whispered, "I'm sorry we bothered you. I know you have special plans tonight."

Andre waved a hand and smiled. "That's okay. I understand Emily well. I was close to animals as a kid too. It's why I became a veterinarian."

"You know," Mrs. Witherspoon said, "I think it's her dad. He gave her Mittens on her sixth birthday, and she misses him, but she isn't alone. I can't wait until Neal can visit home. Every day I hope and pray he's safe." She sighed wistfully. "You're lucky to have the one you love close by."

"No, Mrs. Witherspoon . . . I'm blessed," Andre corrected. "I hope everything goes well with Neal's home visit."

"Thanks," Mrs. Witherspoon said, smiling, "and happy anniversary to you and Eva."

Andre's expression glowed. "Thank you. Have a good evening."

"You too." Mrs. Witherspoon turned her attention to her daughter. "Let's go, Emily. I need to get groceries at the store." She walked toward Emily and exited the office.

Andre pulled his cell phone out of his lab coat pocket. He dialed the number of the flower shop he ordered roses from for Eva. They were to arrive at their home in the afternoon, and he hoped his wife didn't go shopping or anywhere else after leaving work at the daycare. It would be terrible if the flowers got stolen.

They cost fifty bucks.

Someone answered his call.

"Hello, my name is Andre Lucas. I ordered a bouquet of white roses to one forty-three Pasture Road. Have they delivered? . . . They have? . . . Great, thank you."

Andre hung up the call and glanced at the ceiling. "God, please let Eva get them. I work hard for my money." He checked the wall clock for one last time.

6:41 p.m.

Meeting deadlines had always been a struggle for him, especially when it came to spending private time with his wife. Somehow, he had to keep his promise. He needed to prove to Eva he meant those vows to love, comfort, and honor her always, and that he had faith in God's sovereign power of wondrous miracles.

Anything was possible to those that believed, even if one doesn't know how the end result will turn out. Andre grabbed his briefcase and rushed out of his office, striving to fulfill his wife's expectation.

Not showing up could break Eva's heart forever.

2

Eva

THIRTY-THREE-YEAR-OLD EVA LUCAS SNIFFED THE fresh-cut, white roses in the vase and placed them on the dresser in their bedroom. A gentle smile inched up her face and traveled to the deep walls of her heart as she read the small, greeting card:

Whether near or apart, you'll be the only girl who holds the key to my heart. Happy Anniversary to the most beautiful woman I know!

Love you forever, Andre

Her husband was always sweet and kind to her since they first met in high school. She could still picture the teenaged boy he was, buried in an oversized, 76ers sweatshirt with grass-stained, denim jeans, helping her open her locker. After she moved from Seattle, Washington, being a new, shy student in a different school was difficult. But meeting Andre on her way to Mrs. Chapman's ninth- grade English class was one of the best times of her life. Since then, it began a lifetime friendship that grew stronger each summer vacation after the school year ended. They shared many similarities the more they knew each other. They both were biracial, caught in the middle of failed relationships, and moved away from the city to live in the southern state of North Carolina. She didn't know he did chores on a farm before school. But based on his clothes, she presumed he was careless of his appearance or wore his older brothers' hand-me-downs.

When her mother Melanie was seventeen, she met Andrew Martello, a young, Italian landscape artist during a college summer trip to Rome. Their relationship started through their artwork, but they quickly fell in love with each other.

Holding strong traditions, Andrew's mama didn't approve of him getting involved with a black woman. After the breakup, her mom returned to the States a broke, pregnant art student who had no clue where neither she nor her baby's life was going. Eva was raised living on welfare, but her mother's skilled hand and artistic talent also helped save them from poverty.

Eva walked over to the front of the queen-sized bed, wrapped in her lilac, downy robe. Piles of stylish dresses on hangers lay across, covering the comforter of the bed. Although Eva was a shopaholic, tonight finding the right outfit was like trying to pull a stubborn tooth. She tucked her left forearm under her right elbow and nibbled her index fingernail, scanning her row of best outfits.

"Hmm . . ." Eva shifted her eyes from her black, maxi dress to her peach, wrap dress her co-worker Louise bought her for her latest birthday. Either of these would be perfect, but she couldn't choose between them.

"Mrs. Flowers! Can you come here, please?" Eva called.

Mrs. Violet Flowers was a next-door neighbor across the street. She was a heavyset woman who embraced her African heritage. Her silvery gray hair remained in a braided crown bun, and being a widow, she appreciated getting company from the Lucas family.

"Yes?" The elderly woman waddled through the door in a long, silky, purple-and-yellow kaftan dress and strap sandals.

Eva sighed and rounded her shoulders. "I can't decide what to wear."

Mrs. Flowers jerked her head back and chuckled. "It's nerves, honey. You and Andre ain't been out to dinner in a while."

Eva glanced at Mrs. Flowers with a wry smile.

This was true.

Aside from a light goodnight kiss, there wasn't much time for her and Andre to do anything special together after their busy schedules. After their son was born, they were always tired, rushing to get shuteye before Andrew woke them for a bottle-feeding or changing.

"I guess I am a little nervous." Eva raked a hand through her wet, shoulder-length tendrils and sighed again. "I thought to wear my black or peach dress. What do you think?" She held each dress by their hanger and placed them against her average height, petite frame, switching between them.

"Well . . ." Mrs. Flowers curled her upper lip. "I like the peach better, but the material's kinda thin and you may be chilly. The weatherman said it's supposed to be cool with clear skies tonight." She shrugged. "How about you wear your wedding dress?"

"My wedding dress?" Eva raised a brow and laughed. "It's been seven years, Mrs. Flowers. I'm not sure if I can fit it anymore."

Mrs. Flowers sucked her teeth and waved a hand. "Oh, please, honey girl. You don't look like you've gained a pound since Andy was born."

A light bulb lit above Eva's head. "Andy! He's by himself. We're in here talking and he—"

"Don't worry," Mrs. Flowers said calmly, interrupting Eva's nervous jabbering, "that little fellow ain't wandering anywhere. He's in his playpen busy as a little bee."

Relief suffused Eva's features. "Oh, good."

"Now you get dressed while I go downstairs and warm Andy some mini ravioli."

Eva smiled. "All right, but don't do the dishes. I'll get them when we come back!"

Mrs. Flowers exited and closed the door behind her.

Eva walked to the large closet and slid hanging clothes on the rack bar. She found her old wedding dress in the back covered in plastic. Eva pulled it out and studied it for a moment, teary-eyed. Through the years, she marveled how their life had fit together like a jigsaw puzzle.

With her husband's well-paying job, they never had a worry of providing their daily needs or keeping up with bills. They were also fortunate to have their beautiful home, and a caring patriarch—Grandpa Ricardo—who was always there if they needed him. Finally, they had their adorable son Andrew who was a special gift and the latest chapter in their lives.

She removed the wrinkled plastic cover and stroked her hand on the smooth, shiny material. The last time she touched it was after she and Andre returned home from their honeymoon, and she washed and hung it in the closet.

Feeling her dress brought back old memories, memories she was sure neither she nor her husband would forget. For a whole week, she and Andre vacationed in Chihuahua, Mexico, staying in the Wingate hotel. They played golf at the San Francisco Country Club and ate fine dining at the Época restaurant, but Eva's favorite spot was touring the breathtaking Copper Canyon. She smiled and giggled, remembering the first night of their honeymoon.

Excited about their married life, Andre had hurried their luggage into their room. With an amused smile, Eva propped her head with a hand and waited for him on the luxury, king-sized bed. As the last tote bag slid off Andre's shoulder, he caught his breath, holding her gaze. His lopsided grin was priceless, closing the door behind him for their privacy.

Finally alone, the reality of their wedding had struck home and they took the opportunity given them. It was already dark by the time they flew into Mexico, and they couldn't think of a better time to carry out their romance. Eva had melted in Andre's affection. The second his arms embraced her, she knew she had a gem. When their bodies joined, their hearts sang in perfect harmony.

Eva closed her eyes and sighed, brushing her dress against her cheek. Because neither of them had experienced it before, she had cherished their first time most of all.

Eva's iPhone on the dresser rang, interrupting her muse. "Oh, hello?"

"Hey, it's me, Andre. I'm calling to let you know I've closed my clinic."

Eva grinned and played with her damp, wavy hair. "Okay. So, how was work?"

"Perfect." Andre sighed and paused before making his next comment. "Emily came in with her new kitten again."

Eva angled her head and turned down her mouth. "Aww . . . poor little girl."

"Yeah," Andre said, "but hopefully it'll be for the last time until necessary. I finally talked with her to resolve her problem. So, did you get the roses I ordered you?"

"Yes—" Eva handled one of the roses and sniffed it— "and I got the little note you sent with them. It was very thoughtful, considering the fact the delivery man sent me the wrong bouquet on our wedding day. They're beautiful. Thank you."

"You're welcome," Andre said. "You know, I've got another gift for you too."

Eva beamed. "Really? What is it?"

Andre laughed. "Do you think I'm gonna tell you over the phone? It's a surprise. I'll show you at dinner."

"But—"

"Eva," Andre interrupted sternly, "you'll get it at the restaurant."

Eva giggled. "Okay, I'll wait then." She untied the strap of her robe. "Well, I've freshened up, and I'm about to get dressed for tonight. Mrs. Flowers is already here to babysit Andy."

"Okey-dokey. I'll see you soon," Andre replied.

Eva wore a wry grin and cleared her throat. "I hope so, Dr. Lucas."

"Honey, please, don't talk like that. I'll be there, okay?" Andre said. "No more excuses."

Eva sighed over the line and made a half-shrug. "Sure, okay."

Her husband broke the awkward silence between them. "Bebé, te amo . . . tanto."

Eva found another smile and blushed. She always liked when he spoke in Spanish to her. "I love you too . . . but please, don't be late again. It's so embarrassing."

Andre chuckled over the line. "I won't. I promise. Goodbye."

"Bye. Love you!" Eva pressed the end-call button. She exited the master bedroom and skipped down the hallway into the bathroom. Born with her father's good hair, Eva blow-dried and styled hers in a matter of minutes.

When she finished, she returned to the bedroom. Her wedding dress fit her like a glove, so Mrs. Flowers was right about her not gaining weight. Of course, it wasn't exactly a surprise. Eva had always been thin as Olive Oyl since she was a small child. In fact, her mother worried she wasn't eating enough and packed two bologna sandwiches in her lunch instead of one.

Ironically, she had a big appetite for a person so little, and especially for pasta and seafood. Eva dropped her cell phone in her leopard clutch purse and snapped it. She took one last look at herself in the oval mirror of the dresser and fingered a couple of loose strands of her hair into place. Then she trotted downstairs to the first floor of the house. In the living room, an episode of *Barefoot Contessa* was playing on the flat screen above the electric brick fireplace. Mrs. Flowers enjoyed watching her cooking shows on Food Network whenever she was over at their house.

"I'm ready," Eva announced, strolling into the kitchen. She found Mrs. Flowers standing in front of the double-basin sink. Andrew was sitting in his blue highchair, eating his small plastic bowl of Chef Boyardee's ravioli.

Tomato sauce stained his cheeks and 'Daddy Loves Me' bib, but after many failed tactics and tantrums, Eva was just glad he finally wasn't using his hands. She gasped with enthusiasm, her hand over her heart. "Is my little Andy using a spoon?"

"Mm-hmm," Mrs. Flowers said over her shoulder, washing out one of Andy's sippy cups with a scrub brush.

"You're growing into a big boy," Eva said, smiling at her son.

"Raa-vee! Raa-vee!" Andrew grinned and tapped his saucy spoon on the tray of his highchair.

"Yes, I see," Eva said with a chuckle, nodding. "Is it good?"

Andrew ate another spoonful and jiggled in his seat. "Mmm, Mommy . . ."

Eva and Mrs. Flowers laughed at the little boy's wit.

Although he couldn't speak too many words, he was an intelligent toddler who understood what others were saying to him. Eva glanced away from Andrew, realizing Mrs. Flowers was washing the dishes. She frowned and walked to the elderly woman, her hands on her hips. "Oh, Mrs. Flowers . . . I told you I'll wash the dishes when Andre and I come back home."

"It's all right, Eva," Mrs. Flowers said, "staying busy helps me forget."

Eva dropped her shoulders and sighed. She knew exactly what Mrs. Flowers meant by her remark. She was talking about her husband Clyde, the one and only lover in her lifetime.

Two years ago, he was called home after a lost battle with Alzheimer's disease. He was a veteran of the Korean War who enlisted right after high school. Clyde sent money to Mrs. Flowers and her family to help save their farm. Often Mrs. Flowers told Eva past stories about their young courtship, and how she never stopped waiting for her war hero's return.

Eva wrapped an arm around the old woman's shoulders. "I'm sorry, Mrs. Flowers. Mr. Clyde was a good man. I know his loss is tough for you."

"Yes, very. I still miss him," Mrs. Flowers said. "You know, true love never dies. One might try to replace it with other things or people, but it never dies." She felt tears form in her eyes and blinked them back. "Well, I don't want to spoil your happy day. You and Andre enjoy yourselves." She patted Eva's arm around her.

"Thank you, Mrs. Flowers. I appreciate your help. Good night." Eva turned her attention to Andrew. "Good night, baby. Be good for Mommy." She kissed the top of her son's curly black hair and added to Mrs. Flowers, "Make sure you call if you need me for anything. My cell number's on the refrigerator."

"Girl, get outta here. You know I always do," Mrs. Flowers said.

Eva chuckled. "All right, take care." She walked out of the kitchen and exited the house. Outside with her hand on the gold knob, she placed her other to her stomach. A bad, queasy feeling caught her off guard, like a foul smell down a country road.

She took a deep breath and locked the front door. *Don't embarrass me, Andre. Please be on time.*

3
Andre

ANDRE BARGED THROUGH THE SWING EXIT DOOR of Pet Friends Veterinary Clinic and felt a drizzle tap his forehead. Thunder crackled and rolled in the distance. He paused in his tracks and frowned at the sky. Giant thick clouds smothered the fiery, evening sunset, casting a shadowy gloom over the spacious parking lot.

A thunderstorm? Though there was a forty percent chance, the weatherman was wrong this time. Andre took a long breath of the damp, earthy air. His heart skipped a beat. He had to get to the restaurant before it rained.

He left his umbrella at home, and the last thing he wanted was to arrive with his navy tuxedo soaked, not to mention double pneumonia. Andre jogged toward his 2017 blue velvet Chevy Impala and unlocked the doors with his keychain remote. He plopped in the driver's seat and shut the door.

Andre let out a sigh of relief, slipped his cell phone out of his hip holster, and placed it in the car holder clipped to an air vent. More thunder clashed, startling him as he pressed the six-speed engine button. Lightning flashed twice behind the monstrous clouds, giving a quick illusion of a bright summer morning. Andre buckled his seatbelt and glanced at the clock on the panel screen of his car.

6:43 p.m.

Time had always been a key factor, wondering and questioning if he trusted God enough to have another child. Would he finally take that leap of faith? He couldn't disappoint his wife again, and he wouldn't. He hadn't told her all his romantic plans for them, but after dinner, she would find out in the hotel suite he booked for them. There were seven minutes to spare. Maybe he wouldn't be late this time. Andre shifted the gearstick in reverse, speeding out the parking space.

But he was too late.

Steady rain pitter-pattered the windshield and sunroof of his car, blurring his view. Andre turned on the wipers and stared hopelessly, clutching the steering wheel. Within seconds, the dry road across from him became a slick, black stream. *Please, God, not again.* From his wedding anniversary to his son's baby milestones, his number of tardies was ridiculous. He hoped Eva and Andrew knew they were important to him.

Andre bit his lip and shifted into drive, cruising down the sloped, paved entrance to the clinic. He glanced down Lime Street, his attention caught by several blowing car horns.

Traffic was jam-packed.

Just great. Andre gritted his teeth and sighed. Now with the weather against him and traffic crowded, going the longer route was the only option. He turned onto Colonel Highway, taking a back country road. He rode past his grandfather's farmhouse and nearby cornfields.

As he made a smooth sharp turn onto Pasture Road, he flicked on his high beams to better see the flooded street. Andre drove by the Thomas family's place, the rugged remains of a small, wooden shack. Fifty years ago, it caught fire after a lightning bolt struck the wind vane during a thunderstorm. Its roof had collapsed from the burning flames, but the ancient house was still standing despite the tragic disaster.

Andre's mobile phone in the holder vibrated. He stole a glance at his cell while steering his wheel.

Eva sent a text message: *Please hurry. I'm hungry. Waiting @ The Redfish Grill.*

Andre returned a reply via Bluetooth: *OMW. Love you!*

He peeked at the clock.

Five minutes were left.

Andre's smile dropped as he looked up from his phone again. In the burst of lightning, a deer leaped in front of his vehicle in the middle of the street. He gasped and stomped on his brake, his heart pounding against his rib cage. His car's tires squealed, sliding into the white-tailed animal.

"Aaaah!" Andre closed his eyes tightly, gripped the wheel, and braced himself. There was a hefty thump of an impact. The deer smashed through the windshield and knocked Andre in his head. Shattered glass flew inside the car's interior. He slumped over in his seat and lost control of the wheel. The car swerved and scraped against the metal guardrail.

Sparks sputtered from the railing as the car screeched off the road and crashed into a neighbor's front yard tree. Thick smoke spewed from the crushed car like carbonated fizz down a shaken-up soda can. Andre's eyes were open, but nothing more than slits. His vision blurred at the lifeless touchscreen between the front air vents.

His body was stiff and ached with excruciating pain, slouching against the passenger seat. He squirmed and attempted to sit upright, but the weight of the deer on his lap pinned him down. Andre winced and exhaled shallow breaths in a panic. He reached a cut, bleeding hand to his crown and felt a deep gash on his head. Andre studied his hand and nearly fainted at the sight of blood.

"Help . . . somebody . . . help me," he said breathlessly. No one could hear him. Except for the thunder and rain pelting his car, he heard nothing. It seemed all hope was lost. After waiting for what felt like infinity, someone knocked and shined a flashlight inside his car.

"Hold on, sir! We're gonna get you out!" a policeman said, his voice muffled against the passenger window. The officer spoke to his fellow colleagues and walked off from the scene of the accident. Fire truck and ambulance sirens rang and approached the scene. Motor equipment zoomed off, and metal bent and broke apart.

Someone was rescuing him.

Andre was breathing heavy and panicked again. In an instant, his whole life flashed before him: his drug addict parents arguing over him, his childhood on his grandpa's farm, his school and college graduations, his wedding day, and the birth of his son. He wanted to speak again, his thoughts and memories slipping away. Andre bobbed his eyelids, fighting to stay awake.

But as gentle as the wind, darkness settled in and would remain for weeks.

4

Eva

FOR THIRTY MINUTES, SHE WAITED FOR HER HUSBAND, sitting at their reserved, two-seat table. She grinned as a tall gentleman of cinnamon brown complexion in a dark suit entered the golden revolving door with an umbrella. Her heart leaped. *Andre?*

Eva craned her neck above the artificial potted plants on a shelf for a better look. When the man closed his wet umbrella and sat at another table with another woman, her smile faded. Her anticipating of his arrival was becoming more unbearable.

She frowned and lowered herself in her chair. *Where could he be?*

Andre was never *this* late. He should've come by now with his surprise gift. But at the restaurant he was nowhere to be found. Though it was raining, The Redfish Grill was only a five-minute drive from the clinic. She couldn't think of what's more important at the moment than celebrating their anniversary. They had been through a lot together, especially during the birth of their son. Eva thought she'd die, that she'd never get to hold the baby she carried for nine months.

With every shallow breath behind her oxygen mask, her fear was intense and deadly, but she felt Mrs. Flowers' prayers from the waiting room. Because Andrew was born healthy and she lived for another day, a guardian angel had to have watched over them that afternoon.

Hearing Andrew's tiny piercing cry for the first time brought tears to her eyes and a sigh of relief. Since then, it mattered little to Andre if they had another baby. He was just grateful she and their son were alive.

Eva pulled her iPhone out her clutch purse and pressed the side button, lighting her touchscreen. She glanced at the time displayed in big, white skinny numbers.

7:20 p.m.

She willed herself to keep calm as Stefano—her waiter—approached her table. He was dressed in a white dress shirt with a black bow tie, a gold shiny vest, black pants, and polished dress shoes, the uniform of all the waiters.

"Ma'am, are you ready to order?" Stefano asked.

Eva sniffled and picked up her Redfish Grill menu. Her vision blurred with angry tears, staring at the restaurant's slogan above the red rockfish logo: *Elegant Seafood at Its Best*. "I guess I should. There's no telling when my husband will come."

Stefano sighed. "I'm sorry he hasn't shown again. I know how much this meant to you, but you mustn't doubt yourself. Andre loves you a great deal. You have to believe that." He shrugged. "He probably got caught in the storm. I'm sure he intended to be here."

Eva swiped a tear from her cheek and hung her head. "He did, and he promised he'd come, but for some reason he always gets tied up in work." She leaned back with an exhale. "I feel so stupid. I should've expected nothing different from him this year. Andre's always late. It's . . . the way he is." She opened her menu and skimmed the entrée selections. "I'll have the grilled salmon with broccoli slaw, please."

Stefano jotted on his notepad. "Okay. And to drink?"

"Iced water with lemon," Eva said.

The muscular, six-foot-three, Italian waiter scribbled again. "Would you like any of our appetizers while you wait? We have some new tasty crab cakes I think you'd love."

"No, thanks," Eva replied dispiritedly, "the breadsticks on the table will do for now."

Stefano smiled. "All right, I'll be back with your drink." He tucked his notepad in a back pocket of his pants and placed a hand on her shoulder. "Cheer up, Eva. I'm sure Andre's dorky self will come here soaked from head to toe in no time."

Eva glanced at the waiter with a chuckle. "Thanks." She watched as Stefano walked away and disappeared through the French doors to the kitchen. Eva closed her menu and placed it and her phone aside on the table. While waiting, she texted her husband four times, but he responded once. She pinched the bridge of her nose and shook her head. *How could you do this, Andre?*

Six times was a world record. If he was running late, the least he could've done was told her when he called earlier or send a message ahead of time. Instead, he left her hoping like many times before. Perhaps Stefano was right. Maybe Andre *was* held back from the weather, or maybe his lateness had to do with her surprise gift. She hadn't a clue of what it was but thinking like a man she imagined one thing.

Lingerie.

Ever since Andrew was born, she and Andre hadn't been intimate for a long time. They'd only talked about giving their son a sibling to play with, a thoughtful picture

33

never put into focus. Andre's anxiety hindered their venture.

Whenever Eva snuggled him and attempted to grasp his attention, he hesitated or claimed he wasn't ready, pushing her away. But Andre's returned kisses and yearning, teary eyes told her differently. It hurt to watch her husband struggling with his desire because of fear of losing her in childbirth.

Maybe he'd finally overcome his cold feet. Although the outcome was unknown, Eva had told him God could work everything out and allow her to have a healthy delivery. Where was Andre's faith? Seemingly, her near-death experience scared him more than her. And if the worse unfolded, she imagined Andre would never forgive himself.

Eva averted her eyes from the empty chair in front of her. She glanced at other happy customers talking and eating with family and friends. Eva listened to the clinking of silverware and relaxing jazz piano music sifting through the ceiling speakers.

She sighed, grabbed a breadstick from the straw basket on the table, and gnawed on it. On her right, a family of eight was having a dinner party. The birthday boy who sat in the center of attention wore a polka-dotted party hat. Based on his blue helium balloon he had turned twelve.

To Eva's left, she saw a young couple who looked like they had come from a formal dance. The man opened a small box and proposed to the woman, who smiled, said yes, and gave him a light kiss.

Disappointment sagged on Eva's shoulders, crossing her arms. When she finishes her meal and goes home, she would definitely have a word with Andre tonight about breaking promises.

"Here you go, ma'am." Stefano placed a glass goblet of iced water with a lemon slice on the brim in front of her.

She gave a weak smile. "Oh, thank you."

"You're welcome. Your meal will be ready in about ten minutes," Stefano added.

Eva nodded. "Okay. Thanks."

The waiter left to the kitchen again.

Eva took the lemon slice off her brim, squirted juice into her water, and rattled the ice cubes in her glass. She took a sip to wash down the breadstick she'd eaten and put her cup down.

Her cell phone vibrated to life.

Eva's ears grew hot, answering without checking the caller ID. "Where are you? I've waited like an hour!"

"Excuse me?" an older gentleman said over the line.

Eva frowned at the unfamiliar, man's voice. "Wait . . . who is this?"

"Ma'am, this is Captain Victor Pierce of Garden Ridge Police Department."

"Is something wrong?" Eva's heart skipped a beat.

The captain sighed. "Yes, ma'am. I'm so sorry . . . but your husband's been in an accident."

Fear clawed through Eva and ripped her resentment to shreds. Now she'd wait a century if it meant seeing Andre alive and well. Her body tensed, pondering the endless possibilities of her husband's condition.

"Uh . . . thank you for telling me," she said. "Is . . . is he alright?"

"I'm not sure, ma'am," the captain said. "It appears he suffered a deer-vehicle collision. He lost control of his car after the impact and crashed into a tree. Paramedics took him to Garden Ridge Hospital about ten minutes ago. I'm really sorry this happened."

"Thank you," Eva said. She ended the call and sat silently amid the lively commotion in the restaurant. In twelve words her world had turned upside down, and nothing mattered but her husband's life. Had he survived the car accident?

Eva took a pen from her clutch purse and wrote a note on a paper napkin: *I had to leave for an emergency. Thank you for your service.* She took a couple of dollars from her wallet, hid it and the note under her goblet cup, and hurried out the revolving door.

5

Eva

EVA BARGED THROUGH THE HOSPITAL AND PAUSED AT
the reception counter.

She brushed her damp hair from her face and caught
her breath in the midst of the nurses' ringing telephones
and light chatter. "Excuse me, I'm Eva Lucas. My husband,
Andre, was admitted here about ten minutes ago. He was
in a car accident."

"Yes, ma'am," a blonde nurse in blue scrubs said, "he was
taken into surgery. If you'd have a seat in the waiting room,
a doctor will speak with you later."

"Okay, thank you." Eva walked away and sat in the
waiting room. She tied her hair back in a ponytail, clasped
her hands in her lap, and took a few deep breaths. Hearing
about her husband in surgery upset her stomach again. Had
she sensed something would happen to Andre before she
left home? Was her nausea a warning sign?

Questions about her husband swam through her mind. *What if he doesn't look the same? What if I don't recognize him? What if he's in a coma? Oh, no . . . what if he dies under the knife?*

Though she wished for the best, she wasn't prepared for the worst. Eva leaned back in her chair and bounced her leg. She glanced at the CNN news blasting from the flat screen mounted on the ceiling above a vending machine.

Eight other people occupied the sitting area, but Eva felt like she was alone. She bowed her head as tears stung her eyes. "God, please, don't take my husband. *Please . . .*" What would she do if Andre died? He was an important member of her and Andrew's lives and they needed him. As time passed and visitors left the hospital, Eva fell asleep.

An hour later, she finally received an update. Someone tapped on her shoulder, and she opened her weary eyes. Two doctors in white lab coats stood before her.

One, an older African American with a bald spot, looked at her over thick eyeglasses. The other, a lanky redhead in teal scrubs and a surgeon cap tugged down a surgical mask from his face. Based on the men's solemn expressions, Eva could tell she was in for heavy news.

The bald doctor cleared his throat. "Mrs. Lucas?"

Eva rose from her chair. "Yes?"

"Hi. I'm Dr. Edwin Brown, Andre's critical care physician." The bald doctor gestured a hand to the redhead surgeon beside him. "This is Dr. Alex Larrabee, the neurosurgeon who performed Andre's surgery."

Eva shook each of the doctors' hands. "Nice to meet you both." She folded her arms and swayed to keep her composure. "How's my husband? Is he okay?" Her eyes welled up and her heart punched in her chest, longing for relief.

Dr. Brown licked his full lips. "Mrs. Lucas, I don't want to drag this out. Andre's in critical condition. He's . . . he's in a coma. I'm sorry."

A tear spilled from Eva's eye. Her chin quivered, and she lowered her head. The moment the doctor said 'coma,' she felt like her life was sucked into a black hole. With Andre, she was trapped in empty darkness filled with stillness and uncertainty.

"We did CT and MRI scans on your husband, which showed serious damage to the left frontal and parietal lobes of his brain," Dr. Brown added. "It appears he has a common brain injury called Diffuse Axonal Injury or DAI. It's a shearing and stretching of the nerve cells, caused by the acceleration and deceleration of the brain's movement in the skull. We also found a few cerebral contusions or bruising, caused by bleeding on the external tissue of the brain. It's a result of his brain striking the skull in his traumatic car accident."

"Oh, God . . ." Eva stifled a sob with her hand. *No! The doctor's lying! It can't be true. How could this be happening?*

Dr. Brown continued. "An Officer Greg McKee found this on the interior floor of the damaged car." He dug his hand in a side pocket of his lab coat.

Greg McKee? Eva recognized the name as the father of her daycare student Autumn McKee, who was a policeman.

The doctor fished out a small black box and handed it to Eva. "Here, ma'am . . . this belongs to you."

"What?" Eva frowned and took the box from him. She unfastened the gold latch and opened it. Before her eyes embedded in gray velvet was a personalized keychain. It was made of two shiny pennies and a stainless-steel tag linked with key rings to a swivel clip. Each penny was engraved with a tiny heart and a name.

One penny was etched with her name and the other with her husband's name. The tag was carved with the numbers 08.28.10—Eva and Andre's wedding date. Now she understood this was the surprise gift her husband intended to give her during their anniversary dinner. It was the most beautiful, unique keychain she ever saw, designed as a reminder for them.

She whimpered and licked her tears, tracing her forefinger over the penny etched with Andre's name. "Thank you," she whispered and sniffled. "I love it."

"You're welcome. We know Andre wanted you to have this." Dr. Brown sighed and changed the subject back to Andre's medical condition. "Miraculously, he suffered no spinal cord injury. If it wasn't for the weight of the deer pinning his body, police believe he would've been ejected from his car."

"So, he'll be able to walk?" Eva asked.

"I don't know," Dr. Brown said. "Unfortunately, it's too early to tell for sure. For now, he's been transferred to ICU where his trauma team will monitor him. Some of the staff is waiting to meet you."

Eva closed the box and dabbed her knuckle at a tear. "What happened in his surgery?" She turned her attention to the neurosurgeon.

"I performed an external ventricular drain placement," Dr. Larrabee said.

Eva grimaced and darted her watery eyes. "What's that?"

"A catheter was inserted through a hole in Andre's skull into the ventricle of his brain. It's a procedure that will help us track his intracranial pressure. Brain swelling increases pressure in the brain and can cause injury to parts of the brain that weren't affected by the accident. But the sooner we drain your husband's cerebrospinal fluid, the sooner we can prevent further damage," Dr. Larrabee explained.

Eva swallowed a lump in her throat. "What happens if his brain pressure gets too high?"

"Andre would need a decompressive craniectomy," Dr. Larrabee answered. He sighed and elaborated on the medical procedure. "Basically, this surgery involves removing a large area of his skull so his brain has more room to swell. His exposed brain would be covered with biologic tissue, and the bone flap of his skull would be preserved in a freezer. After his swelling subsides, I would replace it in a second surgery called cranioplasty, but we're hoping Andre won't need these procedures."

Eva glanced at each doctor. "Can I see him?"

Dr. Brown nodded. "Of course, but only for a little while. Visiting hours for ICU patients is almost over. Please don't remove his cloth restraints or any tubing. All his medical equipment is there for Andre's safety as hard as it may be to watch. Be careful also to keep noise and physical contact to a minimum. Brain injury patients recover best in quiet settings. Talking to him and holding Andre's hand will be enough for him to know you're there."

"Please make sure you also clean your hands before you enter the room," Dr. Larrabee added. "Your husband's stationed in room I-7. We'll take you there."

"Okay. Thank you, doctors." Eva followed the physicians down the hall toward double doors to the ICU unit. As she passed other distraught patients, she braced herself for the flood of emotions that will overwhelm her the second she stepped in Andre's room. She released a slow breath and relaxed her shoulders as she turned a corner with the doctors. Above their heads, a large sign labeled the wing section of the hospital. *Intensive Care Unit.*

Standing in a circle outside the labeled door were two female nurses and a male nurse in colored scrubs and a middle-aged woman in a dress suit. She observed as they whispered and watched her approaching them. From a tinted window she saw a shadow of a man in a bed in the ICU ward. She placed a hand on the cold pane and peered at the darkness. *Andre . . . honey, is that you in there?*

A hand touched her shoulder, causing her to look away. "Mrs. Lucas, these are members of Andre's healthcare team to support you and your husband," Dr. Brown said.

A Chinese-American woman in blue scrubs extended a hand. "Hi, I'm Jia Li, Andre's nurse practitioner. I'll be keeping track of your husband's intracranial pressure and the recovery process of his level of consciousness."

"Hello." Eva shook the practitioner's hand.

A brunette nurse in pink scrubs introduced herself to Eva "Hi, I'm Nurse Daphne, one of Andre's bedside nurses. I'll assist in Andre's IV medications, nutrition, and other daily needs."

Eva nodded timidly. "Hi, nice to meet you." She looked at the dirty-blond male nurse standing beside Daphne.

"Hello, Mrs. Lucas. I'm Hayden Rivers, another nurse of Andre's healthcare team," he said, shaking her hand. "I know you're facing a difficult time, but I'll give you my full support. Dr. Barbara Washburn is a social worker and also here if you need extra help."

"That's right, Mrs. Lucas," the social worker said in a Caribbean accent. "We want you to know we're here for you. My office is open every day from 7:00 a.m. to 5:00 p.m. I can help guide you toward the best treatment for your husband and answer questions you have." She offered her business card. "You can call me whenever you're ready. No pressure."

"Um, thank you." Eva took the card with a weak smile and put it in her clutch purse. She surveyed the group of people around her and felt their love and concern. "Thank you very much."

"We have Andre ready for you to visit," Nurse Daphne said.

Eva faced Dr. Brown, her eyes filled with worry.

The physician gave a nod, giving his reassurance for her entrance.

Eva squirted sanitizer from a wall dispenser in her palm and rubbed her hands together. She took another breath, entered the room, and closed the lightweight door with her elbow. As she approached Andre's motionless body, she felt like she was in Dr. Frankenstein's laboratory—that her husband was some kind of human experiment.

Wires and tubes from beeping machines, monitor screens, and plastic bags attached on his body everywhere, except his hands and feet. He wore a plastic cervical collar for neck support, and his wrists were tied to the side rails of his bed.

Her heart broke at the sight of him. She sat in a lounge chair at the left of his bedside. "Andre? Andre . . . it's Eva, I'm right here. Honey, please . . . please don't leave me." She leaned forward and got a closer look at his face.

His curly, black hair had been cut for his operation, but other than a few nicks and bruises, he looked normal. Eva held Andre's cold, bandaged hand. She longed for a word, a gesture, or a moan, but he made no sound or move. He was stone-still, and she doubted he'd ever wake again.

"Andre, I'm so sorry." Eva placed a hand to her mouth and sobbed. "If I hadn't urged you to come on time for dinner, you might've not gotten in a car accident. I'm sorry I doubted you were coming as you promised me. Now I know you were . . . you just didn't make it."

She stroked her fingers over Andre's shaved head. "Please, forgive me . . . I love you." She stifled another sob, willing herself to be strong. "Now you listen good, Andre Miguel Lucas, you fight to get better, you hear? Your son needs you . . . I need you." She bowed her head in prayer. "God, please help my husband. Heal his body and mind in Jesus Christ's name. Amen."

Someone opened the door.

"Mrs. Lucas, visiting hours are over," Dr. Brown said.

Eva lifted her tear-stained face to the doctor. She darted her eyes from Dr. Brown to Nurse Daphne. "I'm staying with him."

"Ma'am, I'm sorry but—"

"Doctor, please," Eva interrupted, "it's our seventh wedding anniversary."

Dr. Brown set his mouth in a hard line and sighed. "All right, but only for tonight." He faced his nurse assistant. "Daphne, give her Andre's privacy code number. I'm sure she'd want it."

"Of course, doctor," Daphne said as the physician left the room. She walked to the bedside near Eva. "Mrs. Lucas,

I have Andre's privacy code number for you."

"Privacy code number?" Eva looked confused.

"Mm-hmm," the nurse replied, "it'll help you keep in contact with the trauma team and how Andre's condition is progressing. Under the HIPAA laws, we're limited in giving out patient information. But by using our system, we can grant your request to help you feel you're involved in Andre's care, despite your absence. It helps us to respect patient privacy and the needs of loved ones."

"Oh, okay." Eva found a smile.

The nurse jotted Andre's privacy number, the hospital phone number, and the extension to the ICU department on a sticky note. She gave it to Eva. "Here you go, Mrs. Lucas. The ICU unit is open from 8:30 a.m. to 8:30 p.m. When you call, make sure you state your relationship to Andre and give his privacy code number over the phone."

"Thank you," Eva replied.

"Would you like a blanket?" Daphne asked.

Eva nodded. "Yes, please."

"Okay. I'll be right back." The brown-haired nurse smiled and exited the room.

Eva let out a weary breath and leaned back in her chair. With her husband hanging between life and death, she hoped everything was fine with Andrew and Mrs. Flowers at home. She should check on them, but she was so concerned about Andre, she waited until morning. Besides, she had record proof she could trust Mrs. Flowers since the day her son was born, and the elderly woman always said Andrew was like a grandson to her.

She turned her attention back to Andre and lightly kissed the stitches on his head. "Happy Anniversary, Andre. I received your surprise gift from the doctor. It's beautiful." Eva released his hand wrapped in gauze and turned over to her side in the chair, trying to get comfortable. "Good night. Sweet dreams." Her eyes grew heavy in a matter of seconds. She didn't realize she drifted out until a wool blanket was draped over her and the single ceiling light switched off.

Eva squinted at the nurse in pink in the doorway.

"Good night, Mrs. Lucas," Daphne whispered. "See you in the morning."

Eva closed her eyes, repositioned her body, and waited to doze back off.

6

Eva

SUN RAYS PIERCED THROUGH THE HOSPITAL CURTAIN and beamed on Eva's face. She blinked her eyelids open to the glare of a brand-new day, hearing the beeps and pings of Andre's life support machines. Eva pulled down the tan, wool blanket and straightened in the upholstered guest chair.

She placed her feet on the ice-cold, linoleum floor, startled by its freezing touch. Her body was sluggish and stiff. For the whole livelong night, she had slept in a fetal position, hugging her legs to her chest to keep warm in the cool ICU ward.

Eva massaged and rotated her neck to loosen a tight kink. She leaned forward and checked on her husband. Several hours passed, but nothing changed. Andre still rested peacefully—quiet as a feather fluttering to the ground. *Can he hear me when I talk to him? Is he really listening?* She spoke again.

"Good morning, Andre." Eva yawned. "How did you sleep? I slept terribly." She slumped with an arch in her back and brushed a lock of messy hair from her tired face. Looking at her husband, she chuckled, imagining his witty response.

"Pretty good, but my eyes can't decide when to open," he'd say.

Eva held Andre's hand and wore a wistful smile. "Oh, Andre, I wish you'd wake. I miss hearing you talk."

Seconds after her remark, Nurse Jia entered the room, dressed in her blue scrubs and black Crocs, her jet-black hair tied in a sleek ponytail. She smiled at Eva and kicked a wedge under the door to prop it open. "Good morning. I'm here to check Andre's level of consciousness. I'll be examining him using our healthcare Glasgow Coma Scale."

Jia grabbed a three-ring binder from a slot at the footboard of Andre's hospital bed, unfolded it, and clicked a pen. "The Glasgow Coma Scale is an assessment method to test how well a patient responds to external stimuli. Each day I'll observe Andre's eye, verbal, and motor responses, and rate him based on his physical reactions. The higher the total score, the better his brain's recovery."

The nurse practitioner sighed and added, "However, a low score can mean his brain pressure is stagnant or changing for the worse. The good news is Andre's intracranial pressure monitor can alert us of an emergency that requires the doctor's attention."

"Yes," Eva said. "Dr. Larrabee said Andre could need another operation."

Jia nodded. "That's right. Bleeding or high swelling of the brain is serious and can be fatal. Typically, a score of fifteen means a patient is fully conscious, but a score of three means the patient is in a deep coma." She walked to the bedside. "Good morning, Andre. Can you open your eyes for me, please?" The nurse gently stroked Andre's shoulder and observed him, but his eyes stayed closed. With her ink pen, she applied pressure to Andre's middle finger of his left hand, counting for ten seconds while watching him.

Nothing again.

Jia scribbled on a sheet in the notebook. She placed the binder down and held Andre's hand. "Hey, Andre. Can you try to squeeze my hand?"

Eva gulped and studied Andre's still face.

"Come on, now. Squeeze my hand, Andre," Jia said again, but Andre's hand remained limp in hers. She sighed and jotted another note. Then she took a penlight from her shirt pocket and shined it in Andre's eyes, checking if his pupils contract. Jia shook her head and wrote in her notebook again.

"What's his score?" Eva sensed it was below fifteen.

"Three," Jia said, "same as yesterday in the emergency room, but it's expected. He's had a severe head injury. The impact of the deer plus the head-on collision is like a toxic chemical reaction."

Eva lowered her head with a hopeless exhale.

Dr. Brown strolled into the room with his hands in the pockets of his white lab coat. "How's Andre this morning?"

"No change, doctor," Jia replied. "He's still in a coma."

"Well, that's typical," Dr. Brown said. "Only a small percentage of patients wake the first day after a traumatic accident."

Eva angled her head. "When did he lose consciousness?"

The doctor fidgeted with his thick eyeglasses. "We don't know for sure, but he was unconscious while paramedics rushed him to the hospital. The important thing is to make sure Andre's brain pressure remains under control."

Eva slipped on her white-silk, cameo heels and stood with her clutch purse. Tears stung her eyes, staring at the catheter inserted in Andre's head. "Doctor, how long . . . how long will he...."

"Unfortunately, I can't say," Dr. Brown answered. "Every patient is different. He could be in a coma for a few days to a couple of weeks. Usually, it doesn't last longer than two weeks, but if it exceeds that, there's a possibility he won't recover. I know it's hard leaving him behind, but your husband *will* be taken care of. We'll keep you posted if there are significant changes, and don't forget you can call or visit within our ICU hours for updates too. For now, though, stay calm and take care of yourself."

Eva wiped beneath her eyes and nodded. "You're right. I should go. I need to make calls and look after our son. Our neighbor's watching him right now. Uh . . . thanks for helping Andre."

Dr. Brown smiled. "No need to thank us. It's our job."

"Take care, Mrs. Lucas, and get some proper rest," Jia added.

"I'll try." Eva wore a weak smile and looked back at Andre again. She planted a soft kiss on her husband's cheek.

"I love you," she whispered in his ear. "Hold tight for me, honey, okay? I'll visit you tomorrow." Eva tilted her head and watched him as his ventilator whooshed and paused in the midst of the quiet, sterile room. She drew a long breath and exited. Now outside in the hospital corridor, she felt like she left one world and entered another. She rubbed her hands with sanitizer, turned the corner, and strode down the hall toward the automatic entrance doors.

EVA PLOPPED IN THE DRIVER'S SEAT OF HER TUNGSTEN silver Volkswagen Golf and held her steering wheel, resting her forehead on her hands. Her shoulders bobbed as buckets of hot tears slipped down her cheeks. Feeling hungry and cranky she was a perfect replica of a two-year-old having a tantrum. She couldn't wait to eat breakfast, take a fresh, warm shower, and cuddle in her own bed.

Last night had been a wrestling match between dreadful anxiety and hopeful desire. She sniffled and peered at the dazzling sunrise behind the hospital building complex. Eva bit back a whimper, soaking in her sorrow.

Heartbreaking thoughts beguiled her, weighing her heart with guilt. *It's all your fault! You shouldn't have texted him. You distracted him from the road. It was you! All your fault!* Her mind reflected on everything that happened: the police officer's call, the surgery, Andre's coma, and the diagnosis. It all was like a bad dream, and today still felt like a living nightmare. She took her cell phone out of her purse and pressed the on button.

Eva checked for text messages and missed calls. For a second, she stared at the last text Andre sent her before his car accident: *On my way. Love you!* Although he was late from work often, Eva believed he definitely intended to meet her last night. Stefano was right, and she felt in her heart Andre loved her more than words could say. Her phone chirped off and notifications popped on the screen. Eva swiped her finger and found three missed calls.

One of them was from Mrs. Flowers, and the other two were from Mrs. Gracie Higgins, her director at Sunrise Christian Daycare. Each morning she began work at 6:30 a.m., but it was after seven. Now was a good time to inform them about her whereabouts and Andre's car accident. She dialed the number of her workplace and pinned her phone to her ear.

The dial tone rang.

"Sunrise Christian Daycare, how can I direct your call?" the receptionist asked.

"Oh, hi, Janet. It's me, Eva. Is Mrs. Higgins there?"

"Yes, she is. I'll transfer you to the Teacher's Lounge," Janet said.

Eva smiled. "Thanks."

There was a long pause over the phone line.

"This is Gracie Higgins. How can I help you?" an older woman said. Her voice was low and raspy but filled with a heartfelt welcome.

"Hello, Mrs. Higgins. It's Eva."

"Eva? Eva Lucas? Where are you? What happened? I was expecting you to clock in. Louise was climbing the walls trying to handle ten rowdy kids alone in the two-year-old classroom, but some of them were sent home. It's against regulations to have an unequal teacher-child ratio, and you know this! I allowed their parents to drop off their kids expecting you'd be here!" Her tone was sharp and unmerciful.

Eva felt like she was being lectured by her toxic mother. She grabbed a napkin from her glove compartment and slammed it shut. "Well, I'm sorry, okay! My husband had a car accident last night." She sniffled and wiped her runny nose.

Her director gasped. "Oh, no . . . I'm so sorry. Forgive me, I didn't mean to go off the deep end. I've been under a lot of stress today."

Eva sighed wearily. "I understand, and I don't blame you for being upset. I should've called or sent a message sooner, but I wasn't thinking about it. I guess I . . . didn't care about my job at the moment."

"I don't mean to be nosey, but how bad was the accident?" Mrs. Higgins said.

"Well, right now he's in a coma," Eva answered, "and the doctor said he's suffered a brain injury. Diffuse something. I don't remember what it's called. It's been a long night." She closed her eyes and rubbed her forehead. "I need . . . I need time to cope, Mrs. Higgins."

"Of course," Mrs. Higgins said, "I reckon I can change the scheduling. I'll give you a week, but I'm afraid it's all I can spare."

Eva found a smile. "Thank you, Mrs. Higgins. I'll be back after next week."

"Good, and I'll be praying for Andre," her director said.

"Thank you. Goodbye." Eva exhaled and ended the call. She scrolled through her contacts list and started to redial her home number, but her ringtone jingled off, notifying her of an incoming call.

Eva grinned and answered. "Mrs. Flowers?"

"Hey, morning, Eva. I was calling to find out if you and Andre were all right. How was your anniversary dinner?" Mrs. Flowers said blissfully. She snickered. "Did y'all sneak into a hotel?"

Eva stared into space and hesitated, her eyes welling again.

"Eva? You still there?"

"Oh, yes, ma'am. I'm here," Eva said with a sigh, "We didn't have dinner, Mrs. Flowers."

"You didn't?"

Eva dabbed her eyes with a crumpled napkin. "No."

"Don't tell me Andre didn't show again," Mrs. Flowers said.

"He didn't, but it wasn't his fault. Mrs. Flowers, Andre had a car accident."

Her receiving end filled with heavy breaths and Eva hoped the elderly woman wasn't having a heart attack.

"Mrs. Flowers? You okay?"

"Yes, honey . . . I'm just shocked," Mrs. Flowers said.

Eva sighed and explained the details of her husband's medical condition to Mrs. Flowers. "He's in ICU where his healthcare team is monitoring him."

"Oh, dear. I'm sorry, Eva. Is there anything I can do?" Mrs. Flowers said.

Eva shook her head. "No, ma'am. You've done plenty already. Thanks for watching Andy for me. My mom rarely visits me, and when she does, it's always at the wrong time. I don't know what I'd do without you."

"You're welcome. It's my pleasure. Your little boy lights up my life." Mrs. Flowers chuckled over the line.

Eva grinned again. "What's he doing anyway?"

"He's peeking at me from his playpen," Mrs. Flowers said. "I've already given him his breakfast and bath, so you don't have to worry about it when you get home."

Eva closed her eyes and mouthed a "thank you" heavenward. Though inside she was a mourning widow, this old lady was a saint. She giggled and cocked her head. "Can you put Andy on, please?"

"Sure, honey. Let me put it on speaker."

Eva waited over the line. Her heart filled with joy, listening to her little boy's small voice. "Hi, baby! Have you been a good boy?"

"Yeeeaaa!" Andrew replied on the phone. He babbled baby talk Eva wished she could understand. She gasped with enthusiasm as if she knew her son's every word. "Is that so? You did? Really?" Eva chuckled. "Was he a good boy, Mrs. Flowers?"

Mrs. Flowers answered, taking back the home phone. "Mm-hmm. You should've seen him last night. He was trying to show me how to read 'The Cat in the Hat.' He kept interrupting me during his story time, pointing his little finger at the words in the book."

Eva laughed. "Aww, he'll get it after a while. Hold tight with the little man. I'll be home soon."

"Okay, hon. See you then," Mrs. Flowers said.

Eva ended the call and likewise informed Grandpa Ricardo and Pastor Tyson of last night's incident. Both were surprised, and Pastor Tyson said he'd start a prayer chain for Andre's recovery.

"Thank you, Pastor Tyson. It means so much to me," Eva said toward the end of the call with the preacher.

"No problem, sister. It's the least I could do," Pastor Tyson replied.

"All right. Bye now." Eva pressed the hang-up button and scrolled through her contact list. She stared at her mother's cell number, biting her lip. Calling her mom didn't seem like a good idea. Even after seven years, she still struggled to accept the fact her daughter was married with a husband and a child of her own.

Eva glanced in hesitation from the passenger seat to her iPhone in her hand. She filtered a breath through her clenched teeth and tossed her cell on the empty seat like it was a contagious disease, hoping her mom doesn't call her.

It could ring any minute or second.

For some odd reason, she always knew when something bad happened in Eva's life like she had a crystal ball that told her daughter's misfortune. After the tragic news she's already gotten, the last thing she needed to tolerate was her mother's obnoxious behavior. It was the main reason there had been friction between them since she was a little girl.

Eva rolled her eyes and turned her key in the ignition, praying in her mind. *God, please help Andre get well soon. Amen.*

7
Eva

EVA LEANED HER FOREHEAD AGAINST THE YELLOW-tiled wall and thought she would puke.

Her tears mixed with the sprinkling, hot water trickling down her face and naked, slender body. Since the devastating call from the police, she had cried for an eternity, pondering how she'll adjust to her new situation. Life as she knew it would never be the same, and if faced with the worst, she wondered how she could live without Andre's presence.

After coming home from her overnight stay in the hospital, her week off flew by fast, but Andre was still in his coma. His Glasgow Coma Scale remained at three, and though he wasn't getting worse, it seemed he would never get better. She bowed her head and took deep breaths, trying to keep from losing her mind.

Eva closed her eyes and banged her fists on the tiles. She wanted to scream and question God why he had let something so terrible happen to her husband. But all she mustered was a weak whimper. She turned off the squeaky knob and stood there a moment longer, recalling her past week. Yesterday, she had discussed with Mrs. Flowers Andre's frequent unresponsiveness and her worries he won't wake up.

Their conversation had shifted into another long story about Mr. Clyde and his Alzheimer's diagnosis. It was good to have someone to relate to her emotional pain, but a part of Mrs. Flowers would never know how she feels. Andre was an independent, young man who was a hard worker at the top of his career. He had big plans and desires for her and their son, dreams that now may never come true.

Last Friday wasn't any better.

The electricity and water cut off, and Eva had to make visits to the utility companies and request bill transfers. Aside from her checking account, she didn't know the first thing about paying bills, as Andre had always handled them for her.

Her mother likewise never taught her, much less talk about her grandparents. Getting counsel from a bank teller helped answer her questions.

Eva sniffled and opened her eyes, returning to the present. At breakfast, Mrs. Higgins called her, and she reassured her director she was clocking in for work. She imagined her daycare kids missed her fun-loving attitude, but being happy felt like rock climbing without a safety line. She fought to reach the summit of joy in her life. Each passing day brought her closer to making a harsh decision, a decision she'd never be able to forgive herself in making. Now she understood how Andre felt if she bore another child and died.

Though Eva didn't want to concentrate on the 'what ifs,' life had a way of showing one up when least expected, and no matter what, she had to accept it. Eva grabbed the towel draped over the shower curtain rail.

She muffled a frustrated groan that echoed through her ears. As hard as it was, it was time to pull herself together, especially for her son. Andrew was unaware of his father's accident, but he was also bright and alert. Sooner or later, he'd notice something different, if he didn't already.

Looking at his little, innocent face, a whisper spoke from his maple brown eyes. *Where's Daddy?* Eva pulled back the shower curtain and stepped out of the bathtub, wrapped in her towel. She rolled on her deodorant, rubbed lotion on her body, brushed her teeth, and put her contact lens back into her eyes. Then she styled her shoulder-length hair with her comb and blow dryer and left the bathroom. Eva walked in the master bedroom and paused. Her eyes pooled, staring at Andre's sage green terry robe hanging on a hook beside their dresser.

She wore a wistful smile and pictured her tall husband wearing it after taking a shower. He looked so real before her, leaning on the wall with his arms crossed, giving her a smile. *Andre?* Eva's heart skipped a beat. She scuttled over and handled the collar of the empty robe. Eva closed her eyes and sniffed. It still held the fragrance of his rainforest soap mixed with his cologne. Andre smelled so fresh and enticing. He always used bars of soap whenever he took baths as his grandfather raised him to do.

Once he told her Grandpa Ricardo jokingly said scrubbing with bar soap created more suds and a cleaner bod. A tear rolled down Eva's cheek as she stroked her hands around the collar and soft interior of the robe. She appreciated the anniversary gifts he bought her over the years, but all she ever wanted was his priceless undivided attention again.

She sighed at the queen-sized bed. Her daycare uniform she wore to work lay over the blanket. Each day she and the other teachers wore a yellow T-shirt painted with an orange sunrise, a khaki skirt, and white tennis shoes. Eva got dressed in her clothes and looped the strap of her teacher ID card around her neck. She looked in the oval mirror of the dresser and tied her hair in a side ponytail.

Just 6:00 a.m., it was still dark outside, but the sun was peeking through thick, cumulus clouds huddled in the deep plum-and-gold sky. Today's sunrise reminded her of one of her mother's landscape paintings. Her mom was a handful, but she had a lovely talent Eva admired.

She glanced out the window and whispered a prayer, asking God for a sunny day. Rain would add to the gloominess already hovering over her head. She had grieved for what used to be—now she had to move on toward the future.

"Hey, Eva! Andy's all set! Are you ready, hon?" Mrs. Flowers called from the living room.

"Yes, ma'am! I'm coming!" Eva took her clutch purse from off the dresser and headed downstairs.

"SURPRISE!" THE KIDS SHOUTED AFTER EVA ENTERED THE door.

She gawked with her hand over her racing heart and surveyed the two-year-old classroom. Unlike a typical day of chaos, everything was neat and tidy. All art supplies were in the tin cans on the back shelf, the kids' coats and backpacks were in their cubbies, and the toys were in their labeled plastic bins. Eva read the white banner hanging across the ceiling the daycare kids made for her: *Welcome Back, Mrs. Lucas! We Love U!*

A bright red heart replaced the word 'love.' Painted around the greeting words were colorful, childlike handprints. Each pair of small hands had a name of one of the ten children underneath: Tyler, Autumn, Reggie, Brianna, Dinah, Juan, Sidney, Garrett, Isabelle, and Chase.

Tyler Witherspoon was the quietest student in the class, but he was also a stubborn thumb sucker, a baby habit Eva and his mother strove to get him to stop.

Autumn McKee was an auburn-haired princess. She was also Mrs. Higgins' granddaughter, and soon to be a big sister to a new baby brother. Reggie Gibson was a little gentleman, always doing nice favors for his teachers and female classmates. Brianna Luiz was shy and liked to play by herself, but she had the most contagious giggle Eva ever heard.

Dinah Welch was the main student to watch. She got into trouble for picking on other kids, but she was also the only child in the class who could already write her first name. Juan Diaz was an artist in the making, preferring to color and draw more than play with toys.

Sidney Webb was a motor mouth. She enjoyed talking about her family, which included her parents, her grandma, two older brothers, an older sister, and three dogs. Her stories were funny and entertaining, but sometimes she talked too much, like during naptime. Garrett Fisher obsessed over superhero action figures, his favorite being Batman.

Isabelle Holt was a tender heart, who Dinah called a crybaby. Close to her mommy, she cried every time her mother had to leave for work. Chase Daniels was a lovable teddy bear and being big for his age, the tallest kid in the class.

Eva looked from the banner. Below on the fine motor table were containers of banana nut and blueberry muffins, a bowl of fruit cocktail, a bag of Styrofoam plates, plastic spoons, and small cartons of milk.

Happy tears filled Eva's eyes. "Wow. Thank you. I . . . I don't know what else to say."

"Well, the kids wanted to throw you a welcome back party," Louise said. "So, I asked permission from Mrs. Higgins and she gave the OK." Louise Burnett was Eva's co-worker in her classroom. After a disappointing breakup, she raised her daughters alone. Her sense of humor and good nature helped relieve Eva's stress load during their workdays. She and Eva supervised five kids each, but they had all the children participate in their circle time together.

"Thank you," Eva told Louise.

"You're welcome." Louise smiled at Eva and clapped for the toddlers to get in order. "All right, class! Let's get seated!" She raised an open hand and counted down. "Five . . . four . . . three . . ."

Little boys and girls scampered around the fine motor table and plopped in the colored plastic chairs. Reggie and Autumn raced after the same chair beside Eva as she took her seat. Both were close to her and always fought over getting her attention.

"I wanna sit here," Autumn whined.

"No, it's mine!" Reggie frowned, tugging the chair.

Louise stopped counting. "Reggie, Autumn, it doesn't matter where you sit."

"But I touched it first." Autumn looked up at Louise, peeking through her bangs. Her bowknot headband held her curly auburn hair and matched her bumble bee sweater.

Eva wore a wry smile as Louise rounded her shoulders and sighed wearily. She eyed the long-faced, black boy beside Autumn. "Reggie, can you be nice and let Autumn sit beside me, please?"

"Okay," Reggie muttered. He crossed his arms and plopped in a chair next to Juan.

"Thank you." Eva smiled at Reggie and revived his charming grin.

"Come on, class, bow your heads," Eva instructed.

The two-year-old toddlers wove their hands and bowed their heads. Before every meal, they said their grace together, which Eva and Louise had taught them. With their daycare teachers, the kids recited the blessing over the food:

60

God is great and God is good,
Now we thank Him for our food,
By His hand, we all are fed,
Give us Lord our daily bread,
Amen, thanks God.

Louise opened the containers of muffins and gave the kids one based on what flavor he or she wanted, while Eva served them fruit cocktail from the bowl.

"YES, JESUS LOVES ME! FOR THE BIBLE TELLS ME SO," Eva sang, plucking a ukulele.

All the toddlers sat on the round, blue alphabet rug during circle time. Sidney and Isabelle played tambourines, Chase beat on a bongo drum, and the other kids clapped to the song.

Louise sat opposite from Eva and sang the verse with her, rattling a pair of Mexican wood maracas. *"Jesus loves me! This I know, for the Bible tells me so. Little ones to Him belong, they are weak but He is strong. Yes, Jesus loves me! Yes, Jesus loves me! Yes, Jesus loves me! For the Bible tells me so . . ."*

"Yea!" the children said after the song ended.

"Okay, class, it's nap-time!" Eva took the tambourines from the two girls and the drum from Chase. She and Louise placed the instruments in the clear bin as the children scattered to their blue cots. Across from the quiet reading area were two rows of five beds.

Eva and Louise tucked the kids in with their blankets from each of their wooden, name-tagged cubbies.

Louise draped Chase with his Bob the Builder fleece blanket. "Y'all know the rules. Go to sleep and no—"

"Playing!" the kids interrupted in unison.

Some giggled and snuggled under their blankets.

Eva chuckled and covered Sidney with her pink, Barbie blanket. "Make sure you stay quiet, sweetie, okay?"

"Yes, Mrs. Lucas." Sidney cuddled her teddy bear and shut her eyes.

Louise stood from her knees. "Phew, finally I can relax."

Eva giggled beside her co-worker and watched the children. Louise wasn't exaggerating. From six-thirty in the morning to twelve-thirty in the afternoon a lot happened in a daycare. The kids' nap-time was their only chance of freedom to take a break.

Louise left to the Teacher's Lounge and returned with a Styrofoam plate of food and a paper cup of V8 fruit juice. Then Eva took her turn and likewise came back to the classroom. The teachers sat at the same fine motor table and ate their lunches, whispering over their food.

"So, how's it going?" Louise asked, pouring ranch dressing on her Caesar salad. She placed her sauce cup down. "Mrs. Higgins said you suffered a family tragedy."

"My husband had an accident," Eva said, rolling a rotten grape tomato on her plate with her fork.

Louise's jaw dropped. "Oh, no. Is Andre okay?"

"He's in a coma." Eva hung her head, staring at her plate of salad. "I can't bear looking at him anymore. Seeing him . . . all the tubes and wires on his body . . . it makes me sick to my stomach. It's already been a week, Louise. I'm not sure he'll recover."

Louise touched Eva's hand. "You can't lose heart. Andre's a strong man. He'll bounce back from this."

"When?" Eva's vision blurred, her chin quivering. "I've waited for days, sitting and praying by his bedside, reading him scriptures from the Bible . . . hoping he'll open those gentle, brown eyes of his. Nothing's changed." She blinked, and a tear fell onto a leaf of lettuce on her plate. "And if matters couldn't get worse, Andre made most of the income in our home. By myself, I can barely keep up with our household bills."

She cupped a hand over her mouth and stifled a sob. "I grew up on welfare. There were times my mom didn't know if she'd be able to keep me. I don't wanna be on assistance, but I also want no one to take Andy away from me."

"Don't worry about it. God will work things out," Louise said, trying to raise Eva's spirits. "You might not feel like it, but he's right by your side, girl. He sees your pain and knows your struggles. He might not act in *our* timing, but God's got your back."

Eva gave a half-shrug. "Perhaps, but what condition will Andre be in? Yesterday Dr. Brown talked about the effects of brain injury to me in his office. He . . . he may never be the same again." She drew a fast breath, regaining her composure. "I try to be happy for the kids, but I'm so burned out, and things will get tougher before they get better."

"Well, I'm willing to help whenever I can. You know me." Louise sipped her cup of juice.

Eva frowned and shook her head. "Oh, no, I can't let you do that. You're a mother of four and your daughter Kenya is still so young. How are you supposed to help me and take care of your own family?"

"I guess you got a point there." Louise twitched her mouth. "But I'll at least be praying for you and Andre. You guys are good people, and some of my best friends."

"Thank you, Louise. Thanks a lot." Eva found a smile and dried her cheek with a napkin. She drank from her cup of iced water and bit a Ritz cracker with a slice of cheddar cheese. Although she was heartbroken over Andre's accident, it taught her not to jump to conclusions.

One night had changed her life forever, and there was no telling what numbers would add to the equation. How could she solve the dilemmas that beset her? As bill collectors harassed her with calls, her family's expenses piled up like dirty laundry. Time was moving quicker than she could believe, and Andrew was a growing boy eager to interact with other kids and learn new things.

In a couple more months, she would need to move him

in her own classroom—which meant paying more for his daycare stay. She needed a miracle, and negotiation from the president of the daycare couldn't hurt. At the same time, she understood Mrs. Higgins had to keep strict regulations. Equality was their policy, and that meant treating all parents with the same respect and financial payment, even if a parent's an employee.

"Have you heard from your mother?" Louise asked, pulling Eva out her trance.

Eva darted her gaze from a side window to Louise. "No. We aren't too close." She ate a spoonful of strawberry yogurt from a container.

Louise knitted her brows. "Why not? I'm sure she could help you."

"You don't know my mother." Eva leaned back and pursed her lips with a look of disapproval. "She doesn't just *help* out. She tries to take over everything, including how I take care of my son. She's been nitpicking me since I was a little girl. After coming home from dealing with stuck-up cheerleaders in high school, I literally used to feel like my mom was bullying me too. She made me feel like nothing I did was good enough, or I was incapable of . . . being successful."

"Set her boundaries," Louise said, shrugging. "You might still be her child, but she has to respect your wishes as an adult married woman too."

Eva folded her arms and sighed. "I'm afraid she'll get offended. She can be fussy, which makes matters worse. She's an artist and always traveling places like a nomad. I don't have the slightest clue when she'll visit again."

"You mean, your mom . . . pops up unannounced?" Louise wrinkled her nose.

"Yup," Eva said, "and it hasn't been the first time either." She blushed and glanced both ways, ensuring nobody but her co-worker heard what she whispered. "One time, Andre and I were right in the middle of a private moment and the doorbell rang. We wondered who would come to our house at midnight, and lo and behold, it was my mom, standing in the doorway with luggage in each hand for a two weeks visit."

Louise snickered. "Wow. I know Andre didn't like that interruption."

"Actually, it didn't faze him," Eva said, "I mean, we've agreed to have another child, but it never worked out. Andre was always scared ever since . . ."

"Since what?" Louise said.

"Ever since Andy was born." Eva lowered her head, fidgeting with the hem of her yellow T-shirt. "I contracted an infection in my bloodstream called amniotic fluid embolism. It has to deal with the fluid that surrounds a baby in a mother's womb. Only a small percentage of women experience it at least once. I couldn't breathe . . . I was so scared I thought I would die."

Louise was shocked. "Oh, wow. I didn't know that."

Eva sniffled and lifted her sad eyes to Louise. "I don't blame Andy for what happened. We were both victims in a crazy ordeal, but the doctor said many women who experience this have safe, full-term deliveries afterward." She ate another scoop of yogurt and stuck her spoon in the container. "Somehow Andre thought if I get pregnant, it'll happen again. He was afraid he'd lose me. My mom's arrival had completely turned off his mood. But he was polite and treated my mother with the highest respect."

She sighed." He's only complained once I need to have a serious talk with her about respecting our privacy and our home. Truth is, my mom's lonely. She raised me by herself, you know, and suffered a broken heart, which I don't believe ever healed." Eva leaned back. "I never knew my father, but she loved him dearly. I can only imagine how she felt, his parents rejecting her for her nationality and the color of her skin."

"Why didn't your father marry her?" Louise asked.

Eva held out her hands and shrugged. "He was loyal . . . too loyal to his mother and Italian roots."

"That's too bad." Louise shook her head. "I can understand your mom's pain. I've got four girls of my own and love them to death, but it's hard being a single mother." She sniffled. "It's harder when . . . the father of your kids wants nothing to do with them."

Eva placed her hand over Louise's, feeling empathy for her co-worker. By God's grace, she had a good husband who played the role of fatherhood in their son's life.

But after Andre's car accident, she got a bitter taste of the struggle of single parenthood, a struggle which could last the rest of her life.

8

Eva

P
lease wake up, Andre. I miss you . . .

Eva opened her eyes and stirred under the palm leaf comforter. She hugged her husband's pillow, peering at the young couple in the framed, wedding photo on the nightstand. She and Andre were on cloud nine. They were so happy and perfect together, slicing their four-tower cake. It was made with a vanilla bean fondant and designed with pretty roses around it in white frosting.

A photographer took the picture during the outdoor reception, their guests and loved ones surrounding them in a lively crowd. There was an awesome turnout on the cool, summer afternoon. Neighbors, co-workers, family, and friends answered their invitations and came to show their love and support. It made Eva feel special, as often she felt unloved by anyone, maybe even her mother sometimes.

Moisture surfaced Eva's eyes, studying the photo. Regret was something she didn't want to feel, but she wondered if she should've married Andre. Falling in love wasn't completely pleasant. Pain and hurt also came with it when things went wrong. She didn't worry about the down times then, but she surely focused on them now. Eva stared at the vase of flowers on the dresser she got on their wedding anniversary night. The white roses were wilted, and the leaves were dried to crisp, a couple of petals sprinkled on top the dresser.

Like her marriage, they were falling apart, their beautiful newness wearing away. Eva rolled over and looked up. Her heart jumped in her chest at the eerie shadow looming from the sunlight across the ceiling. It looked like a beast reaching out a clawed hand. But then she remembered the oak tree nearby the driveway. She sat up and glanced out the window beside the bed, relieved to see a naked branch, rattling in the light breeze. All the bright, yellow leaves had fallen off of it as the first day of autumn began.

Andrew whined out of his sleep.

"I'm coming, Andy." Eva stepped out of bed and tied on her lilac robe. She tucked her feet in her soft, matching slippers, left the master bedroom, and rushed down the narrow hallway to her son's room.

Andrew's bedroom was styled with a sailor boy theme. The wallpaper was navy blue and white striped with an anchor and lifebuoy pattern design. Above his white crib was a navy-blue ship helm engraved with his name. Close to a single window in the room, a white, boat-shaped bookcase held Andrew's favorite Dr. Seuss books and framed baby photos. Aside from that was a treasure chest of his toys.

Eva wore a sad face and approached the crib. "Aww . . . what's wrong, baby?"

Andrew was standing with his small hands gripping the edge rail. His pudgy cheeks were wet and glistened in the sunlight. Not seeing Mookie in his crib, Eva discovered what had troubled her son's little soul. Mookie was Andrew's stuffed, brown, plush monkey with Velcro hands and feet.

Andre had bought it for their son for his first birthday. Andrew attached to it and took him everywhere, but last night was the first time he slept without it. For him to not realize until morning, her son must've been exhausted from his crying spell last night. Having his daddy away in the hospital, he wouldn't let her go to save her life.

Eva gasped and knitted her brows. "Uh-oh, looks like Mommy forgot to tuck in Mookie. I'm sorry, honey." She lifted Andrew into her arms, kissed his cheek, and toted him on her hip. "Come on, let's find him. I'm sure he's around here somewhere." She unfastened the anchor latch of his treasure chest and peeked inside. Lego blocks, shape puzzles, electronic learning systems, and a few other stuffed animal friends filled the base of the chest. "Nope, he's not in there."

Andrew moaned in disappointment.

"Shh, we'll find him, Andy." Eva exited her son's room and journeyed downstairs to the living room. Mookie was on the gray carpet floor near Andre's tan recliner where she had rocked Andrew to sleep. The stuffed monkey must've fallen from her lap when she stood to sneak Andrew in his crib. Eva bent down, picked up Mookie, and handed him to her son with a smile. "Here you go, Andy."

Andrew sniffled and cuddled the soft monkey to his face. "Mookie . . . mine."

Eva chuckled. "Yes, he's yours, baby. Now, let's get breakfast." She carried her son into the kitchen and sat him and his monkey in his highchair.

The digital phone on the counter rang.

"Hello, Lucas residence." Eva held the phone in the lock of her shoulder and took a carton of eggs from the refrigerator.

"Hello, Mrs. Lucas, this is Dr. Brown." His voice was thick and raspy.

Eva put the phone on speaker. "Hi, doctor. Are you feeling okay?" She placed a frying pan on the electric stove.

Dr. Brown cleared his throat. "Well, I'm a little under the weather, but I can't complain."

Andrew babbled and drummed his hands on his food tray, tuning out the adult conversation.

"Shh, be quiet, Andy." Eva glanced at her son with her forefinger to her lips. She focused back on the phone call. "Sorry, doctor. My son wants to be gabby this morning. So, how's Andre?"

The doctor hesitated.

"Dr. Brown? You still there?" Eva grabbed a bowl from the dish rack and cracked an egg in it.

"Oh, yes, Mrs. Lucas, I'm here. It's just I'm trying to find the right words to tell you about Andre."

Eva frowned. "Tell me what?"

"Mrs. Lucas . . . it's going on four weeks." Dr. Brown sighed. "For the sake of you and your son, it's time you think ahead about your husband. Could you meet me in my office, please?"

Fear plunged in Eva's stomach. "Okay, sure. I'll be there after work today."

"Good. I'll meet you later, Mrs. Lucas."

"Bye, doctor." Eva gulped and ended the call.

Nobody had to say anything. Yesterday afternoon she had received an important letter about Andre's health coverage, but she buried it under junk mail.

There was no need to read it. She already suspected matters had taken a turn for the worse, and she hoped to God she'd have the strength to go through whatever was coming next.

SILENCE SUFFOCATED EVA WITH EVERY PASSING MINUTE. Wrestling with her apprehension, she fiddled with the metal clip of her clutch purse and surveyed the lifeless waiting room. Dr. Larrabee and a male specialist she didn't recognize from Andre's trauma team were performing a serious exam on her husband. Although Dr. Brown hadn't gotten into detail of everything, she sensed something about it differed from a normal Glasgow Coma Scale test. She squeezed her eyes and wove her hands under her chin. *God, please let me get good results from this exam. Please . . .*

Andre had to be okay. He had to get better and come home again. For some time she had prayed faithfully and believed God would work a miracle, and she refused to let her hope die. Before she left Andre's bedside, she kissed his cheek, and it was warm to the touch. His black, curly hair had grown back over his stitches, and that couldn't happen to a dead person, could it?

"Mrs. Lucas, the exam is finished now. Dr. Brown is waiting for you," Nurse Jia called.

Eva walked to the doctor's office.

"Please, come in," Dr. Brown said, sitting behind his wide desk.

Eva sat in a chair in front of the doctor. She observed as Dr. Brown stood and closed the door of his office for privacy.

Her heart pounded. "Please, tell me. How did the exam go?"

Dr. Brown filled his seat again and laced his hands on top of his desk. "Dr. Larrabee and his assistant performed a brainstem exam on Andre. Your husband passed the test."

Eva grinned. "Really?"

"That's not a good thing, Mrs. Lucas," Dr. Brown said.

Eva's smile faded. "Oh, it isn't?"

Dr. Brown's wide forehead wrinkled. "No. His result should've been negative but based on the fact his Glasgow Coma Scale hasn't improved the past three weeks, it makes perfect sense." He leaned back in his chair; his mouth hung open a second without words. "Were you contacted by your health insurance company?"

"Yes," Eva said, "they sent me a letter, but I never read it." She glanced at the floor.

"Why not?" Dr. Brown asked.

Eva gritted her teeth and squirmed in her chair. "I . . . I haven't had the time."

"Well, your health insurance company knows you've been struggling to pay your husband's medical bills," Dr. Brown said. "Life support is expensive, and I'm aware you have a toddler son at home. The funds you use to sustain Andre's well-being could help you with other things. Therefore, they set a maximum day limit."

"But it still hasn't been a month yet since his accident," Eva replied.

"That's true," Dr. Brown said, "but supplying Andre with life support is clinically unprofitable now." The doctor slipped off his eyeglasses and licked his lips, bracing himself for his next words. "Mrs. Lucas, I'm afraid Andre's suffered brain death."

"Brain death?" Eva inclined her head, leaning forward. "Can you fix it?"

"No," Dr. Brown said, fidgeting with his glasses, "his brain will probably begin liquefying within the fourth week. Even if he wakes, he'd be no more than a vegetable. The trauma team and I have done everything we can for him."

Eva's eyes swam with tears. "So . . . what are you saying?"

Dr. Brown drew a long breath and exhaled. "I'm so sorry, Mrs. Lucas, but your husband . . . your husband's dead."

Adrenaline rushed through Eva. "No!" She jumped from her chair and paced the floor, debating her claim like a lawyer in a courtroom. "Andre's not dead! He's still breathing . . . his heart is beating—"

"Mrs. Lucas, your husband's connected to the ventilator, which artificially supplies oxygen to his heart. Without it, he can't breathe, and his heart would stop beating in a few hours or so. The only things worthwhile you can do now are . . . hope for a miracle or donate Andre's organs and let him rest in peace."

"You'd like that wouldn't you, doctor," Eva scolded, crossing her arms. "My husband sliced open like an operation game—his eyes, heart, and lungs taken from his body."

Dr. Brown flared his nostrils and sighed. "Please, don't take it personally. It's not about money. There are just a lot of people waiting for transplants. Your husband could save someone else's life. In Andre's case, no paperwork is necessary. Your consent to remove Andre from life support will help to proceed with transplantation."

"Is that so?" Eva glared over her shoulder at the doctor. "Well, I'm not giving it!"

"Listen, I know you're upset," Dr. Brown said, "but Andre registered as a donor, which already gives legal consent to the Organ Donor Foundation. I think the fair thing to do would be what he would've wanted, and not yourself."

Eva plopped back in the chair. She stared at the doctor. "All right, I'll consider it, but I'm not making any promises."

"That's fine," Dr. Brown said. "Whatever you choose, I'll support you one hundred percent. Andre will remain on life support for three more days. Just take your time and think about your decision. However, after the last days of his life support, the transplant team can still continue transplantation. It would be less painful if you give your blessing."

Eva took a long breath and sighed.

When Dr. Brown told her Andre was dead, a part of her had died—her hope and faith that the impossible was possible. Though it was her choice to make, she couldn't imagine ending Andre's life. Since the day they said "I do," they had become one, and pulling the plug to her would be like committing suicide. But one thought reigned above her final decision of Andre's fate.

How could she live without her husband?

9
Eva

B EFORE CHURCH SERVICE, EVA VISITED THE EMPTY sanctuary and fell on her knees in front of the altar. She crouched and sobbed with her face to the carpet floor. Deciding what to do about Andre was hard, but knowing she'd have to let him go was harder. Her mind went blank, and all she could do was allow her river of heartache to overflow. Seven years wasn't a complete decade.

Her marriage with Andre was sweet and delightful, but much too short. Together they were supposed to watch Andrew have his first day of pre-K, graduate from college, and grow old to witness the next generation. Her sobs echoed in the wide, spacious room. Footsteps came from behind her. Pastor Tyson must've overheard her from his office and come to check things out.

A thick hand with stubby fingers touched her shoulder. She raised her tear-streaked face.

Pastor Tyson knelt nearby, his expression filled with concern. "Sister Lucas, what's wrong? Is it Andre?"

"Yes." Eva sniffled and wiped beneath her eyes. "The doctor said there's nothing else he or the healthcare staff can do. He wants me to donate my husband's organs for recipients on the National Transplant Waiting List."

The pastor sighed. "Well, what do you want to do?"

Eva shrugged. "I don't know, pastor, and I have one day left to decide. I wish I could change things, but I can't. And I don't understand why a loving God would want my husband dead." She studied the pastor's face. "Why did this have to happen?" Her chin quivered.

"Sister, I can't answer that," Pastor Tyson said, "but I know there is always a reason for everything. You'll know in due time. You believe and trust God." He patted her shoulder, stood, and started to leave to his office.

"Wait!" Eva called.

The bald pastor paused and glanced back. "Yes?"

"Can you pray for me?" Eva said.

Pastor Tyson smiled. "Sure." He joined Eva on the floor. "You ready?"

Eva nodded and closed her eyes, her hands in prayer pose. "Go ahead." She relaxed her shoulders and waited for the pastor to begin.

Pastor Tyson bowed his head. "Father God, I ask you to help this young sister. Give her the strength to accept whatever your will is for her husband. Please, guide her in her decision-making that she does the right thing. Comfort her through her grief and provide for her and her son whatever they stand in need for. Protect them and bless them, in Jesus Christ's name. Amen."

"Amen," Eva echoed, stifling a sob.

"Be encouraged, sister, and never forget the Lord has the last say," Pastor Tyson said.

Eva nodded and bit her lower lip.

The pastor left and entered back into his side office. Since his prayer, Eva felt a little better, but the reality of her husband's departure was still around the corner. She exited the sanctuary and returned home again.

AFTER EVA STEPPED OUT THE SHOWER AND TIED ON HER robe, she sat on Andre's side of the bed. She picked up the framed picture of her husband on his nightstand and stared at the photo of him in his white lab coat. Since her discussion with Dr. Brown in his office, she had come to terms with the chance her husband would never come home. *What should I do, Andre?*

Eva shook her head and sighed.

Out of nowhere, his kind voice spoke to her mind as clear as day, "Do what you know is right." She gulped and willed her tears to stay back. It was a hard pill to swallow, but it was the truth. As much as she hated to admit, Andre was a proud, registered donor, and after death, he wanted others to remember him for giving the gift of life to someone else.

Her vision blurred, talking to Andre's photo. "Okay, honey. I'll do it . . . I'll give my consent." It was a picture, but it was more than an object to look at and hold. The photo held Andre's spirit, his optimistic attitude of seeing the bright side of unfortunate things.

The longer she stared at his picture, the more her frown turned to a smile. She was thankful she collected photos of him. When the surgery was over and his casket buried off, she wanted to cherish his handsome face, to keep it locked in her heart forever like treasure in a safe.

She wondered who would get Andre's organs after the operation. No matter who, she hoped it to be people who take care of them and not take her husband's sacrifice for granted. Her sixteen-month-old son was about to lose his daddy without a word in it edgewise, and the thought of it broke Eva's heart. Truth is, it was the main reason she had a hard time choosing what to do. Raised without a father in her life, she had wanted for it not to be the case of her own child or children.

Eva placed Andre's picture back on the nightstand. She cracked open the door of the master bedroom and poked her head in the outside hall. The aromas of maple sausage and fresh, brewing coffee wafted in the air. Mrs. Flowers insisted on cooking her a big breakfast to lift her spirits, but she didn't feel it was necessary.

Eva tiptoed down the narrow aisle and peeked in Andrew's bedroom. The little boy was still asleep. He was so peaceful and calm, so she didn't bother him.

She came downstairs and entered the kitchen. "Good morning."

With a spatula, Mrs. Flowers added one last pancake to a stack on a plate. She looked over her shoulder with a half-smile. "Good morning, hon. How you feeling?"

"I'm hanging in there." Eva wore a weak look. "I'm . . . gonna take Andre off life support."

Mrs. Flowers paused and sighed. "Finally decided, huh. I know it was complicated."

"Yeah," Eva said," but it's what Andre would've wanted. It doesn't make me happy, but I love him too much not to respect his wishes." She dragged a chair from the kitchen table and sat down. "Thanks for cooking breakfast."

"You're welcome," Mrs. Flowers said. "You've had a lot on your shoulders since Andre's accident. Having to make a tough decision, I thought the least I could do was give you one less thing to worry about."

"Well, I appreciate it," Eva said with a smile.

"Is Andy up yet?" Mrs. Flowers offered Eva coffee.

Eva cupped the warm mug. "Nope. He's still knocked out. Andre's absence has been hard on him. Andy's been antsy lately. He's a bright kid and knows something's wrong. I told him his daddy was in a deep sleep, but I'm sure he doesn't understand what I mean. It's getting tougher for him to fall asleep at night." She blew off the steam and took a sip.

"Poor child." Mrs. Flowers sucked her teeth.

"I can't tell him his daddy died," Eva said. "Someplace inside won't let me say goodbye." She stared in her mug.

Mrs. Flowers joined her at the table. "I understand what you mean. When you're used to someone always there, it's hard to imagine them ever leaving, especially when it's someone you love. But life happens. People come and go every day. That's why time is so precious to us."

Eva raised her head and looked in Mrs. Flowers' eyes. If she could turn back the clock, she would in a heartbeat, and had Andre known ahead of time about his accident, she knew he would too. She took another sip and glanced at her brown leather wristwatch. "Well, it's getting late. I'd better wake Andy for church." She sighed wearily and forced herself from the table. "I know he's gonna be cranky, but he'll likely fall back to sleep on the ride there."

"Probably." Mrs. Flowers chuckled.

Eva headed back upstairs.

THE CHURCH GREW QUIET AS EVA ENTERED AND SAT ON A pew with her son, but she wasn't looking forward to the bawling faces of the congregation. What she needed was encouragement through her bereavement and not a load of tears and pity.

Pastor Tyson stood behind the pulpit and began his Sunday sermon. He opened his bible and slipped on his wire-framed eyeglasses. "Good morning, church!"

"Morning," a few members said.

"Today in my office I thought to myself about the story of Job," Pastor Tyson said. "His experiences are a great lesson for us and showed how quickly turning points can change one's life. But through the pain and heartache Job suffered, he refused to curse God. You know, we look to God for miracles or good things to happen, but the minute trouble comes, we sometimes forget He exists."

Eva squirmed and wrapped her arms around Andy in her lap. She was feeling like the pastor was criticizing her, but rather than tiptoeing to the ladies' room, she listened to the whole message. It turned out it was what she needed to hear, a wake-up call to the good effect of hardships. That though we had no control over life, the struggles we go through only make us and the relationships we share with others stronger. Eva never thought about her situation that way.

But since becoming "the breadwinner" of her family, she'd learned how to step up to the plate in ways she never would've if Andre hadn't gotten injured. She also conceded how much she missed her mom, and her desire to strengthen their mother-and-daughter relationship. The closing of the service ended with the church choir singing the gospel song "My Help" by the Brooklyn Tabernacle Choir.

Eva closed her eyes and swayed in her seat, allowing each note the lead alto singer and the choir sang soothe her inner soul. Their harmonies were magnificent, and during the final triumph finish, Eva nearly thought she would fly to the clouds. The congregation crowded on the wooden pews applauded after the song ended. Some stood, while others bounced happily and waved their hands and paper fans, chanting hallelujahs and amens.

A tear dripped from Eva's chin.

Regardless of what happened, the Lord would carry her through. After a few uplifting remarks, Pastor Tyson said the benediction and dismissed the congregation. Eva greeted and hugged a couple of people. Even despite some of their doses of compassion, she could tell everyone wasn't sorry for her.

Some were glad of her misfortune, but Eva ignored their sarcastic comments. Vengeance belonged to God, and in due time, He would handle them in his own way. Besides, there were more important things to think about, such as giving her consent tomorrow. It would be the last time she sees her husband in the hospital on the machines.

Before she leaves, she would make sure to tell him five simple words. *Goodbye, I'll love you forever.*

10

Eva

THE PIT OF EVA'S STOMACH FELL AS DR. BROWN AND a middle-aged man in teal scrubs entered the hospital conference room. She looked up as the critical care physician introduced a lean, suntanned man.

"Mrs. Lucas, this is Peter Sullivan. He's the family care coordinator of the Organ Procurement Organization," Dr. Brown said.

Eva shook the coordinator's hand. "Nice to meet you."

"Likewise. I give my condolences for your loss," Peter said.

Eva gulped. *Condolences?* While Andre was still in the hospital on the ventilator, it felt like the coordinator spoke a foreign word. Was she really about to end her husband's life forever? She leaned back in her chair and wove her clammy hands on the table.

"I'll leave you two alone to discuss matters." Dr. Brown left as the coordinator sat in a black swivel chair near Eva and placed a manila folder on the long, polished table.

"I'm here to discuss your husband's social history. Do you feel ready to answer a couple of questions for me, Mrs. Lucas?" Peter said.

Eva nodded. "Sure."

"Great." Peter opened his folder. "I also have paperwork for you to fill out."

"Paperwork?" Eva frowned. "I thought all you needed was my consent."

Peter pulled a pen from a chest pocket of his shirt. "Yes, it's true, but this is to protect us in the court of law. You don't know how many lawsuits have been about families who claimed doctors stole their loved ones' organs without permission."

"Okay, I understand," Eva said.

Peter nodded. "Good. I guess we can begin." He slipped a form and a packet of paperwork from the folder and clicked his pen.

Eva answered the coordinator as he slashed X marks in the boxes to Yes or No questions and jotted notes on the form. She knew her husband's background info like the back of her hand. Unlike his parents, Andre never indulged in drugs or alcohol, so the interview was a breeze.

Afterward, the coordinator explained everything about the Organ Donor Foundation paperwork. The closer he got to the end of the packet, the faster Eva's heart pounded in her chest.

"If you'd sign here, we can confirm the donation today." Peter handed Eva his pen.

"Thank you." Eva took it and stared at the blank dotted line. Unshed tears formed in her eyes as she scratched her cursive signature and gave the coordinator back his pen.

"Thank you, Mrs. Lucas." Peter caught a glimpse in Eva's sad eyes and lowered his head in a moment of silence. "I know this is hard for you, but organ donation can make the grieving process much easier for families."

"We'll remember your husband, Mrs. Lucas," he added. "I'll get you in contact with the recipients of Andre's organs."

"Mm-hmm," Eva muttered with a nod.

Peter gave a half-smile. "You can go sit with Andre after our discussion."

"Thank you." Eva snatched a tissue from a Kleenex box on the table and dabbed her eyes and flushed nose.

"Do you mind telling me things about him I can share with his recipients?" Peter asked.

"All right," Eva said, "well, he worked as a veterinarian. Since he was a boy, he loved animals. He was kind and enjoyed making people happy. He was a good father and husband and always helped those in need." She chuckled. "He wasn't always on time, but he tried. His job tied him up a lot, but I know he still loved me and our son."

"That's wonderful," Peter said, smiling. "Well, I've gotten the information I needed, Mrs. Lucas. Thanks for your generous offer."

"You're welcome," Eva said.

She and Peter stood and pushed in their chairs. Eva drew a long breath and exited the conference room. She marched to her husband's ICU room for the last time.

When she got there, Hayden stood along Andre's bedside, filling a specimen cup from a syringe.

He turned around and gasped at Eva's presence after the door shut. "Oh, I didn't know you were here."

From the distance, Eva saw Andre's bare thigh and stepped backward. She blushed and clutched the strap of her sunflower tote bag. "Sorry, if I startled you."

"That's okay. I was just getting a sample for a urinalysis test. Dr. Brown wants to ensure Andre's kidneys are healthy enough for successful transplantation." He capped the tube and stuck a label on it. "Sorry about your husband. So, how are you holding up?"

"How would you feel?" Eva asked with attitude.

Hayden wore a hangdog expression and looked away.

"I'm sorry." Eva closed her eyes and sighed. "I didn't mean to be rude."

"You've been through a lot of pain, Mrs. Lucas. You have the right to be angry." The male nurse straightened kinks in the tubing of Andre's Foley catheter, peeled off his rubber gloves, and threw them in the trashcan. "If I were you, I'd feel the same way."

"Are you finished with him?" Eva glanced from Andre in bed to the nurse. "I can wait outside."

Hayden pulled the hospital blanket back over Andre's lap. "Nonsense, I'm all done." His sneakers squeaked as he walked up to Eva. He touched her shoulder. "I'll leave you alone with Andre until Dr. Brown arrives to take him for chest x-rays."

Eva found a smile. "Thanks."

"Let me take this sample to the lab." Hayden left.

Eva approached Andre's bedside as the ventilator hissed in the dreadful silence. She sat in the upholstered chair next to him, the same chair she had been praying and reading scriptures to her husband in for the past three weeks. Today marked the fourth week since Andre was in his coma, and the week the transplant team would remove his remains for other awaiting patients. She leaned forward with a pensive smile, watching Andre.

Over time, his skin had changed from a healthy cinnamon brown to sallow beige. He had also lost weight, and his stubble beard cast a five o'clock shadow around his chin and square jawline.

"Andre . . . it's me, Eva." She held his hand and wove her fingers with his. "I told Andy about you, but I know I'll have more explaining to do when he gets older. He misses you so much. Sometimes I can hardly get him to sleep at night." She sobbed and shook her head in bafflement. "Part of me still refuses to believe you're dead. But . . . I know I must move on. I'll miss you." She stroked her other hand over Andre's glossy, dark locks and softly kissed a corner of his lips. "Goodbye, honey. I'll love you forever." She sniffled and walked to the door.

Shortly after, Dr. Brown came into the ICU ward.

Eva dried her tears. "Oh, hi, doctor."

"Hello, Mrs. Lucas. Is there anything I can do to help ease your pain?" Dr. Brown said.

"No, I'll be fine." Eva's stomach revolted. "Excuse me . . ." She barged past the doctor and rushed to the nearest women's room.

Eva hurried into a stall and hovered over a toilet. For a moment she fought the violent jerks and tried to keep from puking, but the reverse motion made her feel sicker. Soon, Eva had coughed up her breakfast she'd eaten in the morning. She remained in the stall a good ten minutes, struggling to gather herself together.

"Mrs. Lucas! Mrs. Lucas, come quick!" Nurse Daphne called into the restroom.

Tremors shook Eva's body. She exited the stall and wiped her mouth with toilet paper. Eva frowned at the elated face of the brunette nurse in purple scrubs, poking her head from behind the swing door. "What?"

Daphne grinned. "It's your husband. He's awake!"

Eva widened her eyes. "He is?" She thought she would faint. Was this some kind of joke, or was this nurse telling her the truth? At the moment she wasn't in the mood for someone playing games with her emotions.

"Dr. Brown listened if Andre's heart was still beating, and out of nowhere, he moaned and opened his eyes. It's a miracle!" Daphne said.

Eva felt breathless. "Oh, my goodness." She placed a hand over her mouth and broke down as what Pastor Tyson said in the sanctuary echoed through her mind. *The Lord has the last say . . . The Lord has the last say . . .* She couldn't contain the joy bubbling up inside her, much less stand straight. Her legs were flimsy as spaghetti, leaning against the opening of the stall.

Daphne ran over and squeezed Eva in her arms. "I knew it! Your husband's still alive. He's alive!"

Eva stared in disbelief. "Are you serious? I . . . I can't believe it."

"Come on, you can wait for the results. Nurse Jia will call you when he's ready." Daphne looped an arm around Eva and walked her out of the restroom.

"MRS. LUCAS?" PETER STRODE IN THE WAITING ROOM WITH the paperwork.

"Yes?" Eva rose from her seat with her sleeping son in her arms. Since her husband had awakened from his coma, what would the coordinator say now?

Peter tilted his head and folded in his mouth. "Uh . . . I heard about your husband's recovered consciousness, and in the conference room, I got the impression you didn't want to donate Andre's organs."

"No, I did not," Eva confessed. "I'm sorry."

The coordinator held the organ donation packet horizontal in his hands and tore it in half and the halves into two more halves. "I've talked with Dr. Brown about the dead donor policy of my Organ Procurement Organization, which forbids our transplant team to remove organs on non-deceased patients. Therefore, the organ donation has been cancelled, Mrs. Lucas."

"Thank you," Eva said humbly, "but if time permits, I'll make sure Andre helps to save others' lives."

"Have a nice day, Mrs. Lucas," Peter said.

Eva offered a thoughtful smile. "You too."

The family coordinator exited the waiting room.

Eva filled her chair and contemplated the patients Andre would've saved whose lives were still on the line. As much as she was glad her husband had a second chance at life, she prayed God would make another way to spare those people on the waiting list too.

"Mrs. Lucas, you can come in now," Nurse Jia said, catching her attention.

With a timid smile, Eva handed her son and his stuffed monkey to Mrs. Flowers. "It's best for Andy to stay here. We don't want to overwhelm him."

Mrs. Flowers sat the little boy in her lap. "I was thinking the same thing. Best wishes."

"Thanks." Eva stood and wiped her palms on her ruby wrap dress with big white flowers and followed Jia through the hospital corridor. They turned the corner and arrived at the same door labeled I-7 of her husband's ICU ward.

Eva clipped her tinted aviators on her collar. Her heart was in her throat as the nurse practitioner insisted she walk in first. For weeks she waited and hoped for this moment, and now that it arrived, she found herself afraid. Why was she scared to see her own husband?

Jia read the worry in Eva's eyes. "It's okay. The doctor and I will be right beside you."

Eva found a calm smile. "Thank you." She and the nurse shared a side hug, and then she rubbed on sanitizer and entered the ICU ward. The life support machines were still in the room but were off and had been pushed away against the wall. There wasn't a beep, whoosh, or ping, as Andre could breathe on his own.

She sheepishly watched him lying in bed and huddled near the doctor. Her husband hadn't spoken to her, his drowsy eyes suspicious of her presence. Staring at his face, she felt her eyes get wet. Although Andre was alive, he was a long way from a full recovery.

"He's out of it, but his vitals are stable." Dr. Brown turned his attention from Eva back to his patient. "Hey, sir, can you stick out your tongue?"

Exhaling wheezy breaths, Andre slowly stuck out his tongue, comprehending the doctor. Thrilled by Andre's response, Eva and the doctor exchanged smiles. Her husband's intelligence had remained intact despite his car crash, which was a good sign.

Jia wrote in Andre's record notebook.

"Hi, I'm so glad you're awake," Eva said, looking over her husband.

Awe transformed Andre's face, his lower lip drooped. "You . . . nurse?"

Eva frowned. "No, Andre, it's me . . . Eva, your wife."

Her husband kept a blank face.

"Don't you remember me?" Eva's heart sank, staring at him.

Andre was puzzled and hesitated, trying to recall her.

Eva released a shocked breath and faced the physician with a terrified look.

"I'm afraid he's lost his memory," Dr. Brown said.

Eva fled from the ICU ward. Her emotions burst like an exploding volcano, disappointed the man she loved no longer remembered her.

"Mrs. Lucas! Mrs. Lucas, please!" Dr. Brown chased after her down the hallway.

Eva squeezed her eyes shut and sobbed, leaning her head against the cold wall. "He doesn't know who I am. I prayed so much for him to be made whole. He's supposed to be in better condition than this. And what's up with his speech? He talks as if . . . he's unsure of himself."

"Broca's aphasia," Dr. Brown said. "It's a speech disorder that makes it difficult for someone to express themselves. It's caused by damage to the Broca's area in the frontal lobe. Reading and writing can also be a challenge. Speech therapy can improve it to some extent. However, his speech will likely remain impaired." He continued. "You must be reasonable, Mrs. Lucas. Andre suffered head trauma. It's common for patients to suffer from amnesia after severe car accidents, or not recognize loved ones. It's most likely due to previous swelling of his brain against the skull, causing an imbalance in cognitive processes."

"What am I supposed to do?" Eva said.

"Be patient with him. He can emerge from his present state. His memory loss could be temporary. You of all people should be grateful. Brainstem death is an irreversible and fatal condition. There's no explanation other than God for him waking again."

"I am grateful, Dr. Brown, but—" Eva inhaled a breath and craned her neck, crossing her arms—"what if he never remembers me again?"

"Let's not deal with that now," Dr. Brown said. "You must have faith Andre's memory will progress, among other things."

Eva grimaced and inclined her head. "What do you mean?"

Dr. Brown tucked a hand in a pocket of his lab coat and sighed. "Andre's . . . a quadriplegic. I performed different exams shortly before you came in, and he showed no signs of sensation in any of his limbs."

Eva's body felt leaden. Her husband didn't know who she was, he could barely speak, and he was paralyzed from the neck down. Though thankful he awoke, she was also troubled. How could a five-foot-six and 129-pound woman handle caring for a six-foot, disabled man by herself? It was a lot different than aiding him through a common cold. Andre needed twenty-four-hour care, and she wasn't confident she had the body strength and time to tend to him with her full-time job.

Her eyebrows furrowed. "But . . . how could he be paralyzed if he has no spinal cord injury?"

"Paralysis can happen in various ways," Dr. Brown said. "Although spinal cord injury is the primary cause, it can also affect patients due to stroke, or even multiple sclerosis. In Andre's case, it's because of his closed head injury. There's a loss of messages traveling from his brainstem to the motor cortex in his frontal lobe."

The doctor slipped off his glasses and cleaned them with a hankie from the chest pocket of his lab coat. "In fact, a brainstem injury is as severe as a spinal cord injury. The brainstem is a small part of the brain but controls heart rate, blood pressure, body temperature, and breathing. It's why for a long while Andre had been on life support."

Eva cocked her head. "Oh, I see. It's like someone cutting a plug in an outlet with scissors."

"That's correct." Dr. Brown adjusted his glasses back on. "The motor cortex is a crucial part in the frontal lobe that involves the execution of voluntary movements, such as walking. With physical therapy and lots of practice, your husband can recover his mobility. Brain tissue has a remarkable way of repairing itself over time, which is another key factor of him regaining consciousness."

"So, now what?" Eva said.

"Now since Andre's stabilized, we'll move him to the Acute Care unit to ensure he's oriented with his new situation. You might also want to video record Andre's progress. Many families do this, as the patient may not recall being in the hospital. Even though he can breathe on his own, he'll remain on a feeding tube for now. With his present condition, it's a good idea for you to speak with Barbara Washburn." The physician put a hand on Eva's shoulder. "We can discuss more in my office. Please, join me?"

Eva responded with a nod and followed the doctor.

Dr. Brown swiped his ID card dangling around his neck over a security scanner. He held open the door for Eva and then sat at his desk. The doctor pulled two caregiver brochures from a drawer of his desk and handed them to Eva. "These brochures explain the steps of caring for someone like Andre, such as bathing and eating."

"Thank you." Eva took the brochures.

"Your husband's condition is sensitive, and after his discharge will require an attentive caregiver. As a quadriplegic, he'll need to be rotated every so often in his sleep to prevent other complications, such as bedsores, blood clots, and muscle atrophy. The less he moves, the stiffer his muscles can become, which can be painful. It's important he stays active, and he'll still need a urinary catheter and to be on a bowel program."

Eva frowned. "What's a bowel program?"

Dr. Brown reclined back and laced his hands over his potbelly. "A bowel program is a method to help quadriplegics and paraplegics train their bodies on a schedule who suffer from neurogenic bowels. It's tougher for paralyzed people to reach a toilet themselves and disposing of stools can also be difficult. Drinking plenty of water and eating fiber and protein foods are ways to help make it easier for the disabled. Laxatives are also helpful, but should be used with strict caution, and the same is true with catheterizing procedures."

The doctor cleared his throat. "Andre also has a neurogenic bladder. It means his brain doesn't signal to his bladder, causing him to suffer episodes of incomplete leakage or retention. I'm sure you know while comatose he was on a Foley catheter. Your husband can still use this type, but I recommend he catheterize in ways that put him at less risk of urinary infection."

He spoke on. "Using clean intermittent catheterization is one of the most common. However, in Andre's case, he'll need help until possibly regaining use of his arms and hands. The directions for this are explained under the Bladder Health category in the *In-Home Personal Care* brochure." He sighed. "Because of his memory loss, Andre may be uncomfortable with you at first, not to mention the fact you're his wife. I suggest you hire a professional caregiver to tend to his personal needs. From him or her, you can learn how to build Andre's trust and care for him yourself."

Eva bit her forefinger nail. "How much will that cost?"

"I'm afraid the prices vary." The doctor took a slow breath. "Most caregivers request a payment range of nine to fourteen dollars per hour."

"I don't know if I can afford it," Eva said with a weak look. "Plus, I work in the daytime."

"Well, there are part-time caregivers. Perhaps you could hire one while you're at work during the day, and care for Andre yourself at night."

"I suppose," Eva said with a shrug.

"I'm sure Barbara Washburn will help you," Dr. Brown said.

Eva twisted her mouth. *Barbara Washburn . . . why does he keep mentioning her?* She knew the doctor was trying to give good advice, but she refused to resort to financial handouts as her mother did. *How can she go back on her word?*

"Barbara's an understanding person," Dr. Brown added, "who I promise will do whatever she can for you. Try calling her."

Eva nodded but didn't make another comment.

"I'm deeply sorry about Andre's disabilities, but don't forget there's still hope," Dr. Brown said. "If he could wake after several weeks in a coma, it must be possible, right? For amnesic patients, it's crucial not to pressure them into remembering the past. Showing old pictures have been a better, proven way to stimulate their memory. You should try it with Andre."

"All right, I'll try it. Thank you, doctor." Eva offered a handshake.

Dr. Brown shook Eva's hand. "You're welcome. I wish Andre the best recovery."

Eva exited his office and headed back to the waiting room. Next week would be hard on everyone, but especially Andre. Although he arose from his oblivious cocoon, he became a different man.

Confusion swirled around him like a biting wind, and she wished she could do something to help him—to comfort him in his misplaced world. But their marriage changed the moment she looked in his hollow eyes, and it would take a while before he could trust and love her again.

11

Eva

AGAINST HER WILL, EVA SWALLOWED HER PRIDE AND dropped by Dr. Barbara Washburn's office. After ignoring the social worker's phone calls, she didn't know whether she'd invite her in or cast her away. But she finally acknowledged working extra hours at her job wasn't bringing home enough bacon to cover her expenses.

She straightened and knocked on the door.

"Come in! Come in!" Dr. Washburn chirped.

Eva entered and studied her surroundings. Her nose tingled from the pungent scent of perfume in the office. She found the ebony-skinned woman behind a wooden desk, dressed in a lavender blouse. Her flared collar draped over the top of a white blazer. Her thick, salt-and-pepper hair was in a stiff bouffant that made Eva wonder how much hairspray she used.

Dr. Washburn smiled, a gold front tooth sparkling in the sunshine. "Oh, Mrs. Lucas! Please, have a seat, dear."

Eva wore a weak smile and sat in a leather chair in front of the social worker. She gripped her clutch purse in her lap, hoping she wouldn't fall into a trap. Welfare had its gains and losses. As a working recipient, the second she got a raise benefits given to her could be taken away. And after confiding her confidence, she didn't want to end up hanging on a thread.

The social worker made a steeple with her hands. "I'm glad you came. I express my sincere sympathy for what happened to your husband. I know you've been having a difficult time. How have you been since Andre's brain injury?"

Eva glanced at the ceiling fan and exhaled slowly. "Well, I've cried a lot, but I'm trying to stay strong for our son."

Dr. Washburn nodded. "That's good. How did Andre's accident happen?"

Eva gulped and studied her lap. "He collided with a deer and also suffered a head-on collision with a tree in someone's yard. When I got the news, I felt like someone ripped my heart out of my chest. I didn't know what to think." Tears clouded her vision.

Dr. Washburn pulled a tissue from a Kleenex box on her desk and handed it to Eva.

"Thank you." Eva sniffled and swiped beneath her eyes.

"I can only imagine how you must have felt," Dr. Washburn said. "Know none of what happened is your fault. It's typical to blame ourselves, but sometimes we suffer misfortunes. The good news is your husband has survived the worst and is on the road to recovery. What was Andre like before his accident? It's useful to the trauma team to rebuild the original life your husband had."

Eva sniffled again. "Andre was an outdoorsman and grew up on his grandfather's farm. He liked fishing, hiking, and horseback riding. One time he taught me how to ride a horse when we were teenagers." Her lips curved in a warm smile. "He was always thoughtful and loved nature. We used to take long walks through the Woodland Forest and climb the Eagle Haven Mountains where we'd sit and talk until sunset." She gazed outside the window to her right, longing for the past to rewind and somehow become the present.

"He sounds like he was a wonderful man," Dr. Washburn said. "And I'm sure he still is, despite his accident. Having therapy will improve Andre's disabled condition. He must relearn many everyday tasks, which means he'll need physical, occupational, and speech therapy. Would you be okay with that, Mrs. Lucas?"

Eva sighed and let her guard down. "Yes, ma'am."

"Good. Because of your husband's disability, I'm sure you and Andre qualify for benefits." Dr. Washburn rolled her desk chair toward her computer. She typed on her keyboard and surfed up the Social Security Administration website. "There are two main government programs that can be beneficial to you and your family. One of them is Supplemental Security Income or SSI, and the other is Social Security Disability Insurance or SSDI."

She faced Eva. "Supplemental Security Income is a welfare program. If you and Andre are eligible, the SSA gives you money each month to help pay for things, such as food and utilities. Along with SSI, most people also get Medicaid, which can help pay the expenses of Andre's therapy, medical equipment, and other things he'll need."

"Guess I have no choice," Eva muttered under her breath.

Dr. Washburn bit her lip and looked away from her computer screen. "Mrs. Lucas, after you've rejected my calls, I know you've been against relying on welfare. But if you're struggling, there's no shame in asking for help. It's the best thing you can do for your family. However, to qualify, there are strings attached."

Eva frowned. "Such as?"

"Well, aside from disability, one must also have low assets and low income. For married couples, you must have below three thousand dollars of assets. Now, this is for money in the bank and doesn't include your house or car."

"I got paid from my job last week," Eva said. "With the deductibles, it was seven hundred and ten dollars, and Andre has nine hundred left in his bank account."

"Do you have proof in documentation?" the social worker asked.

"Yes, ma'am." Eva unclamped her purse and handed Dr. Washburn a folded copy of her latest pay stub and Andre's bank summary.

Dr. Washburn put on her reading glasses and unfolded the slips of paper, examining them. "Okay, let me add the total." She tapped on her calculator. "With your and Andre's assets, it gives a total of one thousand six hundred ten dollars, which is below three thousand. Now since Andre isn't working, I imagine your monthly income is below the federal benefit rate. To be eligible for SSI in 2017, the monthly income for married couples must be below one thousand one hundred and three dollars. This will include half of wages and twenty dollars of unearned income."

"Am I eligible? I work nine hours per day at the daycare and make eight dollars per hour," Eva said. "Andre's grandpa tries to give us money, but we never accept it from him. He's already done enough helping us pay off the rest of our house mortgage."

"Let me calculate your monthly wages." Dr. Washburn added another total. "Awesome! I divided your monthly wages by two, and it's approximately seven hundred twenty dollars, below the federal benefit rate. Do you know if Andre's receiving social security disability insurance?"

"I'm not sure," Eva said, "he just woke from his coma, but I assume he's eligible. His employer took a premium from his check every month while he worked at Pet Friends Veterinary Clinic."

Dr. Washburn angled her head, twirling a pen between her skinny fingers. "How long has Andre worked there?"

"Eight years." Eva crumpled her tissue in a ball and held it in her lap.

"That's great. It looks like you and your husband qualify for both insurance benefits," the social worker said, smiling. "I'll need your consent to ask some interview questions so I can fill these applications online for you."

"You have my permission," Eva said.

Dr. Washburn turned her attention back to her computer. She typed the information for both applications as Eva answered her questions. After their long discussion, she said, "If your case gets denied, you must request a reconsideration. It means sending your case back to the people who rejected you. It can take three to six months before it's processed. However, I don't believe you'll have to go to the extremes for approval of benefits. As long as you show legitimate proof of your husband's disability by medical records, you should be fine."

The social worker sighed. "But if you have a hearing, hire a good lawyer to file a disability claim. Convincing the social system about your husband's disability can be long and tiresome. It can take an extra one and a half to two years before you receive benefits. If your husband meets the disabled criteria—which he should—he's qualified to receive SSDI."

"What about Supplemental Security Income?"

"Well, if everything goes fine, you'll get benefit checks mailed to you within the next sixty days," Dr. Washburn said.

Eva allowed a smile. "All right, thank you."

"You're welcome. I'm always here to help. If you have questions, call me," Dr. Washburn said.

Eva stood and shook the social worker's hand. "Trust me, I will. Goodbye."

"Bye, Mrs. Lucas. I hope Andre gets well enough to go home soon."

Eva exited the office.

Knowing they had a good chance for insurance benefits helped her breathe a little easier, but her sigh of relief could change fast. Sometimes life had a way of stealing happiness when one thinks things are getting better. Regardless, Eva was never one to give an easy fight. If her claim was refused, she had in mind to write an appeal before Dr. Washburn mentioned the possible drawback.

Andre needed a lot of expensive, medical supplies, and she would do whatever she could to ensure her husband gets well. She cared about Andre, and despite his handicaps, she loved him. Though he became distant and withdrawn, her faith Andre still loved her too hadn't stopped.

Maybe she was fooling herself into believing a lie, or she felt obligated for Andrew's sake, but she believed in striving to keep their marriage afloat.

On their wedding day, she promised to stay by his side through sickness and in health, and that was exactly what she was determined to do.

12

Eva

"MR. LUCAS, I'M HOLDING THE TUBE FOR YOU, okay?" Hayden said from an Acute Care room. Eva strode the linoleum hallway, carrying her son on her hip.

Having others tend to Andre's needs wasn't easy. His caregivers were friendly, compassionate, and helpful to him, but sometimes Eva was a little jealous. Though they meant well, the nurses were aiding Andre with everyday tasks—which as his wife—she felt like she should be doing. From sinus allergies to a twisted ankle, she'd always been the one to nurse her husband back to health but now was a different story.

"Good morning! How's my favorite patient?" an unfamiliar woman said.

Suspicion dawned on Eva's face. She didn't recognize the nurse's voice, but it wasn't Daphne, her husband's former bedside nurse.

Andre groaned.

"Uh-oh, that doesn't sound too good, Mr. Lucas," the woman said. "I'm about to check your vital signs, okay?"

"Yeah," Andre said in a monotone.

Eva started to stroll in but found the cubicle curtain pulled across the hospital room. Andre was in the middle of something personal or exposed, so she shied away and waited outside in the hall. Since the day he woke with retrograde amnesia, their relationship was trapped in a tight corner, and she didn't want him more uncomfortable than he was.

"Looks like your blood pressure's normal, Mr. Lucas. One twenty-seven over eighty-two. You're doing well," the woman said.

Eva glanced below the curtain and saw men's sneakers along her husband's bedside.

"Alrighty, you're all done, Mr. Lucas," Hayden said. "Let me take out the sterile catheter and clean you off. Can you dump out his...? Yeah, thanks."

Eva turned away from the curtain. She wondered if it was a bad time to bother Andre with a hospital visit, but she needed to bond Andre with their son again. For a whole month, Andrew had never visited his father, and he deserved to see his daddy.

Andrew whined as Eva swayed with him in her arms.

The curtain slid back, staggering her with a gasp.

A young, African American nurse was before her. Her small frame and thin bone structure made her look like a college intern in her early twenties. A claw clip held her soft black hair, and her deep brown skin shined without a blemish. She wore Minnie Mouse scrubs and a stethoscope looped around her neck.

The nurse grinned, revealing her pearly smile. "Hello, you must be Mrs. Lucas. I'm Sasha, Andre's acute care

101

practitioner." She glanced at Andrew, her grin still on her face. "And who do we have here?"

"This is Andy, Andre's and my son," Eva said.

Sasha waved. "Hi, Andy. I'm pleased to meet you."

Andrew leaned against his mommy, holding his stuffed monkey underarm.

"How is he?" Eva asked.

Hayden exited the hospital room and stood beside Sasha in his blue scrubs clipped with his name tag.

"Andre's doing fine," Sasha said. "His vital signs are strong and healthy." She put her hands in the pockets of her shirt. "I'll remove his feeding tube next Monday, which is also good news."

"He'll be in Acute Care one more week to make sure he's aware of himself and his name, the time and date, and so forth," Hayden added. "Yesterday I took out his Foley catheter as you requested. I've trained him on a straight intermittent catheter in a urinal on the bed. With help, it can also be done from his wheelchair at the toilet. Either way, he should go four to six times per day to ensure his bladder stays empty, as Andre can't feel when it's full. It's important to protect him from kidney failure. I've also trained him on an enema to help start his bowel program."

Eva frowned. "What's an enema?"

"It's a liquid injection used to stimulate the disposing of stools," Hayden explained. "Has someone given you a caregiver brochure?"

"Yes," Eva said, "Dr. Brown gave me one, but I haven't finished reading it."

"Well, you should," Sasha said, "it will help you to feel less embarrassed and calmer while caring for Andre at home and make him more at ease too."

"I will." Eva angled her head. "So, how will I know when Andre has to . . . you know?"

"We've discovered he gets a sick taste in his mouth and suffers from muscle spasms," Sasha said. "You can also check if his bladder feels distended. If you notice one or all of these signs, he needs to go, even if he's too embarrassed to say so."

Eva wore a weak look. "Can we visit him?"

"Certainly," Sasha said, "but make sure you stay patient with him. He's in a troubled state of mind and disoriented. We'll be nearby if you need us. Try not to take what he might say or do too personal, okay?"

"I'll try." Eva took a deep breath and walked into the hospital room with Andrew. Her husband was sitting up in bed in a thin, teal gown, his hands resting at his sides. He stared at an episode of *The Price is Right* on the flat screen mounted on the ceiling. To his left were a manual wheelchair and a nightstand with an empty plastic urinal on top. On the right side were an adjustable overbed table, a gym bag of his hygiene products, and a commode toilet for easy transfer.

Eva smiled at her husband. "Hi, Andre. It's me, Eva, your wife again. How are you?"

"Fine." Andre glanced at her and sunk his head against his soft pillows.

Eva dropped her shoulder bag on the floor, adjusted Andrew to her lap, and sat in a leather chair next to the bedside. "Phew, this little boy's heavy. He can walk, but he's been kinda clingy lately." She looked at Andre, and for the first time in what felt like ages, her husband inched up a smile.

"Uh, cute. Who . . . baby?" Andre faltered, eyeing Andrew.

Eva's heart danced with joy. "He's our son." Her eyes welled as her husband looked away. "Andre, it's okay if you don't remember him." She stroked his right hand on the hospital bed. "His name is Andrew, but we usually call him Andy. He misses you."

"Daddy . . ." Andrew squirmed in Eva's hold and leaned over, gripping his tiny hand on Andre's thumb. It pained Eva to have to keep their son in her lap. She could only imagine how her husband felt, being unable to hold his own child.

Andre grimaced and bit his lower lip, fighting back tears. "Why . . . here? Go away."

"But I brought pictures to show you." Eva took out a rectangular, brown leather album from her tote bag and opened it before her husband. "These are a couple of photos of me, you, and Andy. That's you at the end of the aisle in the navy-blue tuxedo. I'm the woman in the white dress. Your Grandpa Ricardo is the elderly man beside me in the gray cowboy hat. He walked me down the aisle to you." Her smile dropped. "I never met my father."

Andre studied the Kodak photo vaguely.

Eva caught his muddled expression. To him, it didn't differ from looking at a stock image of strangers in a store-bought picture frame. She sighed and flipped to the next picture, hoping he'd recognize the snapshot of their newlywed photo shoot. In the photo, Andre stood behind Eva with his chin nestled on her shoulder and an arm hugging her waist. The photographer took the picture right when they were in the middle of a laugh.

"Here we are again," Eva said. "After we got married, we took many pictures together. I'm camera-shy, but you were so excited. You wanted the whole world to know it was our wedding day. I can't remember what but . . . you said something funny to make me smile."

Andre blinked and remained silent.

Eva turned past newlywed photos of them making silly faces and stopped at a picture of Andrew when he was a newborn baby in his hospital bassinet. "This is Andy a little after he was born. It was a cold, rainy spring afternoon. You were trying to get to the hospital in time, but there was a terrible accident that caused a traffic jam. I told you I named him after my father."

Andre drew a breath and turned his face. "No more."

Their son whined and squirmed again.

Eva gazed at Andre sadly. "Look, maybe if you see more pictures, your memory will—"

"Get out! No more!" Her husband squeezed his eyes shut and struck his head wildly on his pillows, having a fit. "Get out! Get out! Get out!"

Sasha and Hayden scampered to Andre's room.

"Hey, what's going on here?" Hayden said with a frown.

"Tell her . . . leave alone," Andre said, looking away. "Leave alone!"

Sasha sighed and turned to Eva. "Ma'am, your husband's upset right now. We'll keep you posted about his condition. You can visit another time, but it's best you leave at the moment. I'm sorry."

Eva's face burned. Anger crashed through her like stormy waves striking a rocky shoreline. She closed the photo album, loosened Andrew's grip on Andre's thumb, and stood with their son in her arms. Andrew squealed and broke into a deafening tantrum.

Sasha grabbed the shoulder bag and hoisted it on Eva's shoulder for her. "Sorry . . ." she mouthed softly, her heart breaking for the little boy. She rubbed Andrew's back, baby-talking him. "I know, honey. Hang in there. Your daddy will be home soon, okay?"

Eva glanced at her husband with watery eyes, as Hayden calmed him during the commotion. "Forgive me, Andre. I didn't mean to upset you. I just—goodbye." She scattered from his room before she cried, toting their hollering son down the long hallway.

"I FEEL LIKE I'M IN QUICKSAND," EVA SAID IN MRS. Flowers' living room. "No matter how many times I try to stand, I keep sinking deeper in a pit of hopeless misery." She raked a hand through her hair, stifling a sob.

Mrs. Flowers placed a tray of porcelain teacups and sugar cookies on the table and joined her on the white loveseat sofa draped with a blue, knitted throw. She touched Eva's shoulder, looking at the framed, black-and-white photo of her husband in his army dress uniform on the hearth of her fireplace. "I know the feeling, honey. It was difficult seeing Clyde's memory fading away too. You never think such a thing could happen after knowing someone for so long. But you gotta believe God's gonna heal your heart and work everything out."

"No offense, Mrs. Flowers, but I don't wanna hear about God right now. I don't mean to belittle you, but it's different with my husband and me. I mean, you and Mr. Clyde had decades together before his dementia took effect. But Andre's a young man. He's a father to a precious little boy he doesn't even remember."

Eva eyed Andrew with a small smile. He was sitting on the carpet floor in front of her and Mrs. Flowers, rocking to nursery rhyme songs as he played on his light up, VTech piano. His cute giggles warmed her heart. Deep inside, Andre *had* to love this kid. How could he not care about their son? He was their own flesh and blood, a special gift which had been lent to them.

She folded her arms and sat back. "One night completely wiped out his memory, including his childhood. I don't know if it'll ever come back. I tried showing him pictures to stimulate his mind, but I can tell nothing's familiar, which agitates him. He stares at old photos without an inkling of recall." She hung her head. "I pushed him a little too hard this time. Maybe because Andrew was with me. I don't think he wants me around anymore."

Mrs. Flowers sipped from her cup and frowned. "Now, don't you doubt yourself. Andre loves you."

"How can he love me when he doesn't remember who I am?" Eva faced the elderly woman with a heartbroken expression. "I love Andre . . . so much, but we have no chemistry, and it's never coming back again."

Mrs. Flowers put her cup on her saucer. "Give it time. Take your troubles to the Lord in prayer. Ask God to direct you in what to do. People have their own interpretations of what love is these days, but rarely does anyone think about where love comes from. Love . . . is a divine affection. First John 4:8 tells us God is love. It comes from the Lord, Eva, and nobody can love your husband better than Him. If you want Andre to love you and Andrew back, you must first show love to him. Ask God to place His love in you . . . for him to let you see Andre through His eyes, and I guarantee you'll witness Andre return the same feelings."

"That'll be a miracle," Eva said, rolling her eyes. "He's suffered a bad blow. He hesitates in his speech often, and sometimes I'm afraid of him."

"Well, you shouldn't be. He's your husband. Stay open to Andre, and let him know you're there for him, even if he acts like he doesn't want you near him. It's how God treats us. Sometimes we want nothing to do with him either, but he still shows mercy toward us."

Eva felt a pang of guilt.

Mrs. Flowers was on point. Eva couldn't help listening, absorbing whatever wisdom she could offer to benefit her own marriage, family, and well-being.

"How much longer will Andre be in Acute Care?" Mrs. Flowers asked, changing the subject.

Eva sighed. "One more week. Afterward, he'll begin therapy. His nurses are ensuring he's aware of himself and the basics, what happened to him, and so forth." She furrowed her eyebrows, glancing at Mrs. Flowers. "But I'm not gonna lie. I'm not too comfortable with those female nurses seeing and touching Andre. I mean, I'm glad he has a male nurse who also helps with his toileting and bathing, but it makes me feel weird like . . ."

"Like you're incompetent," Mrs. Flowers said, finishing her statement.

Eva grabbed a sugar cookie. "Yeah. Plus, Hayden isn't always there, so half the time it's a woman nurse who assists him. If anyone tends to Andre's personal needs, it should be me. But I'm scared I'll do something wrong, even despite reading the caregiver brochures. If I ever gain his love and trust, I don't wanna lose it from making a mistake or hurting him." She nibbled her cookie.

"I understand what you mean, but at least Andre will be out soon. What will you do after he gets discharged? He'll need supervision during the day." Mrs. Flowers slurped another drink.

Eva took another bite. "Dr. Brown advised I hire a caretaker to tend to Andre while I'm at work. I have to find the cheapest I can get. Someone of quality, but who doesn't mind getting paid on a biweekly salary."

"How about you place an ad in the daily paper?"

Eva considered Mrs. Flowers' suggestion. "Sure, I guess I could do that. Hopefully, someone would be kind enough to volunteer their services. Let me jot a note." She unsnapped her clutch purse and took out a pen and a scrap of paper. She thought and scribbled an ad idea.

"How's this?" Eva asked, holding out the paper.

Mrs. Flowers leaned over and read her newspaper ad:

CAREGIVER NEEDED FOR DISABLED HUSBAND!

Paralyzed husband with a TBI, (Traumatic Brain Injury)
Work days: Monday through Friday. Weekends off.
Hours: 6:30 a.m. – 3:30 p.m.
Pay: Biweekly – Open for compromise.
Male caregiver preferred. Must have professional experience.
Bring a resume for review.
For more information visit, 143 Pasture Road, Garden Ridge, NC.

"It looks good," Mrs. Flowers said, giving her approval.

Eva smiled. "Great, I'll place it in the classifieds tomorrow."

Finding a responsible caregiver was a big deal and would be a major help for Andre and her. She desired it to be a man though, one who was strong enough to move and rotate Andre until he got a patient lift through his medical insurance. She also wanted it to be someone who would push Andre to stick with his exercises, instead of letting him stay in a wheelchair all day. As Dr. Brown said, the more Andre sits in the same position, the stiffer his body would become, and he didn't need more health issues.

LATER AT NIGHT, EVA BOUGHT TAKEOUT FROM MCDONALD'S and drove home. She wasn't in the mood to cook, and wanted to snuggle in bed, fall asleep, and forget today's visit. From Andre's discharge to her broken marriage, there was so much that consumed her thoughts. But the sun had sunk behind the horizon, and now she was ready to lay back and rest. Eva tucked Andrew and his stuffed monkey under his Cookie monster blanket in the crib. She kissed her son's forehead and stroked his hair. "Good night, baby."

Eva left her son's bedroom and went to bed in the master room. She tossed and turned, struggling to relax. Some nights were harder than others without Andre. She always knew the side he stirred in his sleep, groping his vacant bedside for his athletic, lengthy body. She moaned and opened her heavy-lidded eyes, staring at the pitch-black ceiling.

Car headlights from outside glided across the white plastered surface, keeping her awake. She thought about what Mrs. Flowers said about God's love. She needed help, comfort, and strength to continue on for her son and disabled husband.

Many hours passed as she faded in and out of sleep.

By dawn, she finally built the courage to pray. She climbed out of bed in her silk, peach gown, stood on her knees, and laced her hands. "Dear God, help me. Guide me in what to do about my husband. Send a miracle for Andre and me. Please, help my husband's memory. God . . . you are love. And like Mrs. Flowers said, 'True love never dies.' God, I place our marriage in your hands, guide me to be the sensitive, patient wife I need to be for Andre's sake. I need your help now, Lord. Let your love shine through me and on Andre, and let my husband learn to love me and Andy again. Let him remember us again . . . in Jesus Christ's name, I pray. Amen."

Eva crawled back under the blanket of the queen-sized bed and hugged Andre's pillow. She closed her eyes and attempted to fall back to sleep. A tear spilled in her ear. One tear became two, and then several. Dealing with her husband's situation was one of the toughest dilemmas she ever faced in her life.

It hadn't been an easy road, and especially after her latest visit. Andre never was a hostile man, even over disagreements, but now he had changed. Speaking to her husband became a fearful undertaking, unable to predict his mood swings.

Knowing his brain injury caused his behavior, she didn't want to hold him accountable for his words or actions. Nothing was his fault. He was a victim of a terrible accident and she understood his resentment toward a life he couldn't call to mind. But after Andre's outburst, how and when would they ever get along again?

13

Andre

A NDRE STARED AT HIS REFLECTION IN THE BATHROOM mirror and marveled at the hole in his neck.

For weeks he breathed through a plastic tube without a hint of his existence, and today he would eat his first solid meal. After eating from a bag through his arm, he lost fifteen pounds, and the muscles of his arms and legs had worn down. He was thankful to be alive, but he wished he could get back the brain he once had.

His mind felt like an old, dusty book filled with cobwebs. Names of objects were harder to recall, and the slightest syllable was labor. He knew what he wanted to say, but he omitted the smallest of words. He watched Hayden rinse his toothbrush and squirt an amount of paste on the bristles.

As Hayden brushed his teeth, he tried to piece together the memories of the photos Eva showed him yesterday morning. From an intellectual perspective, he knew the man and woman in the pictures were them at younger ages, but he didn't remember how he felt. He was only told about what happened, unable to relive the excitement he was feeling on their wedding day.

"Can you say aah for me, buddy?" Hayden said.

Andre opened his mouth wide. "Aah!" He let Hayden brush his tongue and back teeth. The foamy toothpaste made him look like he had a horrific case of rabies, but he liked the minty taste.

Hayden filled a paper cup with cold water from the sink. "Now, take a sip and rinse out your mouth for me, but don't swallow." He held the cup to Andre's lips.

Andre carefully sucked a sip and swooshed it around in his mouth.

Hayden watched him, ensuring he doesn't choke. "Great job, man. Okay, that's enough."

Andre spit it out into another empty paper cup held to his lips, and then Hayden wiped his mouth with a paper towel.

The male nurse smiled. "So, are you ready for breakfast?"

"Yes . . . hungry," Andre answered.

Hayden chuckled. "That's good. Mrs. Dorothy Jackson is your speech therapist. She'll help you practice swallowing different foods."

Sasha poked her head in the doorway with a smile. "Good morning! I like your blue cardigan, Mr. Lucas."

"Thanks," Andre replied with a half-smile.

Sasha looked at Hayden. "Make sure you change his bedding."

"Yes, ma'am, I'm about to after I send him over to Mrs. Jackson."

Sasha gave a thumb's up and left from the door.

Hayden flicked off the light switch and rolled Andre in his wheelchair to the cafeteria in the hospital. An old woman was sitting at a square table. Her thin, cottony, snow-white hair was a cauliflower, and her sagging, blotched skin revealed she was at least in her seventies.

On the table were two Styrofoam cups and a food tray of Andre's breakfast—sliced banana, cream of wheat, and a carton of milk. Beside the old lady on the floor was a tan bag filled with supplies with the phrase 'SPEAK YOUR MIND' in thick black letters on it.

She grinned as Hayden pushed Andre to his breakfast. "Hello, Andre. I'm Mrs. Jackson."

"Hi." Andre looked at the food tray and then back at her.

"I've brought activities to improve your speech and memory skills, but first you need energy," Mrs. Jackson added.

Hayden smiled. "I'll leave him alone with you. Have fun, Andre." He patted his shoulder and exited the room, his Nike sneakers chirping on the newly waxed floor.

"Okay," Andre said, glancing over his shoulder.

"First, we'll try a few swallowing exercises. Are you ready?"

"Yes." Andre observed his speech therapist as she showed him different tongue exercises, mimicking her actions. He used one Styrofoam cup to sip water to rinse his dry mouth, and the other cup to spit it out. After his warm-up exercises, Mrs. Jackson took a VitalStim—an electric device to assist swallowing—out of her bag. She stuck the wired patches on Andre's neck. Then she picked up the spoon on the tray and fed him small morsels at a time, training his muscles used for swallowing.

"Can you guess the flavor?" Mrs. Jackson asked, spooning him a scoop of cream of wheat.

Andre savored the taste in his mouth and frowned. "Can't tell . . . don't know." He swallowed and licked the excess from his lips.

"It's peaches and cream. Can you say peaches?"

Andre tried to form the word with his lips. "Pou . . . pee . . . peaches."

"Very good, "Mrs. Jackson said. She spooned him the last of his cream of wheat and praised him for eating most of his meal. The only thing he didn't finish was his banana, which was a little too difficult for him to swallow.

Felicia—a tall, African American cafeteria worker in lime green scrubs pushed a steel cart of cafeteria trays toward them. "Hey, Mr. Lucas! Did you enjoy your breakfast?"

"Yeah," Andre said, smiling.

"He did a great job," Mrs. Jackson chimed in.

"I'll take this for you." Felicia grabbed Andre's tray and stacked it on the cart, wheeling it to the back kitchen. "Have a good day!"

"You too," Andre said.

Mrs. Jackson took out a stack of picture flashcards. "Okay, Andre. Let's go over some words to strengthen your vocabulary." She pulled a rubber band off the cards and held them before Andre. She went over the cards with him, and then flipped through again, seeing how many names of the cards he memorized.

"And what animal is this?" Mrs. Jackson held up a card.

Andre's eyes darted from the picture on the card. He spotted a dark-haired lady behind his speech therapist, pushing a curly-haired boy in a black and white umbrella stroller toward them. His expression closed, and his heart stopped by her presence. *Uh-oh. What's she doing here?*

"Come on, Andre, I know you can do it," Mrs. Jackson said.

Andre tried to focus and ignore her, chewing on his bottom lip. "Uhh . . ."

"Hi," Eva greeted with a smile, interrupting the speech therapy lesson.

Mrs. Jackson grinned and extended a hand. "Oh, hi. You're a relative of Andre?"

"Yes, ma'am. I'm Eva, Andre's wife." Eva shook Mrs. Jackson's hand.

"How do you do, Mrs. Lucas?"

"I'm well." Eva glanced at Andrew under the canopy of the stroller. "Andy and I came from the daycare where I work and I thought to visit. Dr. Brown advised I be present in some of Andre's therapy sessions."

"Fantastic! Please, join us," Mrs. Jackson said. "Andre and I were going over practice cards. These will help him identify with everyday people, places, and things and build his language skills. You can go over them with him at home."

"Okay." Eva stopped the stroller, unstrapped a Cookie Monster backpack from her shoulders, and placed it on the floor.

Andre cringed inwardly as his wife sat beside his wheelchair at the table, hunching his shoulders like a turtle hiding in a shell. Elation suffused Eva's being, but all he could think about was how much he wanted to disappear.

"You look dashing, Andre," Eva said, smiling.

Andre shyly glanced at her. "Thanks."

Eva dug a sippy cup of apple juice from a drink holder on the backpack and gave it to their son.

Andrew took the cup and chugged the juice like a thirsty traveler.

"All right, Andre, back to your exercise," Mrs. Jackson said.

Andre studied the image on the card again. "Um . . ."

His speech therapist offered a hint. "It's called man's best friend and likes—"

"Dog!" Andre interjected.

"Correct!" Mrs. Jackson showed him another card. "How about this one?"

Andre narrowed his eyes, thinking deeply. He saw it before, the name of the animal was on the tip of his tongue. "Uh . . . cow?"

"Not quite. It meows and many of them like milk," Mrs. Jackson said.

"Oh, cat," Andre replied.

"Excellent!" Mrs. Jackson showed him one last card. "Try this one."

Andre peered at the image and blinked. "Ha . . . house."

"Brilliant! You're learning fast." Mrs. Jackson gathered and shuffled her cards.

Eva beamed and placed her hand over Andre's. "Nice job. I'm proud of you."

Heat crept up in Andre's cheeks. "Uh, thanks." He hung his head, barely looking at her face. *Why is she acting so happy and nice to me? I don't want her here. How could she want anything to do with me?* Eva was a beautiful, young woman with her whole life in front of her, and he felt she didn't deserve to have to put up with the likes of him.

Eva faced the speech therapist. "So, how long will you be teaching him?"

"Until his discharge, but I could continue with him in outpatient therapy. It depends on you and your requests. Playing Scrabble is also a great way to help Andre's speech disorder and improve his memory," Mrs. Jackson said.

As his speech therapist and Eva continued socializing, Andre hung his head and let their words sink in his mind. Being ignorant of easy things was embarrassing, and now in his present condition, he felt incapable of advancing Eva and Andy's lives.

Unless he gets help, he was stuck in bed, and the last thing he wanted was to be a burden, especially to Eva. His trauma team of nurses and doctors were good to him and made moving on with life easier. The only world he knew was in the hospital and leaving it behind was a scary thing. To him, love was a mystery, while marriage and fatherhood were duties he never remembered he had.

Maybe he should stay where he felt comfortable. Maybe it was best for him. His wife had wanted him to live with her, but perhaps he could change her mind. Besides, how much stress could one endure?

14

Andre

Y OU'LL GET AN ELECTRIC WHEELCHAIR TO SUPPLY you a sense of independence," Sasha said, pushing Andre's manual wheelchair. His second week in Acute Care had ended, and Dr. Brown felt he was ready to transfer to the next stages of recovery, his physical and occupational therapy. While Sasha wheeled Andre to his new room, Daphne toted his gym bag.

After turning off the Acute Care wing of the hospital corridor, they took him in a homey, motel-like room. A cozy bed draped with a navy-and-gold, moon-and-star quilt blanket centered the bedroom. Facing the front end of the bed was a double-door cabinet with drawers for storage space. Kitty-cornered on the right side of the cabinet was a dresser with a rectangular mirror. A 20-inch plasma TV was on a shelf of the cabinet, and a bathroom through a door was close to the visitor's chair.

Andre inspected the different environment. "Room . . . nice."

The nurses giggled.

"We're glad you like it," Sasha said. "This will be your room until you get discharged home."

Andre wore a wry smile and glanced at his Air Jordan sneakers. What was home? He couldn't recall where he lived, the house address, or what he and Eva's house looked like, but he hoped it was as warm and welcoming as the room he moved to.

"You should have him meet Dylan. I'm sure he'd appreciate it," Daphne said.

Sasha nodded. "I agree." She leaned over Andre and spoke, gripping the push handles of his wheelchair. "I'm taking you to meet your physical therapist, Mr. Lucas."

"Oh, all right," Andre said.

Sasha rolled Andre from his room to the exercise gym. Echoes of voices and clanking metal equipment met him as the nurse took him into the fitness center. For a long time, he thought he was the only one, but as he surveyed the gym, he realized there were others who faced the same or similar challenges.

Men, women, boys, and girls of different ages trained with their physical therapists, striving to adjust to a more fulfilling life. Some patients were amputees, some were paralyzed, and others suffered mental disorders. Inside were three rows of parallel bars and gym mats spread on tables and sections of the floor. There was also a rack of dumbbells and kettlebells, exercise balls, and sets of lift machinery to help support disabled patients.

"Hey, Sasha!" Dylan Phillips, Andre's physical therapist, entered the back door of the gym just in time. He wore a gray T-shirt tucked in black sweatpants with white piping and a pair of white sneakers. Dylan waved and strode to Nurse Sasha and Andre.

"Hi, Dylan," Sasha said, "I wanted you to meet your newest patient, Andre Lucas. He's a quadriplegic, but it could be temporary. Dr. Brown said he's ready for physical therapy. He's been in Acute Care for two weeks and is stable considering his severe brain injury."

"Cool!" Dylan placed his hands on his hips. "Hey, man. It's great to meet you."

"Hi." Andre found a smile. After seeing mostly women around him, he was glad to get in contact with another man for a friend again.

"Well, he's about to have speech therapy, but afterward I'll bring him right over," Sasha said.

"Great, I'll be waiting," Dylan replied.

Sasha dragged Andre's wheelchair and rotated it in the opposite direction, pushing it toward the gym's entrance.

ANDRE RESTED ON THE COOL MAT AND WATCHED the gleaming, fluorescent lights above on the ceiling. He remained motionless as Dylan helped him perform range of motion exercises and Eva arrived to record his first day of physical therapy.

Dylan placed one hand under Andre's left elbow and the other on his wrist. "All right, I'm going to flex and extend your arm to renovate movement of your elbow." He slowly bent and extended Andre's arm a series of times, counting to ten. Then he flexed and extended Andre's wrist, hand, and fingers. Dylan positioned Andre's arm flat on the mat. "Now, I'm moving to your legs."

"Okay." Andre observed Dylan leave his side, and Eva inch forward, filming him.

"How are you?" Eva asked with a smile. "Do you feel like your joints are getting looser?"

Andre gave a half-smile. "Fine. A little . . . maybe."

Dylan walked further at the end of the mat table. The physical therapist lifted Andre's left leg, having one hand under his knee and the other holding his ankle. He gently bent and extended Andre's leg, moving his hand on top his knee during every flexion of his leg.

Eva panned her Sony camcorder to Dylan. "What's this exercise called?"

"Oh, this is Hip Passive Range of Motion. It helps in increasing flexibility and building his leg muscles." Dylan placed Andre's left leg down on the mat.

Andre peeked below his waist and couldn't hold his burst of laughter.

Eva giggled and turned the camera back to him. "What's so funny?"

Andre's voice trembled, struggling to keep a straight face. "Leg . . . my leg . . . aaahhh."

Eva rotated and zoomed the camcorder to Andre's left leg, which was shaking uncontrollably. She and his physical therapist joined him laughing.

"Muscles spasms," Dylan said to Eva. "It's a common effect of paralyzed people when they're stretching their muscles, but it can also be a sign for pressure sores."

"Oh." Eva chuckled and smiled.

"How long . . . before I walk?" Andre asked.

"It can take from six months to a couple of years."

Andre sighed dispiritedly. Two years sounded like a long time.

"But be encouraged," Dylan added, "with hard work and practice you *can* walk again."

Andre hoped his physical therapist was right. If he gets walking, he could return to work and support Eva and their son. He stayed on the table as Dylan climbed on the mat over him and performed lower extremity stretches with his legs to improve his blood circulation. Afterward, Eva shut off the camcorder and along with Dylan helped Andre sit upright on the table for core exercises.

"I want you to try to pull your body toward me, hold it, and then lean back," Dylan said. He glanced at Eva, cupped his hands under Andre's elbows, and leaned a distance away from Andre. "Eva, guard his back."

"Right," Eva said with a nod.

Andre took a breath and bowed his head, attempting to push himself forward. His limp, numb body leaned back before he could reach Dylan or hold the position. Eva caught Andre in her hands, keeping him from falling over the mat table.

"Try again," Dylan said. "You can do it."

Andre focused hard and licked his tongue on the corner of his mouth, struggling to inch forward toward Dylan. He fell back against Eva's hands again. "I can't . . ."

"Try."

"I can't," Andre slurred again.

"Don't give up," Dylan coached.

Andre tried three more times. The third time he gradually inched closer to Dylan, ignoring the burning pain in his lower back and closing the gap of distance between them.

"That's it," Dylan said, grinning. "You're doing well, man. Just a little more."

Andre inched a tad closer and held the forward position a few seconds.

"Three . . . two . . . one . . . and relax," Dylan said.

Andre leaned back against his wife and let out a slow breath.

Eva embraced him from behind with her arms around his waist and pecked a kiss on his cheek. "Yes, you did it! Good job, honey."

Andre inched up a smile as Dylan commended him with a pat on his back, realizing his torso was still strong despite his paralysis. Although he needed help for many daily tasks, his chance to regain mobility was showing some promise.

He was excited about how he would progress the next weeks ahead. Not having a spinal cord injury, he imagined he'd be out of his wheelchair quickly. Yet,

Andre understood the man he was had transformed, and if his walking ability restored, he wasn't confident he could pick up life where he left off.

15

Eva

THREE WEEKS LATER

HEARING ANDRE LAUGH WAS PLEASANT MUSIC to Eva's ears, but some visits was worse than others. His mood changed like the phases of the moon. October was nearing its end, but Andre remained a complete quadriplegic. With his gradual recovery process, there were more dark eclipses than full moons. She was feeling her composure slip from under her like a trapdoor. Eva entered the rehab gym, pushing Andrew in his stroller.

As soon as she walked in, she saw her six-foot husband standing with the help of his physical therapist, a nurse, and a sling of a hydraulic lift strapped on him.

Dylan sat on a stool with wheels and guided his feet from the back. Nurse Hayden rolled the lift at the front as her husband took slow, wobbly steps across the hardwood floor. Regardless of how bad Andre felt, Eva was so proud of the minor progress her husband made, and she prayed his faith of walking alone would come back again. Hope fluttered through Eva. It was always good seeing him out of his wheelchair. Until the first time his trauma team worked with him in a standing position, she'd almost forgotten how tall he was. Her smile slipped, noticing his impassive expression. As much as she missed him, his face told her he wasn't looking forward to a home or church visit.

Dead silence was growing between them, threatening to split them apart. No longer could she make him smile or laugh. Careful not to offend him, nothing she tried worked. Showing pictures of his past collided with his pessimistic attitude. She was failing to rekindle the spark in their relationship. Now his trauma team was the only ones who could raise his spirits.

"He's progressing well, Mrs. Lucas," Dylan said, "but he still has a long journey ahead of him."

Eva stole a glance at her husband.

Andre grimaced and bit his lower lip as if holding back an outburst. Was she crowding him? Did she expect too much of his recovery? She wanted Andre to understand she cared about him, but she also didn't want to intrude his space to physically and mentally heal.

"Well . . . at least he's getting better. I . . . I should be on my way." Eva wore a weak smile and wheeled the stroller backward a couple of inches.

"Hey, you're taking your husband, right?" Hayden said, reminding her. "You called and requested him to attend church today."

Eva paused and gulped. "I uh . . . changed my mind. I think he'd rather stay here until his discharge, right Andre?"

Her husband responded with a nod.

"Besides, I have so many things to settle before he comes home," Eva added.

Hayden frowned with concern. "Okay, well, you and Andy take care."

Eva peeked at Andrew under the canopy. "Come on, let's go, baby."

Andrew giggled and babbled what sounded like an asked question.

Eva sighed and exited the gym as another nurse entered. She flinched when the door slammed shut behind her. Her heartbeat banged in her chest like a boxer hitting a speed bag. Why was Andre so quiet toward her? Was he angry? Or was he depressed? Lately, he had the demeanor of a prehistoric caveman, at least whenever she was around. Eva went to use the women's room.

When she came out of the stall, she gripped the edge of a sink and speculated how Andre would adjust at home and his treatment when she's away. She heard of disgusting cases of disabled and handicap patients abused by their caretakers. She hoped and prayed nothing like that ever happened to him, especially with their marriage already on the rocks.

Eva raised her head and studied her sad reflection in the wide mirror. Heavy bags drooped under her cocoa brown eyes from waking early for work and lack of sleep at night. She was exhausted, and Andre wasn't discharged yet.

It was the twenty-ninth of the month—a little over two months since Andre's arousal from his coma—and he still had a week and four days before his release date. She turned on the faucet, splashed cold water on her face, and dabbed it dry with a few paper towels.

Crying wouldn't change the way things were, and neither would worrying herself. She filled her lungs with a brave breath and straightened her posture. She had cried her last tear over her husband's attitude. If Andre pitied himself, she wouldn't join him.

And if he was determined to remain a hard shell, two could play at that game. No matter how much he tested her, she refused to allow her compassion to make her crack

126

under pressure. Eva checked her brown leather wristwatch. It was eight o'clock—almost time for church service. She strode to the swing door and left the bathroom, going back home.

A CAR HORN BLEW OUTSIDE.

Eva hurried to a front window in the living room and peeked out the curtained blinds. A 1956 mint green and white Chevy Bel Air was rumbling on the paved driveway of the house. Mrs. Flowers had returned from the gas station and volunteered to take Eva and her son to church this morning. Eva took her clutch purse from the couch, strapped Andrew's Cookie Monster backpack on one shoulder, and lifted her son out of his playpen.

When she exited the front door, Mrs. Flowers switched off the engine and got out of her car. The old woman stepped out her comfort zone of African attire with her Sunday best. Wearing a marigold skirt suit, a black pillbox hat, and gold flats, she looked like a cut-out photo from *Ashro* magazine.

"Mrs. Flowers? Is that you?" Eva joked and closed the front door.

"Yup, it's cool now," Mrs. Flowers said, "I can't be wearing my thin day dresses with the weather changing. Summer's gone, and winter will be here before you know it, honey."

"You got that right," Eva agreed, walking to the driveway. Mrs. Flowers cackled and opened the back car door.

"Thank you," Eva said.

"You're welcome. I never forgot my days of motherhood. It definitely keeps your hands tied," Mrs. Flowers replied, as Eva buckled Andrew in his car seat. Since she rode with Mrs. Flowers sometimes, there was already one on the back seat for him to use.

Eva joined Mrs. Flowers in the front of the car, taking the passenger seat.

Mrs. Flowers turned on the radio and scanned the static stations. A gospel men's quartet blared through the speakers, singing the first chorus of 'Amazing Grace.'

Their four voices mingled in harmony, the background music comprising of a waltz drum beat and a church organ striking slow chords. *"A-maaa-zing grace! How sweet the sound. That saved a wretch like meee! I once was lost, but now am found, twas blind, but now I see . . ."*

Mrs. Flowers hummed to the melody and pulled her car out the driveway, tapping her thick fingers on the silvery steering wheel. She glanced at Eva. "So, have you received news about your SSI benefits yet?"

Eva sighed. "Nope. All the waiting is driving me nuts, but I guess I should hear soon next month. Since Andre gets discharged in November, it'll be perfect timing."

"How's he anyway?" Mrs. Flowers said.

Eva shrugged and studied the blurry view of red-orange maple trees outside her foggy window. "Who knows? He won't talk to me."

"He's going through," Mrs. Flowers said, "I'm sure he'll open up when he comes home."

"That's the problem." Eva crossed her arms over her chest. "He acts like he doesn't *want* to come home. It's the way he looks at me . . . I'm trying to keep it together, but he's getting under my skin."

Mrs. Flowers focused on the country highway and took a deep inhale of sweet sap in the breeze. "Do you love Andre?"

Eva was startled by her question but assumed the old woman was making some kind of point. "Of course," she answered without hesitation.

"Then stay patient with him," Mrs. Flowers said, giving her a look. "Eva, honey, I know you've been dealing with a hard time juggling responsibilities, but you can't always look at things from your perspective. Patience is the key to a lasting marriage."

"I know that," Eva said, "it's why I changed my mind about taking him to church today. I might've invaded his space too much. Andre's always been a strong person, but he needs time to grieve for the past and release his emotions. As far as I know, he hasn't cried since he learned he had an accident."

Mrs. Flowers sucked her teeth and maneuvered into the left lane. "It's hard to grieve for a life you don't remember."

Eva's shoulders sagged. "I guess that makes sense." She arched her brow. "Do you think his memory will come back?"

"Maybe," Mrs. Flowers said. "Somehow I believe a piece of the old Andre is still inside him; and in due time, he's gonna show himself."

Eva sighed. She wished she had Mrs. Flowers' confidence, but the reality of Andre's mental state and condition had kicked into gear. She looked back outside at old farmers, harvesting and selling pumpkins to the community. One of them were giving a group of people a hayride in a cart connected to a John Deere tractor, riding them through the dirt grooves of the orange, ripe patch.

Before Andrew was born, one autumn she and Andre had taken a ride with neighboring friends. They had so much fun together, laughing and talking among their neighbors in town. As they passed the pumpkin patch, Eva hung her head. Their hayride felt like it happened yesterday, but after weeks went by, she had accepted her husband wouldn't remember their past again.

Pastor Tyson read in the Book of Genesis chapter thirty-two. He preached when Jacob wrestled until daybreak with his thigh out of joint, and how God blessed him. From this, he advised the congregation to never give up on faith and to fight through their prayers to receive God's blessings.

Help me, Jesus. I need you. Eva bowed her head and closed her eyes in meditation. It was easier said than done, but she believed God could do anything but lie and fail. Getting through to Andre was becoming more difficult, but with the Lord's help, nothing was impossible. The choir rose from the balcony chairs in their royal blue robes and sang "Tis So Sweet to Trust in Jesus."

After their song, Pastor Tyson ended the service with a closing prayer. Eva held her son's hand and walked him through the crowd toward the lobby doors. She wanted to get away and hide, but the pastor called her name.

"Sister Lucas!" Pastor Tyson said, waving over bobbing heads.

Eva turned around and gave a timid smile. "Hello, pastor."

Pastor Tyson grinned, shaking her hand. "Greetings, sister. How's it going? How's your husband doing in therapy?"

Eva opened her mouth. "He's . . ." She felt like her tongue was snatched out. Fallen in defeat, she had no words to express Andre or herself.

"How about we talk in my office?" Pastor Tyson said.

Eva nodded and followed the pastor along, walking her son beside her.

"Hi, Andy." Pastor Tyson smiled at her adorable son and patted the little boy's head as they walked back up the carpet aisle.

"Hiya," Andrew said with a big grin, waddling next to his mommy. He licked his tongue across his bottom lip.

Eva allowed a smile as Pastor Tyson laughed. She couldn't help herself. Andrew was her ray of hope, and she loved those rare moments of hearing his tiny voice, especially when she understood him.

Pastor Tyson opened the door to his office, and Eva took a breath and entered to exchange words with him. Now was a better time than never to consult her religious leader on behalf of her marriage.

She needed all the support she could get.

16

Eva

S ORRY I KEPT YOU WAITING, MRS. FLOWERS," EVA said, sitting in the passenger seat of the car. She mentioned she talked with Pastor Tyson in his office and he suggested she be open-minded about Andre's feelings. Eva finished saying the pastor prayed on behalf of her and Andre's marriage and her husband's post-injury recovery.

Mrs. Flowers waved it off and turned her key in the ignition. "That's okay, honey. I understand." She switched her gear in reverse and pulled out of the parking lot. From the church, the drive back to Eva and Andre's home on Pasture Road was a fifteen-minute ride.

"Goodbye, Eva!" Mrs. Flowers said out the driver's window.

"Bye, Mrs. Flowers! Thanks again!" Eva waved and watched the mint green automobile careen in the one-door garage of a pale blue and white, single-floored house across the street. She looked at her son, holding him on her hip again. "What do you say, Andy? You hungry?"

Andrew stuck a Velcro hand of his stuffed monkey in his mouth.

"I'll take that as a yes." Eva chuckled and stepped through the door.

Her eyes widened at the quiet house.

Overnight, a tornado had struck the living room.

The house was a complete wreck, an emblem of how chaotic her life had been the past month. Little boy clothes dangled over Andrew's playpen and were on the floor. Countless mail and newspapers buried the side tables, and library books covered one side of the couch. On the center table of the room were her silver Dell laptop, an empty Domino's Pizza box, and a Canada Dry ginger ale soda can.

Eva dropped her jaw, blinking in shock. "Whoa, looks like Mommy's got a lot of cleaning to do." She sighed wearily, sat Andrew on the book-free end of the couch, took off his puffer jacket, and hung it on the coat hanger. "Now you stay here and keep your little hands off those books. I'll be right back, okay?" Eva trotted to the kitchen next door to the utility room and grabbed a laundry basket. She returned and found her son in the same spot, laughing hysterically.

She knelt and wore an amused smile, tossing her son's clothes in the basket. "Hey, baby, whatcha laughing at, huh?"

Andrew caught his breath and regained his composure. He snapped his monkey's feet together and pulled them apart, cackling again.

Eva guffawed at her son, aware for some odd reason the sound of Velcro tickled Andrew to death. There wasn't a doubt in her mind Andrew's infectious laugh couldn't lift anyone's mood, even Andre's. She thanked God for the special little boy she was blessed to have, and for the joy and comfort he provided during such a difficult time.

Someone rang the doorbell.

Eva's heart skittered, shutting off her laughter. *Who's that?*

Her face made a perplexed expression as she answered the door, peeking through the crack. A young, Caucasian man who looked in his twenties was outside on the brick, paved walkway. He had a manila folder with a sheet of paper hidden inside it and a friendly, chipped-tooth smile across his face. His eyes were irresistible and kind—orbs as blue as glacier ice.

Clouds of frosty breath spewed from his lips. "Hi, I'm Skye Garrison." He pulled something from a back pocket of his Levi jeans, and for a split second, Eva held her breath.

"I read your ad in the paper?" Skye raised a brow, holding a folded newspaper.

"Oh, yes, of course." Eva let out a sigh, relieved he didn't pull out a gun. Living alone in the house, she had been edgier without Andre there. She listened as Skye spoke on.

"I thought to stop by, and say I'm interested in working for you," he added. "I have experience in caregiving. Would you like to read my resume?"

Eva smiled. "Sure, come in." She motioned for his entrance.

Skye wiped off his suede hiking boots and came in the toasty-warm house, taking off an orange toboggan hat. Wisps of chestnut brown locks covered his head. He had more hair than Eva had expected under a small knit cap, styled in a wavy haircut that reminded her of Shaggy from *Scooby Doo.*

He gawked at the living room.

Eva blushed as she closed the door behind him. "You'll have to excuse our messy home. I've been too tired to keep up with housecleaning. You can have a seat in the tan recliner."

"Thank you, ma'am." Skye unzipped his red, bubble jacket and sat in the recliner. "I typed it last night." He opened his folder and handed his resume to Eva.

She took a seat on the couch, crammed next to Andrew and skimmed the document. "You worked in a nursing home five years? You look so young."

"I know. I'm twenty-four. It started as volunteer work for community service during high school. I interacted with the residents and assisted in bingo nights, but then I got hired for a paying job at the same facility when I was nineteen. I got trained by nurses to improve my skills, but I'm fairly capable of caring for your husband."

"I see. So, why do you want to work for me?" Eva said.

Skye laced his hands and sighed. "Well, I enjoy helping the old and disabled, which is rare for young people today, but my grandma's one of my best friends. I can do a lot of good in taking care of your husband and being his friend. I was in his shoes, Mrs. Lucas."

He continued. "Six years ago, I had an accident while riding my bike. I had the right of way at a pedestrian crosswalk, but a man in a garbage truck fell asleep at the wheel. He struck me. In a flash, I was lying on the ground. I remember nothing after that except being in the hospital with my mom. I found out later I suffered a brain injury."

Eva marveled at Skye, realizing part of her prayer had been answered. Before her eyes was a living, breathing miracle she believed God had sent to her for Andre's sake.

From first meeting Skye, he looked like any normal, young man. She didn't have a clue he suffered a brain dysfunction, and witnessing his healthy presence increased her hope Andre would recover too.

"The doctor told my mom I had a subdural hematoma. It's a pool of clotted blood from a ruptured vessel between my brain and skull," Skye added. "I was paralyzed on one side of my body and suffered many life-threatening seizures. Doctors didn't think I'd make it, but my mom refused to lose hope. It might be a long journey, but your husband can get better, Mrs. Lucas."

"Thanks," Eva said, "I'm sorry about your accident. How old were you?"

Skye took his resume from her. "Eighteen. It was a little after I graduated high school." He slipped the document back into his folder.

"Well," Eva said, smiling, "you're the only person who came to visit me, and I can't think of a better candidate to assist my husband than you." She leaned back and sighed. "However, there are some things about Andre's condition that might change your mind."

"Like what?" Skye asked.

Eva darted her eyes, nibbling her lip. She informed Skye Andre's a quadriplegic with a neurogenic bladder, has a bowel program, and uses catheters. "Are you comfortable performing these procedures?" she asked after their discussion.

"Yes, ma'am," Skye answered, "I've done them before on other bedridden patients in the nursing home. These daily tasks can be uncomfortable. The important things are to make sure you use good sanitation and keep the patient calm."

Eva let out another sigh of relief. "Oh, well, I guess that settles it. How does seven twenty-five per hour sound?

Skye rubbed his chin. "Make it eight twenty-five and we've got a deal."

Eva tugged her earlobe. She wasn't confident she could give that much, but she was too desperate to complain. She gave a lopsided grin. "Eight twenty-five it is. I'll give you the information you'll need about Andre's daily schedule later." She wore a wry smile. "I hope you don't mind, but I prefer to wait to tour you around the house. My husband suffers from memory loss, and I don't want him to feel like he's the only one new to our home."

"That's fine, Mrs. Lucas," Skye said.

Eva grinned. "Great! You can start on November ninth. That's when Andre gets discharged from the hospital."

"Okay, I'll look forward to meeting your husband." Skye glanced at Andrew crawling into his mommy's lap. "I'm guessing he's your son."

Eva wrapped her arms around Andrew. "Yes, this is Andy."

"Hi, Andy," Skye said, waving childlike at him.

Andrew drew back against his mommy and avoided eye contact, playing with her fingers.

"Don't you wanna say hi?" Eva glanced down at her son.

Andrew blinked and remained quiet, staring.

Skye chuckled. "That's okay. I'm sure he'll get used to me the more he sees me around." He stood and stretched out his arms. "Guess I'll show myself out. Thanks for the job."

"No, thank you for accepting it," Eva said with emphasis. "Even though I don't like to admit it, I need help. I'm sure you noticed the minute you walked in. I imagine it will be harder when Andre comes home."

"Don't worry—"Skye walked to the front door—"I'll be glad to help. See you in November."

"Bye, Skye. Thanks again," Eva replied.

Skye gave a soldier's salute with a dopey grin and exited the house.

What a nice guy. Eva chuckled and shut the door. With Skye's help, it would relieve her from some strain of taking care of Andre, at least during the daytime. At night, she would have to be her husband's caregiver and monitor him when he sleeps, making sure he's rotated to avoid him getting bed sores.

She was glad she was a bookworm. Eva had checked out books from the public library, perusing about how to transport paralyzed people from a wheelchair. Online articles she found while surfing on her laptop were helpful in broadening her knowledge of Andre's brain injury and disorders.

Eva rose from the couch with her son. "I'll finish cleaning later. Come on, let's get something to eat, Andy." She carried her son to the kitchen and sat him in his highchair. For lunch, Eva heated a bowl of Chef Boyardee mac and cheese and four chicken nuggets for Andrew. For herself, she ate a turkey club sandwich and finished a half a bag of Lays potato chips. Later, she played mega Legos with Andrew in the living room.

Unlike her, he hadn't developed a building strategy, and instead observed their pretty colors and rattled them around on the floor. Finally, Eva and Andrew watched the movie *Curious George 3: Back to the Jungle*. By the end credits, her son was fast asleep, cradled in her lap. She put him to bed for an afternoon nap.

"Sleep tight, Andy. I love you." Eva pulled a baby blue, fleece blanket over Andrew and his stuffed monkey and kissed him. She tiptoed out of Andrew's room and entered the master bedroom. It was so silent in the house she heard her shadow's footsteps. She missed those secret whispers she and Andre used to share during Andrew's nap time, peeking at him in his crib and admiring how much their son had grown.

Knowing Andre had become reticent toward her, she understood she'd have to endure a long wait for friendly relations with him. The next months would be a trial by fire, but now with a relatable guy like Skye by her side, she had faith everything would work out fine.

17

Eva

CAN A MAN FALL IN LOVE WITH HIS WIFE TWICE? Eva stared behind Dr. Brown at her husband and sighed hopelessly as the critical care physician offered her last-minute advice. Andre was sitting in his ruby-and-gray, electric wheelchair nearby the entrance. He was in his own universe, admiring the hazy morning through the glass automatic doors.

November had arrived, and it was finally time for Eva to bring her husband home. His life was at stake and had survived, but she questioned if their relationship would do the same.

Though Mrs. Flowers said it depended on her to ignite the flame, a happy marriage wasn't one-sided. It involved the shared exchange of good communication and affection from both spouses—qualities Eva doubted Andre would give. Since completing his physical therapy, Andre made little to no recovery of his mobility. Aside from his face and neck, his thumbs were the only parts of his body he could feel, but his depressed mood concerned Eva the most.

"Have you considered placing him on an antidepressant?" Dr. Brown said, catching her off guard.

Eva shifted her eyes back to the doctor. "Oh, no, doctor. To tell you the truth, I'm kind of skeptical of medications." She glanced at her husband. "Andre's already been through a lot. I don't wanna risk him suffering side effects through the process of curing his depression. I've gotten him to smile and loosen up before during his therapy. I wanna try to pull him out of his low mood myself."

"Fine," Dr. Brown said with a smile, "but if all fails, consider getting him a prescription. Many brain injury victims suffer from major depression, especially those who became paralyzed. If left untreated, he may develop suicidal thoughts or attempt to kill himself. Be sure to keep a close eye on him while he's in your care." The physician turned his back and looked at Andre. "Did you hire a daytime caregiver?"

"Yes," Eva said, "he and my husband's grandfather should be here any minute. Grandpa Ricardo's bringing his Ford truck to load up the electric wheelchair."

"Great," Dr. Brown said, "well, I guess this is goodbye." He held out a hand. "Please call if you have more questions."

Eva shook the doctor's hand. "Absolutely, and thanks for your help."

Dr. Brown walked over to her husband and smiled. "Take it easy, Andre. One day at a time, okay?"

"Okay, doctor," Andre slurred, not making eye contact.

Dr. Brown patted Andre's shoulder. "Farewell, man."

Eva gulped and watched the doctor walk away down the hospital corridor, holding her husband's gym bag. Until Grandpa Ricardo and Skye come, she was left alone with

Andre, a tricky situation which resulted in flare-ups or dead silence.

She inhaled a long breath and approached him. *God, help, Andre. Please, let him speak to me.* Eva stood beside his electric wheelchair and gripped the strap of the gym bag, joining her husband in the outside view. "It's . . . pretty foggy, huh."

Andre made no comment.

Eva glanced from him to the doors again. "Listen, we both have to live together. We have a little boy who needs us . . . so we should try to make this work, right?"

"Whatever . . ." Andre muttered.

Eva pursed her lips and sighed. There was no telling when Andre's distant attitude would change, but at least he spoke to her. It was the first time he had in two weeks. Eva hadn't visited him again since the day she changed her mind about taking him to church with her. Being treated like she was invisible, there wasn't a point to anymore.

A holly green 1967 Ford pickup and an orange Jeep Wrangler crawled into two parking spots beside each other in front of the hospital.

Her face brightened as an old Hispanic man with a gray, bushy mustache and a young, white man with a brown, shaggy haircut strode toward the entrance. The automatic doors slid open and clamped behind them.

"Hey! Buenos dias, Eva!" Grandpa Ricardo spread his arms wide.

Eva giggled. "Buenos dias, Papa." She hugged her husband's grandfather and squeezed her eyes shut to dissipate the tears she felt forming. "Oh, I'm so glad you're here." Eva stepped back and looked at her hired caregiver. "And you too, Skye."

Skye buried a hand in a pocket of his jeans and waved the other. "Nice to see you, Mrs. Lucas."

"Andre, this is Skye Garrison. He'll be your daytime caregiver at home," Eva said.

Skye grinned. "Hi, Mr. Lucas. It's a pleasure to meet you. We have more in common than you realize."

"Hey," Andre replied lowly.

Grandpa Ricardo pulled a pack of Big Red chewing gum from his checkered, western shirt and frowned at Andre. "What's the matter, nieto? Eres infeliz?"

Eva's smile faded "Um, I'm afraid he doesn't remember how to speak Spanish."

"Oh . . ." Grandpa Ricardo sighed. "Well, maybe I teach him. I did before, you know. He couldn't speak a word as a boy, but he became a pro speaker by the time he was ten." He folded a stick of cinnamon gum in his mouth, chewed, and put the pack back in his chest pouch.

"I'm sure he could"—Eva glanced at Andre—"if he tries." She dropped her shoulders with a heavy exhale. "I don't wanna be late for work. We better go home."

"Okay," Skye said, "we'll help him get in your car outside."

"Thanks." Eva turned her attention to her husband. "You can lead the way, Andre."

With his right thumb, Andre pushed the joystick knob of his wheelchair forward, riding himself through the automatic doors. Eva, Grandpa Ricardo, and Skye walked outside and followed behind him. As Grandpa Ricardo backed his pickup truck near Eva's car, Eva and Skye stood with Andre at the parking space. In the pickup's flatbed were a traditional manual style lift and a sling mesh, and connected to the back end was a scooter carrier.

Grandpa Ricardo climbed out of his truck and rubbed his weather-beaten face. "All right, muchacho. Help me with my grandson."

"Yes, sir," Skye said.

Eva opened the car door, pushed back the passenger seat, and stepped out of the way as Grandpa Ricardo and Skye helped Andre transfer from his wheelchair into her car. It took a while before they found a solution as they struggled to get Andre's long legs inside her compact vehicle.

"You may need to get a wheelchair van with transfer features, Mrs. Lucas," Skye mentioned, buckling the seatbelt over Andre's lap. "It'll make it a lot easier." He placed his hands on his hips, catching his breath.

Eva nibbled her lip. "Yeah, I've considered doing that, but they're so expensive."

Grandpa Ricardo rolled the manual lift from the passenger car opening and closed the door. "Do you want me to help? I can get it for you."

"No, it's okay, Papa," Eva said "We'll manage. The lift alone works wonders."

Grandpa Ricardo chomped his gum. "Suit yourself. We'll meet you at the house."

"Okay." Eva ran around her car and sat in the driver's seat. She flicked out her switchblade key and put it in the ignition.

"What . . . that?" Andre asked.

Eva faced him and studied the curious look on his face. She followed his gaze to the custom keychain dangling from her car key. "It's a gift you got me for our seventh wedding anniversary. Before your accident, you were going to give it to me." Her hopes rose. "Do you remember it?"

Andre drew his eyebrows together and tilted his head, rummaging through his memory.

Longing whispered through Eva as he observed the shiny pennies and steel tag glittering in the sunlight. *Come on, Andre. How could you not remember this?*

"No," Andre said finally, "but it's pew . . . beautiful."

Eva swallowed a lump. "Yeah . . . I think so too." Her heart sank, but she wouldn't cry. What good would it do anyway? Her husband's brain was like a reprogrammed computer, not a file of information saved from his prior life. She started the engine, put the gearstick in drive, cruised out of the parking space, and U-turned around the hospital complex to the gate exit.

"WELL, HERE WE ARE. OUR HOME," EVA SAID, UNBUCKLING her seatbelt. She faced Andre who was dumbstruck, looking at their two-story gray house with black shutters, centered in a small, grassy lawn. Evergreen shrubs were bunched on each side of the front door, and in front of the vehicle was a two-door garage with a single window.

Andre looked at the black roof and the puffy clouds behind it arrayed in yellow-orange sunrise. "It's . . . nice."

Eva unclipped his seatbelt for him and stepped outside. She turned around to the trunk of her car and took out Andre's gym bag and a folded manual wheelchair. Having two floors in their home, Andre needed one to use after being ascended with the stair lift installed in the house. Eva walked to the passenger side and opened her husband's door again.

After Skye and Grandpa Ricardo guided Andre's electric wheelchair into the house, they helped him into his manual wheelchair. Taking her husband out of her car was easier than getting him in, as they handled it with ease.

"There you go, nieto," Grandpa Ricardo said, removing the sling from under Andre.

"Thanks, Papa. Thanks, Skye," Eva said. "I appreciate your help."

Grandpa Ricardo's thick mustache rose when he grinned. "De nada. I'm always there for you and Andre too." He looked at his grandson in the wheelchair. "Maybe someday you come stay on the farm with me, aye? I have plenty of chores for you to do."

"I'd like to visit your farm," Skye chimed in.

Grandpa Ricardo's eyes lit up. "Would you, lad? Well, you're welcome anytime." He slid Eva a guarded look. "Let me know how things go and be patient with him."

144

Eva smiled. "I will, Papa, and thanks for your help again."

Grandpa Ricardo hugged Eva and kissed her cheek. "Guess my work here is done. Adios, Eva."

"Adios, Papa," Eva said.

Grandpa Ricardo walked away and glanced back at Andre. "Goodbye, Andre."

"Bye," Andre muttered, staring down at his Air Jordans.

Grandpa Ricardo sighed as if a weight fell on his heart.

At that instant, Eva realized she and Andrew weren't the only ones affected by Andre's brain injury, but his grandfather who raised him from a young child on his farm was hurting too, as much as them. He settled in his Ford pickup, cranked on the rattling engine, and drove out the smooth driveway, revving off Pasture Road onto East Boulevard.

Eva waved and observed as the green-and-white truck rode around a corner hidden by a crowd of red-leaf maple trees. It had been a while since she and Andre stopped by Grandpa Ricardo's farm. Maybe it would be a good idea to visit, especially for Andre.

Skye called for her attention.

She gathered her thoughts. "Oh, sorry. I guess we should go inside. Let me show you around the rest of our home so I can go to work." She held the handles of Andre's wheelchair and pushed him into the house, leading the way as Skye toted Andre's gym bag.

Skye struck up a conversation. "I never mentioned it until now, but I like how you coordinated the colors dark brown, teal, and tan together in your living room. It makes the room stand out and pop."

Eva was flattered. "Thank you. Interior design was one of my secret hobbies, and probably the career I should've pursued instead of childcare. But, dealing with kids is also fun, and I have my good moments in that field too." She stepped backward and spread her arms in welcome,

145

dropping them at her sides. "Well, you know this is the living room. Let me show you the kitchen."

She toured Skye and Andre to the kitchen where Mrs. Flowers had greeted them "good morning." She was drinking a cup of hot coffee at the four-seat table, watching Andrew eating his bowl of banana oatmeal for breakfast.

"How is everyone?" Mrs. Flowers sipped from a mug.

"Fine, ma'am," Skye said, smiling.

Eva grinned and gestured to the old woman. "Skye, this is Mrs. Flowers. She lives across the street and babysits Andy sometimes. If you ever need help with our house and I'm not here, she'll be able to help you. She's practically a part of our family."

Skye shook Mrs. Flowers' hand. "Good to meet you, Mrs. Flowers."

"You too, sonny," Mrs. Flowers said.

Eva slapped her forehead, thinking of what's next. "Uhh . . . oh yeah, the utility room is right around the corner from the kitchen." She turned squarely and pointed at a glass door behind long white blinds. "Outside here is the patio and—" Eva turned another angle, facing an arched entrance—"the dining room is right through this walkway. Let me show you guys." She pushed Andre's wheelchair and toured the dining room. Making Skye and Andre comfortable in the house was important to Eva, but especially for her husband.

"All right, it's time we go to the second floor," Eva said, after exiting the guest bedroom on the first floor.

Skye helped Andre into the stair lift, which slowly took him to the top of the hardwood staircase. Then Skye toted the manual wheelchair upstairs and adjusted Andre back into it again.

Watching the caregiver lift and move Andre was making Eva tired, but Andre depended on them, and she and Skye had to do their best to cope with the process. She sighed and presented the rest of the house, including the master bedroom, Andrew's room, and the bathroom.

"And that's all the rooms," Eva said, after finishing her house tour. "Now I've got to go to work with Andrew. I'll be back between three-thirty and four in the afternoon. My cell number and Andre's daily schedule are on the refrigerator in the kitchen and don't forget, you can ask Mrs. Flowers for help about the house."

"Super," Skye said.

"If Andre takes a long nap, he'll need to be rotated to—"

"Prevent pressure sores," Skye said, finishing her statement.

"Oh, and make sure he keeps up with—"

"His range of motion exercises," Skye said, completing her thought again. "I know what to do, Mrs. Lucas. You don't have to worry. I'll take good care of your husband. Everything will be fine."

"Sorry. I was double-checking," Eva said. "I'll call home during my lunch break to check how the first day is going."

"Okay." Skye arched his brow, watching Eva standing with Andrew in her arms. "You are going to work, aren't you?"

Eva darted her worried gaze from Andre in his manual wheelchair to Skye. "Uh, yeah. I'll leave right now." She took a few steps and paused, looking over her shoulder. "Bye, Andre."

Andre sat with his elbows on the leather armrests of his wheelchair. He wouldn't look her direction, much less say goodbye.

Eva blinked and plastered a smile, but she knew Skye read the sadness in her face. She turned and hustled downstairs. Although she wanted to avoid placing her husband on meds, she faced a difficult test of patience.

Getting Andre out of his depression would be tougher than she thought.

18

Eva

I FEEL LIKE I'M HIS ENEMY," EVA TOLD LOUISE DURING her lunch hour. "Andre wouldn't say goodbye to me when I left, and he barely said it to his grandfather. We're disconnected, and I don't know if it'll ever end. It's like he's in a bubble and nobody's invited inside." She shook her head and sighed. "What if I can't get him to open up to me? Maybe I shouldn't have stayed away for so long during his last weeks of therapy."

"He's probably scared," Louise said.

Eva frowned. "Scared of what?"

Louise shrugged. "I don't know. Maybe he's afraid he'll be reliant on others forever, or he'll fail to meet his responsibilities as a husband and father. He's placed in an obligated position and recalls nothing of how his life was. He just knows you said you're his wife, Andy's his son, and you want his memory to come back again. Imagine the stress and pressure he must feel, especially seeing you struggle to take control over everything yourself."

"Well, he can at least pay attention to me. It's rude not to speak to your wife when she talks to you." Eva ate a scoop of chicken noodle soup from her Styrofoam bowl.

"Do you have plans for Thanksgiving break?" Louise asked.

Eva wiped her mouth with a napkin. "I've been so busy lately. I haven't given it much thought. Mrs. Flowers will invite us to her house with her family, but I doubt I'll be in the mood. It'll make me think of old times, and I want to love Andre for how he is, not how he was anymore." She scooted out her plastic chair from the center table in the classroom. "Can you keep an eye on the kids a minute? I promised I'd call home."

"Sure." Louise drank from a can of Coca-Cola.

Eva tiptoed out of the room and gently shut the door. She exited and stood on the sidewalk in front of the stone daycare surrounded by a wooden fence. She leaned her back against a giant, green, crayon pillar of the entrance and dialed the home number on her iPhone.

"Hello?" Skye's voice cracked through the receiving end.

"Hi, Skye. It's Mrs. Lucas. How are things going?" Eva heard the television blaring in the background.

"Everything's cool," Skye said, "Andre just had lunch. He said he wanted beef stew, so I warmed a can for him with crackers. He's watching Animal Planet. After his episode, we're gonna review vocab cards. He's coming around, Mrs. Lucas."

Yeah, to you, Skye, Eva thought. She peered at the yellow-and-blue playground set in the distance. "Has he had a restroom break?"

"Uh-huh. He went about fifteen minutes ago," Skye said.

Eva glanced at her watch. "Okay, I guess I'll catch you later. Tell Andre I said hi."

149

"All right, Mrs. Lucas," Skye said.

"Bye, Skye." Eva hung up the call and shut off her phone. She let out a sigh of relief that Andre was doing fine, but she was feeling like she had two babies instead of one. Suddenly, she felt like Andre's mother, but it was her job to ensure he was taken care of, even if someone else did it.

Eva returned back to the classroom.

"How's everything at home?" Louise asked.

"Fine, Skye says. He's Andre's caregiver and seems to be doing a good job." Eva plopped at the center table across from her co-worker.

"But?" Louise raised her brows, aware there was more on Eva's mind.

Eva let out a slow exhale. "But . . . I'm worried about tonight when I come home. Andre probably thinks Skye will be living in, but I haven't told him yet *I'll* be caring for him overnight. I'm hoping Skye told him already."

"Maybe he did," Louise said, "men have a way of discussing women, a buddy trying to talk sense into his friend about how to treat his wife."

"Perhaps," Eva replied. "I guess I'll find out after work." She took a sip of her bottle of water and screwed on the cap. She pondered what Louise said minutes earlier. Maybe Andre feared failing her as a man. The day he first woke from his coma, she never forgot the stunned look in his eyes. It was as if he couldn't believe someone like *she* was his wife. She didn't know whether it was because of her appearance or her personality, but Eva didn't always find herself attractive or interesting.

During her teenage years, she didn't look like Esmeralda that's for sure. Somehow, Andre still saw the beauty in her. It was one of the many things she loved and appreciated about him.

His kind heart.

Though her husband had problems managing his time, he *truly* loved her.

EVA NOSED THE FRONT END OF HER CAR TO THE GARAGE and shut off the engine. She gripped her hands on her steering wheel and glimpsed in the rearview mirror. Andrew was asleep, slouched in his car seat like an old man in a recliner. She stepped out of her car, unclipped her son, and toted him into the house.

"Hello, everybody!" Her expression hardened, surveying the empty living room. *Where are they?* Footsteps approached nearby her. She took a swift look at the staircase as Skye came downstairs to the living room.

He stopped at the last step with his hand on the banister knob. "Hi, Mrs. Lucas."

Eva smiled. "Hi, Skye. Where's Andre?"

Skye jerked his thumb behind him. "He's taking a nap upstairs. It's been about two hours. I just rotated him and came from using the bathroom. I hope you don't mind, Mrs. Lucas."

"No, it's okay," Eva replied, "see you tomorrow morning."

Skye nodded. "Bye, Mrs. Lucas." He shut the front door.

Eva walked upstairs and placed Andrew in his crib. She strode the narrow hall and pushed back the door of the master bedroom. Her husband was on the queen-sized bed. His chest rose and fell with soft breaths.

She tiptoed in and sat on her bedside.

Eva untied her tennis shoes and slipped them off as Andre squirmed his head on his pillow. She looked over her shoulder at him.

His eyes fluttered open, staring at her.

"Hey, did you sleep well?" Eva said, smiling.

Andre readjusted his head on his pillow. "Where . . . Skye?

"Let me explain something first." Eva sat upright beside him on the bed and crossed her ankles. "Andre, Skye's a

151

daytime caregiver. I should've mentioned it before, but it worried me you wouldn't want to come home if I told you. It means . . . he's here during the morning and afternoon, and I'll be caring for you tonight."

"No. Skye—stay—here," Andre faltered.

Eva sighed. Why did their relationship have to become so complicated? Something had to be done. Tension couldn't live between them forever. It was time to draw the line. She turned her body, lying on her side toward him. "Andre, I'm sorry, but he can't stay. Besides, caring for you myself at night will save us money." She touched his right hand. "I promise I'll take good care of you."

Eva stood from the bed. "I'm about to start dinner. Do you wanna go back downstairs?"

Andre frowned and sighed wearily. "Yes."

Eva rolled the manual wheelchair alongside the bed and placed the sliding board in the seat. She carefully turned Andre on his left side and applied her pillow behind his back for support. Three other pillows she stacked on top each other at the end of the bed. Eva slid Andre's legs down and lifted his upper body right side up, resting his head on the pillows.

"You okay?" Eva asked.

"Yeah," Andre said.

Eva grabbed a gate belt on his nightstand and wrapped it around Andre's waist. "I'm about to transfer you. One . . . two . . . three . . ." She enveloped her arms around Andre and clutched the gate belt, pulling him onto the slide board and into his wheelchair. She let out an exhale. Her back ached a little, but not enough to complain about. She slid the board from under her husband and adjusted his hands in his lap and his feet on the footrests of the wheelchair.

"How many times did you use the restroom?" Eva adjusted her husband back against the seat.

"Three," Andre said. "Skye took me . . . before he left."

Eva nodded. "All right. I guess you can wait until later." She pushed Andre out of the master bedroom and down the hall to the stair lift. Eva operated the lever, lowering him down the flight of stairs. At the end of the staircase, she sat him back in his electric wheelchair and turned on the television to keep him occupied while she cooked dinner.

For Andre she made baked tilapia with fresh green beans and brown rice with gravy. Dr. Brown advised she ensure her husband has a good diet with lots of protein and fiber to build his muscles and help with his digestion. She made mashed potatoes with fish sticks for Andrew and heated a frozen pasta meal for herself.

Eva sat in a chair in front of her husband and fed him as much as he would eat before having her own food. She tried to get Andre to chat with her about his first day with Skye, but he made little to no feedback. Andrew made most of the noise, babbling and drumming the tray of his highchair with his spoon. Before bedtime, Eva gave Andrew a bath, dressed him in his PJs, and tucked him in his crib.

Now it was a matter of getting her husband ready for bed.

Eva knocked on the door of the master bedroom. "Hey, are you tired yet?"

"A little," Andre said.

Eva opened a middle drawer of the dresser. "What do you want to wear tonight? You have a lot of pajamas to choose from." Regardless of his disabilities, it was important to her she gave her husband some independence.

She took out a pair of blue-striped pajamas. "Are these okay?"

Andre nodded. "Sure."

Eva flapped out the PJs and laid them across his manual wheelchair. She walked around and stood over him as he lay on the bed. As she slipped his arms out of his sweatshirt, his pupils were huge. She could tell he was nervous, so she smiled to help him relax. A large birthmark stained his left bicep. It was shaped like the continent of Africa, and about two shades darker than his cinnamon brown skin. Eva hadn't seen him shirtless for so long, she forgot it was there. She pulled his shirt off over his head, grabbed his nightshirt, and buttoned it on him. Afterward, she tugged off his sweatpants and put on his matching PJ pants for him.

"There, nice and cozy." Eva tossed his dirty clothes in the straw hamper. She returned to his bedside and helped him sit up and transfer back to his wheelchair.

"Uh, I'm taking you to brush your teeth," Eva said. She would get to the real purpose for their departure, but she didn't want to ruin his calm mood. Eva wheeled him out of the master bedroom to the bathroom.

Unsure she could assist him without making a mess on the bed, she didn't trust using the plastic urinal the hospital lent him. She flicked on the light switch and picked up his toothpaste and red toothbrush from the sink holder. When she finished brushing his teeth, she gave him the chance to speak his need to cath for himself.

"Do you have spasms?" Eva spotted his grimaced face in the reflection of the medicine cabinet mirror.

"No." Andre squirmed and smacked his lips as if he had a bad taste.

Eva turned around to him, leaning against the sink counter. "Um . . . do you wanna go before bed?" She cast a glance from the toilet to Andre, and he quickly got her message.

"Uh, no, I'm fine." Andre gulped.

Eva angled her head and sighed. "Andre, you haven't used it since 3:00 p.m. It's nine o'clock at night. I know you have to go again."

She sat on the lid of the toilet in front of her husband's manual wheelchair and wove her hands. "Listen, I know you don't remember me, but you don't have to be embarrassed. I promise to be as gentle as possible."

"I said I'm fine." Andre looked away at the linen tower.

"You're supposed to cath at least four times a day to prevent kidney damage." Eva placed a hand on his knee. "I don't want anything worse to happen to you."

"Okay," Andre muttered, reluctantly glancing at her.

Eva stood and raised the lid and seat of the toilet. "All right, let me wash my hands and gather your supplies." She stepped behind Andre's wheelchair, pushed him to the toilet bowl, folded the footrests, and positioned his feet flat on the floor. "There you go. It'll be over in a jiffy."

She took a grocery bag of used catheters from under the sink cabinet and put the bag on the metal shelf above the toilet. Her husband never reused a catheter to avoid a urinary tract infection, so instead Dr. Brown advised they get disposed in a bag and thrown out on trash day. Eva washed her hands thoroughly and dried them with a sheet from the paper towel holder.

She exhaled to calm her rapid heartbeat and unzipped Andre's gray carry pouch. Eva took out a new intermittent catheter, a lubricant packet, a Betty Hook to keep his clothes from getting wet, and two wipe packs. She placed these supplies aside on top of the sink counter and grabbed two latex-free gloves from a box on the metal shelf. Snapping on the rubber gloves, she stole a glance at Andre and saw discomfort cloud his face. He was scared stiff, unusually ashamed for her to see his male anatomy.

But she didn't blame him.

If she got in a car accident, suffered a brain injury, and no longer remembered her husband, she'd be the same way. Unease grew in the atmosphere, but Andre wasn't the only one nervous. Despite reading the directions in the brochure, she worried about hurting her husband. His daily routine required great care and cleanliness, and one wrong move could cause infection or damage him for life.

She picked up the Betty Hook first and stood behind Andre's wheelchair. "You can close your eyes while I catheterize you."

Andre drew a long breath "Okay." He squeezed his eyes shut, his right thigh jittering.

Eva tucked the Betty Hook into Andre's pajama pants and underwear and fastened the long flat end under his wheelchair seat, exposing him. She took a wipe sample, tore it open, and pulled out the wet wipe. After Eva cleaned him off, she tossed the used wipe in the toilet.

She grabbed and opened the lubricant packet and intermittent catheter from the sink counter. Then she lubricated the thin, plastic tube and slipped her arms under Andre's armpits, still standing behind his wheelchair. She slowly inserted the catheter inch by inch. *Please, God, don't let me hurt him. I'll never forgive myself.*

Her heart drummed against her rib cage. *Oh my gosh! How can he not feel this?* She thought she was going to freak out.

"Are you okay?" she asked with concern.

"Yeah . . . put it in." Andre didn't sense it was already halfway inside him, and Eva realized just how paralyzed her husband was below his waist.

She exhaled to relax and proceeded with the insertion until urine poured from the funnel end of the catheter into the toilet bowl. *Phew. Thank goodness.* She let out a sigh of relief. As the flow dwindled, she slid the catheter in one inch more to ensure his bladder was empty. "Okay. You're finished. I'm taking it out."

"Good," Andre said with a relieved exhale.

Eva chuckled at his reaction. "How did I do, Mr. Lucas?" She carefully removed the catheter and put it in the plastic trash bag.

"Fine, I guess." Andre opened his eyes and wore a half-smile. "You're okay . . . nice woman."

Eva smiled. "Thank you." She cleaned him off with the other wipe and tugged up his pants.

If she could get through to Andre during such a sensitive procedure, they could mend their marriage too.

156

She flushed the toilet, took off the gloves, and washed her hands again. After many tense days, tonight was the beginning of rebuilding their relationship. But with Andre's fluctuating mood, she pondered if it would continue improving.

19

Eva

HAPPINESS COURSED THROUGH EVA AS THE POSTAL worker stuck envelopes in their tan mailbox. The mailman whistled as he walked back to his delivery truck, climbed in, and zoomed to their next-door neighbor's house. She opened the front door and stepped outside in the chilly morning in her lilac robe and slippers. Eva got the mail and sifted through the letters, searching for good news. Sixty days had almost passed since Eva met with the social worker, and she and her family needed those SSI benefits to make ends meet.

She went inside and sat on the couch in the living room.

Aside from fast food coupons and household bills, there didn't seem to be anything from Dr. Washburn or the

Social Security Administration.

Eva bit her lip. *Come on. Where is it?* She flipped Burger King coupons behind the stack and found a letter from Dr. Washburn. Her heart leaped. Eva grinned and ripped the envelope open like a child who found a hidden birthday present.

She unfolded and read the typed letter:

Dear Mrs. Lucas,

I'm writing to inform you your disability claim has been approved. After much discussion and review of your medical records, the SSA has agreed to supply you and your husband with financial assistance.

You and your family will begin receiving SSI benefits and SSDI benefits on November 25th. If you have questions, please call or email me.

Sincerely,

Barbara Washburn

Eva closed her eyes and placed the letter over her chest in gratitude. "Thank you, God." She never thought she'd be so excited to get financial support, but that changed when she became the only working member of her family. She raced upstairs to the master bedroom and told Andre their claim was approved.

"Good for you." Her husband clenched his jaw.

Eva's smile dropped. "No, Andre. It's good for both of us." She approached him and sat on the bed at his feet. "I don't understand . . . I thought you'd be glad. You can get more things you need to get better."

"Better?" Andre frowned and gritted his teeth. "I'm— not—getting—better!"

Eva flinched from the bed with a gasp. Tears shone in her eyes as she stared at her husband. "I'm sorry . . . I'm sorry for the circumstances you've faced with and your accident, but don't take it out on me! I'm trying to help you."

Andre avoided her gaze, ignoring what she said. Every time Eva thought they were getting along, darkness crept in and killed their friendly relations, separating them. Her husband's mood swings were becoming harder to deal with. How could she keep offering love and support, if all she received back was anger, depression, and selfishness?

Not once has Andre apologized for his nasty attitude, and she got a hunch he was taking her compassion and sweet nature for granted.

"I'm going to the grocery store to get a few things. Maybe you should come," Eva said.

Andre shook his head. "No, thanks. I'll . . . stay here."

Eva swiped her eyes. "Fine. You can wait for Skye. He'll be here in a few minutes." She left and closed the door. Since the day Andre got out of the hospital, her husband hid at home, not wanting the public to see him, and especially with Andrew along.

Feeling no good as a parent, he left the responsibility of his son all to Eva. The shoes of fatherhood were too big for his feet, easily annoyed whenever his son was cranky, noisy, or misbehaved.

EVA ENTERED BI-LO ON WILBUR STREET, SAT ANDREW IN the front of an apple-red shopping cart, and wheeled it to the bread aisle. In the middle of the walkway, a tiny, Caucasian woman with strawberry blonde hair had a cart piled with food.

Two children were trailing behind the woman, stepping on the red square floor tiles and skipping the white ones. One kid was a toddler-sized girl wearing a sparkly tiara and purple tutu. The other was an older boy about eight dressed in a Little League baseball uniform.

Eva grabbed two loaves of Wonder bread and caught a better look at the short lady close to her.

"Frankie?" She gaped.

The reddish-blonde woman looked in her direction and gasped. "Eva?"

Both of the women grinned and laughed, bumping into each other.

Francine Nichols and Eva were close friends at Garden Ridge High School. Being four-foot-eleven, Francine was called 'shrimp' or 'shorty' by her school peers, teased for her small stature. Together the girls endured the hardship of bullying for getting good grades and labeled as outcasts.

Francine grinned. "Hey, it's been a long time. How are you?"

"I'm hanging in there. My husband . . . he had an accident a couple of months ago," Eva said.

Francine's smile faded, tilting her head. "Oh, Eva. I'm so sorry. How bad was it?"

"Well, he lost his memory." Eva tossed the loaves of Wonder bread in her cart. "I showed him old photos and talked with him, but nothing works. He's been like a seesaw, and he's ashamed to be in public. It's so overwhelming. Each day I feel like a dark cloud is hovering over me. I'm tired and I need some relief."

"That's tough. Maybe you should hire a caretaker," Francine said.

"I already have," Eva said, "but daytime care is all I can afford. It's expensive paying a live-in caretaker. And besides, where would he stay if he lived with us? We have only three bedrooms, and my husband needs a bed to himself as a quadriplegic. As of now, he stays in the master bedroom and I stay in the guest room. There's been a strain in our relationship for a number of reasons."

"Wow. I'm sorry to hear that." Francine took a loaf of Italian white bread and placed it in front of her cart. She glimpsed back at her children and snapped her fingers, noticing them getting too far away from her. "Piper! David! Get back here. Now!"

161

"Yes, Mom!" David chirped. He and his little sister raced toward Francine's grocery cart.

"And no running!" Francine ordered. "Someone mopped these floors and I don't want y'all to slip and fall."

David and Piper slowed to a steady walking pace the rest of the way back.

"Kids, they're such a mess sometimes," Francine said, rolling her eyes.

"Tell me about it." Eva chuckled and looked at her school friend's kids. "So, how old are they?"

"Four and eight. Their dad's name is Jake. He was a charmer, but also a jerk. After he lost his job, he drank late hours of the night. We had plans to marry, but they went out of the window. I guess we couldn't make it work." Francine shoved her curly hair away from her face.

Eva frowned. "I'm sorry, Frankie, but maybe you'll find the right man someday."

"Are you kidding?" Francine widened her brown eyes. "I'm done with men. I'm fine living with my kids alone. You really have to know what you're doing before standing at the altar, and it's better to be safe than sorry later." A smile danced on her lips. "So, who's the kid in your cart?"

"My son Andrew," Eva said. "He'll be two next April."

Francine chuckled. "He's a cutie. I imagine he looks like his daddy."

"Yup," Eva replied, "just with more hair. Though, I plan to have Andy's first haircut soon."

The two young women laughed again.

"I married Andre Lucas," Eva confessed.

Francine pinned Eva with her eyes. "Andre Lucas? You mean scrawny, little Andre?"

Eva giggled. "He's not so scrawny anymore, Frankie. I have a picture of him." She opened her clutch purse, took out a photo from her wallet, and handed it to Francine.

"Oh, my. He's changed. Andre looks so . . . dreamy." Francine wore a flirty, teasing smile. "I can see why you fell for him." She gave Eva her picture back. "And you . . . you're fabulous. Slender with a good height and everything."

"You're beautiful too, Frankie," Eva said.

"Me?" Francine curled her upper lip. "I look like I belong in the *Wizard of Oz*. All I need is clown makeup, a colorful puffy dress, and dwarf shoes, and I'm an official resident of Munchkin Land."

"Don't talk about your height again," Eva said wearily. "You remember what I told you when we were in school."

"Yeah," Francine said flatly, rolling her eyes, "small people can do big things."

"Well, they can," Eva said with a giggle.

Francine's whole face lit up. "You know, our second class reunion is next week. Why don't you come?"

Eva wrinkled her nose. "Hmm . . . I don't know."

"Come on, please, Eva. It'll be fun. We can pick up on old times. I missed you at the first one. I felt so out of place like I was in high school where I left off ten years ago. All the popular classmates bunched in their circles the same old way, and I was all alone."

"What about Alan Murphy? He always ate lunch at our table," Eva said.

"Eva, Alan died two years before the first reunion," Francine replied.

Eva's heart stopped. "Really?"

"Mm-hmm," Francine said with a nod. "Nadine's the head sponsor of our class reunions. She said his wife told her he committed suicide. 'Everything seemed so perfect,' his wife said, but then one afternoon, she found him dead in their bedroom. He shot himself."

Eva gasped and placed a hand over her heart. "Oh, no . . ." Alan was one of the funniest, brightest kids in school, but now he was buried six-feet under before his fortieth birthday. She had never forgotten the embarrassing time two of the football players set a prank on him. They locked Alan in his locker when he had to use the restroom. He nearly wet his pants after she solved his locker combination and helped him out.

His frustration hurt her gut, kicking his locker before he walked to his class. With her husband's emotional problems, hearing about Alan's death made her fearful. Perhaps she should take Dr. Brown's offer and have him prescribe Andre an antidepressant. Maybe it would help him recover his mood, but compromise and reasoning with Andre was always a challenge. Regardless, she prayed her husband never stoops as low as taking his own life.

"So, will you come?" Francine urged, snatching Eva out of her train of thought.

"Uh . . . I'll think about it," Eva said.

Francine smiled. "Thanks, Eva. You're the best friend ever."

Eva gave a wry smile and massaged her neck. She had seen none of her other classmates in many years and reuniting with them now made her edgy. Her former crush Caleb Williams had moved away to New York with his dad after high school graduation.

So, it was the girls who bullied her that worried Eva the most. On the other hand, she definitely could use a break from running like the energizer bunny. Always on the go for others, it had been a while since she's had leisure time for herself.

Eva and Francine exchanged cell phone numbers.

"I'll catch you later, Eva," Francine said.

Eva wore a weak smile and waved. "Uh, sure."

"We gotta check out," Francine told her kids.

"Can I have Cocoa Pebbles?" David asked, tagging alongside his mother.

"No," Francine replied, pushing her cart away.

"Why not?" David whined.

"Because I said so, and don't question me when I tell you...." Francine turned off the aisle and the light chatter with her son faded in the store's commotion of country music and other shoppers.

Eva laughed and imagined her and Andrew years later when her son gets older. She looked at him in her shopping cart and poked his tummy, making him giggle. "You won't be bugging Mommy to buy you cereal, will you?"

"Nana . . . nana." Andrew moved his face close to his mother's and placed his tiny hands on her cheeks, squishing them together.

Eva chuckled and kissed Andrew's nose. "Okay, okay. We'll get bananas."

Andrew clapped and grinned. Eight little white teeth were in his mouth like shiny pearls in a clamshell, four at the top and four at the bottom. More would pop up soon, and Eva could already hear her son's hollering over sore pain and itchy gums. She put in two loaves of Sara Lee wheat bread and rolled her pushcart from the bread aisle. After bagging a bundle of bananas, she went to the baby aisle and got a pack of Huggies for toddlers. She couldn't wait until Andrew was potty-trained to use the toilet himself.

It would save her the trouble of buying pull-ups every month. A single pack cost as much as her cell phone bill, and she could use the extra dollars to keep up with her monthly payments. Eva checked out and loaded the groceries in the trunk of her car. She buckled Andrew in his car seat, and studied the little boy for a moment, playing with Mookie.

She marveled how two people from two states over two thousand miles apart could meet, become friends, fall in love, and together create the endearing life before her. Her eyes were glossy, encircling her arms around her son. "I love you so much, Andy, and no matter what, your daddy loves you too. He . . . he's just frustrated right now. But someday . . . someday he'll hug you, and kiss you, and love you the way he used to do."

Eva swiped her hands over her damp cheeks. She closed the back door and sat in the driver's seat. At home, Skye helped bring the bags of groceries into the house and fill the kitchen cabinets and refrigerator. Visiting on the weekends, like Mrs. Flowers, the young man had become a part of their family, and Eva wanted it to stay that way.

She placed a can of Campbell's tomato soup in the cabinet above the stove hood and beamed at her son. Andrew waddled over to Skye, hugging his pant leg like he was his big brother. It was the most adorable thing Eva had seen in a long time.

"Hey, Andy." Skye glanced down and smiled at Andrew.

Eva chuckled with a hand on her hip. "Well, that was a surprise."

"Lovie . . . lovie." Andrew reached out his little arms.

Skye looked at Eva like he wasn't sure what to do.

"He wants you to hug him," Eva hinted.

"Oh, okay." Skye lifted Andrew and embraced him. "Hi, Andy. Boy, he's heavy."

Eva giggled and watched the scene. She imagined Andre holding her son, standing tall, healthy, and in his right mind. It was a heartwarming picture—a dream which she wished would come true. An hour later, Skye left home, and the late afternoon and evening were like a prison sentence of seclusion. Once Andre performed his daily exercises and routines, there wasn't much he could do, but sit and stare at images moving across a television screen.

As time passed, Eva witnessed the nerve and willpower slowly dying out of him. It was in his droopy face, his shorter responses, and his dull, sad eyes. It was in his barely touched three courses of meals, and his distressful moans she overheard at night. Eva couldn't understand what was taking long for Andre to walk independently, or at least feed himself, but she strove to stay patient with him.

SUNDAY MIDNIGHT, EVA CAME OUT OF THE GUEST ROOM in her robe and slippers and snuck in the kitchen for a late snack. She flicked on a lamp on a coffee table and curled up on the living room sofa with a small bucket of Edy's mint chocolate chip ice cream, her favorite flavor. Eva grabbed the family album on the middle table and opened it in her lap, flipping through the pictures of old memories. A tragedy of life had avalanched their marriage, burying the bricks that built the foundation of their relationship.

Now it was as if the pivotal chapters of their friendship never existed. They were strangers who shared a framed certificate nailed on the wall, and in heart-wrenching silence lived in the same house. It was hard to laugh and connect like they used to—and getting harder to love as husband and wife. Whenever Eva saw Andre's stiff, motionless body in his wheelchair, the same old question echoed in her mind. *Why did this happen?*

She ate a scoop of ice cream and turned a page. Eva smiled faintly at a snapshot from their honeymoon. In the photo, they were sporting their tinted aviators in a side hug, standing at the peak of Copper Canyon on a sizzling August afternoon. She remembered the sun's heat beating their backs as they climbed the rocky ravine, following a Mexican tourist guide from a nearby village to the top. She flipped to another picture of Andre, laughing and playing airplane with Andrew when their son was nine months old.

With a Christian, witty, loving man who would risk his life for her if he needed to, she had no reason to overthink anything. The second she said 'I do' to him, Eva felt a sense of relief. She turned to a third photo of Andre and her outside in their front yard on a snowy day, sharing a kiss. Oddly enough, she didn't recall this one or who had taken it. Behind them was a snowman they had built together.

Pain gripped Eva's chest, touching the picture. They hadn't kissed or been affectionate in months, but how could they? Andre had been so distrustful of her the mere thought of touching him intimately was like trespassing property. Her throat thickened as she fought back tears. Eva closed the book and placed it back on the table. She ate another spoonful of ice cream, musing over her present life. Just as her husband was a different man, she didn't feel like the same woman either.

No longer did her husband surprise her with pretty flowers with message cards, or tell her he loved her. No longer did he ask about her daycare job or how she was feeling, carry her in his arms, or playfully chase her around the house. There wasn't a sign Andre was still in love with her. To him, she was nothing more than a kindhearted caregiver who was thoughtful enough not to leave him in a nursing home.

A tear coursed down Eva's chin, shuddering her out of a trance. She drew a gasping breath and dried her cheek and chin, looking at the dinging grandmother clock beside the fireplace.

Two hours had passed, and she thought to rotate Andre again. Eva looked in her bucket of ice cream. She had sat and moped for so long it had melted into a milkshake. Eva rose from the couch and put it back in the freezer in the kitchen. She tiptoed upstairs to the master bedroom where her husband slept and approached the bed. She always hated to wake him, but he was at least tolerant enough to accept the routine.

"Andre," Eva whispered, rubbing his shoulder. "Honey, it's time to wake up again. Last time."

He moaned in his sleep.

Eva pulled the blanket off of Andre and positioned his right arm hanging off on the bed. She turned his body onto his right side and tucked a pillow behind his back. In addition to the pillow under his head, a third pillow she placed between his legs with his top knee flexed. Last, she recovered him with a cool sheet and the comforter.

"There . . . sleep tight, okay?" Eva said.

"Mm-hmmm," Andre replied drowsily.

She watched his body rise and fall as he drifted back out. Eva walked toward the door but then stopped and returned to Andre's bedside. She stroked his smooth, freshly-trimmed haircut and kissed his forehead.

"I love you," Eva whispered, longing for Andre's reply. She wore a wistful smile and tiptoed out of the master room, going back to bed alone.

20

Eva

"MRS. LUCAS, I'M AFRAID I CAN'T WORK TODAY," Skye said through her receiving end.

Eva grimaced and adjusted the home phone in the lock of her shoulder. "What? Why not?" She peeled a banana and cut slices in Andrew's plastic blue bowl of oatmeal, hoping Skye wasn't quitting his job.

Skye sighed over the line. "I suffered a loss in my family. My grandma passed away in her sleep. Her burial service is today, and she wrote in her will to be put to rest in her hometown Beaufort, South Carolina."

"Oh, I'm sorry, Skye. I send my prayers to you and your family," Eva said.

"Thank you. I'm sorry I didn't tell you sooner," Skye replied. "What will you do now?"

Eva puffed her cheeks and exhaled. "I guess I'll call my director and ask to have today off. I mean, what else can I do? I can't leave Andre here alone."

"I feel terrible about this, Mrs. Lucas," Skye said.

"Well, you shouldn't. It's not your fault your grandma died."

"I know," Skye said with a sigh, "but you do so much. I know how much you need help. Is there anything I can do to make up for my absence?"

Eva recalled her class reunion. Yesterday she received an invitation text message from Nadine Sterling. She assumed Francine gave Nadine her cell number. The social gathering was taking place in five more days, and she figured taking a breather from her stressful, everyday life would do her body good.

She inched up a smile. "Actually, there is. I reunited with an old classmate in the grocery store, and she wants me to attend our second class reunion with her. I thought it could be fun, a way to take my mind off my troubles at home."

"Good idea. When is your class reunion?"

"It's November eighteenth at seven o'clock, which is this Saturday coming. It would be great if you could fill in for me and watch Andre during this night for free," Eva said.

"Sure," Skye replied, "I'll come in on the eighteenth to make up for today."

"Awesome! I appreciate this, Skye. Caring for Andre has been . . . complicated. You don't understand how much I needed it." Eva ran her hand through her hair.

"You're welcome," Skye said.

Eva poured cold milk from a jug in Andrew's bowl of oatmeal and stirred it with one of his easy-grip spoons. She walked to her son's highchair. "Okay. Goodbye, Skye, and take care."

"You too," Skye said.

Eva pressed the end call button and looked at her son. "Well, Andy, it looks like we're staying home today."

"Oo-me! Oo-me!" Andrew babbled, drumming his hands on his tray. She smiled and put the bowl of oatmeal in front of her demanding little man.

Eva caught another thought. "Mrs. Flowers will also need to be here. I can't be two places at once. But first, I need to call Mrs. Higgins and ask to call out." She dialed the number of the daycare and spoke to Mrs. Higgins who allowed her the day off. Afterward, she phoned Mrs. Flowers. As always, the elderly widow gladly came over and kept a close eye on Andrew while Eva got Andre ready for the day.

EVA UNDRESSED ANDRE, STRAPPED HIM IN A FULL BODY mesh sling, and attached the shoulder straps to the cradle of a patient lift machine. She pressed her foot on the push pad and carefully transported him into a soothing, warm bath. Eva sat on the sill of the tub and lathered up a washcloth with a bar of unscented soap. "Can you close your eyes, please?" she said politely. "I don't wanna get soap in them."

Andre narrowed his brows and eyed her like a scared kitten. Today marked the first time she was washing him, as Skye had always been the one to do this for him.

"It's all right. I won't hurt you." Eva reassured him with a smile, putting his mind at ease.

Andre gulped and closed his eyes.

"This will take a second." Eva gently wiped the cloth over his forehead, cheeks, and neck. She rinsed out the rag in a separate basin of water and swiped the soapy suds off his face. "You can open your eyes now."

Her husband fluttered his eyelids and studied her in awe, squinting from a beam of daylight piercing through the window behind the metal shelf.

Eva wondered what he was pondering at that instant, but she was too distracted herself to ask. She gazed at him with a tender smile, admiring his sculpted, well-built physique. Maybe he wasn't able to walk yet, but since Skye took trips with him to the city gym, he had gotten back into shape. Despite his ailments, outbursts, and muddled brain, he still took her breath away.

With a slight shake of her head, she got a hold of herself and looked at his face, remembering the first thing she loved about him. His sepia-colored irises always reminded her of red desert sunsets, orbs of light at the horizon of rolling sand hills.

Eva sniffled and ached for her husband, combating the pain of unrequited love.

He drew in a long breath and relaxed his shoulders. "Put . . . put back . . . hospital."

"What?" Eva frowned.

Andre sighed tiredly, and she felt his hurt of struggling to speak. Having Broca's aphasia, he was unable to retrieve certain small words. He swallowed hard and attempted to talk again. "No more . . . no more burden. I want . . . divorce." He hung his head.

Eva's heart split in half. She clamped her lips together and angled her head. "Andre, look at me."

Her husband stared down at the sudsy water covering his lower body.

Eva lifted his chin and looked in his eyes. "Andre, you're not a burden and we're not getting a divorce. I married you for keeps, and I meant it. We've had a rough time these past months, but we're gonna get through this together."

She stared teary-eyed at her husband as he removed his chin from her hand and looked away. She needed to be careful about what she said around Andre and over the phone. Although he couldn't move, he could hear and was aware it tired her to take care of almost everything herself.

Originally, she considered admitting Andre into a nursing facility, but her affection willed her to keep him with his family at home. Besides, their son Andrew needed him, whether or not he recovered his memory. Eva raised his left arm out of the tub and cleaned under and over it and his bare chest.

When she finished giving his bath, she moved him with the patient lift to his shower chair. From head to toe, she rubbed and dabbed his body with a soft, clean towel. Andre took her gentle, loving care with ease and nearly fell asleep, watching her dry him off in silence.

"What do you want to wear? Your burgundy or navy sweater?" Eva asked, pulling a new pair of boxer briefs on him.

Andre blinked his drowsy eyes and hesitated to answer. "Uh . . . red one."

"Okay, burgundy it is." Eva smiled and dressed him in a white T-shirt, his V-neck burgundy sweater, and a pair of khaki pants.

"GOOD MORNING, ANDRE," MRS. FLOWERS SAID, OBSERVING him buzz past her in his electric wheelchair and go into the kitchen.

Eva plopped beside the old woman on the sofa.

"How'd the bath time go?" Mrs. Flowers asked.

Eva rounded her shoulders, watching Andrew put a jumbo puzzle of colorful shapes together on the carpet floor. "It was a little tense, but okay, I guess."

Mrs. Flowers leaned forward and scrutinized Eva's hopeless expression. "You look troubled. Has Andre told you something?"

"Yeah—" Eva closed her eyes and rubbed her forehead— "he thinks he's a burden to me. He wants a divorce and for me to put him back in a hospital. I . . . can't believe this."

"Well," Mrs. Flowers said, "he knows you've taken on a lot of responsibilities of him and Andrew."

"I know, but divorce?" Eva replied. "How could he ever suggest such a thing?"

Mrs. Flowers shrugged. "Andre has his personal reasons. Remember, he still doesn't recall ever marrying you. It doesn't matter how kind you try to be to him, nothing will change that fact."

Eva threw Mrs. Flowers a furious look. "But does that mean we should get a divorce?!"

"No," Mrs. Flowers said, "but you must understand where he's coming from . . . him seeing you take care of his needs each night must disturb him, especially since he knows you also have a child to take care of. Maybe he feels like he's taking time away from you spending it with Andrew."

"That's ludicrous," Eva said, crossing her arms, "and not a good reason to call a marriage quits, even if I believed in divorce."

"Maybe, but not to him," Mrs. Flowers said. "Personally, placing Andre in a nursing facility wouldn't mean you're a bad person, Eva. It would mean you're doing what he feels would best meet his needs. Because you've told him a lot about his former life, he probably feels terrible seeing you and Andrew suffer the losses of what he used to provide." She put a hand on Eva's shoulder. "Perhaps you should let Andre be with people he remembers from rehab who understands him if his condition doesn't improve."

A lump formed in Eva's throat. "No. I can't let him go. It's taking a while, but Andre *will* gain his strength and walk, and he *will* get his memory back."

"God willing," Mrs. Flowers muttered.

Eva rose and strutted into the kitchen. "What do you want for breakfast, Andre?" She turned around and waited for his response.

Her husband tilted his head with a long face but said nothing.

Eva bit her lip and thought.

Cheerios with sliced strawberries came to her mind. Before Andre's car accident, he ate it for breakfast every single morning, and sometimes for an afternoon snack. She took a deep breath and clasped her hands together. "Okay, I'll make you cereal." She grabbed a glass bowl from the dish rack and the cardboard box from on top of the refrigerator. Eva poured an amount of cereal into the bowl, the O-shaped oats clinking against the glass surface. She added milk and slices of strawberries into the cereal and brought the bowl with a silver spoon in it to the table.

"Will you say grace?" Eva said, strapping an adult bib on him.

Andre frowned. "Say grace?"

"Never mind. Just eat." Eva spooned Andre a scoop of cold cereal.

Milk trickled down his chin. He frowned and chewed a few times, and with his eyes pinned into hers, let the food ooze out of his mouth. Mushy cereal fell onto the bib around his neck.

Flames of anger shot through Eva, gritting her teeth. She banged her fist on the kitchen table, making the salt and pepper shakers rattle and dance. "Now why'd you do that? If you didn't want cereal, all you had to do was say so! I pay your bills and work my tail off for you and this—" She dropped the spoon in the glass bowl and smacked a hand over her mouth, regaining her bearings.

Eva blinked back tears and shook her head. "I'm sorry, Andre. I didn't mean that . . ." She stood in front of Andre and held the armrests of his wheelchair, urging his response. "Andre, honey, are you hungry? Can you hear me?"

Her husband wore a straight face and avoided her gaze, dissociated in a stillness she couldn't understand.

She unstrapped the bib, tossed the yucky mouthful in the flip trashcan, and washed off the bib in the kitchen sink. "I'm gonna ask you one more time, Andre. What do you want for breakfast?" She glanced over her shoulder at Andre, but he stared like a lifeless mannequin. She twisted off the faucet and turned around, gripping the marble counter behind her. "Andre, baby, please. Please, don't do this. If you're depressed, tell me. Talk. Don't shut me out." She covered her eyes and wept bitterly.

Despair dragged her down, and her high hopes vanished in thin air like rising vapor. The more Andre detached himself, the more she was getting convinced her husband would never get better. If he couldn't accept and love himself for the man he'd become, how could he love her and their son again?

With a negative mindset, he would remain stagnant in his misfortune and never sprout to a renewal of emotional recovery.

They would forever be enemies because of a stormy night that stole their happiness. If she could go back to their seventh wedding anniversary, she would change their evening to a simple candlelit dinner at home.

But that wasn't possible.

Life and time wouldn't allow it, and there wasn't a doubt Andre's brain injury damaged more than his mind. It had also deeply wounded his heart. Eva walked out of the kitchen and marched toward the staircase to pray for him. As she started upstairs, the doorbell dinged. She paused and shared a suspicious look with Mrs. Flowers, both wondering who had come to the house.

Eva wiped her wet eyes and opened the door, her heart skipping a beat.

Her mom had arrived.

21

Eva

WHAT ARE YOU DOING HERE?" EVA STARED AT her mother with a dropped jaw. She blinked in disbelief at the slim, fifty-one-year-old woman in the front doorway. With her flawless, caramel brown skin and youthful face, Melanie Conway could pass for a woman twenty years younger, if it weren't for her gray pixie cut. Her tan leather jacket and jean pencil skirt accentuated her curvy figure. She held a duffel bag in one hand and a vintage suitcase embellished with country and state travel stickers in the other.

"I'm homeless and lost my apartment, so I came here," Eva's mom said. "I was wondering if I can stay with you until I get back on my feet. I got stuck in bad traffic before I reached Seattle-Tacoma's airport. My flight got delayed because of a severe thunderstorm, so I stayed overnight and flew in this morning." Her mother darted her eyes, looking over her ruby, oval-framed glasses. "Are you gonna stand there like a popsicle or let me in?"

Eva pursed her lips with a hand on her hip. How could she reject her mom after the sacrifices she made for her? Although they had their squabbles, she was the backbone that inspired Eva to grow up into the strong-willed, assertive woman she had become. She sighed and relaxed her shoulders. "Alright, you can come in."

"Thank you," her mother said. "Can I get help with my bags?"

Eva took the duffel bag and stood back as her mom entered with her suitcase. She glanced heavenward as she shut the door. *God, please let things work for my good.* Ever since Thanksgiving last year, she detected her mother's jealousy of her friendship with Mrs. Flowers. Who would've thought enjoying an old widow's sweet potato pie better than your mother's was a big deal?

Her mom wiped her leather, knee-length boots on the welcome mat and sized up the elderly woman on the sofa, holding her grandson Andrew in her lap. Her voice dropped a notch. "Oh . . . hi, Mrs. Flowers."

"Hello, Melanie," Mrs. Flowers said.

Eva shifted a nervous glance from her mom to Mrs. Flowers and sensed tension lingering between them. "You can put your things in the guest room with me. Andre's staying in the master bedroom by himself."

Her mom's dark brown eyes went round, jerking back her head. "How come? Did y'all have a fight?"

"It's a long story. I'll explain it in the guest room." Eva toted the duffel bag and led her mother to the guest room on the first floor. A twin-sized bed draped with a blue-rose comforter was on one side of the room, and beside the bed was a comfy blue chair. A pinewood dresser and nightstand set completed the guest bedroom.

Her mom placed her suitcase on the twin-sized bed. She twisted her face and scanned the small, fairly simple room as if she were looking for something. "Only one bed? Where will you sleep?"

Eva shrugged and put the bag on the floor. "No biggie. I'll sleep in the blue chair or on the couch. So, how long you plan to stay?"

Her mom popped the silver latches of her suitcase and opened it. "I'm not sure, but I've got the time to spare." She eyed Eva with suspicion. "You aren't rushing to get rid of me, are you?"

A muscle twitched in Eva's jaw, rubbing her arms. "Uh, no . . . stay as long as you need. You can put your clothes in the middle drawers of the dresser."

"Thanks. Where's Andre?" Her mother took a stack of folded clothes out of her suitcase and placed them on the bed.

"He's in the kitchen. He's . . . depressed," Eva said. She informed her mom about Andre's car accident, his brain injury, his paralysis, and the emotional toll everything has been having on him.

Her mother frowned. "Oh, Eva. I'm sorry this happened. Why didn't you call me?"

Eva shrugged with downcast eyes, but she knew exactly why she didn't phone her mother about her husband's incident. If she had, her mom would've boarded a plane and flown in the next day. Then she would've interfered in how *she* thinks her daughter should handle her husband's medical condition, instead of letting Eva decide for herself.

Her mom held her at arm's length. "Eva, sweetheart, you can talk to me about anything."

Anything? Eva chewed on her bottom lip, shifty-eyed. It was easier said by her mother than done. After being interrupted and ignored many times during arguments, Eva had her doubts, but she didn't bother retorting to her mother's kind remark.

"I don't want you to feel you can't express yourself." Her mom looked sideways and dropped her arms to her sides with a sigh. "If I had known about Andre, I wouldn't have bothered to come here. You know what . . . I'll check in a hotel." She loaded her stack of clothes back in her suitcase.

Eva spoke up. "No, Mom! It's okay . . . you can stay. We can make adjustments."

Her mother faced her again. "Are you sure?"

"Yes," Eva said, "as long as you promise to respect my wishes."

"Which are?" Her mom arched a brow.

Eva drew a long breath and exhaled. "I want you to promise you'll let me make my own decisions without interfering in my personal affairs. And you'll keep your critical opinions about whatever I do to yourself unless I ask for your help."

"Oh, alright . . . I promise," her mother said hesitantly.

"And you'll respect my marriage and my home," Eva added and cringed.

Her mom wrapped her arms around herself. "Fine . . . you have my word."

Eva smiled with relief. "Good. I'm going back to the kitchen. Would you like a cup of coffee?"

"Sure," her mother said, "I'll be out after I finish unpacking."

Eva left from the guest room and returned to the living room.

"How's your mom?" Mrs. Flowers asked.

Eva sighed. "She's okay."

Mrs. Flowers' expression softened. "I hope she doesn't think I'm trying to take her place. I mean no harm to you and your mother's relationship, Eva."

"I know, Mrs. Flowers. You don't have to tell me," Eva said.

Mrs. Flowers stood with Andrew and placed the gabby, little boy back into his playpen. "Well, maybe you know, but your mom's face was so green it settled a weight on my heart."

181

"She'll get over it," Eva said, rolling her eyes. "I'll talk to her."

"Thanks," Mrs. Flowers said, smiling, "and when you do, let her know a friend of mine would like her to paint a special portrait for her son's birthday. He's visiting home from the army for Thanksgiving. I don't know your mom's phone number, so I could never get a hold of her."

Eva grinned. "How nice! I'll tell her later." She let out a slow breath. "Well, let me talk with Andre. Hopefully, I'll get through to him." She returned to the kitchen and sat in front of her husband again. "Honey, are you hungry?"

"Yes," Andre said finally.

Relief spread over Eva's face, and she chuckled. "Finally, we're getting somewhere." She laced her hands on the table. "Now, what do you want?"

"I want . . ." Andre lowered his eyes and thought a moment. "Eggs . . . cheese . . . scrambled."

A corner of Eva's mouth lifted.

Though Andre suffered from a speech impediment, sometimes she found his thinking facial expressions and hesitations cute and likable.

"Okay, coming right up." She stood and whipped up a plate of scrambled eggs with cheese and switched on the coffee maker on the counter. Eva placed the plate of Andre's food on the table and strapped a new clean bib around his neck.

Andre blinked and watched her cut the eggs with a fork. "Sorry."

Eva stopped and studied him with his head hung in shame. She didn't know if he was saying it to her or to himself, but she accepted his apology anyway. She found a smile. "It's okay. Now eat up." She stuck a morsel of egg on the fork and attempted to feed him, but Andre continued talking.

Her husband's eyes danced, looking in hers. "I wish . . . remember you . . . Andy . . . just don't."

"Shh, it's alright, Andre. Come on, eat," Eva said softly.

Andre took in the mouthful, chewed, and swallowed, but Eva couldn't get what he said to leave her mind. Despite his limitations, she realized he was curious about everything she and their son were to him, even though he couldn't recall their past life together. And for the first time, she believed maybe Mrs. Flowers was right.

The man she married was trapped inside.

THE COFFEE MAKER FINISHED BREWING, AND EVA FILLED two glass mugs, one for her and the other for her mom. She stirred in hazelnut creamer in each coffee mug and joined her mother at the kitchen table. While they drank, they caught up on lost time and talked about what had been happening in their lives the past months.

After Eva recapped Andre's therapy in the hospital, her mother shared devastating news. One night someone broke into her mom's private studio and stole most of her art equipment, and she hasn't sold a single painting in weeks.

"I feel like a total failure," her mom said. "Nothing's been going right lately. Sometimes I think I should quit painting and do something else."

Eva grimaced. "Oh, no, Mom, you can't do that. You shouldn't give up on your painting because you suffered a loss, or even because everyone doesn't value your talent. And you're not a failure either."

"Thanks, hon, I needed that." Her mom sipped her mug.

Eva traced the brim of her mug with her forefinger. "I hope you don't mind, but Mrs. Flowers said a friend of hers wants you to paint a portrait for her son's birthday. She said her friend told her he's coming from the army to spend Thanksgiving with his family."

"Is that so?" Her mother raised her eyebrows.

Eva nodded. "Yeah. I mean, I know you do landscape paintings, but you've done a few portraits of people before. It could be interesting."

Her mother curled her upper lip. "Humph, I don't think so."

"It's not because of Mrs. Flowers, is it?" Eva asked drearily.

"Of course not," her mom said. "I just don't like painting people. It's too complex."

Eva snickered. "Complex? I always thought landscapes harder. You have to add details to everything, including blades of grass."

"Well, with me, *people* portraits are more difficult," her mom countered. "If you don't control my life, I won't control yours, deal?" She sipped from her mug again.

Eva zipped her lips and felt bad vibes, getting the cue there was no talking her mother into doing a favor for Mrs. Flowers' friend. "Fine . . . I'm sorry."

"Who takes care of Andre while you're at work?" Her mom's facial features slacked.

"Skye Garrison," Eva answered. "He's a friendly young man, who likewise endured a brain injury when he was in his teens. Because he had to attend his grandma's burial in South Carolina, I had to stay home with Andre today. But he'll be here the rest of the week, including Saturday night. I'm going to my class reunion."

"Really?" Her mom sounded surprised. "Are you sure you should go? Won't Caleb Williams be there? You were kinda sweet on him."

Eva clamped her lips. "Mom, Caleb moved away to New York with his dad after graduation. Besides, he's probably already married off, and I'm not attending for him anyway." She beamed. "Last week, I came across my Francine Nichols in the grocery store. You remember Frankie, don't you?"

"Uh-huh . . . tiny girl with reddish-blonde curls, and a bubbly personality," her mother said. "Y'all had sleepovers every Saturday and always partnered together for school projects. She was the smallest ninth grader I ever saw . . . almost needed a magnifying glass to see her."

Eva frowned and giggled. "Mom, she wasn't *that* little."

Her mom placed her mug on the table and chuckled. "She was close. So, what inspired you to attend this year?"

"Frankie," Eva said, "she wants me to attend to keep her company during the occasion and for us to take a trip down memory lane. She might bring a yearbook. I never got one for many reasons. I wasn't the prettiest sight in twelfth grade."

Her mother sucked her teeth. "Please, Eva. You were a pretty girl then and you're pretty now."

Eva shook her head and drank the last of her coffee. Some people changed over time, and she was one of them. What were her other classmates doing now? And most of all, who was still alive?

Hearing about Alan Murphy's suicide from her friend Francine, she still couldn't believe it was true. Aside from the turnout of her class reunion, she also pondered whether she and her mother would get along the next couple of weeks.

Eva trusted her mom would keep her promise, but grasping her envy toward Mrs. Flowers, she questioned if letting her stay was a big mistake.

22
Eva

IT HAD BEEN FIFTEEN YEARS SINCE EVA STEPPED FOOT into Garden Ridge High, but everything looked the same. Built in 1942, the school was a strong, three-story structure of tan sandy brick and concrete stone that survived the test of time. After the entrance, Eva strode the gray linoleum hallway between two rows of evergreen lockers. She approached the double end doors to the noisy cafeteria. Inside, the buzz of conversation and laughter mingled with American Idol alum Kelly Clarkson's "A Moment Like This."

Eva gripped a cold handle and peeked in a rectangular window of one of the green doors. Many of her classmates were present in their fine or casual wear, huddled in social groups and wolfing down refreshments. Eva searched for

Francine but couldn't see her. Her heart shuddered in her chest.

She felt like that shy, teenage girl who first enrolled at Garden Ridge High School in ninth grade, afraid of what her teenage peers think of her.

Stay cool, Eva. It's just a reunion. She wiped her sweaty hands down her black maxi dress and entered the cafeteria. People eyed her with inquisitive and surprised faces like she had an extreme makeover.

Eva's face flushed as she observed the lunchroom. On the food service tables were party platters, deviled eggs, fruit kabobs, and two punch fountains. A gigantic cake with *Woo hoo Class of 2002* written on top in green cursive icing was the centerpiece of one of the tables.

Between green and white balloons, a sparkly banner read '2nd reunion for Class of 2002' and hung above the announcement stage. Painted on the base of the stage was the face of the school mascot—a grizzly bear with green eyes and sharp teeth.

Eva looked at a front round table to her left, holding her leopard clutch purse underarm.

"Hey, Eva! Over here!" Francine waved a hand.

Eva fixed her eyes on another round table close to the fire exit. She grinned at her school friend.

Standing beside Francine was a plump, older woman with rosy cheeks and dark gray hair in a side bun, dressed in a violet suede suit and two-inch heels. As soon as the older woman waved, she raced over to them, her platform heels clacking in a hustle across the checkered, green-and-white floor.

It was Mrs. Chapman—her ninth-grade English teacher.

"Oh, my goodness, it's Eva Conway," Mrs. Chapman said in a thick, southern accent.

"Mrs. Chapman! Hey, I'm glad you're here." Eva embraced her teacher.

Her English teacher was teary-eyed. "Honey, it's good to see you too. You and Francine were my favorite pupils. How are you?"

Now didn't feel like the time to talk about her husband Andre, his car accident, or her strained marriage, so she left those things out of the conversation.

"I'm well, ma'am," Eva said. "Do you still teach here?"

Mrs. Chapman's bangs bounced as she nodded. "Yup, I'm still teaching ninth-grade English in room one-twenty."

"Wow. That's great," Eva said.

Mrs. Chapman glanced from Francine back to Eva. "You both turned out to be beautiful, young women. It's nice seeing you girls again. I'm going to the refreshment table."

"Okay," Eva said, smiling.

Mrs. Chapman walked off and greeted a tall, redhead woman in a light yellow, off-the-shoulder dress a few feet away.

Francine smiled. "We were looking at old pictures in my senior yearbook."

Eva drew nearer to her friend. She skimmed Francine's yearbook, flipped a page, and laughed. "Haha! That's me!" She pointed at her student photo labeled with her name, her birthday, her school activities, and some of her likes and dislikes. "Eva Rose Conway . . . May 19th. . . Art and poetry club . . . favorite subject English . . . likes reading and making origami." She faced Francine. "Where are you?"

"I'm toward the end of the list . . . page sixty-five." Francine turned a couple of pages of the black-and-white photos of students until she came to hers. "There I am!" She poked her forefinger to a picture of a small girl—who unlike her classmates—looked no older than fourteen. "Francine Nichols . . . February 6th . . . Girls soccer . . . favorite subject biology . . . likes candy and talking on the phone."

Eva and Francine laughed.

"You always did have bubblegum and Airheads in your pockets," Eva said, chuckling.

Francine snickered. "I guess so, my parents ran a candy shop." She handed Eva a black sharpie pen. "Can you sign my yearbook? I never got your signature." She turned to the back of her yearbook where several other students had scribbled their names and little farewell messages.

"Sure, why not?" Eva took the pen from her friend and jotted her name and a quote of best wishes.

Francine smiled at Eva's signature and note. "You have the prettiest handwriting. Thanks for signing my book. I had bought my book kind of late and searched for you and Andre on prom night, but I didn't see you guys."

Eva sighed. "We weren't there. We stayed home."

"Why? It was *so* obvious Andre liked you," Francine said with a cute smile. "I thought he would've asked you out to the dance."

Eva held out her hands and shrugged. "He didn't see the need to go and thought us attending prom might've led to other things."

"Oh, I guess he had a point there," Francine said. "I didn't do nothing wrong, but believe me, there were a few couples who did things they shouldn't have that night." She pinned Eva with her eyes. "Need I say more?"

Eva shook her head and crossed her arms. "Uh-uh, I'm aware of what you mean."

Someone tapped on Eva's shoulder.

Eva spun around and studied the redhead woman who spoke to Mrs. Chapman. She placed a hand on her hip. "Let me guess, Nadine Sterling?"

"Correct." Nadine angled her head. "Long time no see. I love your updo and dress. I didn't recognize you. How's it going, Eva?"

"I'm good," Eva answered. "What about you?"

Nadine snarled. "Meh, I guess I'm okay. I mean, I have a successful career as a district attorney, but relationship-wise, it hasn't gone well. Let's just say I haven't found my Mr. Right yet."

"How's Sammie Cooper?" Eva asked.

If anyone knew about Sammie, Nadine would. Sammie was voted 'Homecoming Queen' in their senior class, a blonde bombshell cheerleader. One of the most popular students in school, teenage boys flocked around her like flies on a horse's tail, but she never swatted at them. Sammie received them gladly. She had liked to be the center of their attention, which may have been because her parents gave her none at home.

They were divorced, and her mother was a cougar and party animal, dating lots of younger men. Eva remembered finding Sammie crying in the girls' room, telling her how lonely she felt. It was the first time they'd talked without Sammie teasing her. She and Nadine used to hang out with their other girlfriend Tasha Burke, the girl Caleb Williams had taken over Eva to their senior prom.

Nadine sighed wearily. "Sammie's . . . sick in the hospital. She has cervical cancer."

A pang shot Eva's chest. "That's terrible."

"Yeah," Nadine said, "but she's fighting and determined to get better. Well, I gotta go. Excuse me, ladies."

Eva and her friend watched Nadine walk away to the entrance and welcome two gentleman wearing suits and ties to the class reunion.

"Poor Sammie." Eva frowned.

"Yeah, and poor Nadine too," Francine added. She closed her yearbook. "She told me she suffered three failed marriages. Three, can you believe that? None of them resulted in children."

"What happened?" Eva faced Francine.

"Her first cheated on her, her second left her, and her third she found out later didn't want children, so she broke up with him too," Francine said dryly. She shook her head. "You're lucky you found someone who truly loves you."

"Sure . . . I guess so," Eva said gingerly.

Francine twisted her face. "What do you mean, guess?"

"He's not the same anymore." Eva sighed and rubbed her arms. "Since his accident, he doesn't remember our wedding day."

Her friend cupped her shoulder. "At least you have great memories to look back on. Everybody can't say that about their marriage. I'm gonna get a cup of pineapple punch. Want some?"

Eva allowed a smile. "Sure, thanks."

Francine trailed off to the refreshments.

Eva sat at the round table her friend left her yearbook on and flipped through the other pages of student photos toward the back. Her eyes landed on a picture of an African American teenage boy grinning wide with a boxed, fade haircut. She skimmed the info beside his picture:

Caleb Williams
Birthday: *Feb. 8th*
Nickname: *The CW*
School activities: *Boys basketball - Point guard*
Likes: *Girls, cars, chocolate, and seafood.*
Dislikes: *Losing at anything, homework, and Brussel sprouts.*

EVA'S HEART STOPPED. SHE SHUT THE YEARBOOK, LOOKING at her school friend getting two glass cups of punch. Her former feelings toward Caleb were of the past, and she had no intentions of reliving them. She was a married woman with a lovable son. And though her marriage had turned upside down, as Francine said, she had made lots of happy memories with her husband Andre.

As Francine returned with the cups of punch, Eva spotted a good-looking, black man in a brown vest outfit and blood-red bow tie stroll in the cafeteria. Her cheeks blushed, and she wanted to hide. It turned out the one she should've been most nervous to find at the class reunion was her high school crush, instead of her female rivals. The man joined a group of men who greeted him with handshakes and high-fives, other teammates of the boys' basketball team.

The group of men rooted with their hands in a circle.

"Gooo Grizzlies!" they said, raising their hands like they used to during their games.

"Here you go, Eva." Francine handed her a cup.

"Thanks," Eva said, distracted.

Francine smiled and drank from her punch cup, eyeing the guys of the basketball team. "Looks like Caleb Williams made it."

Caleb turned his attention from his friends and made a double-take in Eva and Francine's direction. His long gaze passed through Eva's whole being, and though for once she wanted to remain unseen by him, he noticed her.

Francine was excited. "Hey, he's coming our way!"

Oh, no . . . Eva gulped and placed her punch down. "Listen, Frankie . . . maybe I shouldn't have come." She stood from the table, her knees wobbling.

"Don't tell me you're leaving already." Disappointment contorted Francine's face.

Eva kept a nervous look-out at Caleb, grabbing her purse. "I'm sorry. I can't stay here, Frankie. I have to go now." As Stevie Wonder's "Kiss, Lonely Goodbye" resounded from the speakers, she rushed out the fire exit before Caleb arrived at their table.

Eva jogged in her heels to her car. She had her worries about coming to her class reunion, but her pride prevented her from taking heed of her mother's concern. As a teenager, her mom always had to prove her wrong about everything, and she couldn't bear another moment of her interfering skepticism.

"Eva?" a man called behind her.

She stopped fidgeting her purse for her car keys and slowly faced him. Although a tad bit older, Caleb held the same charm. His smooth, dark brown skin and clothing made the thought of a tootsie roll come to Eva's mind. Over the years, his black, coiled hair had been trimmed to a short, low-cut style. He was five-foot-nine—not as tall as her husband—but his robust build proved he was as physically fit.

"Eva Conway?" Caleb was wide-eyed.

"Hi . . . Caleb." Eva gave a shy smile and lifted a shoulder. Getting married hadn't stopped her attraction to other men, and she understood his surprised reaction to her changed looks. The last time he saw her she was a twelfth-grade teenager with a face speckled with pimples, metallic braces, and glasses as big as petri dishes. There wasn't a wonder why a popular guy like him had chosen Tasha Burke over her to their senior prom.

"It's Eva Lucas now," Eva corrected.

Caleb inched forward and slipped his hands in the pockets of his pants. He arched his brow. "Where's your ring? You don't have one on your finger."

"Maybe not, but I have a certificate," Eva said with a smirk, tilting her head. "Wedding rings are a tradition that doesn't keep couples together. They give an excuse for them to break apart."

A giggle came from Caleb's lips. "I know, right?" He stroked his thin mustache above his upper lip, still baffled. "Wow, I can't believe it's you. I mean, you look so—"

"Different, I know," Eva interrupted. "So does Andre."

"You've got to be kidding me. You married Andre Lucas?" Caleb said.

Eva nodded. "Yes. We have a son who's almost two. His name's Andrew." She slumped her shoulders. "Though, things have been hard lately." She hadn't told a soul of her graduating class about her husband's condition. But seeing Caleb brought out the truth of what she'd been harboring inside.

"A brain injury paralyzed him, but the doctor said it could be temporary. So far though there hasn't been a change," she said.

193

Caleb's forehead furrowed. "Oh, no. That's awful. I hope he gets well."

"Yeah, me too." Eva folded her arms. "So, when did you come back in town? I wasn't exactly expecting you."

Caleb chuckled. "I moved back two years ago. I'm a real estate agent and designer. What do you do for a living?"

"I'm a daycare provider for Sunrise Christian Daycare. It was my mom's idea," Eva said. "Honestly, sometimes I wish I pursued interior design."

"I figured you were a teacher," Caleb said. "You were always so smart. There's no doubt I would've never finished high school if you hadn't helped me study."

"So, are you married?" Eva asked.

"No," Caleb said, "I enjoy the single life, but who knows? Maybe I'll settle down with the right woman someday."

Eva wore a wry smile. "I'm sure you'll come across her."

"Perhaps I will." Caleb grinned. "You know, I have textbooks about interior design lying around my house. I used them to study before I took and passed the NCIDQ exam myself. They might be helpful in getting you on track with pursuing the career."

Eva twitched her mouth. "Um, thanks, but I'd be fooling myself into ever becoming an interior designer. Besides, my mom says it's a waste of time and money. She doesn't think I can make a sufficient living from it."

"It doesn't hurt to try," Caleb said. "I know from experience the process is long, and the sooner you start studying, the better and sooner the results. It's up to you. I'm not pushing you into doing this, but I believe there's no problem in wanting more, or doing something different for a change."

Eva's mind reeled. She had been a daycare teacher for ten years, wiping runny noses, calming down tantrums, and singing so many kiddy songs she heard them in her sleep. She enjoyed her job and loved her daycare kids, but she had felt like she was living a lie by denying her calling. Maybe working toward her dream career was a good idea, a way to help build her, Andre, and Andrew a more promising future.

"You know what, why not?" Eva said.

"Great. I live on two-thirty Gold Street. You can get the books there, but if I'm not home, you can call me and I'll come right over." Caleb dug in a side pocket, took out his wallet, and pulled a business card from it. "Here, just in case."

Eva smiled and took his card. "Thank you." She read the business title. "Coleman Housing . . . I've heard of it. It's the housing business Andre and I mortgaged our home from. I guess you've followed your father's footsteps in real estate, huh."

"Precisely," Caleb said. "It's a legacy. I gave up a basketball scholarship to keep it in the family. Like your mom, my dad had an influence on my future plans. He thought I needed a more *secure* profession, only in my case, I believe he was right. One injury can end an athlete's career forever."

"That's true," Eva agreed, "but you were a great basketball player. I always liked watching you on the court during game days."

Caleb smiled. "Thanks, I still play sometimes, but only for fun." His smile faded. "Well, I suppose you'd like to go home. Nice talking to you."

"Yeah, good night." Eva turned to her car and took out her keys but changed her mind. Because she and Caleb had talked and matters appeared to be innocent between them, there wasn't a need to leave.

"Then again, I'll stay a little longer." She walked to the exit door to the cafeteria, which Caleb opened before she could herself.

"Um . . . thank you." Eva's skin flushed as his body stood behind hers.

"My pleasure." Caleb watched her enter the cafeteria and followed her inside.

23

Eva

WAS IT A CRIME TO FOLLOW ONE'S DREAM? Getting more criticism than encouragement, her mom led Eva to believe it was illegal. She didn't know whether her mother's struggles as an artist had to do with it, but she concluded to reach her goals she had better keep it secret. Sharing to her mom about her studying to become an interior designer would ruin her excitement, and risk splitting them further apart. Eva loved her mom and appreciated everything she did for her, but she had to be what she wanted to be, and not what her mother thought was best for her.

Orange oak leaves swirled in the whistling wind into Caleb's front yard and fluttered onto the light brown roof of his home. Eva locked the doors of her car parked along the sidewalk and marched up the curvy, paved path. She took a deep breath and rang the doorbell, marveling over his peach and brown brick, luxurious house.

Caleb poked out his smiling face, hiding behind the opened door. "Hey, Eva! You can wait out here. Let me get the books for you."

"Okay," Eva said with a timid smile.

Caleb left the door ajar and slipped back inside.

Eva buried her face in her plaid scarf and rubbed her hands for warmth, trying to endure the chill in the air. Being thirty-six degrees outside, she hoped he wouldn't take too long to come back, and especially with her son left in the back of her car.

About three minutes later, Caleb returned, opening the door. He held a stack of three thick textbooks. "You can read them as long as you want." He released the heavy books into Eva's winter-gloved hands.

Eva grinned. "Thanks."

"The red book is about *Design Elements and Principles*, the blue one is *Color and Lighting Theory*, and the yellow is *History of Interior Design*. All three subjects you must know to pass the NCIDQ exam," Caleb said. "But if you enroll in the Art Institute instead, you still should know and learn these areas of study."

"Thank you. I appreciate this," Eva said. "I've wanted to get into interior design when I was younger, but I didn't know where to start besides choosing colors. Everything my mom said always felt right, but later I ended up regretting giving up on my dream job."

"I'm sorry about your mom," Caleb said. "It's unfortunate she thinks you can't make a living being a designer. I think it's delightful to style and sell a lovely home for a family they can be proud of."

"Me too," Eva agreed.

"I wish you the best success, and I know you can do it. You're a bright, young lady, Eva," Caleb said.

Eva wore a half-smile. Since she was in grade school, she was always a little brainiac, her classmates asking her for help with their English papers or math homework. But for once, she wished Caleb would tell her the truth how he felt about her in the past, instead of sparing her feelings.

When their senior prom came, Caleb told her last-minute he forgot he already asked to take Tasha Burke. But Eva knew it was an excuse to prevent him from keeping his promise of walking arm in arm with the "nerd girl" to the dance.

"Uh, how's your husband?" Caleb asked.

Eva shook her head and sighed. "He's still having a hard time. For some reason, it's taking longer for Andre to walk than we expected. Sometimes he speaks to me, and other times he's silent. I've tried to help him cope and talk him into taking an antidepressant, but he doesn't want one. I'm not sure what to do about him anymore."

"Oh, well, maybe Andre will come around soon." Caleb gave her a quick once-over. "I can tell you've been stressed out over him. Take care of yourself."

Eva cradled the books and waved. "Yeah, you too. Bye." She strolled to her vehicle as Caleb closed his door.

HER MOTHER WAS PAINTING BAREFOOT IN THE LIVING room when she entered the house, sitting in front of a bleached canvas on a wooden easel. Under the easel were sheets of old newspaper to cover the carpet if she spilled paint.

On television she was watching an episode of *The Joy of Painting* with Bob Ross, attempting to copy his portrait of a forest landscape. Her mom added green and yellow paint from her palette to her fan brush and made quick, fast strokes on the bottom of the canvas, listening to Ross' gentle instructions to ensure she did them right.

"Looking good, Mom," Eva said, closing the door with her foot. As usual, Andrew was knocked out in her arms after coming home from working at the daycare.

Her mother smiled. "Thanks, hon."

"Where's Andre and Skye?" Eva asked, rubbing her son's back.

Andrew moaned in his sleep and turned his drowsy head on her shoulder.

Her mom rinsed her fan brush in a can of water. "They're in the kitchen. Skye's giving Andre an afternoon snack."

"Alright, I'm going to put Andy in his crib." Eva started up the staircase.

"Where were you?" her mom said.

Eva stopped in her tracks and glanced back.

"It's four thirty, and you've never been this late," her mom added.

Eva felt her defenses rising, but she kept her calm. If her mother distrusted her whereabouts, she wouldn't give her a reason to meddle in her business. "Traffic was busy on Garfield Drive," she answered. Garfield Drive was where her daycare was located, a small, narrow street next door to the Garden Ridge Police Department.

"Oh, alright," her mom said.

Eva turned her back and let out a relieved exhale. It wasn't a lie she told her mother, but she was thankful she wasn't thrown more questions. She walked upstairs to her son's room and put him to bed to finish his nap. The textbooks she got from Caleb were still in the trunk of her car. At night, she would sneak out to get the books, study, and hide them in the dresser. Eva pulled the blanket over her son, alarmed by a sudden call from downstairs.

"Mrs. Lucas, Ms. Conway, hurry quick!" Skye said.

Eva frowned and hurled downstairs to the kitchen. She and her mother shared a gasp the minute they saw Andre.

Her husband had a spoon in his right hand between his index and ring fingers, feeding himself a bowl of tomato soup. It was a small miracle, like watching Andrew stop eating with his hands again. After months of her husband having everything done for him, he was fighting for his independence.

"Andre," Eva mouthed, her eyes filling with tears.

"I was about to feed him after I brought his drink to the table, but he tried to pick up his spoon. I realized he was attempting to feed himself. He was frustrated, but he kept trying until he could do it. His hand and arm exercises are working, Mrs. Lucas."

"That's terrific," Eva said.

Her mom smiled. "I saw utensils cuffs for paralyzed people to help with eating online." She faced Eva. "You should get a pair for Andre. It would make eating a lot simpler for him, and he could use them to brush his teeth and hair too."

"Well," Eva said, "that depends on if Andre wants them." She sighed and folded her arms, looking at her husband again. Maybe his physical body was healing, but would his mind? If Andre never walked again, Eva wanted him to love and bond with her and their son Andrew above everything else. It didn't matter if Andre was stuck in a wheelchair the rest of his life, or if they never had another child. What mattered was them living happily together and rebuilding their family household.

"Do you want the utensil cuffs, Andre?" Eva said.

Her husband continued eating.

Skye frowned. "Hey, man, your wife's talking to you?"

Andre avoided eye contact with anybody around him.

Eva's mom was confused. "Andre? What's wrong with him?"

"Andre . . ." Eva grimaced with her hands on the table. "Don't you dare ignore me."

Her husband remained silent, and a time of achievement had become another time of devastation. Eva whimpered and fled from the kitchen, running back upstairs to the master bedroom. She slammed the door and cried on her pillow, tired of feeling invisible. Why did Andre treat her like this? Was it his brain jury? Or was it something more?

Maybe he blamed her for his car accident. No matter what, she was determined to follow her dreams. She would allow no one, not even her disabled husband to hinder her efforts. Besides, Caleb owed her his help in interior design after all she's done for him in school, and she was sure he knew this himself. But with her mother in the house, she had to be careful her mom doesn't find the books.

Knowing her mother, it would be a total disaster.

24

Eva

HER MOTHER KNOCKED ON THE DOOR OF THE bedroom. "Eva, can I come in?"

"Why not?" Eva rose from lying stomach-down and sat up on the bed. She wiped her tears as her mom stepped inside and closed the door.

"What do you want?" Eva hoped her mother wasn't about to criticize how well she treats her husband. Ever since Andre was sent home, she had done nothing except strive to be loving and supportive toward him, but Andre refused to keep their communication thriving and alive. He was the one that felt she was incompetent to care for him and the one who suggested they get a divorce.

"I came to check on you," Eva's mom said. "Has Andre always been so quiet?"

Eva snickered. "He's doing it on purpose. Andre's been shunning me since he got out of the hospital. It's not every day, but he does from time to time. That's why I told you he's depressed. It feels like he's never gonna change his attitude, but part of me feels like it's more than his brain injury. It's like he's testing how much I love him."

"Why would he do something so spiteful?" Eva's mom asked. "That's not the Andre I know."

Eva tilted her head and scowled. "Mom, Andre's *not* the same man I married. He has a different mind, a different personality . . . the Andre we knew is gone." Her expression softened and she sighed, rounding her shoulders. "Of course, there are times when I feel like. . ."

"Like?" Her mother perched on the bed beside her.

Eva wore a wistful smile. "Like the old Andre is still there. Sometimes I look in his brown eyes and I think he's there, and he loves me and Andy so much, but he's . . . hurting so badly . . . and he's too ashamed to let it out." She bowed her head and wept.

Her mom wrapped an arm around her, rubbing her back. "Maybe he is. Andre was always a brave person, but I guess he had no choice. He's been through a lot as a child with his parents, and he wanted to be a better man than his father was to him."

"One day he said he wants a divorce," Eva confessed.

Her mom was stunned. "He did?"

Eva nodded. "Yeah, do you think he's right?" She raised her face to her mother. "Do you think we should divorce?"

"No way," Eva's mom said with a frown, "Andre's lost his memory. He doesn't know what he's talking about, and I'm sure if he could remember his past life with you and Andy, he'd never consider divorce. The love and marriage you and Andre had together have been too precious to let go, and it still is. Both of you are going through a storm. But when the dark clouds pass away, the sun *will* shine again."

Eva covered her eyes and let out a slow breath. "I sure hope it's soon. This whole situation is wearing me out."

Her mother stood. "It'll pass. If Andre truly loves you, he'll change his behavior and be willing to recover your relationship, even if he can't recall his memories. He knows you've been taking care of him, and that takes guts after how he's treated you. It's given him a lot to consider . . . you being there for him . . . helping with his needs." She walked to the door. "I'm gonna cook dinner. You can stay in here for a while. Andre seems to need more time alone to recuperate. Maybe you do too."

Eva gave a half-smile. "Thanks for your help, Mom."

"You're welcome, hon." Her mother exited the room.

Relief filled Eva. It had been a long time she felt the support of her mother, or comfortable enough to open to her about her feelings. Ever since Andre's condition, their mother-daughter relationship was making progress. Maybe Eva was wrong and she didn't have to hide her studying and ambition. Maybe her mother would apologize for discouraging her in the past and allow her to choose her career for herself.

No, I can't risk it. Eva shook the thoughts from her head. She took off her tennis shoes, draped herself with the blanket, and drifted asleep.

IT WAS SIX O'CLOCK WHEN EVA AWOKE.

She left the master bedroom and entered Andrew's room to check on her son. Eva flicked on the light switch and found the white crib empty. She figured he was in the dining room having dinner with everyone else. Eva ambled down the staircase to the living room. The television showed a commercial on the flat screen. It was about an interior design student who attends The Art Institute of Charlotte, grasping her attention.

"Eva! Dinner's ready!" her mom called.

Eva glanced away. "I'll be right there!" She looked back at the TV until the commercial ended, inspired to enroll in the university's Interior Design Bachelor of Fine Arts program. She strolled through the entryway to the dining room and sat at the six-chair table across from her husband.

Her mom had made shepherd's pie with gravy and steamed broccoli with onions for dinner. Andrew was in his highchair eating a bowl of Spaghetti-O's and meatballs with a sippy cup of milk. Andre was in his manual wheelchair, struggling to use his left fist to place his fork in his right hand.

"Need help?" Eva grabbed a plate from the center stack.

Andre slipped her a guarded look. "No, I can do it myself."

Eva stared at her husband with surprise. Her spirits buoyed. It was the most words he said in weeks without hesitations or having to think clearly before he spoke. She was glad he responded to her, but she felt his resentment in the tone of his voice.

"I'm sorry, Andre," Eva said. "I was just trying to help." She faced her mother. "Everything looks delicious, Mom. Can I have the broccoli?"

Her mom passed her the bowl across the table.

"Thanks." Eva spooned a serving on her plate.

"Skye said you owe him a late check," her mother said.

Eva smacked her forehead. "Oh, no! I forgot. What'd you tell him?"

"I told him you weren't feeling too well, but you'll pay him tomorrow," her mother answered.

"Nah, I'll call him after dinner." Eva cut a chunk of shepherd's pie from the dish and added it to her plate. Her husband already had his food on his plate, so she put the dish aside. She watched Andre feeding himself, using a side of his fork to cut his food in smaller pieces. From the time they ate dinner to the time Eva's mom brought out apple pie with whipped cream for dessert, she and Andre didn't speak to each other.

Her mother discussed the weather and made a list of corny jokes, trying to break the ice between them. Andrew was the only one who thought her jokes were amusing, making funny faces and giggling, but Eva appreciated what her mom was doing. After dinner, she helped her mother put the food away and clean the dishes in the kitchen.

"Thanks for trying, Mom." Eva tucked a wet plate on the rack.

Her mom raised an eyebrow. "Trying what?"

"To get Andre and me to talk friendly with each other." Eva mocked a laugh and placed another plate on the dish rack. "And do you know what the funny thing is?"

Her mom pursed her lips. "What?"

"Regardless of Andre's attitude," Eva said, "he still needs my help to use the restroom, at least, until Skye shows him how to do it himself. He told me he'll teach Andre to self-cath when I called him on the phone. I'm hoping he'll listen to my advice and take advantage of the urinal the hospital gave him. It would save him the trouble of taking his wheelchair to the bathroom, but he's so stubborn."

"He's a man," her mother said, "a majority of men have a dominant nature, but maybe it's a good sign Andre is getting better."

Eva cocked her head. "How so?"

Her mom rinsed a soapy plate in the basin sink of water. "Well, because he's gaining back more of his independence, maybe he'll stop feeling sorry for himself."

Eva shrugged. "Maybe. I'm gonna check on him." She walked off and picked up Andrew from his playpen in the living room. "Alright, little one. It's time for you to hit the sack." She glanced at Andre, who was focused on a Monday night NFL football game. "Thanks for watching him."

"You're welcome," Andre said, staring at the television.

"Pee-pee poo," Andrew said and whined.

"Uh-oh." Eva felt his bottom and noticed his sweatpants were damp. "Come on, sweetie, you need a new pamper." She carried Andrew upstairs and changed him on the baby table in his bedroom. She tossed the dirty pamper in her son's diaper genie and switched Andrew into his Cookie Monster pajamas. Before Eva put her son to bed, she sat in the rocking chair with him in her lap and read him *Peekaboo Bedtime* by Rachel Isadora, one of his favorite stories. Then she laid him in his crib with his stuffed monkey and kissed him goodnight.

Their son was nineteen months old now, and she marveled how much he developed in his mind, speech, and mannerisms. He could understand and say more words, he could build with his Lego blocks, and he was budding a sense of humor. It saddened her Andre was missing out on their son's growth process before his eyes, but she prayed and believed he would escape his maze of depression and change soon.

EVERYONE WAS SLEEPING AND THE COAST WAS CLEAR.

After slipping into a pair of clothes, Eva tiptoed out of the guest room and went to the living room. She snuck outside and brought the textbooks Caleb gave her into the house. Eva sat on the brown sofa, put on her glasses, and read the yellow book first: *The History of Interior Design*. She flipped to chapter one and used a neon green highlighter to mark keywords she'd need to know in her vocabulary. Eva learned about many designs from the Renaissance era.

Turning ahead, she discovered the book also had text about other styles from the Victorian age to Contemporary Modern. There was so much for her to read and learn, and Eva was so excited she read chapters two, three, and four, highlighting and jotting annotations of notes. When she finished chapter four, she bookmarked chapter five and opened the red book next: *Design Elements and Principles*. She was more intrigued with this book, which was about basic features to consider when one designs a room and creative ideas based on them.

By the time she read in the blue book *Color and Lighting Theory*, it was eleven o'clock and she had fallen asleep. One in the morning, Eva awoke, hid her textbooks under her clothes in the bottom drawer of the dresser, and climbed back on the couch. It wasn't until sunrise she realized she hadn't set her alarm clock. Eva peeked at the digital clock on the nightstand.

6:45 a.m.

She jumped from the couch to get her son and herself ready to leave for the daycare. Embarrassment seized her as she arrived late to work, but she apologized to Mrs. Higgins and promised it would never happen again. Afterward, Eva received news from her director two more of her students were leaving her two-year-old class. One of them was Juan Diaz, and the other was Autumn McKee.

"Please, excuse me for my lateness. I had a long night," Eva said to Autumn's parents.

Greg looped an arm around his wife Amy, dressed for night duty in his lieutenant police uniform. At thirty, the tall and thin man was already going bald in the center of his jet-black hair. He nodded. "It's okay. We understand the pressure you've been under with your husband."

Eva thought to mention it had nothing to do with Andre, but she bit her tongue. She glanced and smiled at Autumn, playing at a toy kitchen set with two other girls in the dramatic play area. No one could say she wasn't Amy's daughter. They both shared the same bright, reddish-brown hair.

Amy grinned. "I'll be seven months tomorrow. Greg and I've been working hard to keep our mortgaged home, but I need a serious vacation."

"I don't blame you," Eva said, "it's hard being pregnant and working at the same time. I've been there, and now, I'm pulling the weight alone again. I'll be praying everything works out for you and Greg and your delivery."

Amy smiled and placed a hand on her protruding belly, bulging out her sweater. "Thanks, I'll continue praying for you and Andre. I know times have been tough for you, but we appreciated you caring for our daughter. You're a great teacher."

"Thank you, Amy." Eva felt a tug on her khaki skirt, causing her to look down.

"Mrs. Lucas, I'm gonna miss you." Autumn poked out her lip. She had turned three last month and was moving to Mrs. Drummond and Mrs. Timberlake's three-year-old classroom.

Eva brushed a hand over Autumn's hair and sighed. "I'm gonna miss you too, sweetheart. I'll visit you every chance I can get."

"You promise?" Autumn said and sniffled.

"I promise." Eva managed a smile.

Greg shook Eva's hand. "We'll never forget you and everything you've done."

Eva looked in his soft, bluish-gray eyes and saw he meant each word. "I'll never forget you either, Mr. McKee. I can't thank you enough for finding my husband and calling in help after his accident. If you hadn't, he might've never had a chance."

"You're welcome again. Have a good afternoon." Greg held Autumn's hand and walked her out with his wife.

"You too." Eva waved. Her heart wrenched as Autumn stared back at her. She would miss the friendly, little girl, and her innocent, blue eyes swelled Eva's heart with remorse. Why in the world did she feel guilty?

25

Eva

EVA OPENED THE REFRIGERATOR AND SHOOK HER head at the Styrofoam tray and slice of sweet potato pie wrapped in plastic. On Thanksgiving Day, this time Mrs. Flowers didn't invite Eva and her family over and instead gave leftovers from her family's annual gathering. But her mother hadn't eaten hers yet. She figured her mom thought Mrs. Flowers was trying to get on her good side. Eva sighed. It would be a quiet ride to and from church this morning, but at least Andre was willing to come this time.

It was important for her husband to recover physically and mentally, but it was also critical for him to regain spiritual strength too. For a long time, Eva hadn't been able to attend church because of her disabled husband wanting to stay out of sight and Skye being off on weekends. Joy blossomed within her when he told her he wanted to go today, and she expected it would be the start of Andre mending his troubled heart.

She took out a jug of orange juice and poured herself a cup. "When are you gonna eat your Thanksgiving dinner, on New Year's?"

Her mom was cooking breakfast at the electric stove. "Why don't you eat it? Mrs. Flowers gave the leftovers to you, not me."

Eva turned and sipped from her glass cup. "Mrs. Flowers gave each of us a plate, including Andrew. She was trying to be nice."

Her mother's expression hardened. "I don't need her kind gestures. I'm fine without them, and that's what you need to learn to do too, young lady."

Anger roared through Eva, banging her cup on the counter. "What do you have against Mrs. Flowers?! What did she ever do to you?!"

"Do *not* raise your voice to me!" her mom countered.

Eva stepped forward and glared at her mother. "Why don't you say it? You're jealous I have a better relationship with her than my own mother!"

Her mom slapped her across her face.

Eva fought back tears and ran out of the kitchen. Though she was hurting inside, she told her mother the truth that had been eating her up for years. It was the reason her mom was displeased with Mrs. Flowers' presence when she first entered the house.

It was why she didn't want to paint the portrait for the son of Mrs. Flowers' friend, and why her Thanksgiving dinner from three days ago was still in the refrigerator. Eva went into the guest room and shut the door. She hated how her mother treated Mrs. Flowers, and especially a widow who lost her husband.

If her mother placed herself in Mrs. Flowers' shoes, she'd realize the woman who she thought was trying to take her place was simply an old, lonely woman. Eva dried her eyes and opened the bottom drawer of her dresser. She laid out her amethyst and white floral dress to wear for church. Then she bathed Andrew and dressed him in an evergreen sweater and blue jeans. After Eva took her son in the kitchen to have breakfast, she entered the master bedroom to check on Andre. He was in his manual wheelchair, adjusting on a sky blue, long-sleeve dress shirt.

Eva brightened.

Her husband needed help with small objects and a few tangible doings, but he was getting much better at daily tasks for himself. She was grateful she had less to do than when he first came home.

Andre looked at her reflection in the mirror of the cherry wood dresser. "Can button shirt . . . fix collar, please?"

"Sure." Eva walked to his wheelchair and fastened each button. "You look handsome."

"Uh, thanks," Andre said with a weak smile. He tilted his head and frowned. "Okay? What happened . . . mother?"

Eva rolled her eyes and closed the last button of his shirt. "She's got problems. It's something about being jealous of Mrs. Flowers . . . or my relationship with her."

"Oh," Andre said lowly.

Eva pulled down his neck collar. "Do you think you can fix your tie?"

Andre lowered and shook his head.

"Okay." Eva put his blue necktie on for him and tied it in a knot. "Perfect. You're all done. There's breakfast downstairs."

"Not hungry. Going . . . brush my teeth." Andre wheeled himself out to the bathroom.

Eva squared her shoulders and exited the bedroom. Where was God? Sometimes she felt like He wasn't listening to a word she said. Praying for Andre the past year became a worn-out routine and she didn't know him too well anymore. But after all his stressful and depressing days of seclusion, she realized the only way he would allow love to enter was if he wanted it himself.

"PRAISE THE LORD! CAN I GET AN AMEN IN THE HOUSE?" Pastor Tyson gripped the pulpit and bounced with a spring in his step after the choir finished singing "Jesus Is Mine."

"Amen," the congregation said.

"I said, can I get an amen in the house?" the pastor repeated.

"Amen!" the congregation said louder.

"It don't matter how you feel, or what you're going through. You can always depend on the Lord Jesus," Pastor Tyson proclaimed through his microphone. "Please turn with me in your bibles to the book of first Samuel chapter seventeen. . ."

Eva glanced at her husband, sitting in front of the other side of pews. He didn't look happy, which worried her. Her mind drifted off with concerns for her husband. She hadn't paid too much attention to the pastor, but somehow his sermon swerved from the triumph of David against Goliath to his downfall of lust and sin. After King David remained in Jerusalem, he saw a beautiful woman bathing, and temptation took root and grew into a heap of trouble.

One evening also affected Eva's life, and she got a feeling the pastor's message was a warning to her. Should she have gone to Caleb's house? Was getting the books a bad idea? She didn't mean to destroy her marriage, but what about Caleb? Although he was never interested in her when they were teenagers, he was also a single man known for playing the field.

Eva gulped and listened as the pastor expounded David's experience. He said how one mistake can lead to another and advised to always be honest and ask for forgiveness for one's sins. Eva cast a look at her husband again, who had his head hung low.

As Pastor Tyson read in First Corinthians chapter seven verse eleven, Eva was sucked into a daydream, remembering how Andre used to be. Sometimes he read bible verses to Andrew in his lap, telling their son how Jesus loves him more than he can himself. Andre loved God and had taught her to do the same at the end of their senior year. If it wasn't for him, she would've never gone to church.

Building a relationship with Jesus Christ guided her to make wise choices. It also allowed her to find the strength to love not only others boldly, but also herself. From a child to a young woman, Eva wondered why none of her grandparents bothered to visit her, and why they couldn't accept she was here and love her. Maybe her mother and father had her out of wedlock, but it wasn't her fault. She was a harmless child, who wanted to spend time with her grandmas and grandpas like other normal children.

As a young girl, Eva suffered from great depression for feeling ugly and never having a boyfriend. But it appeared saving her heart for a man worthwhile paid off. In high school, she had wanted to be popular, but after attending her class reunion, it seemed a simple life was the better choice. Many of her classmates were divorced or raising fatherless children. Despite his changed lifestyle, she was grateful for how Andre had worked hard to make her and their son's lives better.

The night of senior prom, Eva accepted Jesus Christ. In her bedroom, she cried and asked God to forgive all her sins. She also prayed for God to help her save herself for a good man who truly loved and respected God and her. Later, Pastor Tyson baptized her for the remission of her sins, and she had strove to serve the Lord ever since. Now having seen her adult life, she realized her prayer had been answered, regardless of the present decline in her marriage.

"Sister Lucas . . . Sister Lucas, the pastor called you to the front," a fellow woman beside her said, pulling her out of her muse.

Eva wore a dazed look. "Huh?"

"Pastor Tyson asked you to come forth," the church sister whispered. "He has a presentation for you and Andre."

"Oh?" Eva found Andre in his manual wheelchair beside the pastor. She rose from her pew with Andy and strolled down the aisle. "What's this about?"

Pastor Tyson smiled. "The church and I know of you and your husband's financial struggles, and we couldn't help but offer a helping hand. Therefore, we've raised a donation of two thousand dollars to be presented to the Lucas family."

Eva wore a sad frown. "Oh, no, you didn't have to—"

"We wanted to do this," Pastor Tyson interrupted. "Please, say you'll accept our donation. It's the least we can do."

Eva faced the congregation seated on the church pews. "Uh, thank you. Thank you so much."

"Yeah . . . thanks," Andre added.

The congregation clapped and cheered for them, but Eva darted her eyes with uncertainty. Would the church's generous offer conflict with the benefits they were already receiving? There was one way to find out, and it would be from a letter from the Social Security Administration.

26

Eva

THE FIRST DAY OF DECEMBER ROLLED IN, BUT NO check arrived from social services.

Eva drove into the driveway at home. Her wipers swished off the flurries sprinkling from the gray, cloudy heavens. Today marked the first snowfall. She switched off the engine and sat in her driver's seat with her head leaned against the neck rest. Her heartbeat pulsated as she exhaled heavy breaths.

Stress burdened her like never before. Though the church meant well, she hadn't spent enough of their donation in time, and the SSA counted their contribution for her monthly payment.

Eva peeked in the rearview mirror at Andrew.

A smile tugged at her lips. She liked to watch her little boy sleep, bundled up in his winter toboggan, red-and-black plaid coat, red mittens, and black boots. He looked like a tiny lumberjack. He was so endearing. She couldn't understand why Andre hadn't tried to know his son more. Of course, he'd been so mentally absorbed in his own problems he forgot others were emotionally suffering too. But Andrew still wanted to play with his daddy. It was in his smile and alert eyes when Andre buzzed around in his electric wheelchair and in his strong grip whenever he crawled over and touched Andre's leg or feet.

Maybe she ought to be thankful Andre at least smiled at their son, but since gaining use of his hands and arms, he never tried to hold him. Having little hand dexterity, he was scared he'd drop Andrew and cause him to get hurt. But there were other ways he could show affection toward Andrew besides giving a hug. Eva unbuckled her seatbelt and snatched her key out of the ignition. She never thought she would be, but she was thankful for her mother's visit to town. Despite their differences over Mrs. Flowers, it allowed her to focus on her studies of interior design and finally prepare for the spring semester.

Last Sunday's quarrel had stuck in her mind her whole work week. Her mom had never slapped her before, and neither had she apologized for hitting her. After church service, Eva didn't eat lunch or dinner and went to sleep early to wake later to study at night.

Mrs. Flowers was coming to the house less out of fear she was ripping Eva and her mother apart, and with her husband's aloof behavior and no change in him through prayer, she felt like nobody understood or cared about her pain and loneliness.

Eva climbed out of her car and unclipped Andrew from his car seat. Carrying her son, she unlocked the door and entered the cozy, warm house. Andre was in his electric wheelchair, playing UNO with Skye while watching a dog show on Animal Planet.

"Hi, fellows," Eva said, closing the door.

Her mom walked in the living room, kneading a dishtowel. "Eva, can I talk with you privately, please?"

Eva's heart felt light. "Sure, just let me put Andy upstairs." She turned her back and let out a relieved breath, glancing skyward. For the past seven days her mother had given her the silent treatment, and she reckoned she was finally ready for them to move on. Eva trudged up the staircase to her son's bedroom and laid him down, placing Mookie under his arm. She came downstairs again, awaiting her mother.

"She's in the guest room." Skye tossed a card on the middle pile of a coffee table. "Change the color to . . . yellow."

Andre inspected his hand and slammed his cards. "Gah!"

Eva chuckled at her husband, stepped into the guest room, and shut the door. She wove her hands and smiled. . "I accept your apology."

Her mom peered at her like she was an alien. "Apology? What apology?"

"For Sunday about Mrs. Flowers." Eva's countenance fell. "Isn't what this is about?"

Her mother cackled. "If you think I'm giving an apology, you've got another thing coming, honey."

Eva's stomach knotted. *Oh, God. Here we go again . . .* She squeezed her arms around herself as if trying to contain the burst of rage she felt fueling inside of her.

Her mother walked over to the dresser, opened the bottom drawer, and pulled out the three textbooks Caleb gave her.

Eva's chest tightened so much she couldn't feel her heart beating.

"The Art Institute of Charlotte called about their spring semester. And while doing laundry, I discovered your little secret. What are you doing hiding these books?" Her mom was stone-faced, glaring at her. "And where did you get them?"

Eva's chin bobbed. "I knew you'd try to talk me out of going back to college to become an interior designer, just like you did when I was younger. And the books . . . I got them from an old classmate."

Her mother crossed her arms. "Who?"

Eva gulped and straightened. "I got them from Caleb Williams. He's an interior designer and real estate agent. He allowed me to use them to study."

Her mom raised a brow. "Have you ever considered he may be using you?"

"Using me? What are you talking about?" Terror crossed Eva's face.

"Being generous and kind to . . . womanize you," her mother said, "either that or to make someone else he's interested in jealous."

Eva grimaced and shook her head. "Caleb wouldn't do that."

"How do you know? When he was a teenager, he didn't exactly have a good reputation." Her mother tossed the books on the twin-sized bed beside clean, folded towels and studied her reaction.

Eva glanced from the bed to her mom again. "Maybe not, but he's always been kind, too nice to admit he wasn't interested in me when we were kids."

"Who says he's not interested in you now?"

Eva gagged at her mother's startling question, trying to catch her breath. "Why do you keep making accusations? You're just trying to stop me from pursuing interior design." Fury ignited her as she gathered the books on the bed in her arms. "You know, I have all this pressure on me! I'm always doing something for someone, but hardly ever get to do anything for myself! The least you could do is encourage me, instead of criticizing what I'm doing!" She turned her back and marched from the guest room, her mother trailing her from behind.

Skye and Andre were frozen in shock, observing the fiery argument.

"Eva, come back here!" Her mom pulled her arm. "Eva, listen!"

Eva gave her mother a dirty look. "No, you listen, Mom! You made a promise to keep your critical opinions to yourself! You're my mother and I thought to take your word, and let you stay in our home, but . . . I guess you were lying the whole time."

Her mom frowned. "Where are you going?"

"I don't know, but I can't stand another second of your insolence!" Eva left and the front door slammed shut.

27

Eva

SATURDAY EVENING

Eva? What are you doing here?" Caleb said, holding his doorknob.

Eva held his three textbooks with tear-streaked cheeks. "I came to return your books. I think . . . I shouldn't be going back to college, but only because of Andre and my son." She sighed. "They both need me more than they ever did before, and I imagine it will be hard to continue with my studies after my mother heads back to Seattle."

Caleb waved a hand. "Nonsense, you can keep them. Maybe when things simmer down, you can pick up on your studies. I don't use them anyway."

"Are you sure?" Eva shrugged.

Caleb nodded. "Yeah. I don't have any use for them." He studied her expression. "Are you okay?"

"It's my mom." Eva hung her head.

"Do you wanna come in and talk about it. I'm a good listener," Caleb said.

Eva sucked her teeth. "It's not a good idea. Besides, I don't wanna bother you."

"Nothing you say will bother me, Eva. We're friends," Caleb said.

Eva arched a brow. "We are?"

"Sure, we are," Caleb said. "Now, come in out of the cold and sit down."

Eva gave a half-smile. "Okay."

Soothing warmth embraced her the second she entered his house. She sat on his Chesterfield, brown leather sofa in front of a brown-and-black marble table. Her eyes scanned across her environment in the living room.

Red-orange flames danced on the artificial wooden logs in an electric fireplace. Tribal masks hung on the walls, and knick-knacks of elephants, giraffes, and lions decorated the TV stand, bookshelf, and wine chest. Looking around, Eva felt like she left North Carolina and stepped into an African Safari.

Caleb joined her on the couch and closed his HP laptop on the table. "Excuse me, I was skimming through house listings in the area when you arrived." He grabbed a dish filled with gold-wrapped Ferrero Rocher chocolates and offered it to Eva. "Would you like one? They're delicious."

Eva shook her head. "No, thank you." She looked around again. "You have a beautiful home."

"I'm pleased you like it." Caleb placed the candy dish back on the table. "So, what's wrong with you and your mother?"

Eva puffed out a breath and leaned back against the smooth curves of the sofa. "We don't get along well. She's always interfering in my business. At the moment, she's homeless and I allowed her to stay as long as she promised to respect my boundaries, but she still didn't again. I was clear, assertive, and everything, but she broke her promise."

She licked her lips, thinking deeply. "It's like she believes she's entitled to because I'm her daughter and she raised me. Sometimes I think it's because she's unhappy herself, and she assumes whatever I work to achieve will lead to heartache, like what happened with my father." She hung her head. "My parents broke up because my mom wasn't welcomed in my father's Italian family."

"I always wondered what your heritage was," Caleb said. He rubbed his chin. "So, you're half Italian?"

Eva's cocoa brown eyes reflected the flames in the fireplace, looking at him. "Yes. My father's from Rome, Italy. He was a handsome and talented landscape artist, Mom said. It's all I know about him. I gave my son his name Andrew when he was born."

"That's nice. I'd love to meet your son someday," Caleb replied, smiling. "I'm sure he's cute as a button."

Eva chuckled. "He is, and he's such a clown sometimes. He likes to make me laugh."

"I bet he got his looks from you," Caleb remarked.

Eva crinkled her nose. "No, not really." She stared ahead with a dreamy smile. He got them from his father."

"It's been a long time since I've seen Andre," Caleb said. "Maybe I could visit him sometime if he'll be willing to see me."

Eva smiled and placed her wavy hair behind her ears. "Sure, I think he'd like that."

Caleb stood and grabbed two shot glasses from the rustic mantel above the burning fireplace. He perched back on the couch and put the glasses on the table. "Care to have a drink?" Caleb handled a bottle of Calvados beside his laptop and filled one cup to the brim, casting a sidelong glance at Eva.

"Oh, no thanks. I don't drink." Eva clasped her hands in her lap.

Caleb cocked his head with a playful grin. "Aw, come on. A little drink can't hurt. Besides, it's practically fruit juice. I don't drink heavy, nasty stuff like hard liquor."

"What is it?" Eva said.

"It's called Calvados, a French fruit brandy made from pears and apples. It's my favorite. I'm sure you'll like it too." He held the glass of brandy. "Here, smell it."

Eva took a sniff and bit her lip. A Christian woman and teetotaler, she consumed nothing stronger than a can of ginger ale. Her mother would be furious if she found out she drank alcohol. "Well, it does smell good, but it wouldn't be safe. I have to drive home and—I should get going now." She jumped to her feet and flinched backward.

"What's the rush?" Caleb looked at her in disapproval. "Ever since you were a teenager, you've always been uptight and afraid to try new things. You hardly ever let yourself have fun. You've let your mother dictate your entire life. You know, parents aren't always right."

Eva thought about what Caleb said and found some truth. She was always a goody-two-shoes. Always taking her mother's advice and sticking her nose in books, major reasons she didn't have many friends growing up.

"You're right." She sat back down and sighed. "I'm a boring person."

"I don't think so," Caleb said, staring at her. "You're . . . afraid, but you don't have to be. You can trust me. Chill out, it's only one drink." He handed her the shot glass.

Eva took the glass from Caleb and glanced at him with a nervous smile. She knew she shouldn't drink, but it felt good to make a rash decision without her mother butting in or talking her out of it. She gulped the brandy and giggled, already feeling the alcohol work its way through her system. "That *was* good. It does tastes like apple cider."

"I told you," Caleb said, grinning. "You want another one?"

"Hey, why not?" Eva said in a carefree tone.

Caleb refilled her glass and poured in the other for himself. "How about we propose a toast?" He held up his shot glass of brandy. "For all the times you helped me pass Mrs. Chapman's vocabulary tests."

"Cheers!" Eva laughed and tapped her glass to Caleb's. They drank from their glasses together, but two simple drinks had become two others for Eva.

Caleb reclined back with an arm around the sofa, crossing one foot over his thigh.

"I was expecting Tasha Burke at our class reunion," Eva said. "You and she were close. What happened between you two? I thought y'all got married."

Caleb shrugged. "Tasha became a model and lives in New York. I left to avoid seeing her with another man."

"Oh, I'm sorry. I shouldn't have asked." Eva cringed inwardly.

Caleb laughed and scratched his temple. "No, it's okay. I like the way my life is. Things wouldn't have worked out between us anyway."

There was a moment of silence, and then Caleb spoke again.

"Eva?" he said.

"Yes?" Eva faced him and placed her shot glass on the table.

"I know you won't believe this, but I think you're so beautiful. Andre's a lucky man. You've changed so much, and it makes me ashamed of how I treated you in the past. I knew you had a crush on me. I'm sorry. I should've told you the truth, but I was too embarrassed."

"The truth about what?" Eva asked.

Caleb sighed. "You know, how I felt about you back then?"

"Oh, that." Eva lowered her head.

"I liked you, Eva," Caleb added unexpectedly.

Eva raised her head and studied his eyes in awe. "You did?"

"Yeah . . . a lot," Caleb whispered and scooted closer to her on the couch.

Eva sprung from the sofa, nearly losing her balance.

Caleb grimaced. "What's the matter?"

"I need to go home. It's . . . late," Eva said and smiled weakly.

Caleb didn't pressure her to stay this time and smiled back. "Okay, maybe we can chat some other time. I'll show you out."

"Thanks." Eva strode to the door and stepped outside in the frigid night.

"Don't forget the books," Caleb mentioned, "I said you can have them." Holding the textbooks before her, he flexed his brow with a wry smile.

"Oh, yeah. I forgot." Eva blushed and plastered a timid grin, taking the books from his hands. Her stomach throbbed with a warm, fuzzy feeling.

Caleb looked concerned. "Uh, can you drive?"

"Yeah, I'll be fine," Eva said, clutching the books to her chest. "Good night, and thanks again."

"No problem." Caleb shut the door.

Eva drove away, but she would go to a convenience store before returning home.

"THAT'LL BE THREE DOLLARS AND NINE CENTS," THE CASHIER lady in a red T-shirt said.

Eva fished the total out her clutch purse. All she had left was change. Her expression winced, and she giggled. "Sorry . . ." She placed a handful of quarters, nickels, and dimes on the checkout counter and sifted through them with her forefinger. "There's one dollar . . . two dollars . . . three dollars . . . and ten."

The cashier lady scraped three rows of quarters and a dime off the counter and wore an amused smile. "Thank you, ma'am." She popped open her drawer, dropped the coins in their proper slots, took out a penny, and ripped the paper receipt. "Here, you go. One cent is your change."

"Thank you." Eva took the penny and her receipt. She swiped the pack of spearmint Icebreakers she had brought from the counter and exited the swing door.

Eva settled in her car and gazed inside the brightly lit Circle K store. *Am I crazy?* She must've been out of her mind to drink late in the night, and especially after arguing with her mother. But maybe what she needed was a little booze to ease her stress load. One thing for sure, she was wired and felt better than she had in days.

Spending time with Caleb was nerve-racking and comforting at the same time. He understood how she was and what she was feeling, and it thrilled her he confessed he liked her when they were teenagers. She opened the pack of mints and tossed two in her mouth. Her mother had a nose like a bloodhound. But maybe if her breath smelled fresh her mom wouldn't be able to tell she had brandy.

She cranked her engine, reversed from the slanted lot, and careened down the street. The ride back wasn't long, and Eva was grateful. She swerved a little on the road, but she safely pulled into the driveway. Knowing her mother was probably waiting for her in the living room, she dumped four more mints into her mouth. She remembered the patio door. Maybe she could sneak through there instead of the front door. Eva got out of her car and snuck in the backyard.

It was either that or burn in humiliation.

Luckily, the patio door was unlocked. Eva slipped her thin frame through the door opening into the pitch-black kitchen, rattling the long, shading blinds. Either someone forgot to lock it, or she was falling into her mother's trap. Eva slid the door shut and fastened the latch.

Like a teenager who passed her curfew, she tiptoed toward the arched entryway to the living room. The light switched on in the kitchen before she made it mid-way. Eva turned around and saw her irritated mother in her soft white robe and slippers.

Her mother pursed her lips and crossed her arms over her chest, tapping her foot.

"Mom, before you hound on me, don't forget I'm a woman and responsible for making my own decisions," Eva stated.

Her mom smirked and walked to her. "I was waiting to make sure you come home safely. I'm not gonna ask you where you've been, Eva." She sniffed her daughter's breath and frowned. "Spearmint?"

Eva shifted her eyes and nodded. "Uh, yeah. I came from the store."

Her mother gave her an once-over. "I tucked Andy in bed, and Skye helped with Andre. I'm going to sleep. You won't have to put up with me too much longer. I'll be gone soon. Good night." She strode past Eva a couple of inches and paused for another remark. "Oh, there's aspirin in the medicine cabinet, in case you'll need it."

Eva cringed as her mother left the kitchen. Though she was thankful her mom didn't nitpick her, guilt consumed her from within. Drinking wasn't something she was accustomed to doing, and part of her wished Caleb hadn't influenced her to take a swig. The other half of her was contrary to what her mind knew was wrong, as temptation and morality battled within her.

She wanted to visit Caleb again.

28

Andre

ANDRE WAS FALLING DOWN.
He hollered and swung his arms, hoping for something to break his fall.

He landed and opened his eyes.

It was dark. Very dark.

Gray smoke arrayed the blackness.

A woman's scream echoed. Her voice was familiar. He heard it before, but he couldn't place from whom it belonged. He struggled to his feet and peered in the distance.

There was a scorching lake—orange, steamy, glowing lava mixed with cakes of ash.

Stepping stones rowed across it to a large, rocky cliff.

A young woman in white was at the peak. Her wrists tied, her slender body chained to a chair. He couldn't see her face, as it was veiled by her hair. She called for help again, fighting to break loose. Not a soul was in sight—but Andre.

He had to save her.

Andre coughed from the smoke and stepped on the first stone. It sank. He panicked and leaped to another stone and another as they sank, trying not to lose his balance.

He made it halfway to her and smiled.

Hold on! I'm coming! His voice echoed, and the beast heard him.

It knew he would come for her.

The ground shook when Andre reached the last stone.

He widened his eyes at the horrific sight before him.

He could barely breathe, and he couldn't move.

A gigantic king cobra burst up from the cliff like a jack-in-the-box, hindering Andre from saving the woman. It was multicolored with red eyes. It turned its hooded head and looked at him, licking its split tongue.

Then it struck down to bite.

He cried in terror with an outstretched hand, his voice fading in the darkness.

Andre gasped from his sleep and stared at the dark ceiling. He gulped, paced his breathing, and tugged his damp sleeveless undershirt from his sweaty chest, recalling his whereabouts. Andre frowned and tried to piece together the nightmare he had.

Although he loved many kinds of animals, he despised snakes. He sensed something was wrong in his waking life, but he didn't know what it was. Unable to interpret the dream, he shut his eyelids and released a long sigh, falling back to sleep.

AT SUNRISE, SKYE KNOCKED AND ENTERED THE MASTER bedroom. "Good morning, Andre." He flicked on a bedside lamp.

"Ugh . . ." Andre squinted at the bright light and held his right hand over his eyes. His disability was a conjoined twin that followed him everywhere and his life had become the same routine. Andre was tired of feeling worthless. He saw no purpose in being alive, nothing to make him feel profitable.

"Come on, man. It's time to get up," Skye said, pulling the blanket off Andre. "You've got a big day ahead of you. Grandpa Ricardo called and you'll be staying with him for a little while."

Andre sat up in bed, supporting himself with his arms behind his back. Unless he looked down he wouldn't know his legs were there. He hated having to use a wheelchair to help him get around. He wanted to stand on his own two feet and walk like any other normal human being. His range of motion and leg exercises helped keep him from getting stiff, but he still hadn't regained complete mobility.

He screwed up his face. "What?"

"You're going over to Grandpa Ricardo's farm," Skye said. "Your wife got called by your grandfather. He thinks maybe if you stay busy, it'll help make you feel more useful. Because you like animals, it could also help you feel better." He rolled Andre's wheelchair close to the bed and locked the brakes. "For starters, you can transfer yourself this time. I'll stay if you need me."

Andre wore a weak look. "But . . . I can't."

"You won't know unless you try, man. Here, using this will help." Skye placed the wooden slide board on the bed. "You have a majority of your upper body strength. Just remember what I taught you. You can do it, Andre."

Andre puffed his cheeks and exhaled slowly. He gripped the slide board and positioned it under his buttocks and partly on his wheelchair. He bit his lower lip and tucked his flimsy hands under his long legs, adjusting them along the bedside. Andre scooted his bottom across the board inch by inch until he got into the wheelchair and yanked the board out from under him.

"You did it!" Skye grinned.

Andre sighed. "Maybe, but it took a while."

"You know your schedule," Skye said. "We'll begin your exercises after you freshen up and get dressed."

"Alright." Andre grabbed his portable urinal from the nightstand and set it in his lap. Then he took his gray pouch of supplies, unzipped it, and placed it on the bed.

"I'll give you your privacy. Call me if you need help." Skye exited and closed the door.

Andre rolled his eyes and sighed. Emptying in a plastic container made him feel awkward. He remembered being uncomfortable as the bedside nurses catheterized him in the hospital. Now having more liberty for himself, he didn't take the small things he could do for granted, but losing sight on what he couldn't do was still a hard test.

"I'm done!" Andre called.

Skye cracked open the door and peeked inside.

Andre leaned forward and pulled up the back waistline of his pajama pants.

"Okay." Skye took the filled container to the bathroom. Meanwhile, Andre gathered his clothes for the day from the dresser, choosing what he wanted to wear. Someone knocked again, and he checked out who it was.

Eva gave a smile, looking in from behind the door. "Hey."

"Hey," Andre replied.

"Did Skye tell you about Grandpa Ricardo?" Eva asked.

Andre nodded. "Yes, he told."

"You'll need to pack clothes in a suitcase." Eva entered and opened the large, side closet, taking out a navy-blue suitcase with wheels. She laid the bag on the bed and unzipped it.

Andre watched her with a hopeful heart. With his sudden departure from home, did he accomplish his goal? Had he finally gotten Eva to give up? He needed to find out.

"You want . . . get rid of me?" Andre said.

Eva paused and frowned at him. "Of course not. This is a vacation, something to get your mind off your troubles, and maybe help your memory."

Andre went poker-faced. "Oh, okay."

"I'm about to go to work," Eva said. "I'll take you over at Grandpa's Ricardo's farm this afternoon. If you want, you can pack before I get home."

Andre placed his long-sleeve gray shirt, underwear, and jeans in his lap and rolled himself in his wheelchair. "I'm taking a bath." He sighed and left the bedroom. Nothing he did had gotten Eva to quit on him. Both highly impressed and deeply overwhelmed, staying on the farm with his grandfather was his last chance to relieve her of him.

AS THEY PASSED THE DEAD, GOLDEN STALKS OF CORNFIELDS, Andre stared out the passenger window of Eva's car. He looked to his right at an old wooden house with a collapsed roof. His eyes didn't want to leave it the farther it got in the distance as a moment of déjà vu came over him. Had he seen it before? Andre turned his attention to a white farmhouse and red barn as Eva cruised into a wide, lush, green pasture, surrounded by a barbed wire fence.

She shifted into park and turned off the engine. "Look familiar?"

"No, not this farmhouse." Andre blinked and frowned.

Chickens behind a fenced-in coop beside the farmhouse pecked in the dirt and strutted around as Grandpa Ricardo fed them grain from a tin bucket.

"Hola! Buenas tares!" Eva climbed out of her Volkswagen.

Grandpa Ricardo put down his bucket and waved. "Hola, Eva!"

Eva ran over and gave Andre's grandfather a hug.

Andre observed them discussing matters, but they were too far away to hear what they were saying. Together they walked over in a side hug. Grandpa Ricardo helped Andre into his manual wheelchair, and Eva took Andre's luggage from the trunk of her car.

A ramp for Andre to roll himself into the house was built on the side of the porch. Like his own home, it would take time before he got used to living on a farm. But when he inhaled the earthy air, he became comforted by the great outdoors.

"Welcome back, nieto. Guess you'll be living with me a few days, aye?" Grandpa Ricardo grinned.

Andre cocked his head, shading the radiant sun from his face. "Can you . . . tell me my parents, please?"

Grandpa Ricardo tilted his cowboy hat back a tad and slipped a handkerchief from a pocket of his striped shirt. "Your parents lived in Philadelphia. Their names were Derek and Marie, my daughter. They fought and did bad things. I took you in when you were five and raised you on my farm." He wiped his dirt-smeared forehead. "Maybe you'll feel useful here. There's a lot to do."

"Maybe," Andre said with a half shrug.

Eva let out a slow exhale, trying to dissipate her tears. "Well, I better go before Andy has a fit." She started to leave but turned around and hugged Andre. She hadn't embraced him in weeks, afraid of invading his space.

Andre hesitantly wrapped his arms around her and closed his eyes. For once, out of nowhere, he felt a strong connection with Eva and wanted to stay in her arms, his hidden feelings rising to the surface. Although he couldn't recall marrying her, he was drawn to her beauty since he arose from his coma, and her compassion and generosity had made him fall in love with her. But with his angry outbursts and ailments, he didn't feel he deserved her affection.

"Goodbye, Andre. I'll miss you," Eva said, looking in his eyes.

Andre swallowed a hard lump. *Go ahead, Andre. Tell her . . . tell her how you feel.* His heart grieved and called out to him, but he restrained his emotions. "Yeah, uh . . . bye, Eva."

His wife waved and left from the porch.

After she sped off down the country highway, Grandpa Ricardo introduced Andre to Carlos, Hank, and Bob, his hired hands. The three men worked for his grandpa's corn farm and were clearing the dead stalks for the new crop season. His grandpa also showed him the farm animals in the barn, teaching him the Spanish names for them. There were two spotted cows named Wilma and Thelma, and two pigs named Prissy and Twinkle, but Andre's favorite part was when he met the four horses.

Grandpa Ricardo named them unique names according to their colors. Two of the horses were male and the other two were female. Black Thunder was an American Quarter with a silky, dark mane and tail that sparkled in the sun. He was the top dog of the pack, as he was the main one his grandfather went horseback riding with in the pasture. Gold Star was a Colonial Spanish Mustang and a sweetheart with her tan coat and brown mane and tail. Grandpa Ricardo told him she was the horse Eva liked to ride when she came by to visit.

Gray Cloud, a gray thoroughbred, was stubborn compared to his other four-legged companions. But he was big, strong, and dependable. Last, there was Brown Sunset. She was an Arabian filly and the youngest of the group, always prancing around and searching for adventure. With his grandfather, Andre helped groom the horses, learning how to brush them and clean their hooves.

Later for dinner, Grandpa Ricardo made Mexican black bean soup and homemade biscuits. While listening to his grandfather share stories from his youth, Andre had two bowls and two biscuits. Ever since he received some use of his hands, his appetite increased, and he was ready to eat whatever meal was set before him. It turned out his first day went better than he expected, but after he tucked into bed, he was haunted in his sleep.

The nightmare began again.

29

Eva

WHAT COLOR IS THIS TRIANGLE?" EVA SAID, holding a construction paper shape. She and Louise had gathered the daycare kids around the alphabet circle rug. They reviewed shapes, colors, and numbers one through ten with their new class. All the toddlers watched them and their instructions, eager to shout out the answers.

Even Andrew paid attention. When he first transferred in the two-year-old room, he clung to Eva like a leech, stressing over the fact he had to share his mommy's attention in the class. But now Andrew made friends and was growing up into a sociable, little boy.

"Yellow!" the kids said.

Eva clapped and beamed. "Great job, everyone!"

Louise raised another shape. "What color is this square?"

"Red!" the kids answered.

The phone in their classroom rang.

"I'll get it." Louise took the call as Eva continued talking among the class.

"Okay, kids, I've got one more. What color is the circle?" She held the round shape and grinned.

"Green!" the kids answered.

Louise glanced at Eva with her hand over the receiver. "Eva, it's for you. A man wants to speak with you."

"Oh, okay." Eva took the phone from Louise.

"Hi, Eva," the man said.

Eva knitted her brows. "Caleb?"

"Yeah, it's me," he said, "I'd like to apologize for the other night in my home. I knew you didn't want to drink and I shouldn't have pressured you. It was inconsiderate of me."

Eva was taken aback. "Oh . . . uh, thanks and I accept your apology."

"I couldn't help but call you." Caleb sighed. "I don't want to ruin our friendship. I let it happen once in the past, and I'm not gonna do it again."

Eva's mouth curved into a smile. "Thanks, I appreciate that." She glanced at Louise and her two-year-old class. "Listen, I'm in the middle of teaching my class, so I have to go right now." She removed the phone from her ear, but Caleb spoke through the line again.

"Wait up!"

Eva cradled the phone to her ear. "Yes?"

"Mr. Coleman, my boss, is having a dinner for his real estate agents at the Redfish Grill tonight. He allowed us to invite one friend or family member. I'd be more than happy if you come."

Eva thought about the invitation. She loved to eat at the Redfish Grill, but she hadn't gone there since Andre's car accident. She was too scared it would evoke memories of the terrible incident that occurred on that dreadful night.

But Eva knew she shouldn't allow one disaster to prevent her from enjoying her life, and she figured it was a good time to face her fears.

Her company with Caleb helped her cope with her present situation. He was always willing to hear whatever she had to say without judging her or making false claims, and she liked that about him. Eva shifted her eyes around the classroom, trying to make a decision. The last time she spent an evening with him, she drank alcohol, something she thought she'd never do.

Her mind wrestled with conflicting thoughts. *Don't do it, Eva. Think about your husband. Caleb's underhanded. You know what happened last time.* She closed her eyes and sighed, biting her lip. *No way. You're just having dinner. What harm can come from this? Besides, your husband doesn't care about you. He'll never know about it anyway.*

Eva gritted her teeth. She felt like she had an angel on her right shoulder and a devil on her left.

"Hello? Eva, are you there?" Caleb said.

She shook her head and focused back on the phone call. "Um, sure. What time?"

"How about nine o'clock?"

Eva darted her eyes, unsure of herself. "Uh . . . that's fine."

"Awesome. Nine it is," Caleb said.

"Alright . . . goodbye." Eva hung the phone on the hook and stared into space.

Louise walked over. "Everything okay?"

Eva spun around with a startled look. "Yeah . . . I'm fine." She returned to the circle rug and sat down, but her mind was restless with worry, wondering if she made the wrong choice. Caleb's attention and friendship eased the pain of forgotten love, and his invitation flattered her.

On the other hand, her mother wouldn't like her having dinner with another man, but was it a dinner date or a friendly night out? Besides the two of them, other people with their loved ones would also be present. Wouldn't it create a different atmosphere compared to a romantic tryst? Eva thought so, but she would find out.

ALL THE LIGHTS WERE OFF, AND SHE TIPTOED DOWNSTAIRS, dressed in her canary yellow, floral print, maxi dress and off-white pump heels. Her hand touched the cold knob of the front door, and as she expected her mother caught her again, flicking on a lamp in the living room.

"Where are you going, Eva?" her mother said.

Eva faced her mom, who was sitting on the sofa in her robe and slippers again.

Her mother lifted her brow with suspicion.

"I'm going for a drive." Eva drew a breath and craned her neck.

"Where?" Her mother's jaw tightened.

"Just *out* . . . I need some fresh air," Eva said.

Her mom pressed her lips together, eyeing her clothing. "I hope that's all. You're pretty dressed up for going for a simple drive. I'll listen in for *my grandson* Andrew. Good night." She stood from the couch and walked around the corner into the guest room.

Shame corroded her insides. She couldn't believe it. Her mother thought she was having a love affair, but if she was, it was her personal life. She was an adult woman capable of thinking for herself, and her mom needed to accept she wasn't her shy, little girl anymore.

Eva swung open the door and exited the house. While driving to the restaurant, Eva felt a million butterflies fluttering in her stomach. As a teenager, she had longed to spend a date with Caleb.

Though she saw tonight as an innocent, social meeting, she couldn't deny, her former crush still existed. Caleb Williams was the first boy she liked, and the only popular guy who at least smiled or spoke to her in school. His wide, ivory-white grin and wink used to make her heart throb. She remembered how amazed she was watching him play basketball in the gymnasium after the cheerleaders' pep rallies.

He never missed a shot and passed and dribbled like nobody's business. All the girls were crazy about him, but back then Eva was equal to his own shadow, tagging along behind him and rarely noticed for her actions. Eva parked in a lot and entered the five-star restaurant, welcomed by an upbeat piano jazz melody playing from the ceiling speakers.

She surveyed the dining area and spotted Caleb outside a large window. He was standing at an outdoor table near the shore of Horseshoe Beach, waving his hand. Business people in formal suits and dresses filled the rows of chairs across and beside him, and she was relieved. Caleb had told her the truth as she expected, and there were no worries.

Eva laughed and passed through the glass door to the outdoor dining tables. "Hi! I wasn't expecting everyone to sit here."

"Hey, Mr. Coleman thought it would be pleasant to view the beach while we dine. He went to the restroom, but he'll be back." Caleb placed a hand on her shoulder, introducing her to his comrades. "Everyone! This is an old classmate and friend of mine, Eva Lucas."

Two African American women and two Caucasian men greeted her with smiles and waves. Sitting next to each one of them was a relative or close friend they had invited.

"Eva, this is Rachel, Paige, Vance, and Lou," Caleb said, pointing to each of the real estate agents.

"Please, take a seat and join us," Rachel said, smiling.

Caleb pulled out a wrought-iron chair for Eva.

"Thank you." She sat and placed her clutch purse aside on the table.

Caleb grinned and returned to his seat, which was across from hers. "I'm glad you made it."

"Me too." Eva smiled. A breeze washed over her face and shoulder-length hair as she looked at the peaceful sandy beach. "It's lovely out here."

Caleb joined her in the view as roaring, foamy waves tossed and broke from the shoreline, serenely ebbing away. "It sure is."

Eva opened her menu. "So, what's your favorite meal here?"

Caleb faced her and was about to speak when Mr. Tony Coleman—the real estate broker—returned to the table and made a whistle for attention.

"Welcome associates, family, and friends!" Mr. Coleman said. "I'm pleased y'all made it and were kind enough to bring someone with you." He raised his eyebrows at Eva. "Mrs. Lucas, I'm surprised you're here."

"Hello, Mr. Coleman," Eva said, smiling. "Your associate Caleb Williams invited me. We attended the same high school together."

"Is that so? How are you and Andre enjoying your home?" Mr. Coleman said.

Eva straightened. "Fine, sir. We've been in it a little over a year."

"Excellent!" Mr. Coleman regained his train of thought. "Excuse me, everyone. Where was I? Oh, yes . . . I'm glad so many faces are here tonight. Coleman Housing is a terrific real estate company committed to making sure clients have the best homes on the market. But it would not be what it is today without reliable agents. I appreciate all my agents for their hard work and dedication, which is why I have arranged this dinner of celebration. Let's give them a hand." Mr. Coleman and the guests clapped for the group of agents.

"And," Mr. Coleman added, "I'd also like to increase their shares of the profit from forty percent to an even fifty per agent."

"Woohoo!" Paige cheered and clapped.

"Well, somebody's happy," Lou murmured and laughed. Eva and Caleb chuckled.

"That's all I have to say. Everyone enjoy!" Mr. Coleman unbuttoned his gray suit jacket and took a seat in an end chair.

The applause died down and the agents communed with each other and their invited guests, deciding what they wanted to order.

"Steamed lobster with butter dip and fresh pasta salad," Caleb said, folding his hands on top of his menu.

Eva frowned. "Huh?"

"You asked me what my favorite meal was," Caleb said.

Eva moved her hair onto one shoulder. "Oh, of course."

"What's yours? Shrimp scampi linguini with garlic bread?" Caleb said.

Eva shook her head. "I like it, but no. It's grilled salmon with broccoli slaw. I order it a lot when I come here. Andre and I used to eat out at the Redfish Grill a lot, so he always knew what I wanted." Her eyes moistened, but she willed back her tears.

"You mean, for your anniversary?"

"No," Eva said, "before then. We came to the Redfish Grill together since we were engaged, but that was before he arrived late." She sighed and dropped her shoulders, scrutinizing the tiny print in her menu.

Caleb giggled and simpered. "You need those glasses you had in high school?"

Eva blushed and chuckled. "Apparently, I do." She looked at him over her menu. "My hands were trembling, so I couldn't get my contacts in before I came tonight. I was nervous about having dinner with you."

"How come?" Caleb inclined his head.

A chill rose up Eva's spine. "Well, I guess because getting married hadn't made you ugly to me."

Caleb tilted his head back and laughed. "Some things never change, but you . . . you're different. You look good

243

without glasses. I could hardly recognize you at our class reunion."

"I know," Eva replied, widening her eyes for emphasis. "You looked like you'd seen a ghost."

Caleb sighed and leaned back. "I didn't mean to be so shocked, it's just you're a remarkable person. Like I said, your husband's fortunate to have you as his wife."

"Yeah," Eva said plainly. With Andre's changed attitude, she wasn't too convinced anymore.

An African American waiter with gray, receding hair strode to the outdoor table and stood beside Mr. Coleman's chair. He asked each person's order around the table and jotted it on his notepad. Caleb told the waiter he wanted his favorite meal of lobster with pasta salad and then ordered his drink.

"I'll have lemonade," he said, "but make sure there's no ice."

"Gotcha." The waiter wrote and flipped a page. "And for you, ma'am?"

Eva squinted under the entrees label. "I'll have . . . the fried tilapia with scalloped potatoes."

"Okay, and to drink?" The waiter scribbled Eva's main course.

"Just iced water," Eva said, leaving out her lemon slice.

"Alright, I'll be right back with everyone's orders." The waiter traveled to another empty table and gathered dirty dishes left by the missing customers. He entered the main dining area through the swing door and headed for the kitchen.

"Didn't you want your salmon?" Caleb looked puzzled.

Eva shrugged. "No. I wanted to try something different."

Caleb stared in her eyes and quirked up a playful smile that made her wonder what he was thinking, but she didn't bother to ask. He glanced at the Atlantic Ocean and took an inhale of the salty air. "Have you tried a dessert here?"

"Yeah," Eva said, "their brownie parfait. It's so delicious."

"I've had their key lime pie with whipped cream, but I didn't like it." Caleb grimaced. "Too sweet for my taste buds."

Eva crinkled her nose. "I don't like key lime pie, or lemon meringue pie either. I'm not a fan of citrus-based desserts."

"I bet you like apple pie," Caleb said.

Eva giggled and raised a shoulder. "Well, sure. Doesn't everybody?"

Caleb laughed at her engaging wit and character. He angled his head and gazed upon her a moment. "You know, I wish I had known you better earlier. You're a fascinating woman."

"Thanks." Eva nibbled her lower lip, struggling to contain the thrills flowing inside of her. Tonight was one of the best nights of her life in a long time, and Caleb's sweet, witty remarks topped it off.

AFTER CALEB PAID FOR THEIR MEALS, HE WALKED EVA BACK to the parking lot. Without her contacts, there was no way she'd be able to find her vehicle in the pack with her blurry vision. They stood under a streetlight beside her car. Eva turned off her honking car alarm. She chuckled. "Thanks for *steering* me to my car."

Caleb laughed and slipped his hands in the pockets of his pants. "You're welcome. I enjoyed myself with you and the others. I had a great time."

"Me too. Ever since Andre's accident, sometimes . . . I feel so lonely. Thanks for paying for my check, but it wasn't necessary." Eva clenched her purse.

"Oh, no need to thank me," Caleb said. "I'd do it again."

Eva raised her head and studied him in awe. "Well . . . good night."

"Good night." Caleb gazed in her eyes. "I'm sorry things have been hard on you, Eva. Someone like you . . . deserves the best." He caressed her cheek with the back of his hand.

Desire bottled up inside Eva, but if she stood there a minute longer, she'd do something she'd regret. She closed her eyes, her thoughts of them together wandering out in left field.

Eva sensed Caleb attempting to kiss her. Surrender whispered through her, but she fought the urge and backed out. *What am I doing? I'm a married woman.*

His lips were inches away from hers when she shyly turned her face last minute, making it land on her cheek. Something about his lips on her skin didn't sit right with her, cringing away.

Caleb sighed heavily. "Sorry, I shouldn't have done that."

"No, it was my fault," Eva said with an ashamed frown.

Caleb gulped and shook his head. "Look, let's forget about it and go home."

"You're right. Good night, Caleb." Eva fidgeted her key in her car door as Caleb walked off and sat in her driver's seat. She pressed her hands over her eyes, choking on sobs. Guilt pinched her heart. How could she have let something like this happen? Temptation was getting the best of her, and she needed to bring Andre back home as soon as possible. She was in danger, tied up in a situation that was a tangle of lust and love.

Her crush was blossoming.

30

Eva

I T'S ABOUT TIME YOU GOT HOME," HER MOTHER SAID after she came into the house.

Eva's annoyance flared as she faced her mother. "Mom, I'm a grown woman! I'm not a child anymore! So, can you please stop treating me like one?"

Her mom raised her hands in prayer pose, approaching her with caution. "I'm sorry, but I was worried about you. Were you with someone?"

"That's none of your business," Eva said. "You know, ever since you found out about the textbooks you've been hounding me."

"That's what mothers do," her mom said.

"They also trust their children will make the right choices," Eva retorted. "But instead, you butt in and take over, making decisions based on what you think is best." She grimaced and jabbed a finger on herself. "You don't care about what I want! All you care about is your own happiness!"

Her mother frowned. "That's not true!"

"Yes, it is!" Eva said. "You don't respect my boundaries and you always break your promises. Honestly, sometimes I wish you'd leave me alone!"

Her mother bit her lip, on the verge of crying. "Fine! I'll take the first flight to Seattle tomorrow. If you think I'm nothing more than a pest, I'll leave, but don't call me if you need help." She stormed off into the guest room.

Eva massaged her forehead. She never intended to be so harsh, but a frenzy of emotions overflowed her. She raked a hand through her hair and released a breath. The night was well-spent and she wanted to fall asleep. Her mother's help had been valued, but with Andre recuperating, she didn't need as much support anymore.

And no matter what, she could always depend on her neighbor Mrs. Flowers for anything. But having her mom leave on bad terms wasn't an option. Despite disagreements, she loved her mom, and she refused for them to remain enemies.

She believed God allowed Andre's accident for a reason, an opportunity for her and her mom to finally make things right. She entered the guest room and found her mother folding her clothes and stacking them in her suitcase and duffle bag. "Mom, you don't have to leave."

Her mom continued packing. "I've made my decision."

Eva drew nearer and held out her hands. "Where will you go?"

"I'll get another apartment elsewhere," her mother said. "I've contacted the director of the educational department of an art museum back in Seattle. I'm planning to do a workshop. Maybe it'll help me start my own landscape painting exhibition. Besides, I'm sure you'll be glad to have me gone anyway." She shut a middle drawer of the dresser.

"Please, don't leave like this," Eva said wearily. "Can't we talk calmly?"

"What's the use?" Her mom faced her. "You and I are like oil and water. I've overstayed my welcome, and it's time I go home, wherever that is." She opened the closet and took out her easel.

Eva peered at half of a velvet frame buried under the clothes in her mother's suitcase. She walked over, pulled it out, and studied the framed, colored picture. Shock paralyzed her as she stared at the handsome Italian man smiling in the photo. He stood in front of the Colosseum with a palette in one hand and a paintbrush in the other. On his left was a canvas on an easel, which based on his landscape portrait, was a replica of the gigantic stone structure.

His raven-black, curly haircut and coffee brown eyes reflected the light of the sunny day. Through his heart-shaped face, dark eyebrows, and creamy tan skin, Eva found the resemblance of her son. She imagined it was how Andy would look years later. The sleeves of his half-unbuttoned, baby blue dress shirt were rolled up to his elbows and gray paint smeared one thigh of his khaki shorts. On his bare feet was a pair of leather flip-flops.

Her jaw went slack. *Oh my gosh. Could it be him?* She stared at her mother, holding the picture. "Is this who I think it is?"

Her mom turned around and froze with her tan leather jacket. She glanced at the picture in Eva's hand and sighed dejectedly. "Yes . . . it's your father."

Eva's knees weakened. She plopped on the twin-sized bed and held a hand over her mouth. Waterfalls ran down her cheeks. Since childhood, Eva never saw her birth father. Mixed emotions from surprise to heartache surged through her, and she couldn't believe her mother never showed her his photo before.

"I'm sorry, honey." Her mother sat beside her. "I wanted to show you his picture when you were little, but I was dealing with some things. The sight of your father made bad memories come back."

Eva sniffled and raised her head. "What about the good ones?"

"They came too," her mother said, "but we had few of them, Eva. We got to know each other for only a couple of weeks. When he found out I was leaving, he proposed and I accepted, but you know what happened after that. Your father, Andrew, couldn't bear disappointing his parents, and especially his mother."

Eva wiped beneath her eyes. "Did he . . . did he know about me?"

"No," her mother said, "not until you were one. We wrote to each other, but he stopped mailing letters to me."

Eva frowned. "Why did he stop writing to you?"

Sadness clouded her mom's features. "He told me . . . he got married in his last letter. After that, I never heard from him again."

"Who did he marry?" Eva said.

Her mom sighed and wiped her wet cheek. "Silvia De Vecchi. She's a gorgeous, Italian nude art model he met in a café downtown, but he wasn't happy. Andrew Martello never loved anyone but me."

"You still love him, don't you?" Eva said.

Her mom buttoned her lips and nodded, too hurt to speak.

"What did he say about me?" Eva said.

Her mother drew a breath and exhaled. "He said he was sorry for not being there for you, and he hoped y'all would find each other someday." She brushed Eva's dark hair behind her ear with a wistful smile. "Whenever I look in your eyes, I see your father. I was unable to control my past with Andrew and his family, or with my own parents disowning me when they found out I was pregnant. Because of this, I've become controlling of your life. But then, you fell in love with a man and got married . . . and I felt like I lost your father again."

"Oh, Mom . . ." Eva's face contorted as she embraced her mother, sobbing on her shoulder.

Her mom rubbed her back. "I'm sorry for being pushy, Eva. And I'm sorry for slapping you and being so cruel. You were right. I was jealous of your friendship with Mrs. Flowers, but it's only because I wanted us to be close. I'll make amends with Mrs. Flowers tomorrow." She held Eva at arm's length and continued. "From now on, I won't visit unannounced and I'll respect your marriage and home. I could tell my coming used to bother Andre, but he's a good, patient man who kept his peace."

Her mother held her hand. "I'm sorry for discouraging your passion for design too, Eva. Thinking about how my career has gone, I realize how I made you feel. It hurts when you're hindered from doing what you love. I should've known better. Your father and I are both artists. Creating art . . . it's in your blood. I love you, honey, and I'll . . . I'll trust you'll make the right decisions. Just please be careful. I don't want you and Andre's marriage to fall apart. Lately, I've been concerned about you two so much."

After what happened with Caleb tonight, Eva thought to say her mother had good reason to worry, but she was too ashamed. Feeling vulnerable and troubled with her marriage, she needed her mother's comfort and support now more than ever.

"I will, and I'm sorry too. I love you, Mom." Eva hugged her mother again. Her shoulders bobbed as her mom held her tighter, but she wasn't crying only because of her relationship with her mother. She was also crying because of the threat Caleb posed and her fondness toward him that never died. Most of all, she cried for her hopeless longing for Andre to become the strong husband and father she believed he could be. Somewhere deep inside Andre's broken heart, he had to want to stay in her and

Andy's lives, and for one main reason.
She felt it when they said goodbye.

31

Eva

I'LL PRAY YOU HAVE A SAFE FLIGHT," EVA SAID TO HER mother in the Piedmont Triad International Airport. She gave her mother a side hug, holding Andrew on her hip. Garden Ridge had no airport, so she had driven her mom to the closest one in the city of Greensboro.

Her mother smiled. "Thank you, sweetheart." She tickled her grandson's tummy, making him giggle. "I'm gonna miss you, little munchkin."

Eva handed her son to her mother. Her eyes watered as her mom squeezed and cuddled him in her arms, cherishing the heartwarming moment. She thanked God for her and her mother rebuilding their mother-daughter relationship. If they could work out their differences, forgive, and move toward a brighter future, her and Andre could do the same, right?

Her mom looked over her ruby eyeglasses at Andrew. "Now you be a good boy, ya hear?" She kissed his cheek and gave him back to Eva.

"I'll let you know when we have his third birthday," Eva said.

"I'll look forward to it," her mother replied. "Sesame Street, right?"

Eva grinned and nodded. "Yes, ma'am."

With a playful smile, her mother cast a glance from Andrew to her, pondering what present to get her grandson. "Hmm . . . I'll see what I can find for Andy." Her mom winked at her.

"Cookie Monster is his favorite," Eva noted.

Her mother chuckled. "Alright, I'll keep it in mind when I go shopping. Bye, Eva."

"Goodbye, Mom. Best wishes with your art workshop." Eva shared another hug with her mother. I hope you get your own exhibition at the Seattle Art Museum."

"Bye, Andy." Her mother pinched Andrew's pudgy cheek and walked off with her luggage.

"Grammie, bye-bye," Andrew said, waving his hand.

Eva watched her mother pass through the crowd of passengers in the airport terminal, tossing her suitcase and duffle bag in a drop-off queue. Next, her mom got in the airport security line where two security guards were waiting. She handed one of the guards her ticket and ID and passed through a full-body scanner.

"You're good," a security guard said, giving her mom a thumb's up.

Her mother blew her and Andrew a goodbye kiss and waved for the last time before proceeding to her designated boarding gate.

Eva smiled and waved her son's hand.

Her heart shuddered as her mom left, anxious without her mother's guidance. Her mom had interfered, but her apprehension and concern had always been out of love. She was her mother's child, and as a single parent, her mom was accustomed to striving to keep her from harm. Eva got a pack of Goldfish cheese crackers from a vending machine and waited on a leather chair for the flight departure.

Some minutes after she and her son finished sharing their snack, a flight attendant declared an announcement from an intercom.

Her mother's plane was preparing for lift-off.

Eva walked to a large window and looked outside at the Delta Airlines aircraft. The plane wheeled down the tarmac runway and glided off the road into the gloomy sunrise. Eva touched the ice-cold pane and closed her eyes, a tear trickling down her cheek. *Please, God. Give Mom safe travels.*

She stared at the plane until it disappeared behind the clouds.

Maybe she should've told her mother she almost kissed another man, but their bond was so fresh and headed in the right direction, and she didn't want to spoil it. Even so, what her mother assumed about Caleb appeared to be true. Surprisingly, he found her attractive and was interested in her more than he ever was when they were teenagers.

An uproar of cheers and applause caught Eva's attention. She beheld a group of people near a side food bar, having an impromptu celebration. Amid them was a redhead man with a buzz haircut in a camouflage army uniform and chunky boots.

Unfamiliar with the soldier, Eva frowned in wonder, but then it occurred to her.

Neal Witherspoon had finally come home.

He marched to his blonde wife and children, toting a hefty backpack and carrying a bouquet of red roses in his hand. Neal offered Mrs. Witherspoon the flowers and accepted her kiss and tight embrace as Tyler and Emily screamed and grappled his waist and leg.

Envy ached Eva's heart, snuggling her son. Her eyes glistened with tears as she observed the excitement and joy of the Witherspoon family. She never thought she'd know how it felt to be a soldier's wife, but since Andre's accident, she endured a long wait for the man she loved to return: a desperate need for him to be a hero and rescue her from a battle against sin.

Eva sniffled and slipped into a nearby elevator that opened its doors. She pressed the first-floor button, swiped her eyes, and waited as she and her son descended. During her long drive back from Greensboro, she thought about Andre again. If he didn't find it in his heart to come home today, she didn't know what she would do.

BRINGING HER HUSBAND HOME WAS THE BEST DECISION she could make for herself and their marriage. It would also motivate her to give living with Andre another go. Eva got out of her car and walked up the rickety porch steps of Grandpa Ricardo's white farmhouse. Birds chirped in the naked oak tree in the front lawn. She sneezed from the scents of wet earth and freshly mowed grass. Eva knocked and waited for an answer.

Grandpa Ricardo opened the door. "Hola, Eva!"

"Hola, Papa," Eva said. "How's Andre?"

Grandpa Ricardo grinned. "He's doing good. I've been keeping him busy doing chores and his appetite has also improved."

Eva beamed. "That's great. I came to take Andre home."

"Take him home?" Grandpa Ricardo's unruly eyebrows rose.

"Yeah," Eva said, "I mean, it's been a little over a week. I thought he'd be ready to start fresh . . . maybe we can finally work things out?"

Grandpa Ricardo sighed and twitched his mustache. "Well, you can try. He's been all right here the past few days." He smiled. "Maybe he feels better."

Eva tilted her head with an inquisitive look. "Where is he?"

"He's in the red barn. He likes grooming the horses."

"Thanks, Papa," Eva said. "Can you listen in for Andy? He's sleeping in his car seat."

"Sure thing," Grandpa Ricardo said.

Eva walked down from the porch and passed the chicken coop beside the farmhouse. She strode in the barn to her husband's wheelchair, the dirt ground crunching under her feet. Her nose tingled at the pungent odor of manure.

Wilma and Thelma mooed and chomped, eating their pails of hay. Prissy and Twinkle squealed and oinked at each other like two friends holding a conversation. Black Thunder and Brown Sunset were quiet behind their fenced stables. But when Gold Star spotted Eva, she neighed and bobbed her head, as if greeting her hello.

Eva walked to Gold Star's stable and brushed a hand over the horse's brown mane. She grinned. "Hey, girl. I missed you too."

Andre glanced back at Eva but didn't stop brushing Gray Cloud. Dust particles spread from the horse's gray coat and dissolved in the light breeze.

"Hi, Andre." Eva sat on prickling haystacks in front of Gray Cloud's stable with her keys in her lap.

Andre paused and hung his head. "Hi." He cleaned the dandy brush in his hand with a plastic curry comb in his other.

Eva fidgeted with the custom-made, penny keychain hooked to her ring of keys. "How are you?"

"I'm fine." Andre continued brushing Gray Cloud's long neck in short, flicking movements.

"Andy and I miss you being home," Eva said. "My mom flew back to Seattle today. I'm sorry for the clashes we had

257

over at the house, but my mother and I are doing much better now."

"Glad . . . hear that," Andre bumbled. He coughed from the dust, stopped, and placed the dandy brush and curry comb in his lap. "My arms . . . back tired." Andre grimaced and kneaded his right arm and shoulder with his left hand.

"Let me help you." Eva placed her keys aside and hopped off the haystack.

Andre's expression softened. "Oh, no, it's alright. I'm—"

Eva stood behind him and massaged his arms, working her way further up. From his sigh of relief, she knew he couldn't help giving in to relaxation. She peeked at him with his eyes closed and smirked, kneading his shoulders. "Feel better?"

"Yes . . . uh, thanks." Andre cleared his throat and removed one of her hands from him. "I'd better finish brushing."

Eva wore a weak smile. "Oh, okay . . . sorry." She sat and watched her husband again. "Gray Cloud looks white. You're doing a good job with him." She gulped and figured it was about time she speaks about the reason she came. "Andre, you've been here over a week. Your appetite's increased, you appear to be doing well, and—I guess what I'm trying to say is . . . I'd like you to come home."

Andre stopped again. "I wanna stay here."

"What about Skye and your exercises?" Eva said.

"I quit! Leg exercises . . . not working anyway," Andre replied. "I'm not getting better."

"But . . . you can't," Eva said. "You have to come home with Andy and me. We need you."

Andre glared at her. "What do you need me for? To stare at when you're bored?!"

Eva crumbled inside. His words felt like a knife to her heart. She had brought Andre to his childhood home to help him cope with his new situation and move on in life with her and their son. Instead, it gave the impression of making matters worse. Will she and her husband ever get on good terms?

"Andre! That was uncalled for," Grandpa Ricardo said with a frown, walking in on his grandson's rude comment.

Eva rose. She threw up her hands and backed away from her husband. "No, Papa! You heard him. Let him waddle around in his pathetic pity! Let him do what he wants!" She kicked a clump of dirt and stomped to her car.

"Eva, wait! Don't go!" Grandpa Ricardo placed down a bucket of grain and raced after her.

Eva slammed her car door and revved her engine. She zoomed out the front yard as Grandpa Ricardo chased her vehicle, pleading in Spanish and English to not drive away. But what was the point in staying? Andre said didn't want to come home, and talking to him wouldn't change his stubborn mind. Eva understood Andre suffered through a lot, but she wished he'd show more empathy toward her and not always brood over his own misfortunes.

Her husband had turned into a selfish brat, and having a class of daycare kids, she already had enough tantrums to deal with. What happened to the gentleman she married on their wedding day? Her love and hope for Andre was slowly dying out. If he continued behaving the same way, their marriage would never get resolved.

But if it didn't, Eva wanted Andre to at least make greater effort to be in Andrew's life. Did their son matter to him?

Depression submerged his being so deeply all he focused on was not being able to walk and function like he used to. Eva rode to their house, laid Andrew in his crib, and went in the master bedroom. She cried on her pillow and swaddled herself in the comforter. Her cell phone vibrated on the nightstand.

Eva sandwiched her head in her pillow and stirred from the sight of her phone.

It vibrated two more times.

Please, shut up! Eva filtered a breath through clenched teeth and turned over on the bed. She snatched the phone and saw a Messenger notification in a corner of the screen. Eva frowned and swiped it down with her thumb.

A circle profile photo of Caleb's dark brown, grinning face was beside the text message.

"Caleb?" Shivers ran through Eva's body. Not having her cell number, he must've searched up her Facebook account to get in direct contact with her. Some of his message was hidden with ellipsis dots. She sat up and tapped his message to read all he sent: *Hi, Eva. Sorry to intrude. I'm feeling pretty low and haven't been truthful to u. Need someone I can trust to talk to. You're the only one I feel will understand. Please meet me 3:00 p.m. @ Starbucks on Olive St. so we can talk.*

Eva nibbled her lip and hesitated on what to do. She took a deep breath and typed him back a quick reply: *Feeling low too. I'll be there shortly.* Eva called Mrs. Flowers over to listen out for Andrew and left the house to meet with Caleb to hear his honest confession. She wasn't aware of what he wanted to tell her, but he at least convinced her of one thing.

Unlike Andre, he cared about her feelings.

32

Eva

EVA STEPPED INTO STARBUCKS AND FOUND CALEB sitting at a booth, staring in a porcelain mug. Her face fell as she stood and watched him. She had never seen him so unhappy before. From what she recalled, he was always grinning and parading himself, showing off his pearly, wide smile. He knew he was fine-looking, and being a lauded basketball player, he was always popular and admired by his school peers.

Now he was a successful real estate agent who made big bucks, had a refined red Jaguar X car, and lived in a fancy, two-story home. What was he moping for? She walked to the table and sat on the long seat in front of him.

"Hey, I got your message," Eva said. "It kinda creeped me out, but I got it."

Caleb raised his head and sighed. "Sorry, I didn't mean to scare you." He cupped his hands on his mug.

"What's wrong?" Eva frowned and angled her head. "You look sad."

Caleb took another sip of his coffee.

"You said you weren't truthful. What did you mean?" Eva wove her hands on the table.

He perched his elbows on the table and hunched his shoulders. "I told you I enjoyed the single life, but it was a cover-up of how I really feel. Yes, I was a player, but I've changed over time. Those casual make outs with girls from my teenage years ended not long after graduation. I've wanted to settle down for some time." He sighed and peeped at Eva. "I've suffered three broken engagements with other women."

Eva's jaw dropped, and she blinked in disbelief.

"I know," Caleb said and winced. "I understand you're shocked. I would've mentioned it at the class reunion, but I didn't want you to feel sorry for me." He shook his head and shrugged. "What am I doing wrong? I'm confident in myself and I stand up and take charge as a man should do." He studied the floor. "I thought women valued men like that."

Eva chewed her upper lip. "Well . . . they do, but many women also want to be treated as equals, and not like their incapable of making decisions. Most like relationships with men who can trust them, who aren't jealous, and who treat them like people instead of things."

Caleb's forehead creased. "What's wrong with being protective?"

"It depends on what your definition of that is." Eva darted her eyes, and based on his shifted body language, she knew she struck a nerve.

Caleb pressed his fist against his cheek. "I can't help it if my definition of *protective* doesn't suit some women. I like to make sure nobody's trying to take her away from me."

"You can't be insecure, Caleb," Eva said. "If you want a solid relationship with a woman, you're gonna have to learn not to be possessive and trust her."

He snickered. "That's not what my dad said. He always said, 'To keep a woman, you gotta stay on your toes.' My mom keeps nagging me I need to find a wife. Since my father passed from heart disease, she gets lonely, and she wants me to give her grandkids to fill her big empty house." Caleb peeped at her. "Eva, I know you're married with a son, but the other night in the parking lot made me realize how much I'd love to have a woman like you."

Eva gulped and hung her head. "Caleb, I—"

"Please, just listen a minute," Caleb interrupted, "Eva, if Andre isn't willing to be there for you anymore, maybe it's time for you move on. You should be with somebody who will make you happy."

Eva drew her brows together. "Andre makes me happy!"

"How? By leaving you alone?" Caleb grimaced and leaned back. "If he loved you, he wouldn't allow one incident to ruin his whole marriage, but he would fight for it. He would stay committed to you, and he would do his best to care for you and your son Andrew."

Numbness infused Eva's body. She couldn't help but agree with Caleb. He had spoken the thoughts which had swirled around in her mind for the past year. And as much as she didn't want to admit, lately she found more comfort in another man than her own husband.

"I'm repairing a house on Lime Street," Caleb said, changing the subject. "I'm going over to paint the porch and do other minor fixes today. Would you like to help? With you interested in interior design, it might be a fun learning experience."

Eva hesitated. "Uh . . . sure, I'll come."

Caleb grinned and sighed. "Great, and Eva . . . thanks for the advice. I'm thin-skinned when it comes to criticism, but you told me right. I guess I've screwed up, but I promise I'll do better. Trust me, we're just friends. Don't take what I said out of context, but as a friend, I'm saying maybe think about it?"

Eva nodded slightly. "Alright." She wore a timid smile and relaxed her shoulders. Moving on and forgetting her husband wouldn't be easy-peasy, but it was obvious he wanted nothing to do with her and their son. As Caleb said, they deserved the best, and after Andre's frequent rejection, it persuaded her this wasn't coming from her husband again.

"YOU'VE GOT A SMOOTH STROKE FOR A DAYCARE TEACHER," Caleb said, observing how Eva handled her paintbrush.

Eva chuckled. "Thanks. My mom's an artist, so maybe that's where I get it from. Or perhaps it's from watching my students do arts and crafts." She took her brush, dipped it in the can of white paint, and continued stroking the middle stair of the porch steps while Caleb finished the first one.

"I appreciate you being here," Caleb said. "I didn't think you'd come after what happened last night. I'm sorry for embarrassing you. I should've thought twice."

"I forgive you," Eva said. "Besides, I led you on a little."

Caleb paused with his brush in his paint-smeared hand. "Eva, I hope I'm not meddling, but how long have you and Andre been married?"

Angry tears brewed in Eva's eyes. She stopped and rubbed the sleeve of her denim jacket over her face. "Eight years now. Sadly, our wedding anniversary has become like any other day. We didn't celebrate this year. Of course, Andre also doesn't remember marrying me."

Her strokes became faster and harder. "We had a spat before I met you in Starbucks. I was attempting to take Andre home after he stayed over his grandfather's farm, but he doesn't want to live with Andy and me because he thinks he's a burden." She sighed. "Because of this, he's given up on our relationship, and worse, he doesn't bond with our son like he should be. I mean, how can he not love this kid?"

Eva took her phone out a pocket of her jacket, unlocked her pattern code, and showed her home screen wallpaper image of Andrew to Caleb.

Caleb smiled. "Oh, wow. He's a heartthrob."

"Exactly," Eva agreed with enthusiasm.

"How old was he in that picture?" Caleb asked.

"Andy was nine months. He had learned to crawl that day." Eva put her cell away and finished painting the middle stair.

"Who's watching him now?" Caleb said.

Mrs. Flowers, our neighbor," Eva answered. "She babysits Andy sometimes. Her husband died, and our son helps keep her company. Her children only visit her during Thanksgiving."

Caleb frowned. "That's too bad. Your son must be special. Maybe we could have a picnic and I could meet him."

"Okay . . . I think Andy would like that." Eva wore a half-smile. "He's friendly, and it doesn't take him long to get used to new people." Satisfaction comforted her. Wanting strong male influences in Andrew's life, it pleased her Caleb wanted to get to know her son, and she couldn't wait to introduce him.

A low, chugging engine approached behind them.

Eva looked back as a 1994 white Ford F-150 pickup rode up and parked beside her car. A scruffy, Caucasian man in gray coveralls climbed out of the truck. He took a toolbox from the flatbed and walked toward them.

"Morning," he said in a deep, husky voice.

Eva crinkled her nose at the odor of cigarette smoke from his clothes. "Good morning."

"Hey, you're right on time," Caleb said, "but you'll have to go through the back door. The porch is still wet."

"Gotcha." The man toted his toolbox around back the house.

Eva frowned. "Who was that?"

"That was Max, the plumber," Caleb said.

"What's wrong with the plumbing in the house?" Eva asked.

Caleb ground his jaw. "During my inspection with the previous owner, I discovered the sinks in the kitchen and bathroom don't drain. The pipes are clogged."

Eva made a short laugh. "Unbelievable."

"Yeah," Caleb said, "the owner didn't want to contribute to making repairs, but she expected me to set a high asking price. Nobody would buy this little old house for what she was requesting. I had to negotiate with her until finally, she lowered the cost."

"Have you gotten any buying clients?" Eva said.

Caleb exhaled a mist of fog. "Nope, but I'm sure once the place is fully renovated this house will sell before Simon says."

They exchanged smiles and continued painting.

Eva stole another look at Caleb, her smile fading. The smell of fresh paint made her reflect on another cold, foggy afternoon. After a tech had identified from a sonogram they would have a baby boy, Andre was so excited he wanted to get an early start on preparing their son's bedroom.

Neither of them could agree on what design to choose. She wanted a circus theme, but her husband thought a train theme was better. They fought over their differences like forever until they agreed with Mrs. Flowers' sailor boy design.

Often, Andre wistfully peeked in the empty, finished room, expecting the arrival of their unborn son. Some nights they talked in bed, whispering loving messages to the baby, and marveling over kicking moments he showed sign. She missed those times, but now they were nothing more than a closed album of snapshots and photographs.

Her eyes teared up, and she exhaled a sharp breath to keep her composure, stroking her brush on the rail of the porch.

Ignoring a strong love was hard. And Caleb's shady prior relationships with women made her fearful there was something fishy about his friendship, and a worrisome question she was too scared to ask arose: what were his intentions toward her?

33

Andre

NIGHT FELL AND ANDRE SAT IN HIS WHEELCHAIR on the porch of his grandfather's farmhouse. He studied the waxing crescent moon hanging in the black velvet sky. Listening to the chirping crickets and droning locusts from the backyard woods, he felt a sense of loss, regret, and indecision.

Seeing old photographs wasn't enough for him to identify what kind of man he was. He wanted to step in the shoes of the man smiling and looking back at him in the unfamiliar pictures. It would mean the world to him to know at least a pint of what he had forgotten.

And then, there was Eva.

He didn't recall marrying this compassionate woman, but she had proven she loved him unconditionally. He frustrated, offended, and distressed her often, but she still wanted him to live with her. Andre couldn't understand what she wanted with him, but pondering everything she did for him, remorse pricked in his heart.

How could he be so mean toward her? Why was he so rude and spiteful? He needed to get help and change his mood. Eva was a good, strong-willed person, which he had taken for granted and on purpose tried to shun.

Last Saturday, Eva had told him she called Dr. Brown. She tried to convince him to take an antidepressant the doctor had prescribed for his clinical depression, but Andre refused again, afraid of the chance for side effects. Now she had gone, another week passed, and she hadn't come back for him.

Every day he wrestled with his unstable feelings toward her, and his misery of being only part of the man he was. Having hardship in his marriage, it appeared he suffered a lost love, and it devastated him. He wished he could dive in the cogs of his brain and repair whatever dysfunctions caused him to act and speak the mean ways he did.

But overcoming himself like this wasn't possible.

The front and screen doors opened, and Grandpa Ricardo peeked out in the chilly evening. "Supper's ready, nieto."

"Not hungry." Andre stared at the glowing moon.

"What's wrong, Andre? Are you thinking about Eva?"

Andre bowed his head and sighed wistfully. He was always thinking about his wife—pondering the patience and love she showed toward him and wishing he could remember the normal life they had with their son.

Grandpa Ricardo walked onto the porch and stood beside him. He placed a hand on Andre's shoulder and pointed across the road from them. "Look, there over yonder."

Andre lifted his head and peered in the direction.

"That's Old Thomas family's place. It caught fire some time back." Grandpa Ricardo faced Andre. "I think the house is like you, nieto. Its roof had collapsed." He peered back at the shack in the distance. "But one wonders . . . how this house still stands after all these years. Focus on what you can do, Andre, not on what you can't do. Your inability to walk and speak normally doesn't make you more or less of a man."

"It's hard . . . I can't provide . . . family," Andre faltered, biting his lip.

Grandpa Ricardo turned toward Andre. "Who says you can't? Your only hindrance is yourself." He wore a stern expression. "Respect and cherish your good qualities. Learn and strive to improve your bad qualities. Be thankful for who you are. No matter what, you're a survivor, nieto. Never forget that."

He patted Andre's shoulder.

Andre thought about what his grandfather said. He didn't know what a paralyzed man could do, but he wanted to help make Eva and their son's lives more sufficient and easier.

Grandpa Ricardo held back the screen door for him as he wheeled himself inside.

Without dinner, Andre entered the small bedroom and transferred into bed, musing over what he should do next until he drifted out. Several hours passed, and the dreaded dream invaded his sleep:

Andre was falling again.

He hollered and tumbled down a passage of nothingness, hoping for a ledge or branch to break his fall. He landed face down on his chest and stomach, the impact throbbing through his body.

It was dark. Very dark.

He opened his eyes.

Wisps of gray smoke arrayed the surrounding blackness.

A woman's scream echoed. Her voice was familiar. He knew who she was. He struggled to his feet and peered in the distance.

There was a scorching lake. Orange, steamy, glowing lava mixed with cakes of ash. Stepping stones across it led to a large, rocky cliff.

A young woman adorned in a white, silky dress was at the peak. Her wrists were tied with thick rope, her slender body chained to a chair. He couldn't see her face, but he knew she was there.

Andre, help me! she called, fighting to break loose.

Not a soul was in sight—but him.

He had to protect and save her.

Hold on! I'm coming! Andre coughed from the smoke. He stepped on the first stone. It sank. He panicked and leaped to another stone and another as they sank, trying not to lose his balance.

Don't worry! I'm almost there! His voice echoed, and the beast heard him. It knew he would come for her. It knew he loved her. An earthquake shook the ground when Andre reached the last stone.

His eyes widened at the massive creature before him. He gasped and he couldn't move a muscle.

A gigantic king cobra barged through the cliff, blocking Andre from saving her. It was multicolored with fiery, piercing eyes and sharp fangs. It lowered its hooded head, its face transforming to that of a man. He looked at Andre, viciously licking his split tongue.

Then he struck to bite.

The woman screamed and looked away, her black, wavy hair covering her face.

"Eva!" Andre jumped up in bed and stretched out a hand before him. He panted and winced, waking up with a horrible migraine. It was the third time he had the same nightmare, but this time was a little different. Something was definitely wrong. Andre couldn't place his finger on it, but somehow, he knew Eva was in trouble. Static crackled in his ears. He squeezed his eyes shut and clutched his head.

One after another, snippets of evocative images pieced together in his mind: a colorful flower bouquet tied with a blue ribbon, a tire swing on a peach tree, a ticking wall clock, a vase of white roses, a navy ship helm engraved with Andrew's name, his hand dripping with blood, a deer in car headlights, a penny keychain sparkling in the sunlight. . .

Great emotion engulfed Andre. He opened his eyes as a spark of intellect shocked him. Everything he had been told for days, weeks, and months was true. He didn't remember all he's ever said or done with Eva and Andrew, but now he was fully aware they were his wife and son. It wasn't because of the pictures, but it was because he remembered and adored them.

"Dear God . . . Eva . . . Andy . . ." Andre said, his voice cracking with regret. He pressed his shaky hands over his eyes and hung his head. Andre switched on the light on the nightstand. A framed photo beside the digital clock caught his attention.

He grabbed it and studied the center image of his teenaged self, wearing a black riding helmet, a red western dress shirt, and jeans, mounted on a black colt. Andre panted and turned his head, surveying his whereabouts.

He was in his old bedroom.

Golden little equestrian trophies filled the top shelf of a short, green bookcase next to the closet. On the middle shelf were a collection of books about many animals from domestic farm to the Sahara Desert.

Toy dinosaurs and horses were lined in a row on the last shelf. Beside the bookcase was a small writing desk where he always did his homework after school.

Andre's vision clouded with tears as he placed the picture down, gawking at the items and traces of his childhood.

Grandpa Ricardo barged into the bedroom dressed in his striped pajamas and nightcap. He caught his breath. "Nieto, what's wrong?"

Andre slowly looked over at the old Mexican man with silvery hair and a thick mustache, trapped in awe. "Mi . . . mi abuelo."

"Si, Andre. I'm your grandfather." Grandpa Ricardo's grinned and exploded with laughter. He knelt by the bedside and hugged him tightly, crying tears of joy. Until recently, Andre hadn't spoken a word of Spanish, and the fact he said something without being taught, showed he regained a part of his memory.

They held each other with outstretched arms.

Andre winced from his headache. "Where's Eva? I want . . . go home."

Grandpa Ricardo frowned, gripping Andre at arm's length. "I've tried calling, but she won't pick up. When I visited, Mrs. Flowers said she wasn't home." He sucked his teeth. "Something was off last I saw her."

Andre's heart was in his throat. "I'm scared, Grandpa. I don't wanna lose her."

"You won't," Grandpa Ricardo said. "She loves you. You'll go home tomorrow. Rest yourself now, okay?"

"Tomorrow," Andre agreed with a smile. He lay back in bed, pulling his blanket over him.

Grandpa Ricardo turned off the lamp and left his bedroom.

Thinking of Eva, Andre struggled to fall back to sleep.

He hoped he wasn't too late.

ANDRE STUDIED THE HOARY HEAD OF THEIR TWO-STORY house as his grandpa pushed his wheelchair up the brick pathway. Snow blanketed the black roof, the evergreen shrubs, and the front yard. Another December was coming to a close, and in the short time that whizzed by, it felt like years since he'd been home.

It disappointed Andre his wife stopped visiting him on his grandpa's farm, but part of him didn't blame her. He had been quite a crabby man, making their marriage more difficult than it had to be. A marriage which though he

273

couldn't recall the beginning of, he wouldn't change for the world.

Grandpa Ricardo knocked a gloved hand on the front door.

Eva answered, and her stunned face showed she wasn't expecting her husband. She clamped her lips and crossed her arms over her chest.

"Hola, Eva. Andre wanted to come home." Grandpa Ricardo wore a lopsided grin.

Eva averted her eyes from Andre to Grandpa Ricardo. She flared her nostrils and sighed. "Alright, he can come in. I'll call Skye. I'm about to go to work."

Grandpa Ricardo lifted Andre's wheelchair over the steps and let Andre push himself inside the toasty-warm living room.

Andre observed over his shoulder as his grandfather spoke.

"Do you want to talk?" Grandpa Ricardo arched a brow and set Andre's suitcase inside next to the coat rack.

Eva swayed, her arms still crossed. "No, Papa. We'll be fine."

"Okay," Grandpa Ricardo said, "but I'm here if you need advice."

Eva nodded and closed the door.

"Hey," Andre said.

Eva turned around and faced him, leaning her back against the door. "Hi."

Andre gazed at her as if ensuring he never forgot her again. Warmth filled his chest, and his heart danced from her presence. He pulled off his winter gloves and set them in his lap. "Sorry . . . I missed you . . . Andy a lot."

Eva turned her back to him, rubbing her arms. "Then what took you long coming back?" She hissed and rushed upstairs to the second floor, leaving Andre to sit in silence. He would've told her he remembered her and their son, but at the moment, none of that mattered.

He had to prove he loved them first.

34

Andre

LATER IN THE AFTERNOON, ANDRE PEEKED THROUGH the blinds of their bedroom window and viewed below him. Outside Eva was talking to a black man leaning against a red car. Shock overcame him as she held the man's hands, kissed his cheek, and took their son from the back seat. Apparently, the man wasn't only someone Eva knew, but he had taken her to work and drove her home.

As she carried Andrew, she led him to come into their house. Andre's heart quaked, troubled by the river of separation which had flowed between them. For the past few weeks, he had no clue what happened with Eva or their son, and neither did he know this strange man.

"Hey, Andre! Eva's home!" Skye called from downstairs.

"I know!" Andre stared at the tire tracks imprinted in the snow on the driveway. Heavy steps came up to the second floor. Someone knocked.

"Come in." Andre stared at the closed door

Eva stepped in the room, holding Andrew. "Hi, Andre. Uh, how are you?"

Andre shrugged. "Fine, I guess."

Andrew moaned and brushed his forehead against Eva's chest.

"Andy's sick," she said with a sour look. "He caught a cold from a kid at the daycare." Eva exhaled a long breath, swaying to comfort their son. "Listen, there's someone I'd like you to meet. He's an old classmate of ours and he wanted to say hello."

"Okay." Andre rolled himself from the bedroom, following Eva down the hall to the stairs. At the base of the staircase, the man from outside stood with his hands in the pockets of his trench coat. His rectangular face portrayed a smile meant to be friendly, but Andre didn't trust it.

"Hi, Andre," the man said.

Eva introduced the man to him. "Andre, this is Caleb Williams. He played basketball at Garden Ridge High where you and I graduated."

"Hi," Andre said plainly.

Eva shifted her eyes between the two men, nibbling her lip. "Well, y'all can get acquainted with each other while I tend to Andy." She walked their whining son down the hallway into the bathroom.

Andre and Caleb stared at each other without a word.

"Goodbye, Andre. See you tomorrow," Skye called as he left the house.

Andre glanced away from Caleb and waved. "Bye, Skye. Have a good night."

Caleb cleared his throat, drawing back his attention. "I'm sorry about what happened. Being in your condition must be miserable."

Andre smirked and wove his hands. "It's not too bad. I have . . . own vehicle wherever I go."

Caleb laughed. "I never thought about that." He raised his eyebrow. "But I heard you've been depressed. I can understand you wanting to divorce."

Andre's expression hardened. "What? I don't want to get a divorce."

"That's not what Eva said," Caleb remarked.

Andre was breathing heavy, wondering how he could've ever wanted to do such a thing. But being in an emotional and dazed state, he wouldn't deny he hadn't requested it.

"She also told me you've felt like a burden to her," Caleb added. "Frankly, I don't blame you for feeling that way. It must suck seeing *your wife* do everything you can't." He pinned his eyes at Andre as if urging him to blurt an angry outburst.

Andre gritted his teeth but made no comment.

"Maybe you came home, but you won't win back Eva's heart after how you've treated her," Caleb said. "Yelling at her, ignoring her when she speaks to you, refusing to be with her and your son . . . you're better off killing yourself for your own good."

Andre curled his hands and wanted to jump out of his wheelchair and attack Caleb. He was an evil man full of himself. How did Eva get so close to someone like this?

Caleb inched forward to the last step, glaring up at him from below. "Eva doesn't want you anymore, Andre. I haven't asked her to marry me, but when I do, I'm sure she'll say yes. And she, I, and Andy will live happily ever after, and you . . . you will be dead or in a nursing home."

Andre's blood boiled. Was Caleb telling him the truth? Had he pushed Eva to her limit? Had she given up on him? Why else would she want him to get acquainted with this other man? He closed his eyes and hung his head, ashamed of his behavior.

"Eva's gonna be mine," Caleb whispered deviously. "I assure you I'll take *great* care of your wife for you."

A flash of the cobra snake zoomed through Andre's mind. With terror, he looked in Caleb's eyes. Maybe he was paralyzed with impaired speech and emotional problems, but he was smart enough to understand who this man was. He was the serpent from his nightmare—the man blocking he and Eva from making amends and threatening to break apart their marriage.

"While you were away, we've spent much time together. Uh . . . I hope you don't mind." Caleb licked his lips and smirked, rubbing his hands together.

Andre gulped. His face fell, and his heart shattered to pieces. Had Eva cheated on him? Or was Caleb trying to manipulate his fragile mind?

"Andy's resting peacefully," Eva said, coming back to the staircase. "I gave him some medicine. I'm sure he'll get better soon." She glanced from Andre to Caleb and smiled, ignorant of what they said out of her presence. "So, how did everything go?"

"Everything went fine, right, Caleb?" Andre pursed his lips.

Caleb grinned and lifted his chin. "Right. I'll be leaving now. Goodbye, Eva, Andre." He waved at them and exited the house.

Eva released a sigh. "Phew, I'm glad things went so well."

"Are you kidding me?" Andre glared and wheeled away.

"What? Andre, wait a minute. . . ." Eva frowned and followed him into the master bedroom.

Andre peeked outside the window and watched Caleb speed off in his car.

"What do you mean? What happened?" Eva said.

Rage swept over him, throwing a look at her. "What do you care? You . . . you told him . . . everything that . . . happened . . . between us!" He exhaled rapid breaths, his mind exploding with fury.

"I needed someone to talk to!" Eva shouted, on the verge of tears.

Andre's lips drew back in a snarl. He banged his numb right hand on the armrest of his wheelchair. "What about your mother? Or . . . Grandpa? Or Pastor Tyson?" He shook his head. "You didn't have to talk to Caleb." He glanced down and raised his head with a scowl. "Tell me, what's going on with you two? Why'd you . . . spend time with him?"

Eva looked startled. "We have a lot in common. Caleb gave me textbooks. I've been studying interior design, and plan to enroll back in college soon. He's just a friend! He's a real estate agent and a designer. He's been helping me get hands-on experience with some of his projects for clients."

She sighed. "I wanted you to realize our friendship has strictly been about house design, so I asked him to tell you what's been going on between us for himself. He said he would. I thought he told you those things."

"Well," Andre said, "he didn't. He told me . . . you told him I wanted a divorce." He slumped his shoulders, folded his hands in his lap, and sighed. "Maybe I did, but I don't anymore." He rolled closer to his wife and wore a weak look. "Eva, you gotta listen to me. Caleb's no good. He said many harsh things."

Devastated, Eva was taken aback and sat on an edge of the queen-sized bed. "I can't believe this. Caleb's always been trustworthy and understanding toward me."

"It could've been a cover-up," Andre said. "He was pretty wretched . . . upset to say the least. I'm worried about you."

"Andre, I'll be fine. Believe you me, I've been a little skeptical of Caleb's friendship and his interest in me, so I'll consider your warning." Eva started to walk off.

"Wait," he said, holding her hand. "I'd just like to say . . . I'm sorry how I acted and I'm back to stay. Please . . . don't leave me."

Eva's throat thickened with sobs, looking away. "I'm sorry, but . . . I can't promise that. I need time to think. I don't know how to feel about you right now." She slipped her hand free and turned her back.

"You can have the master room," Andre said and looked down. "I'll take in the guest room." He rolled his wheelchair out of their bedroom. Maybe Caleb was right and he didn't have another chance with Eva. One thing for certain, Andre felt bad distrusting his wife. But if she was only studying for college and getting experience with design, why had she kept it a secret from him?

35

Eva

EVA BROWSED THE ELECTRIC LED SIGN NEXT TO a fenced-in baseball field on Wilbur Street, waiting at an intersection. Bright, golden lights reading Happy New Year blinked twice and slid across the blackboard. Then, an animated image of a baseball player struck a ball with a bat. The ball flew up and filled the whole screen, advertising the New Year in large numbers: *2019*.

She tapped her forefinger on her steering wheel. Every day she left work, she couldn't wait to crawl back into her warm bed and go to sleep. After her spat with Andre on Grandpa Ricardo's farm, she had gotten acquainted with Caleb in the heat of the moment and gave him her cell number. Their friendly gatherings made her feel a mixture of fear and adoration. He arrived at her house and drove her to work the past days, but after Andre came home, guilt wouldn't allow her to ride with him anymore. Caleb said he understood, but apparently, he was offended.

Regardless, she still had fun with him, painting houses, shopping at Lowes and Home Depot, arranging furniture, and welcoming clients into their new homes. Their bond had reminded her of how well her marriage used to be with Andre. She wanted to shun her husband and strove hard to get beyond their past love.

Remembering their former life was too painful with everything changed, but Caleb had made her feel special again. He sent her flowers, took her out to dinner, and encouraged her pursuit of interior design. Enjoying his company, she gradually fell for him. Aside from kisses on the cheek, they hadn't gotten sexually involved, but it frightened her she approached that direction.

Her crush had grown full-bloom into a deeper sense of meaning, but what about Caleb? At their class reunion, she held his attention in the cafeteria, which was staggering. Her dentist removed her braces after high school, and she had gotten eye contacts her sophomore year of college.

Skin acne treatments accentuated the natural beauty of her skin, which according to Andre had always existed. Looking in Caleb's eager, mahogany brown eyes, Eva sensed he was only attracted to her looks, but strangely enough, she didn't care. What happened to her self-esteem? Where was the love of God she showed to Andre?

Pride and unforgiveness had decayed her dignity, and she wasn't feeling exquisite anymore. Her mom always told her there was a difference between love and lust, and Eva had learned the difference the moment Andre bent on one knee, held her hands, and proposed to her on his grandpa's farm. During an August sunset, Eva sat on the tire swing tied to a peach tree in the farmhouse's backyard. She followed his gaze and listened to his words like music notes floating in the breeze. When Andre ended his nervous blabbering, her heart skittered, and she nodded and whispered yes, flinging her arms around his neck. Eva wanted to kiss him so badly, but he placed his fingers over her lips.

Fearing it may lead to an unlawful sin, he advised they wait until their wedding day. Instead, they hiked to the Eagle Haven Mountains where they watched the clouds and talked about their future dreams for each other. There wasn't a need for a ring on her finger. Their promises and conduct were enough to sustain their devoted love and friendship. And when the big day and their honeymoon arrived, Eva understood the reason for their delay. As they came together, there was a pure virtue—the realization their relationship wasn't a matter of trial-and-error.

But they forever belonged to each other.

A tear trickled down Eva's left cheek. She swiped it with her thumb and drew back to present time, smiling at her son in the rear-view mirror. "Hey there, baby."

"Hi, Mommy . . ." Andrew grinned, framing his cheeks in his red, gloved hands. About a week ago, she had taken him to the barber again.

Though he cried and screamed at his first haircut, now thirty-three months old, he handled the buzzing razor like a pro. With his curly, black hair smooth-shaven he was like a mini version of his daddy. Eva focused back on the road and hit her gas pedal when the light flashed green. Just like she and Andre had been with their parents, Andrew was in the middle of their broken marriage. Whatever decision she made, she had to consider not only herself and her husband, but also their son.

Lately, she got the strange feeling she was being watched. Caleb found her in more places than a mere coincidence, grinning and waving at her from different angles in retail stores and in the public library. Every day her iPhone had dinged off and rang nonstop. It turned out messaging with Caleb and giving him her number were bad ideas.

She was getting creeped out and figured it was a major reason for his previous breakups with women. He impressed her with his boasting achievements, and other times she found them annoying. From what she could tell, he liked Andrew a lot the afternoon they had a picnic at the town park. But he had also changed her views on Andre, and now she couldn't grasp how she felt about neither him nor her own husband. Suddenly, Eva felt an urge to read her Holy Bible for direction, something she hadn't done for a while.

She would read it after she got off from work.

LOUISE TILTED HER HEAD. "HOW ARE THINGS WITH Andre? I know you're glad he's home." She smiled tenderly at Eva, snapping open a can of Coca-cola.

"Maybe," Eva said and sighed. "I'm so confused. I'm not sure exactly what to think of him."

Louise made a funny look. "What's there to think about? You love Andre and he loves you."

"I'm not sure, Louise," Eva said. "He has a new mind, a new character which I struggle to understand. He's a little better than before. His speech has improved a lot and he bonds with Andrew more than he used to. But I don't know how much longer I can tolerate his mood swings. I should've had the doctor prescribe him medication, but I wanted to respect his wishes. After all, he's the one who would be taking it, not me."

"It takes time to adjust to physical changes," Louise said, "but Andre's always been one to have fire in his belly and I have faith things will work out."

"I don't," Eva said bluntly. "Last I heard he quit his leg exercises and he and Skye mentioned nothing about him going back to the gym. Sitting in his wheelchair for hours stiffens his body. He needs to practice taking steps again."

She sucked her teeth. "It hurts me he's given up. I know he could walk if he tried harder. And yet, *he's* not my main problem."

Louise bit a cucumber. "What's your main problem?"

"I've spent time with another man," Eva confessed, "but mostly for business purposes. His name is Caleb Williams. He's an old classmate. Caleb claimed he liked me as a teenager, but I think he said it to make me feel good. I encountered him at my class reunion and he's attracted to me. It makes me nervous, but I've also been flattered by his attention." She bit her lip. "He was my high school crush, and I had wanted him to like me a lot. Now since he finally does, I've fallen for him." Eva lowered her head, picking her nails.

Louise placed her long, skinny braids down her shoulder. "Does Andre know?"

"Not entirely," Eva replied.

Her eyes pooled, looking up at Louise. "But he suspects there's something going on. Caleb treated me better than I've been treated in months, but he has another side to him I don't like at all. Recently, I noticed him being almost everywhere I go, and it frightens me. It's a miracle he isn't in our classroom. Because he used to drive me, sometimes I think he might follow me to work."

Louise contorted her face. "Sounds like a stalker. You should call the police."

"I know," Eva said, "but Caleb's been so kind and I'm scared of what might happen. For months, I've wanted Andre to show he loves me as Caleb did . . . the way he used to. Since I heard of his accident, I was there for him through thick and thin, but when will he be there for me?" She placed her hand over her heart. "I mean, I'm thankful he's home and does nice favors, but I want him to be willing to get medical help, so we could get along better. If he truly cared about our love enough, he'd try harder to recover mentally and physically and take the chance to improve the function of our marriage."

Louise leaned back. "I'm sure he didn't mean to be selfish or uncaring. Imagine if it were you that had a car accident and suffered from memory loss. Think about how you'd feel living with a man and a little boy who you don't remember, but who's supposed to be your husband and son."

Eva sipped from a Styrofoam cup of iced water. "I'd feel lost . . . lost and afraid."

"Andre probably does too," Louise said.

"But don't I have the right to happiness?" Eva said. "I've been doing for others and haven't gotten the chance to fulfill my own desires. Caleb's been helping me hone my skills in interior design. It's a dream come true."

"Of course, you have the right to be happy," Louise responded, "I just believe there are other ways to achieve your goals, ways that wouldn't put your marriage at risk."

"My marriage is already at risk," Eva said. She glanced from the rows of sleeping toddlers to Louise. Tears spilled on her cheeks. "I don't know how to put it back together again."

Louise sighed and placed her hand over Eva's.

The same heartache Eva felt over her marriage had followed her into the New Year, and she had grown weary over the whole situation. Andre told her he was a burden, and though she told him he wasn't, his self-indulgent pity sometimes made her feel like he was.

Eva had no intentions of getting involved with Caleb, but maybe Andre would be better living without her in his own home. Maybe he'd be happier, as her presence had been an irritation to him than anything else. It was the perfect solution. Andrew could always visit his daddy, but it was time now.

They had to go their separate ways.

36

Andre

ANDRE CLENCHED HIS TEETH AND WATCHED SKYE count his number of reps, working up a sweat from a handicap, lat pulldown machine at the Body Shop Fitness Center. He inhaled with each pull of the cable handles and exhaled when he released, building his chest muscles, biceps, and mid-back.

The metal weights slid and clanked faster as he sped up his pace, releasing bursts of grit and frustration. Recalling his nightmare and everything he suffered from his health, a soup of emotions stirred within him.

Somehow, he had to prove to his wife he wasn't a sourpuss or helpless weakling. Dealing with depression for him had been like a stubborn rash, but since he returned home, he had reached the rebirth of his manhood. On the morning he saw Eva at the door, he admitted to himself he couldn't let her slip away. Like his physical therapist Dylan said, with hard work, one day he believed he could get out of his wheelchair and walk again.

But if he doesn't, he'll do whatever he could to help take care of his family. Eva had carried the weight long enough and he couldn't bear her supporting their household by herself. Having paralysis and low testosterone levels, he thought he was fooling himself, but maybe someday they'll have another baby.

Since he had no spinal cord injury, he had hopes for a second child, but he also had his doubts and worries. Regardless of the minor differences, their marriage could get back on track. Besides, there was no way he'd allow another man to steal his wife and son.

The night his awareness of Eva and Andrew returned, he felt an emotional connection to them and he realized how much they meant to him. Being freed from a shell of confusion and loneliness, he needed and wanted them in his life, and he couldn't believe he'd ever forgotten them. He didn't know what Eva's plans were toward Caleb, but her commitment during his muddled state of mind showed she wanted their marriage to survive.

Keeping his partially restored memory and recovery a secret, he wanted to surprise her and asked Skye, his grandpa, Pastor Tyson, Dr. Brown, and Mrs. Flowers not to say a word.

"Hey, take it easy, man," Skye said. "Your muscles look like they're about to explode."

The kilogram plate weights clanked loudly as Andre lowered them with a deep exhale.

Skye unstrapped Andre's wrists from the cable handles.

Andre licked his sweaty upper lip, grabbed a white towel Skye handed him, and wiped his face and neck. Wet spots soaked his royal blue T-shirt over his chest and under his arms.

Skye wrinkled his nose. "You feeling okay?"

A drop of perspiration trickled down Andre's left temple. "Yeah . . . I feel great." He dabbed the towel at his sideburn and plastered a smile.

"Are you sure? You look like something's on your mind. What is it?" Skye said.

Andre wrapped his towel around his neck and rolled his wheelchair from under the lat pulldown machine. He looked down and sighed. "I keep having this bad dream."

Skye frowned and sat on the leather seat of a bench press. "What's it about?"

"I'm falling down in darkness . . . and I land in this dark, smoky place."

Skye peered and inclined his head. "Then what happens?"

"I hear a dark-haired woman . . . screaming. Her hands bound . . . someone tied her to a chair." Andre knitted his brows. "There's a lava lake . . . I go across stepping stones and try to rescue her, but every time I try . . . a king cobra comes." He squeezed his eyes shut, his chin quivering. "It . . . it bites her, and she dies." Andre gulped. "I know she's Eva . . . and Caleb's the snake."

"Have you told your wife?" Skye said.

Andre shook his head. "No, she'll think it's silly."

"How do you know?" Skye asked. "Eva's always cared about your thoughts. It might be a warning. Maybe she'll take it seriously. You told me she accepted your warning about Caleb before, right?"

"Yeah," Andre said, "but I think she still hangs out with him sometimes. So far, she hasn't cared much about anything nice I've done for her. I mean, she thanks me, but it's more like an indifferent type."

Skye chewed his bottom lip. "I've talked with Eva, and she's been dealing with a couple of problems too. Both of you should talk privately and stop all this crazy secrecy."

"I'm giving her space as she did me," Andre said.

289

Skye crossed his arms. "Maybe so, but you should be careful and make sure it isn't an excuse because you still feel like a burden to her. Honestly, you should tell her the truth of what's been going on, and especially that you remember her and Andy again."

"Not yet," Andre said, raising his head. "I don't want her to stay with me because I'm trying to fully recover or remember her, Skye. I want her to stay because she loves me."

"If you keep pushing her away, you're gonna lose her," Skye admonished.

Andre sighed heavily. "I know . . . but it's complicated." He blushed and glanced behind Skye at three men joking around and running on electric treadmills, working up their cardio.

"What's so hard about bonding with your wife?" Skye arched his back and cupped his knees.

Andre drank from a bottle of Vitamin water and screwed on the cap. "You're too young to understand." He placed his drink in a holder strapped to his wheelchair.

Skye straightened and made an O with his mouth, getting the picture from Andre's discreet response. "Oh, you're afraid you can't . . ."

Embarrassment consumed Andre, feeling as if the whole world knew his private concern of whether he suffered impotence. He bit his lip and wore a timid look, gripping his neck towel tighter.

"Well—" Skye twisted his mouth—"if you're worried about that, you don't know how much Eva loves you." He stood from the bench press seat and slapped Andre's toned left bicep.

"Come on, it's time to work those quads." He winked and walked past to a leg extension machine.

Andre growled, tilting his head back. He wasn't looking forward to exercising his legs, but he knew it had to be done if he would ever move around on his own again. He pushed his wheelchair to the leg extension machine.

Skye aided him out of his chair and onto the leather seat, placing his legs over the adjustable roll pad. Next, he lowered the roll pad for a less range of movement and set an easy weight, ensuring Andre doesn't injure himself. When Andre was well-positioned, Skye knelt in front him and smiled.

"Okay," he said, "we're gonna take it slow. Ten leg curls at twenty kilograms. You ready?"

Andre puffed his cheeks and exhaled slowly. "Yeah."

"I'm gonna do the same thing as other days. I'll operate the lever," Skye added.

"Alright, but nice and slow, okay? I can already feel the burn with my legs stretched out." Andre reclined on the leather backrest and released heavy breaths.

Skye chuckled and nodded. "Just relax. I told you I would." He gripped Andre's ankles and carefully pushed down so Andre's legs bent over the roll pad. He slowly raised it up and continued the process, picking up on his counting. "Two ... three ... four ... five ... six ... seven ... eight ... nine ... ten. There ... you all right?"

Andre's legs quivered. "You mean, besides my muscle spasms?"

Skye wore a lopsided grin and cocked his head. "They'll stop soon."

"Get me back in my chair, will you?" Andre grimaced. Constantly working out his legs, his muscle spasms hurt and weren't so funny anymore.

Skye pushed Andre's wheelchair closer and helped him back into it again.

"Thanks," Andre said, adjusting his feet on the footplates.

"You know we'll be back tomorrow, right?" Skye reminded. "You need to rebuild your leg muscles, as they've worn down."

"I know." Andre allowed a smile, gripping the rubber

wheels of his chair. "And I can't wait. I don't wanna stay in a wheelchair forever. I wanna get better. God be my helper, I will walk . . . for Eva, Andy, and myself."

"That's the spirit!" Skye gave Andre a high five. "Come on, it's time you practice standing again." He and Andre left from the gym and went to his grandpa's farm.

Without Eva knowing, Grandpa Ricardo had built wooden makeshift parallel bars in the backyard shed. Last week, Andre began practicing standing and taking steps again.

Andre took a long breath and rolled his wheelchair between the two parallel boards. He nodded at Skye in front him, his expression serious and determined. "Let's do this."

Skye grinned and strapped Andre with a gate belt around his waist. He clutched the belt and counted, preparing Andre to stand. "Ready, one, two, three." He tugged Andre out of his chair, which Grandpa Ricardo pulled away from behind him.

Andre straightened his back and gripped his fingerless-gloved hands on the rough, sandy boards. His height was a few inches above Skye's. He inhaled deeply. It always felt good to be on his feet instead of restrained in his wheelchair.

A tender smile curved his lips as he closed his eyes. He imagined himself walking toward Eva on a sunny, spring day: *He saw the blissful smile on her pretty face as he stepped to her in the open green pasture, her raven hair dancing in the wind. He made it to her, and she embraced him in her arms. They gazed in each other's eyes and exchanged smiles, approaching a kiss. . .*

"Looking good, nieto," Grandpa Ricardo said, interrupting his romantic fantasy. "How long you stand this time?"

Andre sighed with longing and snapped out of his muse. He glanced over his shoulder at his grandfather. "Two minutes, Grandpa."

Grandpa Ricardo held a stopwatch and clicked start. "Alright, it's counting."

Andre bobbed his head and exhaled slow breaths, holding his standing position helped by Skye. Each day he felt a little tingling in his toes and feet and an ounce of strength building to his legs.

"Time!" Grandpa Ricardo said, pressing the stop button.

"You can sit down now." Skye held the gate belt and eased Andre back into his wheelchair.

"Great job, man! That's the longest you stood yet. Are you ready to try steps?"

"Give me a minute," Andre said, leaning back his head. He glanced at the wooden ceiling and relaxed his speedy heart rate. "I'm ready."

Skye held the gate belt and counted again, lifting Andre back out of his chair. He stood farther at the end of the boards and observed as Andre dragged his numb, flimsy legs, taking small steps.

Andre's eyes watered, fighting shooting pains in his legs, but he couldn't quit. Somehow he had to get out of his comfort zone of lies and hopelessness, and regaining his mobility and taking medication were two of the ways in which he could do this. Now his marriage and family were worth more to him than holding his adamant opinion. It wasn't easy learning practically everything over again, but in the year and four months since his car accident, he had made a miraculous recovery.

He wished Eva was happier about him coming back home than what she was and gave him more credit than what she did for the progress he made. She couldn't grasp how it felt to be a self-reliant, strong man, and suddenly become immobile and helpless as a child. Or how it was to fall in a chamber of despair so deep he had to look up to see the bottom. Andre wouldn't hold it against her though.

He loved her too much to hold a grudge.

37

Eva

E VA SAT IN THE DRIVER'S SEAT AND TOOK HER HOLY
Bible out of the glove compartment of her car. She
closed her eyes and held it across her forehead,
pleading to God. *Guide me, Lord. Show me what to do.* She
stuck her thumb in the gold-edged pages, opened to First
Corinthians chapter seven verse eleven, and whispered the
verse to herself: *"But and if she depart, let her remain unmarried
or be reconciled to her husband: and let not the husband put
away his wife."* She raised her head and glimpsed outside
her windshield as Louise waved and buckled her baby girl
Kenya in her white Nissan Pathfinder.

Recollection settled in her mind. Pastor Tyson had read
the same verse during his sermon one Sunday ago, but she

hadn't paid much attention. Marriage was an institution arranged by God since the day He presented Eve to Adam in the Garden of Eden.

Eva nodded in accordance to what she read. As a virtuous woman, she couldn't forsake the law of God to please her flesh, even if she wanted to. Aside from separation and living alone, resolving her marriage with Andre was her only option.

Divorce was the law of the land, which allowed married couples to sever their ties, particularly to look for another. When Eva had gotten married, she hoped to be in a committed relationship with her husband, and that they'd work out their differences.

But with a brain injury involved, it was extremely difficult. Andre's stonewalling and inattention wouldn't get her anywhere, and neither would her spending time with another man. Both of them tested each other's vows of commitment. They were in the wrong, and she wanted it to stop.

Eva closed her bible and switched on her engine. She felt the need to talk to Pastor Tyson and consult him in her decision-making. She couldn't say she wasn't attracted to Caleb. If she did, she would be lying through her teeth. Her heart was overwhelmed with yearning, not knowing what to do.

She didn't want to tolerate Andre's bad attitude, but she also didn't want to be by herself. For the sake of her son, she wanted Andrew to keep his father in his life, a privilege which Eva hadn't been able to have as a child. There were too many fatherless children, too many women striving to fill the shoes of both mother and father in their children's lives.

Eva pulled out of the parking lot of the daycare and drove to the church. One of the elders was outside mowing the lawn of the church grounds. She found a smile and waved as he waved to her. Eva rolled down the passenger window. "Hello, is Pastor Tyson here?"

"Yes, ma'am. He arrived about five minutes ago," the old brother said.

"Thank you." Eva got out of her car and took Andrew from his car seat. She entered the church and walked down the carpet aisle, carrying her son. Pastor Tyson was talking with someone in his office as Eva was about to knock. She hesitated and waited on a pew. About ten minutes later, the door of the pastor's office opened. A pregnant, teenage girl and a woman who Eva assumed was the girl's mother exited with tear-streaked faces.

"Hi," Eva said meekly.

"Hello," the woman replied, holding an arm around the girl as they walked by in the middle aisle.

Eva closed her eyes and inhaled a deep breath in her lungs. She stood and tapped a knuckle on the door of the pastor's office. "Pastor Tyson?"

Pastor Tyson looked up from an open Bible on his desk and smiled. "Sister Lucas, how are you doing?"

"Um, I wanted to talk with you." Eva's eyes swam with tears.

Pastor Tyson stood and slipped off his reading glasses, directing them at the chairs in front of his large desk. "Sure, come right in, sister."

Eva entered the office with Andrew and sat in a chair, adjusting her son in her lap.

The pastor closed the door and took his seat in his chair. "What do you want to talk about?" He put his glasses back on, wove his hands on top of his bible, and studied her attentively.

Eva's shoulders sagged.

"Pastor Tyson—"she glanced heavenward and let out a breath—"I have sinned. I haven't done right, and now I'm paying the price for my actions."

The pastor frowned. "What happened? What have you done?"

Eva hung her head and sniffled. She told Pastor Tyson she spent leisure time with another man who she liked

296

during high school and he appears to be attracted to her. "I think he expects me to have a love affair with him, but I don't want to. I mean, I find him attractive, but I never meant for our relationship to be more than friendship."

"Have you talked with Andre?" Pastor Tyson said.

Eva shook her head. "Not really. He knows about Caleb, but not about me spending time in Caleb's house and going to dinner with him. It's been impossible to discuss matters with Andre without him getting upset. It's bad enough he's quit his exercises. I don't think he's doing much to better himself. Whenever I come home, I find the same old thing. He sits in his wheelchair and watches television in the living room."

She sighed. "We hardly talk, and we sleep in separate rooms. At first, it was because of Andre's quadriplegia, but he can move around a lot more than he used to. There's no excuse for us sleeping apart now."

Pastor Tyson leaned back. "So, what's the reason you came here?"

"I'm thinking of separating from Andre," Eva blurted, "I know what the scriptures say, but I guess I was wondering what you think I should do."

The pastor rubbed his chin. "I see." He sat forward again. "Well, I'm afraid my opinion doesn't matter, sister. I can only give you what's written in the Good Book, and Romans chapter seven and first Corinthians seven explains the law of marriage according to God. You're the one who must decide whether to live with Andre or not. You've always been a gracious person, and you and your husband have been in love since high school. Do you want to be alone?"

"No," Eva answered, "but I can't deal with his bad attitude."

"Maybe he should be on meds," Pastor Tyson suggested.

Eva wiped her nose. "I've tried to get him to take some, but he refuses. He doesn't think it will help him."

"Maybe he's changed his mind." A twinkle sparkled in the pastor's eye, inching up a smile as if he knew something she didn't. "Go to him, Eva. Talk with him."

"But he—"

"Go to your husband," Pastor Tyson interrupted, "and try talking to him again, and see if you can't get matters resolved."

Eva exhaled. "Alright, but what if he doesn't respond or listen to me?"

"Don't expect the worse," Pastor Tyson said. "Instead, hope for the best. Remember, Andre came back home to you after weeks of being away. He might listen to your perspective this time."

Eva stood with her son and swiped her eyes. "Okay, I'll try, but if he doesn't listen, I see no other solution than us splitting apart. Goodbye, pastor."

"Bye, sister. I'll be praying for you two," Pastor Tyson said.

Eva left and rode home. Thick gray clouds coated the sky as sundown drew near. Eva unbuckled her seatbelt and stared at their house. *Please, God, let things work out. Let us be in unity.* She sighed and tentatively dragged herself out of her car and took Andrew out of the back seat. Eva strode up the walkway, her heart pounding with the click-clack of her leather winter boots.

Fresh lavender scent met her as she entered through the door. Eva gaped and scanned the living room. Everything was clean and organized, a cozy fire burned in the brick fireplace, and the television was off. Eva closed the door with a suspicious look, wondering what Andre and Skye were up to tonight. She placed Andrew upstairs in his crib and returned down to check things out. As she got closer to the kitchen, the mouthwatering aromas of meaty sauce, various spices, garlic bread, and cheeses wafted through the air.

Her stomach growled.

Italian lasagna was her favorite pasta meal, and Eva couldn't wait to get a slice. Andre and Skye were in the kitchen gathering dishes.

She crinkled her nose with a half-smile and gestured her thumb behind her. "What's going on here?" She shifted her eyes to Andre's caregiver and giggled. "And Skye, why are you wearing my apron?"

The color drained from Skye's face, looking at her. He fidgeted off the flower-print, full-body apron tied on him and tossed it on the counter. "Don't mind me. I make a mess when I cook, and I didn't want to get my clothes dirty."

Eva chuckled. "What are you guys doing?"

Andre pushed his wheelchair to her and smiled. "We made dinner for you."

Eva glanced from him to Skye. "Well, thank you both."

"Don't thank me, Mrs. Lucas," Skye said with a goofy look, "the whole thing was Andre's idea. I was his assistant."

Eva marveled at her husband and his lively countenance. Something was different about him the past couple days. Since they married, Andre had never cooked dinner for her, and especially not her favorite pasta dish. For the life of her, she couldn't figure out why Andre was acting nicer toward her, but then she thought of the prayer she said the night after her first time visiting him in Acute Care.

Her husband who for the longest had been in the dumps was finally shining the love she had shown toward him for the past months. They struggled through many valleys and hills to reach this point, and she thanked God for this evening.

No matter what fun, exciting times she had with Caleb and designing homes, she couldn't pluck Andre out of her heart. Everywhere she went with Caleb something or someone reminded her of a special time *they* had spent together. Maybe her husband was a workaholic, but it showed he was a giving person.

Eva glowed inside and felt a newness sprout within her. "Um, thanks for dinner. It smells amazing." She tilted her head with a flirty smile, a hand on her hip. "I didn't know you could make baked lasagna."

"I couldn't," Andre admitted and snickered. "I Googled an online recipe."

"Oh, well, I guess that explains it," Eva said, rolling her eyes.

They shared a laugh.

Andre gripped the wheels of his chair. "It'll be ready in a couple of minutes."

"Splendid. Andy's upstairs sleeping." Eva smoothed her hands down her khaki skirt. She thought about her talk with the pastor and cleared her throat. "Uh, Andre, can we talk"—she glanced from Skye to her husband—"privately, please?"

"Okay." Andre followed her in his wheelchair to the living room. "What do you want to discuss?" he asked.

Eva sat on the couch and placed her hands together to her chin as if praying for the right words to say. "Andre, I have a confession to make. Caleb and I . . . we've spent time together, besides about our interest in interior design." She beheld Andre's stunned expression and cleared the air before he assumed the worst. "Nothing serious happened between us. We've just gone out to dinner a couple of times, and I talked and had a few drinks of brandy over at his house. Since you came home, I haven't spent any time with him, but he's been stalking me."

Andre's eyebrows rose. "That's terrible! Why didn't you tell me? We should report him to the police."

"No," Eva said and shook her head.

"What do you mean, no?" Andre frowned. "Eva, stalkers are dangerous. I don't want you to get hurt."

Eva placed her hair behind her ears and folded her arms on her knees. "I know, but I wanna give him a chance before we get the police involved. If I talk with him and explain how I feel, maybe he'll leave me alone."

Andre screwed up his face. "What is it with you and Caleb? Why can't you let him be and move on?"

"Because I—"

"I'll tell you why," Andre interrupted. "It's because you love him, isn't it?"

Eva pursed her lips and stared at her husband in silence, annoyed by his hot temper.

"Isn't it?" Andre urged.

"No, I don't!" Eva's cell phone vibrated on her hip, and she knew it was Caleb. Looking at her husband's disturbed face, she fought to ignore the call, but her exasperation pulled her aside. She closed her eyes and let out a breath. "Someone's calling me. I'll be back down for dinner, okay?"

Andre's expression relaxed. "Uh, sure."

Eva stood and strode to the staircase. She went upstairs to the master bedroom and answered the call to stop her phone from buzzing again. "Hello?"

"Hey, Eva. It's Caleb. Listen, we've seen each other in different places, and I've been trying to reach you, but you've always gotten away. Can you meet me in the park tomorrow? I have something important to discuss with you."

Eva searched her eyes around the room. "Oh, um . . . I don't know if I can make it."

"Come on, please. It'll only take a couple of minutes. I really need you to come," Caleb said.

Eva sighed and ground her jaw. Her mother always told her if she didn't want a certain man and his advances to either ignore him or tell him to his face. Pretending she didn't notice Caleb hadn't worked. So, it was time for plan B. By meeting with him, she could explain she intends to stay with her husband and no longer wants to hang around him.

"Okay," Eva said, "I'll meet you after work."

"Excellent! I'll see you then."

"Bye." Eva ended the call and exhaled. She felt nauseous. What Caleb wanted to talk about was her least concern.

She was too worried she made the wrong decision again.

38

Andre

ANDRE YAWNED AND ROSE FROM THE BED IN THE guest room, overhearing the discussion between his wife and Mrs. Flowers talking about Andrew. His son was cranky from growing new teeth and had a low-grade fever, and the elderly woman had come over to babysit today. Eva spoke her perky goodbye, headed off to work, and shut the door, but he couldn't help worrying about her.

Based on her irritated expression and hesitant behavior, he knew it was probably Caleb who called on her cell phone yesterday. Andre could've grilled her again, but he didn't want to ruin the friendly relations between them. Trust was an important part of any relationship. As hard as it was, he had to believe Eva would be wise and make the right decision for herself and their son and marriage.

But that didn't mean he wasn't afraid.

Andre rubbed his hand down his drowsy face and checked the time on the digital clock.

6:20 a.m.

He grimaced and swallowed a gulp of warm saliva. A metallic taste filled his mouth, and his bladder pulsated with a throbbing muscle spasm. No one had to tell him. He knew what he needed to do. Andre looked at the nightstand and saw his gray carry tote, but his plastic urinal was missing. He widened his eyes and panicked. *Crap! It's in the bathroom.*

Andre dragged his wheelchair closer to the bedside and tucked the wooden slide board under his buttocks. He flared his nostrils and tightened his lips as he gradually transferred from the bed into his wheelchair. The struggle took a good five minutes before he got seated and always annoyed him, but it wasn't the time to get upset. Andre leaned to the side and pulled the board from under him. He set his gray pouch of supplies in his lap.

Feeling dampness on the crotch of his burgundy pajamas, he realized he suffered minor leakage in his sleep. Andre rolled his eyes and sighed. *You idiot! I'm such a loser.* He hated having to use a catheter, but it was the only way he could control his bladder. He searched around if there was another container to use.

Nothing.

Andre wheeled himself out of the guest room, careful not to scuff the off-white drywall in the hallway.

Skye entered through the front door right on time.

Andre brightened. "Good morning."

Skye grinned. "Morning, Andre."

"Hey, my urinal's in the bathroom," Andre said glumly. "Can you get it for me, please?"

"Sure." Skye ran up the staircase.

Andre cupped his hands around his mouth and shouted upstairs. "And make it quick!" He thought he would die from his embarrassment. Andre rubbed his forehead, trying to keep from stressing so much. He wished there was more than one bathroom in the house. Holding his water too long was a health risk to his system, and as Eva said, the last thing he needed was another medical problem. He overheard Skye excuse himself from Mrs. Flowers who was giving Andrew his bath.

"I got it!" Skye hurled downstairs with the container and handed it to Andre.

"Thanks." Andre took it from Skye and pushed himself back in the guest room, slamming the door. He wheeled himself close to the dresser, placed his gray tote on top, and fidgeted out his crucial supplies from the bag. His heart hammered in his chest, springing another leak. *Rats!*

"Are you okay, man?" Skye asked outside the door. "You need help?"

Andre hesitated. His eyes moistened as he rubbed on hand sanitizer. He attached his Velcro-strapped urinal on his chair between his inner thighs and clipped the Betty Hook to hold down his pants and boxers.

"I'm good!" Andre answered, though he wasn't positive he'd make it without wetting his wheelchair. He cleaned himself, quickly lubricated the catheter, and inserted it in. When he could finally relieve himself, he thought the flow would never stop. He closed his eyes and felt a tear slip down his cheek. *Why do I have to be like this? It's not fair.* One special night had ruined his life forever. Was he cursed? Was God punishing him for his workaholic mindset? Was he afflicted to spend more time with his wife?

If this was why he suffered so, he was sorry from the depth of his soul. As his bladder emptied, the spasm throbbed less and Andre sighed with relief, fluttering open his eyes. Why hadn't he listened to Eva's advice? She told him constantly to keep his urinal with him downstairs, but he was hardheaded and didn't listen. For now on, he would guard it with his life, or one day he may completely wet himself or suffer from kidney malfunction. Andre sniffled and dried his cheek with the knuckle of his forefinger. These times were always uncomfortable to him, despite not feeling it.

Andre slid out the catheter, cleaned himself, put the wipe in the torn pack, and pulled up his pants. He rubbed more sanitizer on his hands and paused, studying the young man in his reflection of the dresser's mirror. Since his tragic accident, he'd completely lost interest in physical intimacy, and in his condition now, he wasn't sure he could anymore.

It was the main reason he worried about losing his wife. If he couldn't satisfy her sex life, would Eva still love him? He knew she was lonely during his depressed state, and with her late returns from college, he feared she was having a secret affair.

Remorse collapsed on him. He buried his face in his hands and sobbed, recalling his past mistakes. *Please, forgive me, God.* They had wanted another baby, but he constantly made excuses and prevented them from doing so. After the birth of their son, out of fear and lack of faith he couldn't take a hopeful chance. Now he faced possibly never having another child with his wife again.

Skye knocked on the door, startling him. "Hey, Andre, are you finished?"

"Oh, yes! I'm done!" Andre swiped a fist over his teary eyes, rolled his wheelchair over, and opened the door.

"Feeling better?" Skye wore a silly grin.

Andre tittered and handed over his plastic container. "Yeah, relieved."

"I'll be right back." Skye took the urinal upstairs to the bathroom.

Andre facepalmed and sighed. *I'm so sorry, Eva. I love you so much.*

IT WAS THREE-THIRTY IN THE AFTERNOON.

306

Andre held the bridge of his nose and blinked slowly. He and Skye were playing a game of checkers on a side table. Mrs. Flowers was knitting socks and watching the news. On the television, the weatherman was reporting a severe thunderstorm expected to bring ice pellets tonight. Andre watched as Skye double-jumped a black chip on the checkered board, stealing his last red chip.

"Booyah! I win again." Skye's smiled faded, looking at Andre. "Hey, dude, you okay?"

Andre nodded and fluttered his eyelids. "Uh, yeah . . . I'm just tired."

"It's probably from your exercising," Skye said. "Do you want me to help you upstairs for a nap?"

"Yes, please," Andre replied, but he doubted he'd be able to sleep. He pushed his wheelchair to the staircase and lowered his footrests. Skye helped him into the seat of the stair lift and operated the lever. Andre rose over the flight of stairs. After he reached the top, Skye carried Andre's manual wheelchair upstairs and helped him into it.

"Thanks, Skye," Andre said. "I've got it from here." Being accustomed with using his slide board, he could get in and out of bed himself. As Skye went downstairs, Andre wheeled to Andrew's bedroom and stopped himself.

He pushed back the door and rolled inside to the white crib. It was the first time he entered his son's room after coming home from his grandpa's farm. His fatherhood hit home as he surveyed the childlike environment, and he desired to be the best dad he could be with his new life. He looked through the safety rail bars, checking on his son.

The cute little boy was resting with his stuffed, brown monkey under his arm, snuggled in his Cookie Monster fleece blanket. His small body rose and fell peacefully, taking a nap after whining and crying all day. An hour ago, he held and rocked Andrew in the tan recliner in the living room, putting him to sleep. Mrs. Flowers had tried to calm him, but apparently, he wanted his daddy's touch this time.

Holding Andrew was magical and brought joy to his soul. He wished he could stop the pain of his son's teething, but he knew it was a part of him growing up. Andrew's baby years were fading away quickly. Eva had already begun potty-training their son and Andre yearned for the several months he lost bonding with him. Spring around the corner, he and Eva made early plans for their son's third birthday, deciding on a Sesame Street theme.

Andrew was a special gift.

Even in his dazed state, the kid's contagious smile had moved his heart. But he didn't feel qualified to be a father then, plus he had lost track of what a father was. Now aware, he wanted to stay involved in Andrew's life.

He wanted to play catch with his son on hot, summer days, and have snowball fights on cold, winter evenings. He wanted to read him bedtime stories, send him off on his first day of kindergarten, and someday watch him marry the woman of his dreams.

Andre reached between the safety bars and held Andrew's hand, stroking his thumb over his son's tiny fingers. Tears shimmered in his eyes as he made a heavy sigh. Thinking of another man taking his wife and raising his son stirred his spirit.

He licked a tear that fell on his lips and whispered, "Daddy's been missing for some time, but I want you to know . . . I love you, Andy. I promise . . . nobody will take you from me."

"Nobody," he whispered with more vigor. He narrowed his eyes and set his mouth in a hard line. As he studied his son, worry swept over him. He released his son's hand and pondered over his sudden apprehension. A still voice spoke to him. *Pray for your wife.* His breath quickened, and the urge became stronger. *Pray for Eva now!*

Andre hadn't prayed for the longest, but he believed God enough to know it was Him who strengthened and spared one's life. He bowed his head. *Okay, Lord. I'll pray.* He clasped his hands and let out a slow breath. "Dear God, please help my wife. Let her stand her ground and protect her from the attack of the enemy. Please . . . don't let her leave me." He felt tears pouring down his cheeks and sniffled. "Please, forgive me for not being there for Eva like I should have. Renew her love for the man I am . . . not for the man I was. Restore my strength . . . help me on my feet again. In Jesus Christ's name . . . amen."

He opened his eyes, his tears dripping from his chin onto his red San Francisco 49ers sweatshirt. Andre exhaled and wiped them away. Eva was off from work, but he got a hunch she had other plans before coming home.

She was going to see Caleb.

39

Eva

BYE, LOUISE! HAVE A GOOD EVENING!" EVA SMILED and waved at her co-worker in the jam-packed parking lot behind the daycare building. She settled in her car and cranked the engine. Within seconds, the bridge of CeCe Winans' hit song "Never Have to Be Alone" blasted through her car speakers, staggering her. She had forgotten she turned on her radio. Eva decreased the volume and sat listening to the song's ending.

She held her steering wheel and hung her head. The lyrics were counsel to her heart and soul, both about her relationship with God and her marriage to her husband. If she had stayed patient and relied on the Lord for comfort through her difficult time, she wouldn't have gotten in an emotional mess.

And though she had been fond of Caleb, it was Andre who had always been her main man. She had lost hope there was anything left of the man she had married, but yesterday proved Mrs. Flowers was right about him showing up someday. Andre was her soulmate who had led her to the love of God and cherished her before she was aware.

Suffering from memory loss, it surprised her he cooked Italian lasagna, her favorite pasta. She wondered if her husband remembered her but considering he couldn't recall any photos she showed from his past, she thought it was a coincidence. A female radio announcer stated Fred Hammond's "I Will Trust" as the next song for the gospel station, but Eva turned off the radio. She exhaled a breath, pulled out of the lot, and turned her gearshift into drive, cruising out the sloped entrance of the daycare.

Her mind spun with anxious thoughts as she rode to meet Caleb at the town park. He had called her while she was at work in the middle of her lesson plan with her class again, asking if she was still meeting him. She told him she was, and his joyous reaction made her more nervous.

He was totally unaware of her purpose for coming to speak with him, but he was about to learn the truth. Eva regretted the camaraderie she built with him over the months. It made ending their company more challenging, and she prayed he'd be able to take another woman's rejection.

Eva pulled along the sidewalk a little distance away from the park.

Caleb was sitting on a wood bench in his tan trench coat and black gloves, resting one arm on top the backrest. He eyed Eva with his wide grin and waved.

A shiver ran through Eva. She exhaled and put her car into park. Turning away from Caleb was the right thing to do. Besides, having another man in her heart, she'd never be satisfied with him, even if she wanted to swap into a brand-new relationship. Eva got out of her car and stepped on the sidewalk caked with ice.

She strode toward Caleb, her suede boots clacking on the pavement. The town park was a winter wonderland. Icicles dangled from bare oak trees and the center pond and water fountain had crystallized with sugary frost. Piles of snow surrounded the open field and naked grassy patches had discolored to a dried, crisp brown.

But the park still tugged Eva's heartstrings.

Years ago, she and Andre had their wedding day in this same place. She pictured the decorations, the guests, and the sounds from the events: the rows of black folding chairs in the healthy green lawn, the white rose altar where Andre and the pastor stood, the mossy trail sprinkled with rose petals, and the soft piano music playing as she walked the aisle. There were many memories here. How could she ever forget them?

Eva perched on the park bench.

"Hey, I'm glad you're here," Caleb finally said.

She gave a weak smile. "Hey."

Caleb sat squarely facing her. His forehead wrinkled. "Eva, I have to tell you something, and I need you to really listen."

Eva nibbled her lip. "Before you speak, I have something to say too."

"Alright, fine," Caleb said, "but can I go first? It was my request for us to meet here."

She made a slight nod. "Okay . . . what is it?"

"Eva . . . we've spent much time together," Caleb began. "And I know this may be sudden, but we've also known each other for a long time. We grew up together." He dug in a coat pocket and took out a small velvet box.

Eva's heart shuddered. For a guy who had been a player in the past, she knew where his conversation was drifting.

"I know you're skeptical of these, but maybe it'll show how much you mean to me." Caleb opened the tiny box.

A ring lodged in the black interior velvet sparkled in the afternoon sun.

Caleb met her eyes. "Eva, I know what I said before about us being just friends, but the truth is, I love you. I think about you every day. I'll be honored if you become my wife. We have much in common with design. Andrew's gotten used to to me, and I'll treat him as my own son. I'll take care of you two, and we can be happy together. Andre hasn't been too kind to you, but I promise to treat you well always. Will you marry me?"

Like a whisper, Mrs. Flowers' words spoke to her: *True love never dies.* For so long, she had tried to discard her love for Andre and replace her heartache over him with her attention and company with Caleb, but it hadn't worked. It hadn't resolved the question embedded in her mind since the downfall began of Andre's health and outlook on life. How could she divorce her husband when his brain injury and the emotional strain it caused on their marriage was neither of their faults?

Eva's mouth hung open, glancing from the fourteen-carat gold diamond ring to Caleb's face again. She had to admit the ring was beautiful, but she couldn't agree with the proposal. "I'm sorry, but I can't accept your ring nor marry you." She stood on her feet, her heart pounding.

Caleb frowned at her. "Why not? You enjoyed the times we spent together."

"Not entirely," Eva confessed and wrapped her arms around herself.

"What are you talking about?" Caleb stood.

Eva sighed and shook her head. "I gotta be honest here . . . I wanted to forget Andre and our marriage the way he had done me and our son, but whenever I hung out with you, I thought about the life we had and our memories." She turned her face away. "And it doesn't make sense why you're so interested in me either. You never paid attention to me in school, except if you needed help with your homework."

313

"I wanted to, Eva. Believe me," Caleb said with a sobered expression.

Eva gave him a stern look. "Then why didn't you? Was it because I wasn't pretty enough then?"

"No," Caleb said and angled his head. "I had . . . a reputation. I was the point guard of the boys' basketball team. You know how that goes in high school."

Eva grimaced and hissed. "Yeah . . . the popular kids ignore the outcasts." She crossed her arms and inched backward. "I wanted to give you the benefit of the doubt, but now thinking about it, I believe it's true. Andre told me you said cruel things to him."

"That's a dead lie!" Caleb shouted.

"Is it?" Eva retorted. "Andre never lied to me. He always told me the truth, even if it hurts."

She spoke straightforwardly. "Look, I appreciate your help and encouragement with interior design, but I never intended for us to be more than friends. Maybe I should've told you sooner, but I guess I was fascinated a little by your attraction in me, especially since I wasn't expecting it."

She inhaled a breath and looked him in the eye. "I'm sorry, Caleb, but I won't be seeing you anymore, and I'd appreciate it if you stop following me around. I don't want the police involved in this. I'd rather we go our separate ways in peace."

Caleb pursed his lips and held out his arms like a gangster. "Fine! Stay with your stupid, crippled husband!"

"Don't call him that!" Eva's eyes filled with tears. "Maybe he can't walk, but he's more of a man than you'll ever be!"

Caleb's expression hardened, his eyes as sharp as daggers. He bit his lower lip and gave her an once-over she felt like seeped through her clothes. "We'll see about that, won't we?"

Eva wore a haunted look and slowly backed from him as he tucked the ring box in his coat pocket, frightened of his intentions. Witnessing his sudden change from a saint to a savage, a veil of portrayal had been pulled off of Caleb, and his rotten character had been exposed. As she ran away down the sidewalk, he cupped his hands over his mouth and yelled a boastful remark.

"I'm gonna getcha, Eva! 'The CW' always gets what he wants!" Caleb said and chortled. He trailed behind and harassed her with vain fantasies of their togetherness, embarrassing her in public.

"Get lost and leave me alone!" Eva's heart raced in her chest, trotting as fast as she could to her car. Her throat clenched, her heart overflowed with remorse and a fresh love for her husband. Andre was right about Caleb. He was as dangerous as a ticking time bomb, and she should've reported him earlier to police. She needed to go to Andre and apologize for nearly allowing temptation to overpower her.

He was her husband until death, and regardless of his brain injury, memory loss, and his below-average attitude at times, she was still in love with him. His willingness to return home and spend time with their son and his kind actions toward her lately proved he was trying to make amends. Their marriage won't be the same again, but she believed they could reconcile and make new, wonderful memories with their son in the present and future.

After all, it was what Eva always wanted from the start.

40

Eva

EVA JOGGED TOWARD THE HOUSE AND BARGED through the front door. She found Mrs. Flowers and Skye in the living room on the couch, watching an update on the approaching ice storm. She shivered and caught her breath. "Where's Andre?"

Skye twitched his mouth, holding the remote. "He's upstairs."

"How is he?" Eva glanced at Skye and Mrs. Flowers.

"Not too good," Mrs. Flowers said, focused on her stitches.

Skye nodded. "Yeah. He skipped breakfast and lunch today."

Eva ran up the staircase to the second floor and peeked into Andrew's bedroom, calling her husband's name. Andre wasn't in there, but their son was still asleep in his crib.

She continued down the narrow hallway, checking the bathroom and then the master bedroom. Her husband was in the master room in his manual wheelchair. He was looking outside the curtained window behind the bed at the dark, cloudy sky. Since daylight saving time began, it already looked like it was night by the time she came home from work.

"Andre?"

Her husband turned his head and faced her with a hangdog expression.

Guilt dropped on her heart from his unhappy face. She scurried over and knelt before him. Her vision clouded with new tears, holding her husband's hands.

Eva gulped and studied his eyes. "Andre, I'm so sorry. I'm sorry for spending time with another man behind your back. I thought my crush on Caleb was over, but temptation had a grip on me. I almost . . . I . . ." Eva rested her forehead on Andre's knees and closed her eyes. Her shoulders bobbed from stifled sobs. "Please, forgive me."

She felt Andre stroke his hand over her wavy, shoulder-length hair.

"I forgive you," Andre said, "and I'm sorry too. Everything wasn't your fault. You were trying to help me, and I made things harder than they had to be. I was trying to get you to give up. I didn't think you deserved a burden like me."

Eva raised her head and frowned. "Andre Miguel Lucas, how many times have I told you? You're not a burden, and I know you'll get better as time progresses."

Andre's chin quivered. "I'm sorry . . . I'm like this, Eva. I'm sorry . . . I'm half a man."

"Oh, Andre, you're not half a man," Eva said. "You're whole and complete." She placed her hand over his chest. "You have a good heart." Her face contorted with sorrow as her husband broke down. She always hated seeing him cry, but it was a breaking point he needed to reach—a release of

317

the pain and grief he had caged inside for a life he no longer had. She cradled his bowed head and planted affectionate kisses over his shaved haircut.

Andre lifted his face and held her hands, stroking his thumbs over her knuckles. "I'm sorry. I wasn't there for you. I wasn't a bit supportive of your pain or feelings. All I cared about was myself."

"It's okay." Eva stood and hugged him. "We can work things out. I understand you've been distressed and scared about the medicine, but maybe—"

Andre nodded and wrapped his arms around her. "It's okay. I'd rather take meds than lose you." He whispered in her ear, "I love you . . . Eva Rose."

"I love you—wait." Eva sat on his lap and wove her arms around his shoulders. She searched his eyes. "Rose . . . you said Rose. How did you know my middle name?" Her breaths quickened, flabbergasted. "Andre?"

Her husband gulped and looked down. "My memory . . . partially returned. I don't remember everything, just who my loved ones are and a little about their backgrounds. It's how I knew lasagna was your favorite pasta meal. Recently, I've been taking an antidepressant Dr. Brown prescribed me, and it's been helping too."

"Why didn't you tell me this?" Tears ran down Eva's cheeks.

Andre licked his lips and sniffled. "Due to your company with Caleb, I wanted to make sure you stay because you love me, and I also wanted to surprise you. Skye and everyone else knew for a while. I'm sorry I kept everything secret. Do you . . . do you forgive me?"

Eva smiled tenderly. "Of course, I forgive you."

Her husband wore a lopsided grin. He framed her face in his hand and dried a tear on her cheek with his thumb. "Thank you for being my wife and friend, and staying by my side . . . even when I didn't want you to." His chin trembled again. "I felt lost and confused for so long. I can't believe I forgot you. I pray I never forget you again. I love you so much, Eva."

"I love you too, Andre," Eva said.

They leaned their foreheads against each other, gazing in each other's eyes. After being distant over a year in their house, they surrendered to love and shared a gentle kiss. As their lips touched, Eva opened her eyes and saw Skye stroll in on them from her peripheral vision. She gasped and leaped from Andre's lap, turning her attention to him.

"Oops, sorry. Maybe I should've knocked." Skye held out his hands and shrugged.

Eva swiped moisture beneath her eyes and gave a wry smile. "That would've been polite of you, but since the door was open, I don't blame you for coming straight in. What is it, Skye?"

"It's my payday. Every two weeks, remember?" Skye flexed his brows and gave a dopey grin that showed his chipped tooth.

"Oh, sorry." Eva chuckled, took her checkbook out her purse on the dresser, and wrote Skye a check for his weekly wages. She ripped the check strip and handed it to him. "Here, I forgot again."

"Yeah," Skye joked, "I can see why." He glanced from Andre to her.

Eva giggled and blushed, while Andre shyly smiled and looked away, rubbing his nose with his forefinger.

"Well, thanks for the check. Catch y'all later. Good night, lovebirds." Skye snickered and walked out of the room.

Eva put her checkbook in her purse and clipped it, standing in front of Andre. "Um, well, I'm gonna go tend to Andy." She backed away from her husband as if it pained her to leave him, bumping into the chest at the end of the bed.

"Okay," Andre said and quirked up another smile.

Eva walked out of the bedroom and entered back in

Andrew's room. The little boy whined from his nap and squirmed under his blanket as she reached his white crib. "Hey, baby. Mommy's home. You feel all right?" She lifted him in her arms and felt his forehead with the back of her hand.

He was still running a fever.

Eva frowned. "Uh-oh. You're burning up?"

Andrew moaned and rubbed his left eye with his small fist.

"Mrs. Flowers! Are you still here?" Eva called.

"Coming!"

Eva listened as Mrs. Flowers came upstairs and entered Andrew's bedroom. "Has Andy had medicine today?" she asked.

"Mm-hmm, around eleven," Mrs. Flowers said. "About an hour after lunch, Andre rocked him in the recliner and he's been asleep for a good while until you came home."

"Hmm, that was four hours ago." Eva looked at Andrew. "Come on, honey. Let me get you more medicine." She took Mookie from the crib, gave the stuffed monkey to her son, and toted him out of his room to the bathroom. Eva grabbed a bottle of Children's Tylenol from the medicine cabinet.

She put the lid of the toilet down, sat on top with Andrew on her lap, and poured an amount of medicine in the plastic cup. "Here you go, Andy. Maybe more medicine will help bring your fever down." She put the cup to her son's mouth and helped him drink. Luckily, Andrew liked the taste of medicine and swallowed it like juice.

Eva smiled and placed the cup on the sink counter.

"Well, I'm going home now," Mrs. Flowers said.

Eva rocked Andrew. "Okay. Thanks for babysitting."

"You're welcome, hon." Mrs. Flowers smiled at the little boy in Eva's arms. "Bye, Andy. Hopefully, you feel better tomorrow."

"I'm sure he will." Eva put a hand on Andrew's chin and opened his mouth, peeking inside. "Both of his lower second molars are almost in, especially the right one."

Mrs. Flowers hummed and waved a hand. "Little Andy's growing up."

"He sure is." Eva chuckled and grinned.

"Well, I'll see y'all later, but let me know if you need anything," Mrs. Flowers said. "I'm a knock or phone call away."

"Okay, thanks," Eva said.

Mrs. Flowers tapped the doorframe and waddled down the hallway, saying goodbye to Andre.

"Goodbye, Mrs. Flowers!" Andre replied from the master bedroom.

Eva stood and adjusted Andrew on her hip. "Come on, baby. Let's get you some chicken noodle soup." She ambled out of the bathroom and went downstairs to the kitchen.

After Andrew was fed, changed into his PJs, and put to bed, Eva and Andre ate leftover lasagna for dinner in the kitchen and talked about their day. Andre told about his embarrassing incident in the morning. Eva sighed and placed her fork on her plate but didn't bother hounding him too much about it.

When he finished, she discussed her hectic work shift in the daycare. A new boy named Rodney had colored the walls with crayons and yanked a handful of his hair off his head. As she shared about her day, Andre snickered, and she couldn't resist laughing too.

But the atmosphere changed when she talked about Caleb and what happened at the park. Andre advised Eva to file a report, deactivate her social accounts, and change her cell number, which she did after dinner.

Fear chilled her soul, worrying about what Caleb had in mind. Discovering she spent the months with a man who was actually a liar and a compulsive jerk made her skin crawl. It turned out the star basketball player she secretly

admired wasn't as charming as she thought.
He was a monster in disguise.

41

Andre

ANDRE PULLED OFF HIS SAN FRANCISCO 49ERS SWEATSHIRT over his head as Eva leaned against the doorframe of the guest room in her robe.

"Hey, I have room for two. Do you wanna sleep on the queen bed with me?" she said.

Andre slipped his left arm in a sleeve of a satin, green pajama shirt and glanced at her. Heat tiptoed up his spine from her fixed look. He gulped and put his other arm in his shirt, adjusting the collar. "I'm fine in here."

"Can I join you?" Eva asked and drew nearer.

Andre gave a shy smile, fastening his shirt with a buttoning tool. He sighed and wrinkled his face, frustrated with his low hand dexterity. "You don't have to," he said with a shrug.

His nerves bothered him from her unexpected presence. Spending the night in the same bed with her felt like a corny joke. With his knobby knees, flimsy legs, and limp wrists, he didn't feel too attractive.

Andre lowered his head, fidgeting with his nightshirt.

Some things still challenges for him, he dreaded having anyone watch him struggling with simple doings. Andre looked up with shock as Eva closed the guest room door and untied her robe.

As soon as she slipped it off, his cheeks flushed and his heartbeat sped up. She was adorned in a dark, silvery, silk-and-lace lingerie gown, which showed off her smooth, olive skin and graceful figure. She hung her robe on a hook behind the door and undid her side bun to let her wavy, black hair fall down her shoulders.

Andre stared speechless at her as she walked to him, unable to look away.

Eva climbed onto the bed and sat on his left side close against the plain white wall. She pulled back the blue-rose comforter and tucked herself underneath.

"W-what are you doing?" Andre stuttered and blinked in disbelief.

His wife cradled his face in her hands and planted a long, tender kiss on his lips.

Andre closed his eyes and melted in her affection, all his lingering thoughts of doubt vanishing away. He looked in her tearful eyes as their lips slowly broke.

Eva mustered a smile and followed his gaze. "If you're staying in here, I am too. From now on, we're sharing the same bedroom. I love you so much, Andre. I'm gonna keep saying it until you get it through your thick head." She knocked her knuckles on a side of Andre's noggin, making him chuckle. "Now, let's get some sleep, okay?"

"Okay," Andre whispered lovingly. A corner of his mouth lifted as he flicked off the lamp on the nightstand and rested his head on his pillow.

Eva cuddled her slender, petite body closer to him and laid her head on his chest, wrapping an arm around his waist.

"Good night, Andre." His wife sighed, approaching sleep.

Andre kissed her forehead and ran his fingers through the waves of her hair. "Eva?"

"Mm-hmm," she answered drowsily.

He swallowed hard. "Uh, if I can't . . . if I can't, you know, perform, will you still love me?"

Eva shifted and sat up, looking over him in the dimly lit room. "Of course, Andre. Our love goes far beyond physical intimacy."

Andre sighed with relief, and then recalled how things were before. "But we had plans for another baby. What if I can't—?"

"Shh . . ." His wife placed her index finger over his lips. "Don't worry about it. If we run into difficulties, I'm sure there is medical help out there for us, if we need it. No matter what happens I'll always love you. Now, let's take things slowly and get some rest, okay?" She laid her head back on his chest and embraced his waist again.

"But I had this dream—"

"Andre," Eva interrupted and kissed his cheek. "Please, go to sleep."

Andre sighed. "Okay, sorry. Sweet dreams, Eva." Hearing her light breaths and feeling the rise and fall of her body against his, he knew she fell asleep. He held her close and sighed, thankful for the new bridge they had begun to build in their marriage and to know how much Eva loved him.

Crying for the past wasn't easy, but he felt better after finally letting out his feelings. Maybe he'd never recall all the memories of his former life, but there were things he would remember. He would remember how amazing his wife looked in her pretty nightwear, the passionate kiss she'd given him, and how good it felt to hold Mrs. Eva Rose Lucas under his arm.

42

Eva

THUNDER CLASHED AND ICE PELLETS TAPPED THE roof of their house.

Eva awoke from her sleep to Andrew crying in his bedroom. He was terrified of thunder, and his teething and fever added to it was a terrible combination. She rose in the guest room, and Andre jerked out of his sleep with a gasp, feeling her presence leave him. She stirred to her husband and studied his face, seeing the fear in his stretched wide eyes.

"Andy's up. I'll be right back," Eva said. "I'm gonna go check on him. You can go back to sleep." She climbed out of the bed, but Andre grasped her arm, stopping her departure.

He rose in bed to a sitting position. "No, I'll wait for you in my wheelchair." Lightning flashed and cast shadows of the dresser and blue reading chair on the white wall.

"Okay." Eva smiled and stroked his jaw. She grabbed her robe from the door, slipped it on, and tied the waist belt. "I'll be right back," she said again, trying to reassure him. She opened the door and glanced back at him with another smile. A flash of bright lightning struck, her petite silhouette gliding across the wall beside the bed as she exited the room. Booms of thunder followed her as she tiptoed down the dark hall.

Eva entered her son's bedroom and found the little boy standing in his crib, gripping the bar railing.

"Shh, it's okay, Andy," Eva whispered. "It's just a storm." She picked up Andrew and rubbed his back. She felt his forehead, which was still pretty warm to the touch. "The storm will be over soon. Now you be a big boy, okay? I'm gonna get you some juice to help cool your fever."

Eva rubbed Andrew's head and kissed his forehead. She sat her son in his crib and placed his plush, brown monkey in his arms for comfort. "Keep Mookie with you. Mommy will be right back." In the refrigerator she filled Andrew's sippy cups with apple and grape juice, making sure he had plenty of fluids for his fever to drink. Eva left her son's bedroom and traveled the rest of the way to the staircase.

Outside the freezing rain pitter-pattered and whistling wind crackled the branches of the tree in the driveway. Eva crept downstairs to the living room. She couldn't wait to go back upstairs to the safety of her husband's arms. Darkness followed her wherever she went like a prowling beast. She groped on the marble counter and realized she finally made it to the kitchen.

Eva grabbed a sippy cup of apple juice from the fridge and turned around, bumping into Caleb. She gasped and dropped her son's sippy cup on the floor.

"Hello, Eva," Caleb slurred, standing in front of her in the unlit kitchen. A burst of light flickered and revealed him dressed in black. He wore a sneaky grin spread across his face.

"What are you doing here?" Eva shrank back against the cool refrigerator.

"What else? I came for you." Caleb gazed in her eyes. "You're the most . . . gorgeous woman I've ever seen. I hadn't forgotten the feel of your lips on my cheek. I'll be leaving soon, but I had to see you again."

Eva drew a deep, nervous breath. "Caleb, you need to go." She called for her husband.

"Why are you so cold now?" Caleb glared at her. "We're friends, Eva. Good friends..." He held the s of 'friends' longer than needed.

Eva's defenses rose. "Not anymore. I want you outta here now!"

"Come on, don't be like that. Gimme a kiss, Eva. Please, just one." Caleb leaned his body against hers and she smelt the fruit brandy from his breath. "You know you want me," he whispered in her ear, running his fingers through her raven-black hair.

Her heart drummed in her chest, squirming to escape him. "No, I don't! Andre, hel—"

Caleb snatched her face in his hands and forced a harsh kiss on her.

Eva slapped his face, and his strong hands clutched her slender neck quicker than she could blink, cutting off her airway.

"Oh, Eva . . . why'd you do that? I was trying to be nice. If I can't have you . . . nobody will. I'm gonna have to kill you, and then . . . your baby." Frustration eclipsed Caleb. His eyes pooled, gritting his teeth. "I gave you my heart . . . and you . . . you broke it to pieces."

Adrenaline pumped through Eva's body, clawing his hands for air. Her body shuddered with each second as her oxygen became shallower. More lightning flashed, and she felt her life slipping out of her. She thought about her husband Andre, the time she'd wasted, and the truth in her heart she'd known all along. She thought about her precious son Andrew, and his innocent life being stolen after she was gone. How could Caleb do such a horrible thing?

She accepted the mistake she made but killing her wouldn't make matters better. Her mind reflected on her mother who'd flown away after they'd gotten on good terms. For Mother's Day, they made plans to visit the spa and go shopping together, but in a no-win situation, it was nothing more than a wish.

Eva stared in Caleb's fierce eyes, convinced of her fate from her circumstance. What could her husband or son do? Andre was paralyzed, and Andrew was cranky and too young to fight. Having the odds against her, only one possible outcome came to her mind.

This was the way she would die.

43

Andre

I'M COMING, EVA!" ANDRE SAID, ROLLING DOWN THE narrow hallway in his wheelchair. He had messed up too often with not being there when his wife needed him, and he would not do it again. His heart kicked and his palms sweat, panicking over Eva's muffled scream. She was in danger. He'd known it would happen since the past year. His nightmare was a warning of an event to come, and now it was happening for real.

He was the only one who could save her.

Earsplitting thunder exploded and lighting flashed twice. Andre pushed himself through the darkness of the living room and arrived at the kitchen. Two dark forms were by the refrigerator. He heard Eva's dying gasps and Caleb's slurred speech.

Lightning flickered, and he saw his wife standing, a tall man strangling her to death. Andre widened his eyes and wanted to yell or flick on the light switch, but he figured it would've blown his cover. He lowered the footrests of his wheelchair and placed his hands on the leather armrests.

Andre lifted his head skyward. *God give me strength.* He pushed himself from his wheelchair and fought the burning pain of his legs. Supported by the counter, he stood, but walking was the tricky part. Andre took a step and felt his legs get weak. He gripped the counter and leaned forward against it, taking a long breath. *Come on, Andre. You gotta do it.* Andre straightened and limped over, sneaking behind Caleb's back.

"I hate to kill you, Eva, but you're too beautiful," Caleb slurred.

Andre growled and tugged on the man's shirt, but Caleb pushed him on the floor and continued choking Eva.

"Let her go!" Andre demanded, struggling to get back on his feet.

Caleb smirked and released his wife a few seconds after, confident she was already dead.

Unconscious, Eva slid down the refrigerator and collapsed on the linoleum floor.

Andre's heart broke at the sight of his wife. *No. Please, God, no . . .*

"You're too late, Andre," Caleb said and laughed.

Andre roared and watched as the man in black strode toward the patio door. With every fiber of his being, he pushed himself up from the floor and charged into Caleb like an angry bull at a rodeo, knocking him face down. The two men rolled and tussled in a wrestling match, each trying to win the upper hand.

Caleb dragged Andre to his feet, trapped in a standing rear choke. He grasped hold of Andre's arm, squatted, and threw him over to break free. Then he kicked Andre in his face and chest. As Andre turned over with a groan and held his side, Caleb drew a butcher knife from a wooden block on the counter. He rushed to stab Andre in his back, but somebody walloped him, and he and the knife dropped to the floor.

The light switched on in the kitchen.

Kneeling, Andre looked over his shoulder. Behind him stood an elderly woman dressed in a clear raincoat over a butterfly-print housecoat with rubber boots. Her gray hair was set in pink curlers and she held a cast iron frying pan.

"Thank you, Mrs. Flowers," Andre said with an arm around his waist, wincing in pain.

"Any time." Mrs. Flowers raised her chin and nodded. "I saw him break in from next door and called 911."

"Police!" a duo of officers called and knocked.

"I'll get it." Mrs. Flowers glanced from her skillet to Caleb. "Y'all are safe now. He'll be out for a little while. This pan is the best iron skillet one can have." She nodded and added with a grin, "Fries chicken quick in it too."

Andre gave the old woman a hint of a smile.

"Let me get the front door." Mrs. Flowers left.

"Eva . . ." Andre dragged himself over to his wife, crawling up to her with his arm. *Please, God, let her be all right.* He sniffled and his chin quivered as unshed tears stung his eyes.

The skin color of her face drained and her eyelids were dark and closed. Finger marks streaked her neck from Caleb's violent hold, and the thought he lost her laid heavy on his heart.

Andre hung his head and whimpered, brushing her hair back with his hand. Just as his nightmare, Eva had gotten bitten by a snake. He looked up as a sergeant policeman and Lt. Greg McKee walked into the kitchen with Mrs. Flowers.

"Officers, there's the man . . . the one in the black." Mrs. Flowers grimaced and pointed at Caleb as he was waking from her hit.

"Alright, you, get up!" The sergeant arrested Caleb with his hands behind him and read him his rights, leading him outside.

"I'll go get Andy." Mrs. Flowers walked from the kitchen and headed upstairs.

"My wife . . . please, help her," Andre said weakly.

Greg knelt down at Eva and checked for signs of life as Andre fearfully watched. He rested her head and tilted her chin to open her airway.

The lieutenant met his eyes. "She's breathing, but barely."

Thank God. Andre sighed with relief.

"Keep her still. We'll call in an ambulance." Greg placed Eva in a recovery position, laying her on her side.

Andre nodded. "Thank you, sir." He leaned his head against the refrigerator and sat beside his wife, grateful to be loved and alive.

EPILOGUE

I T WAS MY FAULT," EVA SAID, SHADING THE WARM SUN from her eyes. She peered at Mrs. Flowers in their backyard, who was pushing Andrew on his Little Tikes swing set. After testifying in court and Caleb was convicted, she hadn't spoken about her strangulation incident, but she managed to complete her first college semester and was well on her way to becoming a certified interior designer.

Andre placed an armful of Sesame Street-themed gifts on the umbrella picnic table on the patio and limped over to her. By the middle of March, he was walking fairly well again. Yesterday he donated his wheelchairs to his co-worker Karen's teenage son who suffered a spinal cord injury after being struck by a drunk driver. Grandpa Ricardo had passed away, but his legacy of fresh sweet corn lived on as Andre and the hired hands continued working on the farm.

He hugged Eva from behind. "Eva, you can't blame yourself for a man trying to force his affection on you. Maybe it was late, but you told Caleb how you felt and he just couldn't take your rejection. It wasn't your fault." He kissed her cheek.

Eva loosened his arms from her waist, and turned to face him. "Yes, it was—"she glanced at her wedge sandals— "if I hadn't gone to my class reunion, Caleb would've never seen me, and none of it would've ever happened." She leaned her forehead against her husband's chest, fidgeting with the clear buttons of his orange-and-blue Hawaiian shirt. "I don't deserve your love."

Her husband raised her chin with a crooked finger. "Grandpa Ricardo once said, 'Sometimes love isn't something one should have to earn to get.' Sometimes it's free."

A tiny butterfly fluttered past them.

Eva found a smile and felt her eyes get wet. She didn't know which Andre she loved better—the before or the after. She thanked God for this young man, the wisdom he had gotten from his grandpa, and having not only *who* she wanted, but also *what* she wanted in a husband.

"We can't change what already happened or predict what's ahead. All we can do is hope for the best and move forward," Andre added.

Eva embraced him and sighed. "I know, but I'm still scared. I'm afraid he'll come back." Using a crowbar, Caleb had easily broken into their old patio door.

She glanced at the new Innotech terrace swing door a specialist installed for them.

"There's no need to be. God will protect us," Andre said and wrapped his arms around her again. "Besides, he'll be in jail for a long while."

This was true.

Caleb was sentenced to fifteen years and denied parole by the judge. But Eva wasn't the only one responsible for him being behind bars. Tasha Burke and two other women also testified about Caleb's aggressive behavior and verbal abuse while they were engaged with him. Through tears, Caleb had confessed he was raised in an abusive household and saw his father beat his mother many times at home after school. "It was the norm," he said to the judge at the trial.

After his former breakups, he had reached an all-time low. Eva was his last resort, and being rejected by a woman who used to be infatuated with him caused Caleb to lose his mind. Ironically, now he was the one with the crush, only his developed into an obsession. His term in the Mount Road Correctional Institute would be a miserable reflection of bad choices, which started in childhood. Eva felt bad for him and prayed he would find redemption through the Lord during his sentence.

As the breeze blew, Andre swayed with her in his arms and whispered in her ear, "I won't let him hurt you."

Eva lifted her face and gave his waist a squeeze. She smiled. "Thanks, for looking out for me. I'm gonna put the candle in Andy's cake."

"Alright, I'll get the hotdogs for the grill," Andre said.

Eva gave her husband a smooch, and he returned the gesture with a grin. They cuddled and giggled. It had taken a lot of time and patience, but after tests and counsel with the doctor things were looking up for a second child, and the spark of romance had ignited back in their marriage.

Their hardship bloomed a positive effect on their relationship, and she was grateful for how much closer they had become. Still holding each other, they looked toward the patio door and saw Skye step outside on the brick courtyard. He wore lime-green star sunglasses and a party hat with sparkly fringe cocked on his head.

Skye blew a party horn. "Happy Birthday, Andy!" He played a German oom-pah song on the iPod clipped to his denim shorts and performed the Chicken Dance.

Eva and Andre laughed as Skye made chicken beaks with his hands, flapped his bent elbows, shook his hips, and clapped to the polka, accordion music.

Eva laughed. "Skye, you're too funny."

"Hey," Skye said and shrugged, turning off his iPod. "What can I say? I love birthdays." He removed his geeky sunglasses and hung them on the collar of his polo T-shirt.

"Well, I guess you wouldn't mind helping me with the grill," Andre said and winked.

A flush crept in Skye's face. "The grill?"

"That's right." Andre studied Skye's nervous expression. "Don't worry, I'm handling the cooking myself. You can clean the grill when I'm finished."

Skye grinned. "Okay. Sweet."

Andre slid back the patio door and walked in the house as Eva's mother came outside.

"Is the party still going on, or am I too late?" Her mom held a blue gift-wrapped present.

Eva took the gift from her mother and hugged her. "Hi, Mom. It's just beginning." She added her mom's present with Andy's other gifts. They squinted out at the backyard surrounded by a white picket fence. Mrs. Flowers was walking Andrew over by the hand across the bright green, grassy lawn to the umbrella patio table.

Her mother swatted at a buzzing bee and marveled at her grandson. "You know, I can't believe he's three. I still remember when he first learned to roll over."

"Me too." Eva beamed at her mom. "Time flies fast, doesn't it?" She stuck a number three candle in the Cookie Monster cake on the picnic table. It was a chocolate cake made with blue fondant coating and fluffy blue frosting for the fur. The cake decorator added chocolate chip cookies in the blue monster's mouth for a special finishing touch.

Eva lit the candle with a lighter.

"Okay, everyone! It's time to sing 'Happy Birthday' to Andy," she announced.

As everybody gathered around the table, Andre walked through the patio door with two packs of ballpark hotdogs. He placed them on the steel counter of the barbecue grill and snuck a spot in the group beside Eva, singing with the others to Andrew. After the song ended, everyone clapped for the three-year-old guest of honor.

Eva stood Andrew on the bench and looked at him in playful wonder. "Can you blow out the candle, Andy? Go ahead, blow it out."

Andrew puffed his cheeks and blew, but the flame wavered and straightened.

Some giggled.

"Try again, honey. You can do it," Eva said with a smile.

Andrew inhaled deeply and blew again. A puff of smoke vanished in the light wind. Everyone cheered and clapped for him again.

Eva and her husband exchanged smiles, and she knew in her heart this was the life she was meant to have. Together they had gone through many stormy days, but as her mother said, the sun had shined again.

Their marriage hadn't been perfect, but there was a perfect God who had enough grace and forgiveness for their imperfections. However long He let them live, they would have, hold, and love each other for the rest of their lives.

Forever.

Acknowledgements

Firstly, I'd like to thank my Lord and Savior Jesus Christ for allowing me to write this novel and use my interest in writing to hopefully be an inspiration and encouragement to others. Publishing my own book has been a dream I've had since I was a little girl; and honestly, many times I thought I was fooling myself and that it would never come true.

Secondly, I'd like to thank my very first readers of my novel *With You Forever* on Inkitt who added this story to their reading lists and thought to give it a read, especially to usernames Nessa, Gumball, and Markusdoyle from Sweden, who was the few that commented or reviewed, and thought this was a great story. Getting feedback means a lot to us writers as sometimes we can feel like nobody cares about the stories we write, except ourselves.

Thirdly, I'd like to thank different members of the writing community for their pep talks and helpful tips of the craft of writing. Though I don't know y'all personally, your videos or online posts are appreciated and some of the only encouragement I receive.

Fourthly, I'd like to thank HugeOrange for their reasonable editing services, and my editor from their company for reading my novel manuscript and giving me extra tips to improve my story.

I also would like to give a special thanks to Regina Boger for handcrafting the anniversary keychain of my characters and sending me pictures that I could use for my book cover design.

It really brought my story much more to life, and it's a memento that I can always keep as a reminder of this novel.

I'd also like to thank myself for not giving up on this story. Being a writer has its risks and challenges. Writing a book is a tough and sometimes daunting task that takes a lot of time and effort, but I worked hard, saved up my own money, and believed in myself to make my dream a reality.

Lastly, I'd like to thank my family, especially my Mom for listening to my moments of story inspiration and finding interest in them, and my older sister Rochelle for encouraging me that despite hard times of sacrifices I would eventually start getting my books out to the world.

AUTHOR'S NOTE:

Hello Readers,

Thank you for taking the time to read my debut novel *With You Forever*. I hope you enjoyed my book. Writing it wasn't easy. It was an emotional, complicated, and in some cases uncomfortable journey. I had to undergo much research for this novel and go through a couple of drafts before I was able to connect the dots in an efficient way.

As serious as brain injury is, I wanted to make Andre's medical diagnosis, his therapy, and his paralysis disability believable and other things, such as Eva's studies of Interior Design and Caleb's profession in real estate.

So, how did this story come about?

It came around March of 2016. The novel idea was vaguely a wife whose husband gets in a car accident and suffers a brain injury. Their names, the kind of injury the husband suffers, how the accident happens, and where they lived still wasn't too clear, but I knew the idea came for a reason and that it could make a great storyline. Afterward, I thought about a startling but common question: *What is true love? Is it merely telling someone, "I love you?"*

Love has been misinterpreted through the media and camouflaged as sex, money, or wealth for years. We see it every day, but true love has nothing to do with these things. True love comes from God, at least to me it does. Have you ever met someone having everything materialistic they could ever want, but they're still dissatisfied? It's because there is a void only God can fill. So many have lost their way despite all the possessions they had, searching for satisfaction from temporal things in *this* life.

And sadly, some have committed suicide, being unable to discover what they're missing.

Divorce rates are steady growing in the ordinary society and among celebrities in Hollywood. Among brain injury couples, divorce rates are also high; as such a tragedy can be an emotionally overwhelming experience. After brain injury, a spouse or loved one can become withdrawn, or even verbally or physically violent, behaviors which never existed in him or her pre-injury.

My character Andre is an example of this change. He was a friendly, outgoing person. But after his brain injury, he became aloof and withdrawn toward others, including his wife and stayed mostly indoors. According to studies, most brain injury couples that divorce is the result of the husband having been injured.

Therefore, I commend the women who chose to live and stay with to their injured husbands in this situation. I also commend couples who stuck with each other until death, regardless of whether they lived together their entire marriage or chose to live separately for whatever reason. Marriage vows are routinely said at weddings, but only a few actually live them out nowadays.

With You Forever is a novel that represents the meaning of true love and how God intended marriage principles to be from the beginning. It is also a story that shows the beauty in celibacy or abstinence before marriage, which sometimes is frowned upon. Many teenage girls and women feel like outcasts because of being inexperienced, which often results in unwed mothers having to take care of their children themselves.

Let me say to all the young, single girls and women out there: There is nothing wrong with you and it's okay to say no or wait until marriage for that *special* someone. You all are beautiful queens, and if anybody, you should be investing in kings. In other words, "Never settle for less when you deserve better."

My hope and prayer is that *With You Forever* will inspire many teenagers—both boys and girls—to not allow peer pressure to influence them. One of my favorite quotes is, "It's better to walk alone than in a crowd going in the wrong direction."

Maybe this book will prevent someone from becoming another statistic or help lower the teenage pregnancy rate. Maybe it will lessen married couples from getting a divorce over trivial reasons, or inspire a couple to work things out before deciding to go their separate ways.

Or maybe it will encourage or be a comfort to someone whose spouse or other relative has recently suffered a brain injury. I don't know, but I pray this novel blesses all those who read it and is a comfort and reminder that no matter what hardship one goes through, as Melanie said, "The sun will shine again."

Peace be unto you,

M. B.

Monroe, North Carolina
June 22, 2019

DISCUSSION QUESTIONS

What does Andre's birthmark represent about the origin of humanity from the days of Adam & Eve?

What perennial plant does Mrs. Flowers symbolize? And what comparisons of it are there to her personality and her as a widow?

Organ donation is a difficult and painful decision for families to make of their loved ones. Did Eva make the right choice concerning her husband's organs?

What is the meaning of Mrs. Flowers' quote, "True love never dies"? Why can't it ever end?

Toxic parent relationships can affect children later in their adulthood. Why did Eva feel guilty about pursuing her dream career?

What does the snowman in Eva and Andre's winter photo represent? Why was she so emotional about this particular picture?

How does the appearance of the vase of white roses and the town park relate to Eva and Andre's marriage over time?

What is true beauty?

After her own experience with Eva's father, why do you think Melanie worried about her daughter so much?

How are the changes of the seasons significant to the mood of the story?

Why do you think Eva ordered something different when she went out to dinner with Caleb?

How did Andre's nightmare make you feel? And what do you think the lava and stepping stones represents?

If Eva had suffered a car accident and brain injury, what do you think Andre would've done?

How do Andre and Caleb differ as men?

During a wedding, the priest usually says he's joining the couple into holy matrimony. What is a holy marriage?

What does Andre and his brain injury and the Thomas family shack have in common?

How does Andy's child development and Andre's recovery process relate?

What significant lesson did Andre learn about love as a result of his brain injury? What actions of Eva caused him to come to this understanding?

People change over time. What's ironic about Eva's love life compared to Caleb and some of her other classmates?

SIGN UP TO THE MONTHLY NEWSLETTER OR EMAIL LIST!

FOR BOOK RELEASES, FREE GIVEAWAYS, BOOK TRAILERS, DISCOUNTS, AND OTHER SPECIAL OFFERS AND INFO FROM THE AUTHOR:

www.mlbull.com

ABOUT THE AUTHOR

M.L. BULL lives in Monroe, North Carolina, but is from Salisbury, Maryland on the Eastern shore where she was born and raised. She is the youngest of three daughters and an aunt to one nephew. Her passion for writing started during fifth grade in elementary school, and she has enjoyed it since then.

Presently, she writes Christian and women's fiction stories based on characters who make serious changes in their lives through faith and determination, which she prays will encourage and inspire readers to never lose hope through the adversities of life. She is also an occasional blogger who writes about former and present authors and poets of American Literature, commending writers for their talented abilities and great accomplishments in the literary world. Her writing motto is: *Touching Hearts One Story at a Time.*

Aside from writing, she likes playing piano, drawing, arts and crafts, watching classic TV shows, and making her own book trailers for her stories.

With You Forever is her first published novel.

FOLLOW M.L. BULL ON:

WEBSITE: www.mlbull.com

TWITTER: @WordzbyHeart

INSTAGRAM: wordzbyheart3

TUMBLR: wordsbyheart3

YOUTUBE: www.youtube.com/m.l.bull

THANK YOU FOR READING!

Please send a review on Amazon, Barnes and Noble, or other book retailers of my novel and let me know what you thought! If you enjoyed this story, don't forget to share your review on social media with hashtag **#WithYouForever143** and suggest it to other friends or loved ones.

CPSIA information can be obtained
at www.ICGtesting.com
Printed in the USA
LVHW042250190620
658102LV00002B/85